Thyme Out

Katie Fforde lives in Gloucestershire with her husband and some of her three children. *Thyme Out* is her sixth novel. Her hobbies are ironing and housework but, unfortunately, she has almost no time for them as she feels it her duty to keep a close eye on the afternoon chat shows.

Praise for Katie Fforde

'The romance fizzes along with good humour and is a good, fat, summery read'
Sunday Mirror

'lively and engaging'
Woman's Weekly

'Joanna Trollope crossed with Tom Sharpe'
Mail on Sunday

'Warm and cheery . . . delicious'
The Times

'Fforde is blessed with a lightness of touch, careful observation and a sure sense of the funny side of life'
Ideal Home

'Deliciously, horribly recognizable – a stunnig début'
Sue Limb

'I really enjoyed *Living Dangerously*. It was the perfect holiday read. A real tonic and great fun'
Marika Cobbold

'Old-fashioned romance of the best sort . . . funny, comforting'
Elle

'Freshness, good humour and a willingness to entertain'
Elizabeth Buchan, *Sunday Times*

KATIE FFORDE

Thyme Out

Century · London

Published by Century in 2000

1 3 5 7 9 10 8 6 4 2

First published in the United Kingdom in 2000 by Century
Random House UK Limited
20 Vauxhall Bridge Road, London SW1V 2SA

Random House Australia (Pty) Limited
20 Alfred Street, Milsons Point, Sydney,
New South Wales 2061, Australia

Random House New Zealand Limited
18 Poland Road, Glenfield
Auckland 10, New Zealand

Random House South Africa (Pty) Limited
Endulini, 5a Jubilee Road, Parktown 2193, South Africa

Random House UK Limited Reg. No. 954009

A CIP catalogue record for this book is available
from the British Library

Papers used by Random House UK Limited
are natural, recyclable products made from wood grown in
sustainable forests. The manufacturing processes conform to
the environmental regulations of the country of origin

ISBN 0 7126 8090 X (hardback)
ISBN 0 7126 8095 0 (trade paperback)

Typeset by SX Composing DTP, Rayleigh, Essex
Printed and bound in Great Britain by
Mackays of Chatham PLC, Chatham, Kent

To the older women I have known and loved,
many thanks for your wisdom

Crosnes – keep in peat over winter. Plant in March, good soil, water, tender loving care. Flowers in July, August. 5-7 months to grow, lifted early winter, after the foliage has died back. Will keep in sand or peat in cold. White when fresh, delicious.

Acknowledgements

To Frances Smith, of Appledore Salads, who was not only the inspiration for this book, but also a constant source of further inspiration and information. To Sybil Kapoor, who put me in touch with Frances. To Jacquie and Steve Fischer of Fischer's restaurant, Stroud, chef Ben, and Ollie, who allowed me in their kitchen. To Ian Peters of Bilbury Trout farm, who told me about trout bait, and Jane Peters who cooked it for us. To Sandra Ashenford for having a brother-in-law Marcus Ashenford of the Chavignol Restaurant, Chipping Norton, and taking me there. To Kate Parkin, Kate Elton and Anna Dalton-Knott at Random House for being so easy and pleasant to work with. To dear Sarah Molloy who is always so supportive however neurotic and boring I'm being, and lastly, to Desmond Fforde for technical support.

I was enormously helped by two books by Joy Larkcom, *The Salad Garden*, and *Oriental Vegetables*. Frances Smith also did everything she could to keep me on the horticultural straight and narrow, thus all horticultural mistakes are entirely my own.

Chapter One

'Well? Are you going to come in? Or just stand in the doorway with your trug, looking picturesque?'

Perdita was almost paralysed with shock and confusion. How could short, plump, amiable and easy-going Enzo have, almost overnight, turned into the tall, black-browed monster she had divorced ten years before? Somehow she got herself across the threshold.

'And take off those bloody gumboots! This is a professional kitchen, not a farmyard!'

Perdita looked down at her feet and noticed that the floor was a lot cleaner than usual. She looked up at her ex-husband. 'No.'

'So you've got bolshi in your old age, have you? You always were difficult.'

'I'm not at all difficult. Where's Enzo?'

'Fucked off to sunny Napoli, I expect. How the hell should I know?'

Perdita suddenly became aware that it wasn't only Enzo that had undergone a hideous transformation. The rest of the kitchen had been affected too. She had an impression of a strange whiteness. The friendly, busy place she had been delivering veg to for five years had metamorphosed into something akin to an operating theatre. The noise and clutter had all gone, as had the cheery hum of Radio One, a Greek chorus to the hubbub of the kitchen. No one was singing, swearing, or clattering pots and pans. In fact no one seemed to be doing anything.

The other two occupants of the kitchen were still just

recognisable, but looked completely different. Instead of a pair of brightly coloured cotton trousers, be-sloganed sweatshirt and a striped apron in one case, and a pair of ripped jeans and grubby T shirt, in the other, the they wore white overalls and chef's trousers. Janey, the young sous-chef, who looked about seventeen, had tried to confine her Pre-Raphaelite hair under a white cap but, like its owner, Perdita suspected, it was desperately trying to escape.

The grease-spattered, doodled-on calendar, marked with everyone's holidays and birthdays, no longer hung by the telephone. In its place was a smart white board and marker pen without so much as a smiley face to relieve its blankness. The large pots of fresh herbs, grown by Perdita, had disappeared from the windowsill. As had the fat string of garlic, brought over from France by someone, the chilli peppers, too hot to use but so cheerful and the 'boob chart', a list of the mistakes made over the week. The person with the most cock-ups – usually Enzo – brought in some lagers to be drunk after service on Saturday night. The disappearance of the boob chart was the ultimate symbol of the end of Enzo's regime: an evil dictator had dethroned him.

Aware that she had become the focus of attention, and that the evil dictator was wearing a very familiar scowl, Perdita decided to pretend everything was as normal. 'Hi, Janey, Greg. How are you?'

Greg and Janey nodded stiffly, but didn't speak. Janey had taken on the appearance of a rabbit in thrall to a stoat. She didn't offer to put the kettle on or make toast, nor did she start rummaging through Perdita's vegetables, exclaiming with delight or horror at what she found. Her eyes were red with weeping, but whether this was because of the pile of finely diced onions on her chopping board, or Enzo's replacement, Perdita couldn't tell.

Greg, the washer-up and general dogsbody, had his long hair tied back in a ponytail under a white cap instead

2

of a bandanna, and didn't make one of his sexist, racist, politically incorrect jokes, which always made Perdita laugh, in spite of herself.

The whole kitchen seemed under a strange, sinister enchantment – like Narnia under its blanket of snow. It was not hard to find the warlock responsible: Lucas Gillespie.

'You will have gathered,' he addressed his workforce, 'that Perdita and I used to know each other.' He gave her a slanting glance and she stiffened. She didn't want their dirty and tear-stained linen washed in public. 'It was only for a short time, years ago, when we were both very young.'

She relaxed. Lucas didn't want his failed marriage known about either. 'I still am young,' she said.

He shrugged. 'So, what have you got there?'

Perdita looked down at the contents of her trug. 'Your – Enzo's usual order. *Mâche,* various chicories, some Ragged Jack kale, the usual saladinis, lettuces and some pea plants.'

'Pea plants?'

'Yes. An excellent crop.' Excellent for her, anyhow. It was labour intensive, but she made a lot of money out of it. She rummaged in her basket and broke him off a leaf.

He crunched it up. 'Mmm. Does it stand well?'

'Of course. Everything I sell stands.'

'I suppose that explains the exorbitant prices you charge.' He raised an eyebrow. 'I've been looking at the accounts,' he added.

Perdita was offended. 'My prices may seem high, but I offer very good value. And if you don't want to use me, feel free to stop. I've got plenty of chefs I just can't supply at the moment.' They weren't quite so conveniently situated as Grantly House Hotel, in fact they were too far away to make supplying them profitable, but they did exist.

3

'And you reckon you can grow anything?'

'Well, I won't grow anything it doesn't pay me to grow. I've got to make a living, after all.'

'What about capsicums?'

She shook her head. 'Too much heat. Too expensive.'

Lucas frowned contemplatively. 'Stay here!' he commanded, and strode off towards the cold store.

The moment he was out of the room, she asked in a stage whisper, 'What on earth's happened to Enzo? And how did you get lumbered with *him*?'

Janey cast a frightened glance in the direction of the cold store. 'Enzo's retired,' she whispered back nervously. 'We're very lucky to have Chef. He's very well thought of.'

Perdita humphed. To her, Enzo was Chef. It wasn't right. 'Chef is dead, long live Chef,' she muttered. 'What do you think of him, Greg?'

Greg shrugged. 'Not laid back like Enzo was.'

This wasn't surprising. Enzo could be, and generally was, described as 'horizontal', he was so relaxed, an unusual and endearing feature in a chef. But not, Perdita's sense of fair play was forced to admit, a characteristic likely to make one hugely successful. Before she could speculate further, Lucas came back into the kitchen.

'Here.' He handed Perdita a small, segmented, tuber, about the size of a prawn. It was dark brown. 'Can you grow these?'

Perdita was a professional. She reckoned to know her veg – the obscurer the better – but she was flummoxed this time. 'Er – what is it?'

'It's a crosnes.'

'I thought that was a disease,' said Perdita.

'It's named after a French town, but you can call it a Chinese artichoke if you like. It's like a dead nettle with roots you can eat. I brought it back from France. If you can grow it, I'll buy every bit you can produce.'

She examined the tuber he put into her hand. 'Well, I'll

4

give it a go. Have you any idea of what it needs?'

'You're the gardener. But if you're in any doubt, I'll take it back. They're expensive.'

Perdita's fingers closed around it. 'No, no. I'm sure I'll have no trouble. Now, I'll just go and get the rest of your order.'

No one seemed to move while she went back to her van, piled three crates of veg into her arms and came back into the kitchen with them. She took them through to the cold room, and put them away. When she came back Lucas was inspecting some ducklings with signs of distaste, Janey was back to chopping onions, and Greg was pulling trays out of the oven, prior to cleaning it. It was something Perdita hadn't seen before. Which didn't mean that the oven was never cleaned when Enzo was in charge, she told herself, just that she'd never been there when it happened. This happy realisation was banished by Greg's obscene and unwitting exclamation as he lowered himself to the floor and looked inside.

'So,' said Perdita, partly to halt Lucas's progress across the room to see the oven for himself, 'is there anything you want specially for next week?'

'I'll see how good this lot turns out to be first.'

Perdita gave him a snarl disguised as a smile. 'Will you give me a ring?'

He saw through the disguise. 'Yes, but I don't seem to have your mobile number.'

'I don't have a mobile. My home and work number are the same. You can contact me almost any hour of the day or night, though naturally I would prefer it if you stuck to daytime.'

He scowled. 'I can't believe you're running a business without a mobile. Still, if you want to stay in the Dark Ages, don't let me try and stop you.'

'Oh, I won't.'

'And don't let anything bad happen to that crosnes.'

Perdita patted her pocket to check that it was still there. 'Well, if you don't want to order anything now, I'll be off. I've got a van full of baby vegetables for the health farm.'

'Then you'd better go. I'm sure they don't like being kept waiting for supplies any more than I do.'

Perdita ignored this dig. 'I don't suppose Janey could—' before she could think of a good reason why she needed help to carry her empty basket out to the van, Lucas saved her the trouble.

'No she couldn't. She's got a lot to do. If she wants to keep her job. Which at the rate she's going, doesn't seem likely.'

Perdita shuddered, and swore to herself that she would get Janey out of that kitchen as soon as she possibly could. Janey reminded her of herself at that age and she would never have survived working for Lucas. Greg, she hoped, was tough enough to look after himself.

She gave Lucas a nod, and her two friends a tentative wave. She felt a traitor leaving them to Lucas's mercy, but she was nervous lest a moment longer in the place would put her under the same glacial enchantment as the others. A roar from behind her as she fled indicated she had left mud on the floor. Her satisfaction was slightly marred by the knowledge that Lucas wouldn't be the one to clear it up, and would probably take his anger out on Janey or Greg.

She clambered into her van in a confusion of emotions, none of them happy. Had Enzo gone willingly? Or had he been pushed out of a job he loved so that horrible Lucas could take his place? And, the biggest question of all, what the hell was Lucas doing as a chef? When they'd been married, he hadn't been able to boil an egg – neither of them had, which had been part of their problem. He had been a thrusting young stockbroker, determined to become a millionaire before he was thirty. What had turned his interest from blue chips to game chips?

6

She had been a dreamy art student, who just wanted to paint. The ten intervening years had apparently affected Lucas's dreams and ambitions as much as they had her own.

'Well, at least I'm completely over him,' she murmured as she kicked off her Wellington boots so she could drive. She switched on the engine. Over him or not, she was forced to acknowledge that seeing him, with no warning, had been a dreadful shock. She had delivered to Grantly House only three days earlier. Why had nobody warned her that a nuclear winter was about to fall?

She turned the key another couple of times, praying that she wouldn't have to go back into the kitchen to ask for a push. 'Come on, baby,' she crooned. 'Start for Mummy, and I'll buy you a nice new Magic Tree.' Her woollen socks hanging over her toes, she pressed gently on the accelerator, and the van grumbled into life.

'I know you need more than an air freshener, sweet-heart,' she went on, 'but I really can't manage without you just at the moment. And do you really want a major operation at your age?'

The van swerved into a puddle in reply.

The health farm, Perdita's second biggest customer, which took pretty much everything and anything she could produce, was reassuringly the same as it had been on her last visit.

'Hello, ducks,' said Ronnie the manager, as she staggered into the kitchen under a pile of plastic crates. 'Got your usual array of slugs and aphids, have you?'

'Now you know you have far more time to clean them than I do,' replied Perdita amiably. 'Besides, I would have thought the guests here would be glad of the extra protein.'

'You know perfectly well we don't starve anybody here, even if they are on de-tox . . .'

'Which is why you want my fresh-out-of-the-ground veg, full of vitamins and minerals. Anyway, never mind about that. Have you heard about the new chef at Grantly House? I nearly had a fit when I saw Enzo had gone.'

Ronnie, always glad of a gossip, especially when he had more of it than his gossipee, inclined his head in a knowing way. 'Want a coffee, dear? You look a bit peaky.'

Perdita did feel a little shaky. 'Yes, please. Black, lots of sugar.'

'We'll take it through to the office, so we can talk in peace. That grater's getting on my nerves this morning.' The grater, struggling with a white cabbage, chose that moment to scream in agony, underlining his point.

'So?' demanded Perdita, the moment the door was closed behind them.

'Oh, don't sit on that stool, love, it wobbles,' said Ronnie, taking the swivel chair by the desk, refusing to be hurried.

'No, no, I'll be fine here. Now, do tell . . .'

'Hang on. I'll stuff a fag packet under it. I don't know what that chair's doing here. You think they'd give me a decent office. This place would be nothing without me.'

'Oh, Ronnie! Don't keep me in suspense! You're always like this when you've got something really good to tell me.'

'Make 'em laugh, make 'em cry and make 'em wait, we always used to say.'

'Ronnie!'

'OK, OK. Well, the story is that Mr Grantly was in France – you know he's got a place there?'

'Yes!'

'Oh, all right,' Ronnie said huffily. 'Just giving you the background. Anyway, he was there and he met this new young chef . . .'

'Not that young, surely?' Lucas must be about thirty-five by now. In chef's terms, that was ancient.

'Younger than Enzo, anyway. And Mr Grantly thought he was just the person to get Grantly House a Michelin Star, so he paid off Enzo and got this bloke over.'

'But that's terrible! Kicking Enzo out so – this new chef – can sweep in and take over! We ought to picket Mr Grantly! Boycott his hotel! Get the press involved!' Perdita was outraged as well as mystified. Lucas had been addicted to the speed of City life. What had happened to make him take such a drastic career change?

'I don't suppose you can afford to upset Mr Grantly, dear, seeing as he's one of your main customers,' Ronnie pointed out. 'And by all accounts, Enzo's quite happy about it. He never was quite cut out to be a top-notch chef. He did make some awful blunders.'

As Perdita was responsible for telling Ronnie about some of Enzo's more colourful catastrophes, she couldn't deny it. She blushed, feeling as if she had let Enzo down.

'No need to look like that about it,' Ronnie went on. 'Enzo's delighted.'

'Is he? How do you know?'

'He rang me before he left. Said he'd got a very good golden handshake out of it. And, of course, he's been talking about going back to Italy for years. You know that. He's no spring chicken.'

Perdita did know, but she doubted anyone would actually enjoy being disposed of so quickly.

'He said we must all go out there and stay with him. He's planning to open his own place.'

Perdita took a sip of barely liquid sugar. 'So what's this new one like, then?'

'Well, you've seen him, so you tell me. But by all accounts he's gorgeous. All smouldery and dark.' Ronnie gave Perdita a sideways glance. 'Obviously not your type, then?'

'Well, no. Actually, we sort of know each other. Years ago, in a previous incarnation. He was a stockbroker.' Better

9

to tell Ronnie what she wanted him to know herself and hope his sixth sense for old scandal wouldn't be aroused. Ronnie could turn the most innocent encounter into something worthy of the *Sunday Sport*; what he would do with her quasi-elopement was too terrible to contemplate.

'And you didn't get on?'

'No. He was a pig. Um – did Enzo say anything about his wife?'

'Who? Enzo's?'

'No! Lucas Gillespie's. He was married when I knew him.' Which was true.

'Oh? Well, Enzo didn't say anything about whether he was married or not. Apparently he's staying with Mr Grantly until his staff flat is ready, so he's well in there, but I've not heard tell of any wife. What was she like, then?'

Perdita hesitated only a millisecond before abdicating from the role of spouse, giving it instead to the woman for whom she had been abandoned. 'Well, I didn't know her well.' Perdita had met the other woman in her husband's life only once. 'But she was older than me.' That had seemed the ultimate insult – he left her playing with her toys while he went off with the grown-ups. 'And very sophisticated. Dark. Very well groomed.'

'And you didn't like her, either?'

'I didn't know her! But she made me feel very young and naïve. Which I was then.'

'And now you're Ms Sophistication, I suppose.' He sounded sceptical.

'But I'm not naïve!'

'Yes you are. But not to worry, it's part of your charm. So how did you meet the evil Mr Gillespie?'

'Oh, at a party.' Ronnie seemed to want a little more detail. 'I'd only just left school. I hardly knew him at all, really.' This was also true. They had met and married within three months. 'But who I'm worried about is Janey. He'll bully her to bits!'

'If you didn't know him that well, how do you know that?'

'I know Janey. She's young and innocent—'

'And pretty. Remind you of anyone?'

'Stop teasing me, Ronnie. This is serious. We must get her out of there! You wouldn't have a job for her here, would you?'

'Perdita, love, I hope you don't mind me being personal . . .'

'But you're going to be, anyway.'

'But don't you think you spend too much time worrying about other people, and not enough time worrying about yourself? You should get yourself a nice boyfriend, have some fun.'

Perdita looked at Ronnie as if she had never heard this from him before, when in fact he said it nearly every time they met. But this time, it raised an important question: what would Lucas think when he found out, as he inevitably would, that she hadn't got so much as a sniff of a boyfriend, let alone a husband? He would think, conceited bastard that he was, that she was carrying a torch for him. And if the painted sophisticate he had left her for was still around, well, her pride demanded she have someone sensational to hang on her arm – if only for special occasions.

Ronnie, surprised that Perdita wasn't protesting as usual, followed up his opening. 'You're really a lovely girl, just a little bit unkempt. I mean, look at your clothes.'

For once, Perdita looked. The ancient Fair Isle sweater, which was warm and comfortable and, to her eyes, attractive, had once belonged to Kitty's long-dead husband. It hung halfway down her thighs and the hem was partially unravelled. There was a hole in the arm and the welt of the cuff was nearly separated from the sleeve. There was a panel of mud on the inside of her leg running from where her Wellingtons stopped to above her knees.

your hair . . .' Ronnie, seeing that for once his were having an effect, pressed on. 'A good cut and highlights would make all the difference – carry you the hump between light mouse and dark blonde. v. y don't you come here for a makeover? You could get staff discount. The girls would love to get their hands on you.'

Perdita shuddered. 'If you've got in mind some wonderful man who'd make it all worthwhile, I might just consider it.'

Ronnie had long been trying to get Perdita to make more of herself, and made one more attempt. 'You won't find a man looking like Orphan Annie. But no,' he went on, defeated, 'I'm afraid I haven't got anyone up my sleeve. Young single men don't come my way much, more's the pity. And it's no good looking among our clientele. We get mostly women, as you know, and enough of them are single to make any man a sitting target.'

'But you do get celebrities, male ones?'

'Occasionally, but . . .'

'Tell you what, Ronnie. If you let me know if anyone lovely, male and straight comes in, I'll submit to every torture you think I need to make myself beautiful.'

'Perdita, love,' Ronnie said sharply, 'this wouldn't be anything to do with the new chef at Grantly's, would it?'

'Good Lord no!' Frantically Perdita tried to think of a reason for this volte-face. 'It's just that I'm approaching the big three oh—'

Ronnie, who was good at birthdays, frowned. 'Not till next year, surely?'

'Well, yes, but it'll probably take me till next year to get my act together.'

'True,' he agreed brutally. 'Well, if you're that desperate, I suppose you could advertise.'

'No I couldn't!' Just imagine Lucas seeing her lonely hearts advertisement in the local paper! She might as well appliqué a bleeding heart to her sleeve and have done with it.

Ronnie looked hurt. 'Why not? It's all very discreet, you have a box number. There are all sorts of safeguards against perverts. I've met some lovely men through the small ads.'

Perdita bit her lip and sighed ruefully. 'I'm afraid I'm a bit too much of a coward for that. There must be a less scary way to find a man.'

'Perdita, are you sure this sudden change of heart isn't anything to do with this new chef?'

Perdita felt herself blush and knew that Ronnie would have noticed it. 'Only indirectly. Seeing him unexpectedly like that made me look back to how I'd been the last time I'd seen him.' A wreck, but no need to tell Ronnie that. 'I've come on a lot. I'm independent, I've got my own business going, but I haven't got a partner. And I still wear my hair in a scrunchy. I've spent so much time and energy getting my nursery going, I haven't had a date for years. I don't mind ending my life as an old maid, but I want it to be through choice, not because I never had an opportunity for marriage.'

This fairly grown-up-sounding statement seemed to satisfy the eagle-eyed Ronnie. 'You don't get the opportunity because you spend all your spare time looking after Mrs Anson. How is she, by the way?'

'Kitty? Oh, she's fine. Still gardening all day, though I've told her a million times I'll do anything that needs doing.'

'I don't suppose she'd approve of you advertising for a man.'

Perdita frowned. 'I don't know what she'd think, quite honestly; she's completely unpredictable. She would like me to have a boyfriend, though. She's always telling me I ought to have children of my own, and not waste my time treating her like a child. As if I'd dare!'

'She's right, you know, Perdita. That old lady's got a lot

of sense.' Ronnie patted her knee paternally, and got up. 'Now, must get on.'

'So must I. Thanks for the coffee and the chat, Ronnie.'

'Any time, love. And let me know if you fancy a make-over. Or even a few make-up hints.'

'I will.' A makeover, much as the idea horrified her, would be worth the agony if it helped her get a man before Lucas could find out that she hadn't already got one.

'And give my best to Mrs A.'

'Of course. See you, Ronnie.'

'See you, love.'

Chapter Two

Although Kitty and Perdita lived so close that their gardens backed on to each other, Perdita drove to Kitty's on her way home, parked her van outside the house and knocked on the back door.

'Kitty? Are you there? It's only me!' She wasn't really expecting a reply, and so she walked down into the garden where she found her quarry in the vegetable plot, pulling out bean sticks.

'Hello, darling, how are you?' The elderly lady removed her pipe from between her teeth and kissed Perdita's cheek fondly. 'Here, take these and come and look at my wintersweet. I think it's going to flower at last. I've had it for years.'

Perdita took the bean sticks and followed her friend down into the shrubbery. Once there, they studied the emerging blossom. 'You are patient. I would have got fed up and thrown it out if it hadn't flowered before now.'

'By my age you've learnt patience, dear, and it smells heavenly.' Kitty stripped off the surgical gloves she wore for gardening and rummaged in one of the many pockets of her body warmer for her tobacco. The body warmer was the last of many layers of clothes she had on and as she favoured clothes with pockets, her hunt took some time. Eventually, she found the plastic pouch in the pocket of her combat trousers and with it a postcard which she handed to Perdita before pinning a slipping plait back round her head with a hairpin retrieved from another pocket. She gestured to the postcard.

'It's from your father. The places they get to! I expect there's one for you at home.'

Perdita glanced at the picture of a waterfall in the Andes for a moment. 'Kitty, what did the doctor say?'

Kitty opened the pouch and found a tamper. She emptied the pipe with a firm knock against the fence and then began to scrape out the bowl of it with the tool. 'Oh, the usual. It was only a routine check-up. There's nothing wrong with me.'

'Did he say you should give up your pipe?'

'No he didn't,' said Kitty firmly. 'He said at my age there was no point in giving up my little pleasures.'

'Even if they include strong pipe tobacco and malt whisky?'

'It's quality of life they go for now. Longevity is out of fashion.' She hooked out a plug of tobacco with her finger and began to fill her pipe.

Perdita laughed. 'Pity they didn't know that when you hit eighty-five!'

Kitty chuckled. 'I could have been hygienically euthanased and they would have had to let me have a cardboard coffin.' Her pipe full, Kitty tucked it into another pocket where it would stay until she was ready for it later. 'Now come inside and let me get you some lunch. I know you won't eat unless I make you.'

'Nonsense! You're the one who stays out in the garden until it's dark and then is too tired to cook!'

'At least I don't think a few chemicals in a plastic flowerpot constitute a square meal,' Kitty retorted.

Kitty and a gentleman friend, on their way back from their Philosophy evening class, had once called in on Perdita at ten o'clock at night. Kitty was appalled to find Perdita eating so late, and such unhealthy food.

'I don't often eat Pot Noodles.'

'Considering you produce organic vegetables because

you think chemicals are unhealthy, you should never eat them.'

'I'm not completely organic, you know. Only nearly,' said Perdita.

'Don't change the subject, and come and have lunch. I bet you didn't have breakfast.'

Perdita and Kitty constantly accused each other of not eating properly while denying they were both equally guilty. Kitty said she didn't need much food at her age, and Perdita said she was young and poor and couldn't afford to grow out of her jeans. One Christmas they had, coincidentally, given each other microwaves. Perdita used hers for heating up frozen pizzas and Kitty used hers to sterilise soil.

This time Perdita lost the argument about who should cook for whom because of the time it took her to get her hands clean. Unlike Kitty, she couldn't garden in gloves. She sat herself down at the large mahogany table and flicked through the junk mail, marvelling at how fit her old friend seemed. Kitty was eighty-seven and more sprightly than many people half her age. She was Perdita's favourite person in the world.

Perdita's parents lived abroad, having worked their whole careers in the diplomatic service. Perdita had spent her holidays from boarding school with Kitty, who was her mother's godmother, and had been more than that to Perdita. She vividly remembered the first time she had met Kitty. Sent by train to stay with her for the Easter holidays, Perdita had been terrified. For a start she had no idea how to address the person her mother referred to as Aunt Kitty, because no one had remembered to tell her Kitty's surname. She managed to avoid calling her anything for nearly the whole of the first day.

She was shown her room, a large first-floor bedroom with windows in two walls.

'This is always going to be your room now, my dear,'

Kitty had said. 'My other guests can have the attic. If you're going to stay with me during the holidays, you'll need somewhere which is permanently yours. Can't think it's going to be much fun for you, staying with an old lady like me, but your mother said there was no one else she trusted to look after you.'

Perdita subsequently found out that Kitty disapproved strongly of boarding schools and of parents who put their careers before their families, but in the beginning, she had refrained from comment.

Although she had no children of her own, Kitty instinctively knew how to make Perdita feel at home. Probably, Perdita reflected, *because* she had no children. She just treated Perdita like an adult who needed cosseting a little. The name thing was got over very quickly when they were saying good night. Perdita started on the 'aunt' and Kitty stopped her immediately. 'Call me Kitty, dear. All my friends do, and I think we're going to become very good friends.'

Many years had passed since that first meeting, and the love between the two of them had grown and developed. When Perdita's marriage had broken up, her first instinct had been to go to Kitty, who hadn't said, 'I told you so,' although she had warned against Perdita marrying a man she had known for such a short time. She had simply said, 'Men are *bastards*!' and given her a stiff drink.

Now, the role of carer was more shared.

'So, any news from the outside world?' asked Kitty, when she had put bowls of tinned tomato soup and a plate of bread and butter down in front of them both. 'Tell me while I pour more sherry. You can always walk home if you're worried about "drink driving".' She said the words with the derision of a non-driver and fairly heavy drinker, as if 'drink driving' was an invention of the press.

Perdita shook her head. 'No, I've got to get the van home. It's playing up.'

'Again? Why don't you let me buy you—'

'We've been through all that. Now, I'll tell you what happened this morning.' Perdita would have preferred not to bother Kitty with the news, but as she was by no means Kitty's only source of information, she'd hear it eventually. It was better for Perdita to warn her personally. 'Enzo's gone from Grantly House!'

'Michael Grantly never did know when he was on to a good thing. I thought Enzo cooked jolly well. On his good days.'

'Exactly! And you'll never guess who has replaced him!'

'Then just tell me. You seem very excited about it.'

Perdita was concentrating hard on sounding upbeat. Finding Lucas in Enzo's place had been a genuine shock, but she didn't want to worry Kitty. 'Well! It's such a surprise.'

'So, are you going to tell me? Or will you let me die waiting for the news?'

'It's Lucas! Lucas Gillespie! My ex-husband!'

There was a moment's silence. 'I know quite well who Lucas Gillespie is, dear. But he isn't a cook, he's a stockbroker.'

'He's a chef now. Apparently. Ronnie told me that Michael Grantly found him in France, and has sacked Enzo so Lucas can sweep Grantly House into all the gourmet food guides.'

Kitty frowned. 'Well, you seem perfectly happy about it, but I can't see it as a good thing.'

'Of course I'm not *happy* about it, exactly. But nor am I traumatised. After all, it's years since we parted and, thanks to you, I'm now an independent woman. Not the little mouse he left weeping in a heap.'

It had been Kitty who had insisted that Perdita stop weeping and, as much as a distraction as anything else, help her in the garden. Later, when Perdita's green fingers became apparent, she had suggested she had some formal horticultural training. Eventually Kitty persuaded Perdita's father to give Perdita the fifteen grand he would have spent on her wedding had Perdita's mother had her way. With that capital, Perdita had started Bonyhayes Salads. Now it was a thriving, if not exactly lucrative, business.

'No. You've done marvellously, but I can't help feeling it would be nice if you had a man as well as a small-holding.'

'Kitty darling, women don't need men these days.' She glanced at Kitty. 'You've managed without one for nearly forty years.'

'True' Kitty went on, producing a plate of rather sweaty cheese from the refrigerator. 'Lionel dying like he did left me man-less for the rest of my life. But you're a different matter altogether.'

Perdita was indignant. 'Am I? Why?'

'Because although my marriage was short, it was satisfying. You've only known that swine. You should have another bash at it. And you don't want him thinking you've been pining all these years, do you?'

Perdita extracted a catalogue from the pile which took up one end of the huge mahogany dining table which was the hub around which Kitty's life revolved, partly to avoid Kitty's direct gaze. 'Would he think that? After all, he must know that building up a business takes a lot of doing. I just haven't had time for a social life as such. These clothes are quite nice. Have you ordered anything?'

Kitty ignored the change of subject. 'He will think you've been pining because he's arrogant. You need a man to throw him off the scent. After all, you don't want him thinking he can pick up where he left off.'

Perdita shook her head. 'I really don't think he'd even dream of doing that. He left me because he went off me. But you're right, I don't want him thinking I've been carrying a torch. I'd better find a man. The trouble is, there aren't any, not round here.'

Kitty cut the rind off a piece of cheese. 'Do Universal Aunts have a branch for presentable men, do you think?'

'I think that would be an escort agency, and going by the docu-soap I watched the other night I don't want anything to do with one of those. So, unless you've got a guardsman tucked up your sleeve, I don't have many options.'

Kitty chuckled. 'Any guardsmen I know would be over ninety by now.'

Perdita twinkled back at her. 'Well, you know what they say: better an old man's darling than a young man's slave . . . After all, I don't want a relationship, just someone to stop Lucas thinking I'm sad.'

'But why don't you want a relationship? You should! You should be having children by now.'

'I've got a nursery already, I don't need children . . .'

Kitty frowned. 'Really, darling. You do need someone. I won't be here for ever.'

'Yes you will. Now do you want some more sherry? Or shall I wash up? Oh!' Her eye was caught by 'Derek, Vet' who was advertising sailing trousers in the catalogue. 'He's nice. Do you think you can buy the men, or is it just the clothes?'

The next time Perdita went to deliver at Grantly House she was prepared. She hadn't exactly put make-up on, or worn her best clothes, but she had made sure her hair was clean and that her jeans were freshly washed and not too obviously in need of mending. Lucas had greatly increased the order, which pleased her.

She piled up the plastic crates and carried them carefully into the kitchen. This time she was expecting a frigid reception and so it was a relief to find the kitchen so full of bustle that no one was aware of her arrival. There were several people standing round Lucas, who was storming about, throwing his hands up in frustration.

21

'This is a professional kitchen. I don't see any reason why it can't be used!'

'But our programme isn't for professionals,' said a well-spoken young man with floppy hair and an anxious expression. 'It's for entertainment.' He sounded tired.

The word entertainment had caused Lucas's black brow to darken further. 'But I thought the location was approved months ago! Before I was even approached!'

'It was.' The tired young man seemed as frustrated as Lucas. 'But not by me! And it's just not exciting enough.'

Lucas opened his mouth to shout, and then shut it again. Before he lost the struggle to remember on which side his bread was buttered, Perdita decided to announce her presence.

'Hi, everyone!' she said over the top of her crates. 'I've just brought the veg.' Everyone turned towards her. 'I'll just put it all in the cold store, shall I? You're obviously busy.' Nobody moved or spoke, so she picked her way through the group until she got to the other door. 'I don't suppose anyone could possibly open that for me?' She smiled, to indicate that she knew she was interrupting, and just trying to get out of the way as quickly as possible.

The man who had spoken sprang into action and opened the door for her. 'Capodimonte in jeans,' he muttered as she went through it. 'And look at those greens!'

'Who is that lovely creature?' said someone else, making Perdita glad of the cool of the cold store.

'That's Perdita, from Bonyhayes Salads,' she heard Lucas answer.

'I think we really must use her. She'd make a lovely contrast to Lucas. A sort of angel and devil thing.'

Perdita swung the door to, so she couldn't overhear Lucas's reply. It might be more devilish than she could cope with. She stayed in the cold store, stacking boxes as long as she could without risking hypothermia, taking in what she'd heard. So Lucas wasn't satisfied with morphing from a City slicker into a chef, he had to be on television as well. Well, he needn't think she'd be impressed by tricks like that. When she emerged from the cold store, the kitchen was still full of people.

And Lucas, his arms folded, was still scowling, but this time the scowl was directed at her. The man with the floppy hair was also looking at her, but he was smiling, extremely charmingly.

'Perdita?' He took hold of her hand. 'I'm David Winter, and I think you may be the answer to our prayers.'

'She probably lives in a council house,' muttered Lucas.

'Perdita? I may call you that? What sort of house do you live in?'

'Oh, it's a small cottage—'

'Perfect! Is it picturesque?'

'Well, I think it's very pretty, but it's not at all done up, or restored, or anything.' She had a feeling these people thought all cottages were candidates for *Country Living* articles when hers was more like the 'before' picture of a major restoration project. 'I don't seem to get much time for decorating,' she added, emphasising her point.

'Do you think we could go and see it?' asked David. 'We're looking for a location, near here, to use for our cookery programme.' He frowned, seeing that she needed more explanation. 'It's a pilot for a series where professional chefs cook in real kitchens . . .'

'This is a real kitchen,' snapped Lucas.

'But it's completely lacking in heart. I'm sorry, Lucas, but the viewers want a good location nowadays.'

'I thought they wanted a half-decent chef.'

'And I really don't think my cottage would be suitable,' said Perdita. 'It's tiny, not at all convenient, and the kitchen is . . .' How to describe the dank, irregular space with little light and almost no working surface? 'Primitive, to put it politely. And minute – not big enough to boil an egg in.'

'It sounds *perfect*! After all, most viewers have tiny kitchens; why are cookery programmes always set in ones the size of barns?' The maker of several such programmes tossed this rhetorical question into the air.

'Really,' Perdita persisted valiantly, 'my kitchen is *not* suitable.'

'Couldn't we just look at it?' asked David Winter.

'Of course, if that's what it takes to convince you.' Perdita suddenly felt as tired as everyone else looked. 'But I promise you, you'll be disappointed. It's tiny, it's dark and it smells of damp. But I'll take you there if you insist.'

'Don't you usually visit your aunt at lunchtime?' said Lucas.

Perdita wondered briefly how on earth he knew that and then realised that anyone could have told him. 'Well, actually it's her bridge afternoon, so I'm not going to today.'

'I expect she's got a lovely big kitchen,' said Lucas, with enough despair in his voice to inspire reluctant sympathy even in Perdita.

'I'm not having her involved in this,' she snapped, to hide it. 'And anyway, she's not my aunt.'

'So we can go and look at your kitchen.' David Winter sounded pleased. 'I've got such a good feeling about this.'

Perdita groaned. 'Promise not to cry when you see how wrong you are?'

'If we're going, let's go,' said Lucas impatiently. 'Even though it'll be a complete waste of time. Janey, Greg, you know what you've got to get on with. I'll come with you, Perdita. Now for God's sake, let's stop farting about.'

For a moment Perdita considered refusing to take him, but then decided that her van might be just what he needed to bring him down off his pedestal.

'Now, listen to me, Lucas,' said Perdita, when she'd

cleared the front seat of rubbish and Lucas had clambered in. 'You will absolutely hate my kitchen. I'm not fond of it myself, and I don't ever do any cooking, but it's not my fault. It's you who want to be on television, not me, so don't blame me for any of this fiasco. OK?' She switched on the ignition, and, reliably, the van failed to start. Lucas sat in silence while she tried another couple of times. 'Now would you mind getting out and giving me a push? There's a slope here. I can bump start it.'

Without a word, Lucas got out.

Perdita disappeared into the coal shed and came out with a large key. As she did so she heard mutterings of 'adorable', 'perfect', and 'don't you just love those diamond panes?' issuing from the carload of television people. Her heart sank. Her cottage, which did look gorgeous from the outside, had seduced them. She would never now convince them that it wasn't their ideal location.

'It's a bit cramped in the hall,' she said, opening the door and going in first. She led the way into the sitting room so that the half-dozen people could all get in through the front door.

The sitting room was the one place Perdita had made comfortable. There was a large wood-burning stove in the stone fireplace, and weak November sunshine shone in through the windows, catching a small collection of copper items, including a kettle, which stood around the fireside. It also highlighted the dust, which stirred and danced in the draught.

The floor was stripped, and the wide, pale boards ran diagonally across the room. The window embrasure was deep and stone, and what furniture there was reflected the period of the house.

'But it's charming!' declared David Winter.

'You haven't seen the kitchen,' said Perdita doggedly. 'It isn't charming, it's unreconstructed!'

25

'How did you come to live here?' asked David, eager for details.

Perdita sighed. She didn't really want Lucas knowing her life story since he left her, but she had nothing to be ashamed of. 'It was adjoining the land I had for my salads. When it came on the market, I bought it.' She saw Lucas's eyebrow shoot up, desperate to ask, 'What with?' 'I have a mortgage,' she added for his benefit, 'like everybody else.'

'I see. And it was unrestored?' David Winter went on.

'It was pretty much as it is now. I had the stove put in, and it does the hot water and a couple of radiators. But as I said, I don't have much time for decorating.'

She knew most women would have been waxing the floors, sponging and stencilling the walls and covering the chairs with petit point, but all her creative energy went into her garden. Home for her was where she flopped for a couple of hours before falling into the bath and into bed.

'So let's see the kitchen,' said Lucas glumly.

The kitchen was a later addition. It was a lean-to at the back of the house and was small and badly arranged. It seemed to make no concession to cooking at all, though the sharp-eyed would have spotted a cooker under a washing-up bowl of sprouting pea seeds, and a fridge behind a bag of compost and a fork. The room was full of trays of soil, sprouting seeds and tottering heaps of flowerpots waiting to be washed. The sink was stacked with unwashed saucepans and grubby plant labels. The only thing obviously used for its purpose was the microwave, which took up most of the work surface.

'I did warn you,' she said as her guests stood open-mouthed in the doorway. There wasn't room for more than Perdita and Lucas in the kitchen at the same time. 'Now, I could probably manage to make you all a cup of instant coffee before you go home. So your journey wasn't completely wasted.' No one seemed to notice the irony in her voice.

'But it's ideal! Just needs tidying up a bit!' said David. 'Look at that lovely deep windowsill! And the beam!'

'That's not a beam, it's a railway sleeper,' said Perdita, perturbed that David was not put off. 'It was just stuck in to stop the house falling down.'

'Presumably all beams were just "stuck in to stop the house falling down", unless you're in a pub, of course,' Lucas retorted acidly.

Perdita turned on him. 'Do you really want to cook in this kitchen?' she demanded.

'Do you two know each other?' asked David.

'Of course,' said Perdita quickly. 'I deliver veg to Grantly House.'

'I know, but there seems to be some sort of – chemistry – between you.'

'If you mean a hearty dislike, you've got it about right,' said Lucas.

'Hmm.' David stroked his chin thoughtfully. 'You know, people are beginning to get tired of perfect-every-time cookery programmes. A little frisson . . .' He stopped talking and narrowed his eyes as some creative and ground-breaking idea occurred to him.

It made Perdita nervous. 'Honestly, this kitchen is not at all suitable. You must see that.'

'That's a Belfast sink under all those pans,' said someone.

'That's not a Belfast sink!' protested Perdita. 'It was in here when I came!'

David Winter sighed in ecstasy. 'Original – perfect!'

Perdita began to panic. 'Listen, this kitchen is too small for one person. It would be quite impossible to do a television programme in here. Lucas would hate it, wouldn't you, Lucas? And he's your star!'

'Actually,' said the annoying individual who had spotted the sink, 'we could all be out in the passage and still get good shots. If it was cleared up, it would be perfect.'

'Well, it's not going to be cleared up! This is my home and where I work, and I'm not going to tart it all up for you lot!' Perdita wanted to cry.

'Temper, temper,' said Lucas. 'You did offer to show us the place. You can't be pissed off now because they like it.'

She turned on Lucas. 'Are you really telling me that you would be willing to do a cookery programme in a kitchen where there's barely space to boil a kettle? And that's when it isn't full of cameramen, and sound people and God knows who else rushing about?'

'If it wasn't full of junk there'd be plenty of room,' said Lucas.

Perdita stopped wanting to cry and started wanting to kill Lucas, slowly and painfully and, preferably, with several thousand viewers looking on.

'And you'll be in it too. You can tell us all about the wonderful things you grow,' said David Winter, as if offering her a treat.

'I don't want to be on television. I have a job,' said Perdita crossly.

'We will pay to use your cottage as a location,' David went on.

'And you do need a new van,' said Lucas.

David frowned, not wanting to give anyone the impression they'd pay huge amounts. 'Possibly not quite enough for that, but it'd be marvellous publicity for your business,' he added.

Perdita took a deep breath. 'I don't need any more business, and I don't suppose you'd start filming for ages. I will have bought a new van without your contribution by then.'

'Actually, we want to start pretty much right away. The programme's due to go out in the spring.'

Eventually, everyone except Lucas found their way out of the cottage and drove off. Lucas stayed on.

'Haven't you got unspeakably expensive gourmet meals to prepare?' Perdita demanded when she realised he hadn't left with the others.

He shook his head. 'We're not open for lunch this week.'

'What about prepping up?'

'I've left that to Greg and Janey. We'll see what sort of a cock-up they make of it.'

'What makes you think they'll cock it up?'

Lucas sighed. 'Experience.'

'You are such a bastard. I don't know why anyone would want to work for someone like you.'

'Because they need money and experience.'

'The money's crap, for a start.'

'Actually, it's slightly better than most people on their level get paid. They do have to earn it, of course. But there's nothing unfair about that.'

Perdita didn't reply, silently renewing her vow to find Janey something better than working for Lucas.

'I suppose you want me to drive you back,' she said, wanting, quite badly, to make him walk in his black and white checked trousers, chef's jacket and working boots.

'Actually I want to see what you're doing here.' He sensed her resistance. 'Unless you're ashamed of it, of course.'

Perdita was intensely proud of her market garden, and part of her wanted the opportunity to show Lucas how well she had done after he had left her, but she couldn't possibly give in to such an arrogant demand. 'Of course I'm not ashamed of it, but just because we were once married, that doesn't give you the right to demand to see it.'

'I'm sure it doesn't. But what about the fact that I'm one of your major customers and I happen to like seeing where what I buy comes from?'

That was unanswerable. She often showed interested buyers round.

'You'd better borrow a coat, then. Or you'll get cold.'

'You won't have anything to fit me.'

She smiled accommodatingly and went into the hall. 'Yes I will. Here.' She burrowed into a row of hooks and produced a very ancient man's jacket which had once belonged to Kitty's husband. Kitty had left it behind once and it had stayed there ever since. Now she was pleased to see the curiosity in Lucas's eyes.

'It belongs to a friend,' she said cheerfully. 'But you can borrow it.'

Chapter Three

There was nothing she could do about Wellingtons for Lucas, but he managed perfectly well in his steel-capped boots, although he did get them covered in mud. Perdita had often wondered if she should have the path from her house to the poly-tunnels gravelled, but like many things which would have made her life easier but not increased her income, she had never got round to it. She just lived in her Wellingtons. She clenched her teeth on her apology for the conditions underfoot.

'Here's my shed, where I do all my seed sowing, what pricking out that gets done, and where I keep my tender things in winter, things like scented geraniums. Very good for flavouring ice-cream,' she added pointedly.

He grunted, casting his disdainful gaze over the shed, which didn't look very prepossessing, even to Perdita's fond gaze. It had a potting bench, a high typing stool, so she could sit to work, and a radio, which she kept permanently tuned to Radio Four. There was a paraffin heater, which just about kept the chill off by day and the frost off by night, not much more. A tottering pile of grubby, mossy polystyrene seed trays occupied one corner. These she used in rotation, and while awaiting their turn, they dried in heaps. The roof was partly wooden and partly corrugated plastic, and there were puddles where they didn't quite join. A fluorescent strip was the main illumination, but there was an ancient angle-poise over the potting bench.

'I'm surprised they don't want to make their cookery

programme in here,' Lucas said.

'I did think of offering it to them,' Perdita replied with a completely straight face, 'but I wouldn't want them in a space I actually use. Come on, come and see the tunnels and meet the veg.' His sideways glance told her he was wondering if she was mad, and, wanting to encourage his doubts about her sanity, she added, 'They're like my family. I talk to them all the time.'

Lucas scrutinised her carefully to see if she was sending him up. Perdita looked blandly back at him, innocent and guileless. The fact was, although she didn't actually regard her salads as close family members, she certainly chatted away to them, cajoling, chiding, and often, congratulating them—'Who's Mummy's nice little earner, then?'

She opened the door of the first tunnel, lifting it over the rut which had formed over the years.

'Hello, darlings!' she said gaily, having checked that William, who worked for her, wasn't in the tunnel. She didn't want him thinking that his boss had gone dotty. 'Mummy's brought you a visitor.' She stole a glance at Lucas's horrified expression. It filled her with glee. 'Be on your best behaviour,' she went on, nauseating herself as well as him.

Then she forgot to be mad as Lucas helped himself to green morsels, and she gathered groups of leaves and rolled them into cigarettes of zing and flavour.

'Here, try this.' She handed him a leaf. 'But be careful, it's strong.' She knew he would ignore her warning and had the satisfaction of seeing his eyes water. 'It goes well with golden purslane, which as you know, is divinely pretty, but a bit bland. This is practically my favourite.' She handed him an attractive plant with rounded leaves wrapped about the stalk. 'I'd almost grow it for its looks alone, but it has a nice flavour too, fresh and quite mild.'

'I am familiar with claytonia,' said Lucas. 'Or has this particular member of the family got a Christian name?'

Ignoring his sarcasm, Perdita looked him straight in the eye. 'It's very important not to give the plants names, or you get too attached, and it breaks your heart when you have to let them go.' She flirted with the notion of telling him she could hear the plants scream as she pulled them out of the earth, but decided he might think she was too much of a nutter to do business with. 'Come along,' she added briskly. 'There are two more tunnels to see.'

William was at the far end of the third tunnel. He straightened up as Lucas and Perdita entered.

'Hello, Perdita,' he called. 'The mesembryanthemums have put on a spurt. Have you got any buyers for them?'

'This is William, my – right-hand man,' she said as she reached him. She hoped she'd put enough nuance into her voice to make Lucas wonder about their relationship. William was quite a bit younger than she, but toy boys were fashionable these days. 'This is Lucas Gillespie, the new chef at Grantly House. Can we interest you in ice plants, Lucas? They've a different sort of texture which is good in a salad – taste a bit salty.'

Lucas almost admitted to being confronted with something he had never eaten before. 'I know these as flowers. They grow a lot in Cornwall.'

'They do have pretty flowers,' admitted Perdita, 'if rather gaudy, but we remove them as soon as they appear.'

'Isn't that a bit cruel?' asked Lucas, one black brow raised.

Perdita looked down at her hands in mock remorse, hoping William wouldn't ask what on earth Lucas was talking about. 'It's tough being in business,' she said.

William, when she finally dared glance at him, was looking a bit confused but, fortunately, he was shy and therefore unlikely to address Lucas.

By the time Lucas had inspected all the tunnels and

seemingly every plant, Perdita was exhausted, and not only because she kept forgetting she was supposed to see her plants as her children. The project as a whole *was* her baby. She did want Lucas to approve of it, and see it as a good, profitable business. Not, she assured herself, as they walked back to the house together, because he was Lucas, her ex-husband. But because he was the new chef at Grantly House, and therefore a valuable customer.

She didn't offer him tea, although she was gasping for a cup herself, but she did offer him a lift back to the hotel in her van. It had got very dark and a cold November wind was blowing up the valley.

'I'm sure you'll need to be getting back,' she said. 'I've got to call in on Kitty anyway, and see how she got on at bridge.'

'I'm sure she must be an excellent player.'

It was just possible Lucas was trying to be pleasant, and that she only imagined a sneer in his voice, but Perdita couldn't bring herself to give him the benefit of the doubt. 'She's awful, actually. She's only recently taken it up, and although the other members of the club are all terribly fond of her, no one likes being her partner. She has a tendency to think aloud, which gives the opposition an unfair advantage.'

Lucas grinned, and for a dangerous, teetering moment, Perdita was reminded of how he was when she had first met him, handsome, devil-may-care, with a wicked grin. It gave her a nasty jolt. Once she had dropped him home and was on her way to Kitty's, she realised that if she wasn't careful she could quite easily find herself attracted to him again.

Of course she wouldn't do anything about it, and would not even allow herself the teeniest fantasy about luring him back to her, but it highlighted her problem. She was alone, with no focus for her romantic urges, no love object, no one even to have a crush on. It was a dangerous state to be in. She must do something about it.

Later, while she was washing up half a dozen dirty mugs and a few bowls, Perdita found it impossible not to think back to her short, turbulent marriage to Lucas Gillespie, and how she had picked herself up afterwards.

Kitty had been marvellous. She had fought Perdita's corner against her parents, insisting that their daughter didn't share their passion for travel and so didn't want to backpack round the world to get over her heartbreak. She convinced them that living quietly with Kitty, gardening, reading and eating nourishing meals, was what Perdita needed. And much later, when Perdita had done her horticulture course, and Kitty had got Perdita's wedding money out of her father, she encouraged Perdita to buy her first polythene tunnel and set up in business.

Kitty then sectioned off half an acre of her own enormous garden and gave it to Perdita – 'So I don't have to feel guilty about not looking after it.'

Later, Perdita had found herself in a position to buy the tiny cottage at the end of the lane which had once housed the gamekeeper of Grantly House, as well as enough land for two more tunnels.

There were a few spectacular arguments about money; Kitty wanted to finance the whole thing. She disapproved of mortgages, having never needed one herself, and felt that Perdita should let her buy the cottage and the land, the argument being that Perdita was going to inherit all Kitty's money anyway.

With a stubbornness which had surprised them both, Perdita refused. She arranged a mortgage and a bank loan. 'So I'll have more to inherit,' she told Kitty.

It was at college that she had learnt about markets. She realised that she could never make enough to keep herself by growing carrots and potatoes. She needed to grow specialist vegetables for specialist cooks. She went to the nearby health farm and persuaded Ronnie's predecessor that he needed to provide vegetables fresh out of the ground, and if he would only tell her what he wanted, she would grow it and deliver it.

She did the same with Enzo at Grantly House. His requirements had been more esoteric and included specialist herbs, flat-leaved parsley, chervil, coriander, every sort of basil and tarragon, thyme, parsley, dill. He wanted baby leeks the size of her little finger, vegetables too young to die, sprouted fenugreek, alfalfa, and sweet seasoning peppers grown from seed sent from the Caribbean. Her business had flourished.

Now, five years on, certain that all wounds and scars from her marriage were healed, Perdita's first concern was Janey. Lucas was obviously the sort of chef who thought humiliating one's staff was the way to get the best out of them. Even without her own, personal knowledge of just how cruel Lucas could be, Perdita would have been worried about Janey, especially when a couple of telephone conversations with her made it clear that she was developing a crush on Lucas. It was easily done when you were Janey's age, as Perdita knew only too well. Janey must be rescued. Perdita liked rescuing things, and if it thoroughly annoyed Lucas in the process, well, all the better.

With these happy thoughts in mind, she didn't know whether to be pleased or sorry when, the next day, she received a faxed order from Grantly House that was even bigger than the last one. She had no way of knowing how Lucas felt about her personally, but he was a big fan of what she produced.

When she delivered it a couple of days later she dutifully removed her gumboots and padded into the kitchen in her woolly socks.

'Hi, everyone! How's things?' she carolled gaily, in an attempt to sound as she had before Enzo's departure. 'Oh, he's not here,' she went on, more naturally. 'What a relief.'

Greg was scrubbing the bars of the oven, giving Perdita the impression that he'd done nothing but clean it ever since she was last here. Janey was making potato balls with raw potatoes and a melon baller, a process which looked both extremely tedious and painful to the palm of the hand.

'Pommes Parisienne,' she explained gloomily. 'Bloody agony.'

'How can you fancy a man who makes you do such poncy things to potatoes?' Perdita murmured to Janey, so Greg wouldn't hear.

Janey blushed. 'I'm sorry,' she whispered. 'I just can't help it.'

'So where's your lord and master?' asked Perdita, at normal volume.

'He's having a conference with Mr Grantly,' said Janey, throwing down her baller in a gesture of rebellion. 'Let's have a cup of tea!'

'Oh, let's. I'll get the stuff.' She went to the door and put her boots back on. Such a relief not to have to take them off when she returned.

'Is it hell? Is he a bastard?' Perdita, having unloaded six crates of salad and put them in the cold store, helped herself to a biscuit, and heaved herself onto the counter.

'Don't sit there!' Janey screamed. 'He'll go mad! I've just sterilised it. He says he doesn't know how we weren't closed down when Enzo was in charge.'

'Oh sod him.' Perdita said rebelliously, staying put.

'I suppose things had got a bit slack,' Janey went on, reluctantly picking up her melon baller.

'You haven't said much,' Perdita said, turning to Greg. 'How do you like working with him?'

'I don't. I think I'll go back to college and get some qualifications.'

'Well, I expect your mother's pleased about that.'

Greg growled. 'Anything's better than being bossed around by that bastard. I don't know what he's talking about half the time. Enzo was Italian, but at least he spoke bloody English.'

'You could get another job. So could you, Janey.'

Janey sighed. 'It's very good experience, working with someone with such a good reputation. It'll look very good on my c.v.'

'But surely you could work for someone with a good reputation who isn't such a pig? That would look just as good on your c.v.'

'Yes,' said Greg.

'And how come he's got such a good reputation? He's not famous, is he?' Perdita, aware that she led a rather narrow existence, wanted to make sure there was nothing about her ex-husband she ought to know.

'Well, you know about the television thing . . .'

She shook her head. 'Actually, I haven't heard a word since they all trooped out of my kitchen. I sort of hoped the idea was off.'

'Not according to Mr Grantly. CMG himself doesn't talk about it,' said Greg.

'CMG?' asked Perdita.

'Call Me God,' Greg explained. 'It's how he likes to be addressed.'

'Not really?'

'Well no, we leave out the Call Me part.'

'Oh dear. So working with him isn't much fun then?'

Janey sighed. 'I'm just glad I'm not making a television programme with him.'

'Oh, that's so unfair!' said Perdita, recognising the disappointment in Janey's tones. 'Who are they getting?'

'Well, you, of course,' said Janey. 'I thought you knew.'

'Oh *no*! I thought that was just that man's whim, not a serious suggestion. I won't do it.'

'But you must!' said Janey. 'It's such a wonderful opportunity! Think of the publicity!'

'I don't need publicity, Janey. I can hardly supply all the customers I've got already. I don't need any new ones.'

'But you're always broke!' said Greg.

'Well, yes, but I work all the hours God sends. I couldn't handle any more customers.'

'You could expand.'

'I don't want to. I don't mind working hard and I like keeping things in my control. When businesses get too big the proprietor can't keep in touch and things get out of hand. Then they go belly up.' This was almost a direct quote from something she'd heard on the radio.

'You still have to do the telly,' said Janey, who didn't care about efficient business practice. 'It's not fair to Lucas otherwise.'

'Honey, they'd get someone else if I wouldn't do it,' explained Perdita. 'It wouldn't mean the programme wouldn't get made. It might even mean they'd do it here, which is what he wants, after all. You might be in it, Janey.'

'No, Mr Grantly told us they won't do it here. They're dead set on your cottage.'

'For God's sake! You know my kitchen, Janey. Would you set a cookery programme in it?'

'I don't know anything about television,' said Janey unhelpfully. 'If they think it's suitable, it probably is.'

'Nonsense. I think they should find another chef and another set and leave us to get on with our work.' Perdita drained her tea. 'And if Lucas is a prick, you should tell Mr Grantly. He's probably got no idea what a swine he is.'

'Sure,' said Greg. 'Mr Grantly thinks the sun shines out of Lucas's—'

'Out of my what?' demanded the man in question,

appearing like a dark cloud on a sunny day, in the corner of the kitchen.

Perdita jumped off the work surface, jarring her feet in her hurry. 'You don't want to know, Lucas,' she said. 'I've brought your veg.'

'Well, I didn't think you'd come here solely to distract my staff from their work.'

'Hadn't you better go and check it?' said Perdita, who would have been furious if he had suggested that such a thing was necessary.

Lucas snarled, and disappeared into the cold store.

Taking advantage of his absence, Perdita hissed at Janey: 'He's a bastard, don't work for him.'

Janey, aware that she'd got behind with her tasks, frantically dug into a potato. 'I know I shouldn't, but he's so gorgeous! I'd rather be sworn at by Lucas than be – be – be'd nice to by anyone else.'

'Your brains have scrambled! You don't want to work for a man like that!'

'Yes I do! Knowing he's going to be here, however horrible he's going to be, makes me look forward to coming into work in the morning.'

Perdita gave up on the logical approach. It was no good trying to argue Janey out of her lunacy – she knew that from personal experience. What Janey needed was not only another job, but another man to have a crush on. And at that moment, the very chap occurred to her.

'Janey, you don't work on Sundays, do you? Come to Sunday lunch this weekend.'

'But, Perdita!' Janey was surprised. 'You don't cook!'

'No,' said Perdita with dignity. 'But I heat up very well.'

Lucas reappeared. 'Don't forget, Janey, that if you contract salmonella you can't work with food. I'd have to sack you.'

'Oh, I won't give Janey that,' said Perdita sweetly. 'She's allergic to fish.'

Lucas scowled, and even Greg and Janey looked a little disappointed at Perdita's childish pun.

'Was everything in order with the veg?' she went on, unabashed.

'No. You left the cold store in complete chaos.'

She smiled. 'There are rather a lot of crates to take back. I wonder if Janey could give me a hand? I see Greg's busy.'

'And as Janey obviously isn't, she's no loss if she helps you. Don't be long, Janey; you're not paid to shift boxes for the greengrocer.'

'Specialist greengrocer, if you don't mind,' Perdita corrected haughtily, as she went into the cold store to collect the first load of crates.

She went back for a second load. 'I can manage these, Janey. Now don't forget, Sunday. Come about one. You can come too, Greg, if you want to.' She added this more doubtfully. Greg's presence would mess up her plans a bit.

'No, you're all right. I'm having Sunday dinner at my girlfriend's. Her mum does lovely roast potatoes.'

Perdita left before anyone could comment on her abilities in that direction.

'Cooking Sunday lunch can't be that difficult,' she said to Kitty later as she helped her stack flowerpots. 'After all, women have been doing it for generations.'

Kitty sucked on her pipe doubtfully. 'Hell in a bucket, my love. You have to get everything cooked at the same time and the oven's never hot enough for the potatoes.'

Perdita thought about her oven for a second. 'Oh God. Do you have to have roast potatoes? Baked ones wouldn't do?'

'Men like roast potatoes,' said Kitty. 'But anyway, who are you going to ask to be your man?'

'No one. I don't need a man.'

'Darling, won't it be a bit obvious? If you invite Janey and William and no one else?'

41

'The only unattached man I know of within fifty miles is Lucas, and it's him I'm trying to lure Janey away from. Not to mention my feelings on the matter. Besides he'd never, ever come.' Perdita thought for a moment. 'You come, Kitty. You can help me.' Perdita watched her friend searching for a reason to refuse. 'Come on, it'll be fun.'

'Oh, very well. Now come along in and let's have a drink.'

William was almost as reluctant a guest as Kitty. What is it about me that makes people so reluctant to come to my house to eat? thought Perdita.

'William, you're not doing anything much this Sunday, are you?'

'Why? Do you want me to do some overtime? I could probably manage about four hours or so.'

'No, I want to invite you to lunch.' There was a long silence. 'Please,' added Perdita. 'I'm going to do roast potatoes. And roast beef – or lamb – whichever you like, really.'

William seemed genuinely confused. His boss did take him to the pub occasionally – she even bought him the odd bar snack – but she had never asked him for anything which could be described as a meal.

Perdita decided that she had better come clean. 'There's this girl I want you to meet. You don't have to marry her or anything, or even take her out, but she needs to meet a few nice men.' William didn't respond. 'The trouble is,' Perdita went on rather desperately, 'she has a tendency to fall in love with bastards.' This was a bit of a slur on Janey, because as far as she knew, Lucas was the first bastard. 'I want her to see that there are lots of other men out there who are perfectly nice and just as attractive.'

She saw the beginnings of a blush steal from William's beard to his hair and she hoped he wasn't taking her remarks too personally. It would be dreadful if William decided that she, Perdita, had developed a crush on him.

'So you'll come?' she persevered.

William nodded somewhat anxiously.

I must find myself a man, thought Perdita, seriously. Poor William's quite shy enough without having to worry about whether his boss is likely to make a pass at him.

While she was buying organic meat from the butcher in the next village, she did wonder if she could possibly invite him. He was personable, good-looking and young. But even if she had the nerve, which she certainly hadn't, and if he was single, which was definitely unlikely, she couldn't let him witness the ruination of the joint he had so painstakingly explained about, boned and wrapped for her. It would be too cruel.

Chapter Four

Perdita had accepted that roast potatoes were essential, and had borrowed a Delia Smith from Kitty to tell her how to do them. As she handed Perdita the book, Kitty had said, 'If all else fails, stick them under the grill.' It was sound advice, which Perdita would willing have taken had her grill worked. As it was, she would have to rely on her unreliable oven.

Tidying the kitchen had been the worst part. It was so full of horticultural paraphernalia which, for various reasons, couldn't join their horticultural cousins in the shed or the poly-tunnels. Eventually, Perdita filled a corner with as many non-cookery items as it would take, and flung a faded Indian bedspread over them. Thank goodness it was only Janey, William and Kitty, who all knew her well, and had better reasons for loving her than her culinary skills. Kitty was bringing sherry and wine, as she didn't share Perdita's opinion that for wine, good value meant cheap.

The lamb smelt delicious. Perdita had studded it with sprigs of rosemary and a clove of elephant garlic, which, sliced up, was enough to ensure that the lamb both looked like the picture in her recipe book, and would taste distinctly Mediterranean.

She swept the sitting-room floor, and took a stiff broom to the worn and faded rugs which covered it, unfortunately covering everything with dust as she did so. Perdita didn't own a vacuum cleaner, convinced that, not having fitted carpets, she didn't need one. It was only at times like this that she wondered if perhaps she should see what she could find in that line at the next car boot sale she went to.

Having dusted the mantelpiece with her sleeve she dashed out into the garden and picked a huge bunch of late asters and chrysanthemums. They looked wonderfully opulent in her copper jug, which, she told herself, was better tarnished, more subtle.

It took her a while to work out how to seat four people round her little gate-leg table without anyone sitting with the leg inelegantly between their knees. Eventually she managed it, providing that William wouldn't mind having his knee pressed up against the leg. She also hoped William wouldn't mind being the only man.

Still, she thought, it would be difficult for him not to appreciate Janey, with her ravishing hair, green eyes and wide mouth. She didn't need to be self-deprecating to feel that set against Kitty, beautiful indeed, but nearly ninety, and herself, passable, but older than William, and his boss, Janey was bound to shine. Which was the point of the exercise.

In a washing up bowl, usually used to sprout pea seeds, was a hotchpotch of all she had in the garden and in her tunnels – broccoli, cauliflower, spinach, beet tops, Swiss chard, and some Good King Henry, in fact everything that she could find which looked like green veg.

Kitty often wondered aloud how it was that Perdita was such a talented gardener and such an untalented cook. Kitty herself, when she could be bothered, was an excellent cook, feeling that if you've gone to so much trouble to grow the vegetables, surely they should reach the table at their very best.

Perdita perfectly agreed with her, but as she usually ate things raw or stir-fried, the thought of cooking a lot of vegetables which all had to be ready at the same time, daunted her. Kitty, she hoped, would take pity and cook them for her. In case she didn't, Perdita had bought some carrots, which she was roasting in the oven under the meat.

For pudding, Perdita had made Kitty's version of trifle, which took a maximum of ten minutes to prepare and tasted delicious, even if it was very liquid and alcoholic.

Perdita was collapsed in front of the wood-burning stove, which was blazing well, when Kitty arrived. She had walked over with a basket containing the promised sherry and wine, but also some ground coffee and a box of chocolates.

Perdita kissed the wrinkled cheek offered her, and then hugged Kitty hard. Although they loved each other dearly, they usually kept their embraces fairly restrained. But Perdita was overcome with a rush of love for her elderly friend – probably, the slightly surprised friend commented, because she knew that Kitty was going to help her out in a difficult situation.

'Well, you are, aren't you?' Perdita demanded. 'Otherwise I shall just take your goodies and send you back out into the snow.' She took the basket. 'You shouldn't have carried all those heavy things. You should have let me collect you in the van.'

'My dear child,' replied Kitty, allowing Perdita to relieve her of her ancient, but politically incorrect fur coat, 'when I can't walk a few hundred yards with a couple of bottles of wine and a box of chocolates, I hope you'll have me humanely put to sleep.'

Perdita ignored this. 'I hope no one saw you wearing this coat,' she said, taking the offending item. 'They might throw things at you.'

'Nonsense, that coat is even older than I am and it's warm. Why shouldn't I wear it?'

Perdita didn't waste her breath explaining again. 'Well, if you leave it to me I won't know what to do with it.'

46

'I'm not going to leave it to you. It's going to Sylvia, my bridge partner.'

'Oh, you've got a bridge partner, have you? I thought no one ever played with you twice?'

Kitty chuckled richly. 'They don't, but Sylvia kindly takes me to my bridge afternoons and brings me home, so I've promised her this coat. *She* doesn't worry about animals which have been dead for hundreds of years. Now, have I time for a quick pipe before the others come? Then I'll see what a muddle you've got into in the kitchen.'

Kitty smoked her pipe looking at Perdita's flower garden, taking the opportunity to do a bit of dead heading while she was about it, and then went into the kitchen.

'What time are they coming?' she asked, after surveying the scene for a few moments.

'In about ten minutes,' said Perdita, having shot an anguished glance at her watch.

'Have you got those *big* sherry glasses I gave you?'

Perdita, correctly interpreting this as indication that her kitchen and its contents were past praying for, dutifully retrieved the glasses from the back of a cupboard, and gave them a cursory dust with a tea towel.

'I'm very lucky to have all these nice things,' she said, pulling the foil off the bottle of sherry Kitty had brought with her. 'I love these glasses.'

'Not at all. I was very lucky to have you to off-load a lot of unnecessary possessions on to.'

'But they're not unnecessary.' Perdita filled one with sherry and took a large gulp. 'QED.'

'I meant unnecessary to me,' said Kitty, pouring a somewhat smaller measure.

Before Kitty had taken more than a sip, the door knocker rattled loudly. Perdita answered it.

On the doorstep was a distraught Janey with Lucas on her heels.

Lucas saved Janey the trouble of explaining. 'I invited myself. It wasn't Janey's fault.'

'I could have worked that out.' Perdita stood in the doorway, not letting either Lucas or Janey across the threshold.

'I wanted to see how your kitchen functioned when it wasn't full of garden rubbish.' Lucas pushed forward slightly.

'You're welcome to another time,' said Perdita, untruthfully. 'But this is a private lunch party. I'm terribly sorry, but you can't come.'

'Oh, don't be ridiculous! If you're cooking a joint you can stretch it. I'll carve if you can't.' Lucas took a couple of steps forward. Janey's anxious expression made Perdita sigh and step aside to let them both through.

'I suppose I'll have to let you in,' she said grudgingly, adding to Janey, 'How *could* you?'

'Mrs . . . Anson . . .' said Lucas. 'We haven't met for some years.'

Kitty, who had seated herself in the one armchair, regarded him through narrowed eyes. 'No. Well, I don't suppose it'll be a pleasure seeing you again, but I dare say it'll be interesting.'

Perdita was aware of a shudder from Janey and decided, for her sake, to keep lunch as explosion free as possible. 'Well, do sit down everyone, and I'll get us a glass of sherry.'

Lucas removed himself to the window seat and Janey sat on the Windsor chair. As Perdita passed the sherry she realised that poor William would either have to squash next to Lucas, or sit on the floor.

'Right,' she said, after everyone had taken their first sip and was looking to her for the next step, 'I'm just going to have a peep at what's going on in the kitchen and then I'll see if I can fit another place round the table.'

'I don't mind eating separately,' said Lucas, who, she noted, had put on an extremely smart suit for the occasion.

48

She hoped William wouldn't feel out of place when he turned up in corduroys, flannel shirt and jumper.

Perdita went into the kitchen, more for a moment to herself than because she thought she could do anything about the chaos that met her there. Fury with Lucas for turning up uninvited tempted her to throw her carefully grown vegetables into a pot and boil them to destruction. But as that wasn't fair on the others, she decided to let Kitty deal with the vegetables later.

She peered into the oven and saw that the lamb was brown on top, and the garlic and rosemary at least smelled nice. The potatoes were the colour of church candles and showed no inclination to change. 'Sod it,' she said, slamming the oven door, dislodging the leg of the cooker as she did so. It took her several minutes to put back the wodge of cardboard she used to level it.

On her way back to join the others she bumped into Lucas. 'Can I help?' he asked.

'Only by leaving the country,' said Perdita, pushing him backwards out of the room. 'Or you could get the chair down from the bathroom.'

'Where is the bathroom?'

'Upstairs. Not hard to find.' It was only after she had dispatched him thence that she remembered that her bathroom chair was loaded with several weeks worth of unwashed clothes. Oh well. If he would invite himself to lunch, it was his look out if he had to confront her dirty knickers.

William arrived while Lucas was still upstairs. He looked clean but crumpled, and extremely dubious.

'William, how lovely. Let me give you a drink.' She thrust a glass of sherry into a hand which would have looked more at home wrapped round a pint. 'You know my friend Mrs Anson.' Kitty nodded benignly but although William mumbled something polite-sounding, he visibly shied away.

49

'And Janey. She works at Grantly House. I don't think you've met.'

William dipped his head and glanced at Janey from under his eyebrows.

Lucas and the chair announced their imminent arrival with banging and muted swearing as they came down the stairs. Perdita waited until they had appeared before adding, 'And this is Lucas, who also works at Grantly House.' She was about to add that he had invited himself but decided the situation was already awkward enough. 'Lucas, this is William.'

'We met the other day,' said Lucas. 'Hello. Where do you want this chair?'

It had taken Perdita long enough to fit four chairs round the table, she didn't intend to struggle with a fifth. 'If you wouldn't mind just fitting it in somewhere . . . And try to make it that no one's sitting in front of a leg,' she said, knowing this was impossible, but feeling it a just punishment for him.

The room was silent apart from the shifting of chairs and more muted swearing from Lucas. Perdita perched on the arm of Kitty's chair, trying frantically to think of something to say. Judging by the expressions on the faces of her guests, they were engaged in the same task.

'Nuts, anyone?' Perdita said at last. 'I'm sure I've got some somewhere.'

Janey followed her into the kitchen. 'Knives and forks. We'll need some for Lucas. Oh God!' she went on, when they were out of earshot. 'I'm just so sorry! But he heard you invite me—'

Perdita held up a hand to stem Janey's stream of apologies. 'I know, I know, there was nothing you could do, and you've got to work for him, which is hard enough already.'

'And you must admit,' Janey went on, 'he does look lovely in a suit. I do like smartly dressed men.'

This didn't bode well for Perdita's matchmaking plans. William had many admirable qualities, but sartorial elegance was not among them.

'Did you suggest he wore a suit?' Perdita pulled out a pile of stained willow-pattern plates from a cupboard.

'Oh no, I wouldn't dare. I just found him outside my door when I set off to walk here. It was kind of him to give me a lift.'

Perdita discarded a severely chipped plate and substituted it with one less so. 'I could have arranged for William to pick you up.' Though he would have taken some persuading. 'You haven't met him before, have you?'

'Not to speak to, but I have seen him playing skittles down the pub. He's a bit older than me, you know.'

'But *decades* younger than Lucas!'

'So?'

'Oh, never mind.' Her matchmaking doomed to failure, Perdita took another look at her potatoes. 'Do you think they're just a little bit brown?'

Janey shook her head. 'Well, I dare say they were whiter than that before, but no one could call them brown.'

'Oh bloody hell! What am I to do with the wretched things? I haven't got a grill to put them under.'

'You could put them in their tin on the hot plate and sort of fry them,' suggested Janey. 'Or sprinkle them with chopped herbs and pretend they're not roast potatoes at all.'

'Well, that would be true, at least. But I'll try the frying thing first. God! I hope the lamb is cooked.'

When tested, the lamb oozed pink fluid. 'What shall I do? It's probably completely raw. I'll poison us all.'

'It's OK,' said Janey. 'Lamb is supposed to be pink.'

'Everything all right in here?' Lucas's voice boomed from behind them, making both women jump.

'Fine!' snapped Perdita. 'Go and sit down, or pour

everyone else some more sherry. You go and sit down too, Janey. I'm better off on my own.'

'Mrs Anson wants to know if you want her to cook the vegetables,' Lucas persisted, peering over Perdita's shoulder at the mess beyond.

'No. Tell her, thank you, but I'm managing just fine. Now everybody get out of my way and let me get on!'

After Janey and Lucas had gone back to the sitting room, Perdita shifted the sack of compost which prevented the door from closing, and shut it firmly. Then panic lent inspiration. She put all the vegetables into her wok, stirring them violently with a couple of wooden spoons. Then she took Janey's advice about the potatoes and stuck them in their tin on her hottest ring at its highest heat. While everything spat and cracked behind her, she drained the meat juices into a saucepan. Good gravy might disguise poor roast potatoes. She stuck the lamb back in the oven, which she switched off, and – after another quick glance at Delia – flung a handful of flour into the pan with the meat juices.

All three plates of her ancient electric cooker were going full bat, but Perdita concentrated on the gravy, adding salt and pepper, and the heeltap of a bottle of wine she had opened rather a long time ago. It thickened, and turned a purplish colour. She added the vegetable juices from the wok, which did nothing for the colour.

'Oh, for some gravy browning!' she beseeched, knowing it had been on her list and she had just forgotten to buy it. For a mad moment she contemplated sprinting across her land to Kitty's and hunting in her cupboards for some. There was bound to be something, be it in a bottle or a packet, and it would be so old the price would still be in shillings and pence, but Perdita wouldn't have cared.

No, that was ridiculous. She turned over the potatoes and was gratified to see faint singeing at the edges of some of them, but the gravy was still an unattractive pinky-beige colour. In desperation she turned to her own cupboard and found some soy sauce. She tipped in a large quantity, knowing it would make the sauce dreadfully salty, but anything which meant she didn't have to serve gravy the colour of raw sausages was OK by her.

To her huge relief it worked. It even tasted all right. Perdita decided to quit while she was ahead and declare the meal ready. But as she was tipping veg and potatoes into dishes she realised that someone would have to carve the leg of lamb which was now sitting on a bread board, oozing quietly.

Kitty had never learnt to carve. Her husband had always done it, and after he died, she just hacked bits off whenever she cooked a joint. William probably couldn't carve either, which left herself, raised in the Kitty method of removing meat from bones, or Janey. She would die before she would ask Lucas.

She stood in the doorway of the sitting room. The gathering didn't look like a hive of social intercourse. Lucas was reading a book, Kitty had produced her needlepoint, and Janey and William were exchanging stilted sentences, but not appreciative glances. Perdita sighed.

'Janey – give me a hand?' she asked.

Janey, glad to get away, came at once.

'It's the carving,' said Perdita. 'Do you think you could do it? The table's not big enough so we'll have to do it in here. Do you mind?'

'Perdita, I don't *mind* giving it a go, but I've never carved more than a slice of cheese in my life. My dad always does it.'

'Oh. Well, you're a bright girl, good at cooking, I'm sure you'll be able to do it all right.'

Janey ran her thumb over the knife Perdita produced. 'You haven't got a steel, have you? Something to sharpen it with?'

Perdita shrugged. 'Possibly not. I've just got what Kitty gave me. There may be a better knife somewhere.'

The second knife was no sharper than the first, and the handle was loose. 'Perdita, why don't you just ask Lucas? Then if he makes a hash of it,' Janey obviously thought this was highly unlikely, 'it'll be his fault.'

Perdita considered this fairly tempting idea, but decided it constituted a cop-out. 'No. I'll carve myself. It can't be that hard.' She took the knife from Janey and made a pass at the leg of lamb. The knife bounced off it and landed on the top of her thumb. Fortunately it was too blunt to cut her. She stuck the point into the meat the next time and managed to hack her way a couple of inches into it before hitting a bone. 'Bugger!' she muttered.

'Why don't you let me?' asked Lucas, from the doorway.

'OK,' said Perdita, deciding that copping out was better than taking more bits off herself than off the joint. 'We'll get the rest of the meal on the table, you carve.'

While she and Janey brought through plates, gravy, serving spoons and the vegetables, Perdita spotted Lucas sharpening the knife on the back doorstep. Then, while she was finding space for everything on the table, he turned the leg of lamb into a row of tidy pink slices, which he laid out on the somewhat stained and chipped serving plate she had dusted down for it. He brought it in and stood holding it. It looked quite appetising.

'Wow,' she said, forgetting for a moment who she was talking to. 'That looks really nice.'

'Goodness knows what it tastes like,' said Lucas. 'Now where do you want to put it?'

In the end Perdita put a trivet on top of the wood-burning stove and put it there.

'Now, where is everyone going to sit?' asked Perdita rhetorically. 'Kitty, you sit there, with William on one side. Now Janey, sit next to William, and Lucas next to Janey. I'll sit next to Kitty.'

'And me,' said Lucas. 'Shall I serve out?'

'Yes, please,' said Perdita, handing round vegetables.

When at last everyone was served, Perdita and Lucas squashed into their places. They had to sit with their knees sideways and were hideously uncomfortable.

'Do please start, everyone,' said Perdita, too tired to care if she could reach her plate or not.

'Well, here's to our hostess,' said Lucas blandly, his sarcasm as silent as it was obvious.

'Yes, here's to Perdita,' said William, missing the undercurrents, and everybody joined in the toast.

Perdita took a huge gulp of wine and was pleased to note that Kitty's dear departed husband had not let them down; the wine Kitty had found in his cellar was delicious.

And so, by some miracle, was the food. The lamb, undercooked by Kitty's standards, tasted perfect. The potatoes, while not exactly brown, had developed enough of a suntan to be appetising, and the sprinkling of rosemary Perdita had added out of desperation gave them a certain sophistication. The vegetables were crisp and the gravy was tasty. Everyone except Lucas delivered a cacophony of praise for Perdita, all of them knowing that cooking wasn't her thing.

'Darling! This is *delicious*,' said Kitty. 'I didn't think I liked lamb rare, but this is really tender.'

'No thanks to me. That was the organic butcher,' said Perdita.

'Well, the veggies are down to you,' said Janey. 'And cooked just right.' She blushed and glanced at Lucas to see if this comment on culinary matters was acceptable to him.

'The vegetables are fine,' agreed Lucas. 'No marks for presentation, but they taste fresh.'

'So, what about the gravy?' Perdita demanded provocatively.

Lucas regarded her. 'Let's not spoil a pleasant occasion by discussing it.'

'I think it's jolly good,' said William. 'Is there any more?'

'And what is this?' asked Lucas, as Perdita handed him a glass dish.

'It's trifle,' said Perdita.

'I was afraid it might be,' said Lucas.

'Now, now, young man. Don't criticise until you've tried it,' said Kitty. 'That's a family recipe, handed down the generations.'

'I thought you and Perdita weren't actually related.'

'Oh, just shut up and eat it,' muttered Perdita, rather to Janey's surprise.

'Oh,' he said after a spoonful. 'No jelly. I'm almost disappointed.'

'It's delish,' said Janey. 'Can I have the recipe?'

'If you promise not to give it to Lucas,' Perdita replied. 'I don't want it turning up on the Grantly House menu as one of his creations.'

Eventually the meal drew to a close. Coffee and various sorts of tea were made and drunk, and Kitty's chocolates were handed round, and Perdita was just racking her brains for some neutral topic of conversation when Kitty got slowly to her feet.

'Well, I think I should be going . . .'

'I'll give you a lift back,' said Perdita, jumping up.

'Nonsense. No need to break up the party. It's only a step.'

'No.' Perdita knew her old friend was longing for her afternoon snooze. 'You walked here, carrying all those bottles, that's plenty of exercise for one day.'

'I'll drive Mrs Anson back,' said Lucas firmly. 'Then you don't have to leave your guests, Perdita.'

Perdita and Kitty both regarded him through narrowed eyes. 'Have you got a decent car?' asked Perdita.

'Well, it's a hundred per cent better than your van.'

'Lucas has got a lovely car,' murmured Janey, a touch dreamily.

'Very well,' said Kitty. 'If you will be so kind, I would be glad to accept your generous offer.' Kitty, while never having driven herself, appreciated travelling in fast cars. 'No need to see me out, Perdita dear. Lucas will look after me.'

While reluctant to see Kitty driven away by the Demon King, she didn't feel she could object when Kitty herself was so keen, so Perdita just kissed her friend and thanked her again for her largesse with regard to the wine and sherry.

'Right,' said Janey. 'Let's do the washing-up.'

William got to his feet, obviously dying to go home and watch some sport, and added, 'Yes.'

'Certainly not! I wouldn't dream of allowing you to wash a thing. But if you're going, William, perhaps you wouldn't mind giving Janey a lift? She came with Lucas and although I could run her back . . .' She left her sentence unfinished.

'Of course I can give Janey a lift.'

Janey didn't look terribly enthusiastic. 'Well, if you really won't let us wash up, let us just take some of these things out.'

When they were alone in the kitchen, Perdita said, 'He's nice, isn't he? William?'

'Oh yes,' said Janey immediately. 'He's lovely. I really like him.'

'He's much nicer than Lucas, isn't he?'

'*Nicer*, yes, but nothing *like* as sexy.'

Perdita, who had reached a stage in her life when 'niceness' was not an insult, but a characteristic to be cherished, was aware that Janey had yet to attain this maturity. She saw them both into William's car, knowing her matchmaking had not come off. She felt extremely tempted to do what she knew Kitty was now doing, curling up in a chair with the radio on and her eyes shut, but the washing-up would be even less appealing if she waited until dark to do it.

Chapter Five

The kitchen looked like it had been turned over by a particularly untidy gang of burglars, only instead of taking things, they seemed to have brought dirty dishes with them, and piled them on every surface. There was more crockery than Perdita knew she owned, and every glass, plate, cup, jug or dish had been used.

Already depressed by the failure of her matchmaking attempt, and tired from the effort of cooking, she decided, philosophically, that doing the washing-up couldn't make her feel any worse; why save something so intrinsically unpleasant for when she was feeling happy? Besides, the lighting in her kitchen was so bad you couldn't see to do anything after sunset, which was horribly early at this time of year.

She put on the radio and the mellow tones of an actor told her that the classic serial was something Russian and depressing. Par for the course, she thought, and attached a length of hose pipe to her hot tap. This she led into a black plastic bucket on the floor and added a squirt of washing-up liquid. While she filled a second bucket, she loaded the first with dirty plates. When she heard a loud bang on the front door she muttered an expletive and turned off the tap. She knew that by the time she got back to her washing-up, the light would be gone, the water would be cold, and the serial would have got to its tragic denouement. If people wanted to buy salad, they should buy it before lunch, not after.

Her annoyance was rapidly replaced by anxiety when

she saw it was Lucas. 'Oh my God! Is Kitty all right?'

'Yes, of course! She's indestructible. She got me to clean out the gutter before I left. No, I came back to help with the washing-up,' he said.

'Well, you can't.' Relief gave Perdita confidence. 'It's kind of you to offer, but I'm better off doing it on my own.' She took hold of her door. 'Now if you wouldn't mind – my water's getting cold.'

This would have disposed of the most dogged doorstep salesman, but Lucas pushed his way into the house with a combination of force and determination. 'I need to talk to you about the kitchen,' he said.

Perdita, having failed to keep him out of the house, was determined to keep him out of that devil's brew of grease and dirty crockery. 'You can't!' she repeated. 'At least, not in it, and not now. Say what you want to say out here, and be very quick.'

Lucas stalked purposefully towards the kitchen door. Perdita flew to it, barring his way like a Cavalier maiden protecting her hidden lover. 'Really, you can't go in!'

'You're forgetting that I carved the lamb.' Lucas was every bit as ruthless as a Roundhead soldier intent on rape and pillage. 'I know exactly what state the kitchen is in.' Perdita found herself swept aside and watched helplessly as he opened the kitchen door. 'What on earth are you doing?' he demanded, seeing the buckets.

'The washing-up,' snapped Perdita. 'What's it look like?'

'Good God! You're not camping. Why don't you use a bowl, like everybody else?'

'Because I hate washing-up bowls! A bucket is far more efficient. You can actually submerge the stuff, for one thing. I have one bucket for washing and another for rinsing. Then they can drain in the sink. When I've taken everything out of it, of course.'

Lucas shook his head. 'You're mad. Why can't you do

60

anything the same way as anyone else?'

'Why can't you tell when you're not wanted? I'm quite happy with my washing-up. It's nothing to do with you how I choose to do it. I didn't ask you to come back and help me!'

Lucas looked about him. 'No, I know. But you must admit it'll take you hours on your own. And why don't you put the light on? It's black as pitch in here.'

'The light *is* on,' sighed Perdita. 'Can't you see it?'

Lucas saw the single, naked bulb dangling from the ceiling. 'For Christ's sake! No wonder you don't like cooking, if you try to do it in this black hole!'

'I don't try to do it in this black hole! I don't try to do it, full stop! Today was a one-off, never-to-be-repeated experience.'

'Well, I can see why.'

'Well, I'm glad you can see something, because after the sun goes down, I can't! But I can just about manage the washing-up by feel, so if you wouldn't mind buggering off, I can get on with it.'

'Why the hell don't you get some lighting in there?' called Lucas from the sitting room. He came back with a table lamp. 'Where can I plug this in?'

Perdita sighed. 'Unplug the microwave.'

Lucas swept up the large quantity of post, junk mail and important letters, which sat on top of the microwave and put it in a pile on a chair.

'Don't put it there! It'll get lost!'

'It's only junk mail anyway,' said Lucas disdainfully.

'It's not, and anyway, I like junk mail.'

Lucas paused. 'You *are* mad. How can anyone like junk mail?'

Perdita shrugged. 'It gives me something to read over breakfast, and I don't have to do anything about it. And the polythene bags it comes in are useful,' she added, slightly shamefaced about her anti-social preferences.

Lucas tutted explosively. 'For God's sake, woman, get a grip!'

Perdita took a breath in order to tell him, in no uncertain terms, exactly how hard a grip she had on life, and no thanks to him, when she observed that he was getting stuck into the washing-up with a speed and efficiency her kitchen had not previously witnessed. She watched for a moment and then decided that it was her washing-up and not for him to do. 'You're slopping water on the floor. Let me do it.' She elbowed him out of the way and sank to her knees. 'Put the kettle on, if you want to be useful. This water's gone cold.'

With a growl of irritation, Lucas filled the kettle and switched it on. 'I need to talk to you about the cooker. It won't do for the programme, you know. Nor will the lighting.'

'The television people will bring lighting. Even I know that much.' She scrubbed at a dish she would normally have left to soak for a few days. 'And as for the cooker, I told everyone, from the very moment they had the idea of making the programme here, that the whole kitchen was totally unsuitable.' She shifted uncomfortably on her knees, regretting that her bucket idea, though excellent in many ways, involved kneeling on a wet kitchen floor in her best jeans. Lucas sneering at her from on high didn't help matters.

'The kitchen is fine, or it would be if it wasn't such a goddamn pigsty, but the light and the cooker are a disaster.'

'Well, I'm sorry about the cooker, it's the only one I've got, and even if I could afford to, I wouldn't dream of replacing it just to please you and your television company.' She sank the last plate into the bucket of rinsing water and decided to put the many roasting tins out in the garden for the foxes to clean out.

'No. *I* want to replace it.'

'What do you mean?' She retrieved the plate, got up and rubbed her back.

'I mean, I will buy you a new cooker, so I don't have to use that one.'

'Don't be silly. You may be a prima-donna-type chef these days, but surely even you can't be so prissy you can't use a perfectly ordinary electric cooker.'

'That cooker is not ordinary! It should be in a museum. I'm sure it's not safe.'

'Of course it's safe! What's wrong with it?'

He stepped round her in order to inspect it and made aggressive stabs in its direction, switching knobs, pulling out plates and generally attacking it. 'It's only got three tiny burners, the grill doesn't seem to work, it wobbles, and I doubt you can get the oven very hot.'

'It was hot enough to cook the lamb!' she said, not sure what temperature it had got to.

'But not hot enough to roast the potatoes.'

Perdita toyed with the idea of pretending they weren't meant to be roast potatoes but rejected it. She scooped several wooden spoons, a wet tea towel and a colander out of the sink. 'I thought television cooks did things mostly on top. And it's all cheating, anyway, isn't it? I'm sure they just paint things with varnish to make them look brown.'

She was sorry she had her back to him and so missed seeing his eruption of fury. She had to make do with wraparound sound, which was several decibels louder than the recommended maximum. It was odd how, when she had been married to him, his fury had terrified her. Now it just made her want to giggle. She turned and leant against the sink, biting her lip.

'Perhaps you're too scrupulous to be a television cook, Lucas.'

He heard the laughter in her voice and strode towards her, bringing his hands down hard on her shoulders. 'I suppose you think this is funny!'

63

'Well, of course I do! It's hilarious! You coming into my house, *my kitchen*, to do a cookery programme. You must see the funny side! Or have you completely lost your sense of humour?'

It was important to make him laugh, then he might let her go. Having Lucas's hands on her shoulders was unsettling. He always had had the ability to arouse her with the lightest, most innocent of touches. It seemed that he still had.

His mouth twitched, first in one corner, and then it curled into a grin made more attractive by the fact that he tried to suppress it. 'I suppose it is a little bizarre, and not something I would have imagined happening six months ago.' His hands slipped off her shoulders, down her arms and away. 'It must have been a shock for you, seeing me again after all these years.'

Not as much of a shock as this note of concern in his voice. 'Well, yes. But it must have been just as much of a shock for you.'

'Not really. I knew Kitty lived in the area, after all. And I saw your name under Bonyhays Salads.'

'Of course. But if I hadn't delivered salads to you, you wouldn't have looked me up?'

'Why not? I know we parted on bad terms, but I would have hoped we could have got over that.'

She turned away from him and put her hands into the sink, trying to make it look as if she was doing something. 'Bad terms doesn't really cover it, Lucas. You abandoned me for another woman, in the most hurtful circumstances possible.'

'I know, and I'm not proud of it. But you've got over it, haven't you? You seem fine.'

She turned back to him. 'Yes, of course I'm fine. But it's no thanks to you, and you really couldn't expect to swan back into my life and for me to forgive and forget.'

'I didn't say anything about coming back into your life,

64

Perdita. Just that I would have looked you up and hoped we could have been civil to each other.'

'Then it's a shame that's obviously quite impossible, particularly as you've got yourself involved in a television fiasco which seems to need my co-operation!'

'I can do without your co-operation! I can easily find another picturesque cottage where, possibly, you don't have to do the washing-up on the floor! But can you do without the money? They'll pay you for using your kitchen, though not much. They'll give you something, and pay for all the vegetables they use.'

'I run a flourishing business. I don't need my life messed around by a television crew.'

'If your business is so flourishing, why don't you drive a half-decent van? Why don't you have a cooker that works? Surely, even if you don't cook, you'd like an oven to heat up your ready-meals.'

'"Need" and "want" are different things! I have everything I need, and most of the things I want.'

'Then buy a van.'

'I don't want to!'

'But you do *need* to,' he shot back at her. 'And you can't afford one.'

'If I really needed, or wanted, a new van I could use the money you gave me.' She hadn't meant to mention this money. It was a symbol of a time of failure and misery in her life, and she had tried to blot it out of her consciousness. Somehow it flung itself into the conversation uninvited.

Lucas frowned. 'Then why the fuck don't you?'

'Because I would rather deliver my vegetables in a wheelbarrow or in a sack on my back than use a penny of your blood money – money you sent me to make yourself feel better about ditching me!'

'I sent it because I thought you might need it! I could ill afford to do without it at the time! I should have known that you would have fled back to dear Auntie Kitty and she would have picked up the pieces and put your life back together for you!'

This statement – pretty much the truth, though it didn't give her one iota of credit for her own efforts – sent Perdita's anger to heights it previously hadn't known. She stormed out of the kitchen in search of her handbag. It took a maddeningly long time to find, and by the time she stormed back into the kitchen with a cheque, the saucepans and several vegetable dishes were draining in the sink.

'Here's your money! I hope it comes in useful!' She thrust the cheque at him, knowing she would have to do some very rapid financial fiddling to get the money out of the building society, and into her current account before her bank manager summoned her for an explanation.

Lucas handed it back. 'I don't want it. It's yours. Why don't you do something useful with it?'

She refused to touch it. 'I've told you why! I don't want it!'

'Then give it to charity!' He stuffed it into the neck of her jumper.

She snatched it out and thrust it deep into his breast pocket. '*You* give it to charity! I'm sure there must be a benevolent fund for trainee chefs suffering from nervous breakdowns caused by tyrants like you!'

'I think I should tell you that, in chef terms, I am a pussycat. I don't hit my staff with ladles, or throw boiling water over them. And if I shout a bit, or let slip the occasional four-letter word, they're all adults, they don't have to stay.'

'Enzo never shouted at everyone, and he was a brilliant chef.' This wasn't entirely true. Enzo *could* cook like an angel, but more often didn't.

'He was the most hopeless, bloody unprofessional idiot ever let loose in a kitchen!'

'How would you know? You didn't see him cook!'

'Yes I did and I ate his food. When I came to look the place over. I've never seen anything so unprofessional in my life. I'm surprised he wasn't closed down by the Environmental Health officer.'

'Well anyway, at least he was a success as a human being!'

'That really depends on how you define "success".'

'At least he was happily married!' she shot at him, wishing she hadn't a moment later. She didn't know that he hadn't married again. 'Though, perhaps you are too,' she added more quietly.

'No, I'm still divorced.'

'So the woman you left me for left you, did she?'

'No, I left her, actually.'

'Oh.' Perdita suddenly needed to get away from the kitchen, with its sodden floor, crowded surfaces and memories of the awful stress of cooking.

He followed her into the sitting room and sat down in the armchair, while Perdita knelt before the wood-burning stove, and delicately coaxed back some flames.

'So, is there a man in your life?'

Perdita had a log in her hand. 'That is absolutely none of your business!'

'I'll take that as a no then.'

Perdita was dearly tempted to throw the log at his head, but resisted, tossing it instead into the stove, with less care than necessary. 'No! You can't take it as anything! It's just none of your business!'

'You asked me if I was married!'

'No I didn't! You volunteered the information!'

'You volunteer it too, then.'

Perdita sighed sharply and got to her feet before collapsing into the Windsor chair opposite his. 'Like you I'm still divorced.'

'And not engaged, I see.' She looked quizzically at him. 'No ring,' he added.

'I hardly ever wear jewellery. It cuts into your fingers when you're digging and gets clogged up with soil.'

'So, are you engaged?'

'I told you, it's none of your business.'

'So you're not. Knocking thirty and no man on the scene. Dear, dear. Lovely girl like you. What is wrong with young men these days?'

She narrowed her furious gaze. 'I do have a boyfriend, if you must know. But he lives quite a long way away, and I don't see him often.' That should shut him up.

'Oh, I am glad.' Clearly, he didn't believe a word of it. 'Then could I invite you both to dinner with me at Grantly House? I'd like to show you the changes I've made to the menu.'

'Does that mean you'd be eating with us? Or would you be in the kitchen?'

'I'd be in the kitchen. I'd come and talk to you, of course, since you would be my guests, but I wouldn't spoil your romantic evening.'

'Oh, good.'

'So does that mean you'd like to come?'

'Of course, I can't make arrangements without consulting – him.' If she made up a name, it might lead to all sorts of complications.

'Of course not. But in principle you'd like to come?'

'Oh, yes. We'd love it.' Like a snowflake enjoys a visit to hell.

'Good.' He got to his feet. 'Well then, since you're not going to offer me tea—'

'No, I'm not.'

'I'd better get back. Thank you so much for lunch. It was very interesting.'

'Thank you so much for coming. It wouldn't have been nearly so much fun without you.'

'No need to be sarcastic, Perdita. I did help with the washing-up.'

'That was the worst part.'

'Let me change your mind about that.' Before she could think what he was doing, he took the cheque out of his pocket and thrust it down the front of her jumper. Before she could react, he got one arm round her shoulders and then kissed her, so hard and so long that she would have fallen over if he hadn't been holding her up.

'You bastard! How dare you?' she hurled at him, the moment she could speak.

He turned, from halfway down the path on the way to his car. 'The advantage of being the wicked ex-husband is that you don't have a reputation to lose. Nothing I could possibly do could make you think any worse of me. Goodbye, Perdita. See you soon.'

She was so outraged by the kiss and his subsequent remark that she only remembered the cheque when she heard a crackling sound as she turned to stomp indoors. By that time his car had roared off.

She stood in her sitting room, simmering quietly, then slumped into the armchair and stared at the flames which flickered behind their glass doors.

'I'll get the bloody cheque to Lucas if it's the last thing I do. Then I have to find a boyfriend. A big one. Who looks likely to punch him on the nose if he so much as thinks about touching me,' she said aloud. 'Sod him, sod him, sod him!'

Her indignation was not, she knew, because of his rapine kiss, but because of her reaction to it. Not that he had turned her knees to jelly, made her wish the kiss could last for ever, or anything remotely romantic. But she hadn't felt revolted, or raped, or violated, or indeed any of the proper, politically correct emotions felt by women when men forced themselves on them. In fact she had responded to the feeling of a strong man's arms around her.

'It's my hormones, letting me down,' she muttered. 'I

69

have to find a boyfriend – not only to punch Lucas, but for *me*! Because I need a man to hug me. Because, however much you love them, you can't cuddle lettuces!'

It was a few days after the lunch party that Perdita came across Kitty, poring over catalogues.

'Hello, what's all this?' Perdita asked. 'I thought you hated shopping by mail order?'

'I do. It's environmentally unsound, but I've just realised that if I look through these I can do all my Christmas shopping without ever going out.'

'Don't you feel up to going out?'

'I feel up to going out,' Kitty explained, irritated by the concern in Perdita's voice, 'but not inclined to thrash my way through crowds of people.'

As Perdita often felt like this herself, she stopped worrying and looked across at the selection of catalogues Kitty was going through. 'They're mostly plants. Do your friends and relations want plants for presents?'

'Of course. Everyone loves plants.'

'But five hundred busy Lizzies, and five hundred universal pansies. Think of all that planting out! And Christmas is such a busy time for most people.'

'Not everyone raises plants for a living, like you do,' said Kitty. 'Besides, these won't come until March.'

'Well, don't give me anything in a plug I can't make money out of.'

'Well, what would you like?'

Perdita sighed. 'A man. Or, better than that, a table lamp. I've put one in the kitchen now, which does improve things a bit, but it means I haven't got one in the sitting room.'

'That's easy. I'm sure there's a catalogue here with them in. You could choose your own.'

Perdita chuckled and flicked through the clothes catalogue with the attractive male models in it. She still liked the vet in sailing trousers. 'What would happen if I rang up these people and asked to be put in touch with him?' She showed Kitty the picture.

Kitty peered at it. 'They'd think you were a crank and refuse to tell you anything about him. And quite right too. His eyes are too close together.'

'That's only because he's squinting into the sun! But I take your point about being a crank. They'd never divulge details about the people modelling, or no one would do it. I'll have to think of something else.'

'Is it Lucas that brought this on? I must say, he has got very attractive in his old age, hasn't he? I never thought much of him as a young man, but a few years have improved him enormously.'

'Do you think so? What do you want for Christmas, then?'

'Oh, I don't know, but I do want to talk to you about it.'

'Talk then. But you will have to think of something. Otherwise I'll order you some surfinias or whatever they're called.'

'The Ledham-Golds have invited me for Christmas,' said Kitty. 'I wasn't going to say if I would go until I'd talked to you about it.'

Perdita felt a bit flat. She and Kitty usually spent Christmas together, and while neither of them felt it was their favourite time, exactly, it was at least familiar. 'Well, I think you should go. It would make a nice change.'

'I could ask them if they could have you as well. I'm sure they wouldn't mind having an able-bodied person about, but they are all awfully elderly.' By this she meant well over seventy, still a good ten years younger than she was herself. 'It wouldn't be a lot of fun for you, but I don't want to leave you on your own.'

'I wouldn't mind, honestly. I think I'd quite like having it on my own – if I couldn't have it with you, of course. You tell the Ledham-Golds you'll go. They probably need cheering up. Doesn't his sister live with them, or something?'

'That's right. She does the garden and Veronica does the house. Bernard does the crossword and watches *Countdown*.'

'I'm quite fond of *Countdown* myself. It's got a cult following, you know.'

'Hmm,' said Kitty disapprovingly. 'What does that mean?'

'It means students watch it.'

'When they should be doing their work, I dare say.'

'Probably. What about a giant lily? Look, it grows to over six foot high!'

Kitty snorted, disgusted by the notion. 'I'd rather have a knitted bed jacket from the church bazaar.'

'You're so difficult to buy presents for.'

'Just get me soap, darling. Now, are you sure you don't mind having Christmas on your own?'

The thought of being on her own at Christmas really didn't bother Perdita, but she knew it bothered Kitty. She wouldn't allow herself to accept the Ledham-Golds' invitation while she felt Perdita would be lonely on Christmas Day.

No amount of telling her would persuade Kitty that a day spent pottering about at home, dipping in and out of the Christmas specials, was an attractive prospect to Perdita. She worked hard, and had very little time to mooch about and refresh her batteries. A day off when she could legitimately be a slob became more tempting the more she thought about it. But she couldn't convince Kitty.

The problem was solved a few days later when Perdita got a card from an old school friend, Lucy, who had married shortly after Perdita and subsequently disappeared off to the Caribbean. Unlike Perdita she had stayed married, even when an island in the Caribbean had turned into an island off the north coast of Scotland. Her card arrived on the first of December, indecently early.

I'm really organised this year as, you will see from the address, we are supposed to be moving to Shropshire next week,' it said, in gold pen. 'Madness, I know, what with having to do F.C. for the children. It should have been October, but house sales never go to plan. I know the house will be wonderful eventually, but at the moment it's crumbling and ancient and will cost mega-bucks to get habitable. I don't suppose you fancy spending Christmas with us? Seriously, it would be lovely to see you sometime.'

This could be the solution. Lucy had always been what she liked to call spontaneous, which other people felt meant unpredictable, and her throwaway invitation could be a godsend. Perdita, to check her friend was still in the far north, gave her a ring.

After a lot of shrieks and how are yous, and I can't believe the children are that bigs, Perdita said, 'I don't suppose you meant it when you asked me to spend Christmas with you?'

'You're not saying that you want to come? Oh, Perdita! It would be marvellous! I only said it as a sort of joke – but prayer might be more like it. I mean, there'll be no hot water or carpets or curtains, or anything. It'll be hell. You'll probably hate it, but we'd love to have you!'

'And I'd love to come. It would be such fun to see you again and meet your children.'

'Are you sure? Jake's brother is coming. His marriage has just broken up. Can you really cope? There's an Aga, but we're not sure if we'll be able to get it lit in time.'

Having assured Lucy that her new house would be considered luxury by some people who had seen hers, Perdita rang off, suddenly looking forward to the festive season.

Kitty, of course, was thrilled. 'Lovely for you to be with some young people for a change. Pity they live so far away. Moving to Shropshire, you said? Will the van get that far?'

'It will do if you pay for me to have it serviced as my Christmas present.'

'Of course, darling. I've ordered you a table lamp, but Father Christmas can give you that.'

'Or it could wait until my birthday.'

'September?' Kitty shook her head. 'I shouldn't think so. It'll be past its sell-by date by then.'

Perdita chuckled. 'Kitty, it's a table lamp. It won't go off.'

Kitty shook her head. Having recently been severely reprimanded by Miriam, her cleaning lady, about having things in her cupboards priced in pre-decimal coinage, she was making her protest. 'I still think it would be better for you to have it now.'

Perdita kissed Kitty's wrinkled cheek in love and merriment.

Chapter Six

The next fortnight was extremely hectic for Perdita. Both the health farm and Grantly Manor were particularly busy, and other restaurants that were not regular customers wanted things at Christmas. Aware she was likely to get a furious phone call from Lucas when he found it, she decided to bury the cheque she had so far failed to give him, in her delivery box among some handsome, but not very appetising cardoons.

Then she rang Janey to find out when would be a good time to deliver, in other words, when Lucas wouldn't be there. Having been assured that he never appeared before ten o'clock, she got up even earlier than usual and ignored her chores, so she could arrive seconds after the kitchen opened. When Lucas leapt out from behind a door at ten past nine, she couldn't help screaming.

'Ah! What did you do that for? You gave me such a fright! Honestly!' Perdita hoped her indignation and surprise would conceal her anxiety about the hidden cheque. He hadn't ordered cardoons, either.

'The early bird catches the worm.' Before Perdita could heartily agree that he was a worm, he went on, poking a derisive finger through the box she was carrying. 'What have you fobbed off on me this time? Not what I ordered, that's for sure. Oh my God! Cardoons!'

Knowing the cheque was right at the bottom of the bunch of spiky, acanthus-shaped leaves, she managed to look him straight in the eye. 'It's a difficult time of year.

I've got a lot of orders to fill. And not everyone can handle a cardoon.'

'If you think you can flatter me into accepting your rubbish, you're in for a shock.'

'Oh?' asked Perdita sweetly. '*Can't* you handle them, then?'

He leant against the cold store door and narrowed his eyes. 'Bitch.'

Perdita took this both as a compliment and as an acceptance of the culinary challenge, thrust the box into his arms and went to fetch the next lot. She was on her way out after the final delivery when Lucas stopped her.

'Don't run away. You usually have time to waste my staff's time, you can stay for a minute. Can you get us both a coffee, Janey?'

'Say please,' muttered Perdita, on Janey's behalf, confident that his cheque was still safely hidden.

'So, what are you doing for Christmas?' Lucas asked, having carried the two mugs into his office.

Reluctantly, Perdita had followed the coffee. 'Oh, I'm going to an old school friend's. In Shropshire.' It was nice to be able to tell him this. It made her sound like a proper person, not a sad divorcee without a social life.

'And I expect you'll be seeing your boyfriend while you're there?'

Perdita had momentarily forgotten about her fictional boyfriend. 'Oh, yes.'

'What does he do? I can't remember if you said.'

Perdita couldn't either. 'He's a vet,' she said, remembering the catalogue which Kitty was still mulling over.

'Oh. Well, don't forget my invitation. Perhaps you'd like to bring him for New Year's Eve? We're doing a dinner dance. It should be rather special.'

'Sounds fun. I'll have to ask him, of course.'

'Is he working over Christmas?'

'Oh, er – yes.' She searched her brain for inspiration.

She'd never had a pet, and knew nothing about vets except what she'd read in James Herriot. She smiled. 'Lambing starts at Christmas. He's likely to be very busy. Which is why I'm going up there. I can see him between lambs.'

Lucas sipped his coffee, which he took very strong and very black. 'Has he got partners, this vet of yours?'

'Well – of course.' James Herriot had had partners.

'Then I expect he'll be able to get time off over New Year, if he's working all Christmas.'

'Well, it's possible, I suppose. But I'd have to ask him.'

'Of course. You mustn't take him for granted. Eligible men are terribly scarce, so everyone tells me.'

Perdita's coffee was also pretty strong. She took a gulp and said, as blandly as she could, 'They are. You should take advantage of the scarcity, Lucas. There's probably even someone out there desperate enough to take you on.'

He smouldered at her, and Perdita found it quite hard not to respond to the smile which lurked beneath his snarl. He hadn't lost his sense of humour, after all.

She took a few sips of coffee and then broke the silence. 'So, what did you want to see me about? Not just to check out my holiday arrangements, surely?'

'No. It's about this cooker. I really need to replace yours. I can probably even get a cooker firm to give me one, as an advertising stunt: "As used by Lucas Gillespie in the award-winning programme . . ."'

Perdita shook her head. 'If they did that they'd want you to use their biggest, most fancy model, not something small enough to fit into my kitchen. No, Lucas. You have to manage with the cooker I've got, or do the programme somewhere else.'

She stalked out of his office, hearing his low growl and feeling his furious gaze on her back. She tried hard not to appear to hurry.

It was with relief that she set off for the health farm. Ronnie might nag her a lot, but he didn't bite.

'How are you, love?' asked Ronnie, when she staggered into the kitchen at Abbotsford Health Resort. 'Haven't seen you to talk to for ages. Time for a coffee?'

'I've just had one, actually, but I'll have another. So what's new?'

'More to the point,' said Ronnie, pouring water into mugs, 'what's new with you? What's all this about a television programme with Count Dracula from Grantly Manor?'

'You wouldn't have a biscuit, would you? I'm starving.'

'I've got KitKats, but don't let anyone know, and you can only have one if you tell me everything.'

'I will, but there isn't much to tell, honestly. The television company who's filming Lucas – Count Dracula ... that really is a very good name for him – decided, for some inexplicable reason ...'

'Careful where you're spraying those crumbs.'

'... that they want to do the series in my kitchen. In my cottage, with me.'

Ronnie's shriek was gratifyingly loud. 'But it's titchy! Not to mention a pot mess.' Ronnie had glimpsed Perdita's kitchen when he had his customer tour.

'Exactly. I expect they'll see sense before anything actually happens. But Lucas is in a froth because my cooker's not up to much. He wants to buy me a new one.'

'Well, let him! After all, he'll be getting well paid for the telly.'

'I can't – for all sorts of reasons.' Perdita realised how nearly she had let slip that she and Lucas had once been married. 'I mean, one wouldn't want to be beholden to a man like that.'

'I'll take your word for it. But promise me one thing: if

you are going to be on telly, let the girls sort you out first.'

'But, Ronnie! I'm a woman of the soil!'

'There's no need to look like one! You could be a real beauty if you weren't so . . .'

'Grubby?'

'No! Well, I'd have said unkempt, badly groomed.'

'I'm not a horse!'

'So why do you wear a ponytail then?'

'Leave me alone, I'm all right as I am.' She gulped down a last mouthful of coffee. 'Now I must go, I've got an appointment with Derek at the garage, and you know what a ray of sunshine he is.'

Perdita kicked at a piece of rubber tube on the ground, pondering bleakly on how often people said 'sorry' when they actually meant 'thrilled to bits'.

Derek, her grudging but long-standing garage man, had declared her van unfit to go to Shropshire without a major overhaul, which, of course, he couldn't possibly do before Christmas. Derek hated her van and had been nagging her to get a new one for at least a year.

'I just wouldn't want you breaking down over Christmas,' he said, his smile not concealing his *Schadenfreude*. 'You could be stranded in Shropshire for weeks, and then where would you be?'

'In Shropshire, presumably,' said Perdita, 'but I take your point.'

'You need a new van, love, that's the top and bottom of it. It's not worth spending money on, see?' He kicked its rotting under-parts and Perdita saw. 'I'll keep my eyes open for one just a couple of years old for you, after the New Year.'

Perdita faked gratitude as best she could and took her unreliable, unrepairable, but strangely dear, vehicle back home, depressed. She would have to tell Lucy that she couldn't come for Christmas, and face up to the fact that she would have to find the money for a better van. How could anyone work as hard as she did and still not be rich? It wasn't right.

Lucy, who still hadn't moved, took the news unexpectedly badly. 'But, Perdita! You *must* come! I was depending on you!' Then she burst into tears.

Perdita, realising that there was a lot more behind this than one less pair of hands to do the sprouts, listened to her friend sob for a little while, opening a pile of Christmas cards.

'I really hate to let you down.' Eventually the sobs had stopped long enough for Perdita to speak. 'But honestly, if the van's not going to make it, I really don't think I can come.'

Lucy sniffed loudly. 'No, of course not. Sorry to be so silly. Moving is such hell – *Christmas* is such hell – and to have them both together is too awful for words – I keep crying. My mother's coming . . .'

'That'll be a help then—' began Perdita.

'. . . but I don't want her to have to do a thing. She always had Christmas at her house, but Daddy died last year, and I want to do all the things she always did, for her.'

'But, Lucy, you're moving house! She won't expect you to do the Full Turkey! When do you move, by the way?'

'Oh, the day after tomorrow, and I'm still not properly packed. But I so want this Christmas to be special. For Mummy, as well as the children.'

'I'm so sorry.' Perdita wondered if the phone cord would let her reach her box of cards so she could write a few. It didn't.

'I've just had a brilliant idea!' Lucy sounded distinctly happier. 'Geoff can collect you! He's Jake's brother, the one whose marriage has just broken up. He lives in Cornwall. That's not far from you, is it?'

'Only about a couple of hundred miles away . . .'

'But it's on the way, isn't it?'

'I'm really not sure. My geography's a bit hazy . . .'

'I'll ring and ask him if he can pick you up. I'm sure he'll be delighted.'

'But if his marriage has just broken up, he's not going to want to pick up some female he's never met and drive her hundreds of miles.' The thought of being that female, trying to make conversation, was filling Perdita with horror.

'Yes he will. I'll tell him how vital you are to my plans, and he'll be perfectly OK about it.'

Perdita's small enthusiasm for the plan evaporated entirely. 'But *why* am I so vital, Luce?'

'Oh well, cooking, and getting the house straight, and stuff like that—' Lucy's voice broke, and Perdita, certain that Lucy didn't have time to keep bursting into tears, interrupted.

'Well, of course I'd love to help with anything you want me to do, but . . .' she tailed off. Perhaps it would be unkind to tell Lucy that she couldn't cook anything more complicated than spaghetti and wasn't known for her tidiness. 'I could look after the children.'

Lucy sniffed. 'Oh no, the children are being frightfully clingy. They're being torn from their home, their familiar surroundings. But you could look after Mummy,' she added more brightly.

When Perdita rang off, some emotionally charged minutes later, she decided to go and tell Kitty that she wouldn't need to pay for the van's overhaul. As she walked through her own land, to climb over the fence into Kitty's garden, she wondered why Lucy's mother needed looking after.

'Well,' said Kitty, having handed Perdita tea in a huge breakfast cup, with a couple of ginger nuts in the saucer, 'I was a bit anxious about you motoring all that way on

81

your own.' Never having learnt to drive herself, Kitty felt subconsciously that it was dangerous, and that women shouldn't do it.

'It would have been perfectly all right if the van had been reliable,' said Perdita, who understood Kitty's subtext.

'Never mind. I'm glad you're being driven. By a man.' Kitty had the sense not to add the word 'nice'. 'So what are you going to take? I could let you have some mincemeat, if you like.'

Perdita shook her head. 'Lucy might expect me to make mince pies. I can't even manage frozen pastry.'

'Buy a box of chocolate biscuits then; they're always useful. And I'll give you a bottle of Lionel's port. I'll never get through it, if I live to be a hundred and fifty,' she went on, as Perdita protested. 'And you might as well take some Burgundy, too. So, what am I going to get you for Christmas? A table lamp isn't enough.'

Perdita picked up the catalogue which still lurked on Kitty's kitchen table and took a lingering look at the vet in the sailing trousers. 'If you can't tuck a nice man into my stocking, I would love a new spade.'

'You're not taking that rust-bucket to Shropshire, are you?' Lucas demanded when Perdita delivered the last salads he was going to get before the New Year.

'No, I'm getting a lift.'

'With your boyfriend? That's nice. What kind of a car has he got?'

'I don't know,' said Perdita without thinking, and then added quickly. 'He's changed it recently.'

Janey, who was making roses out of butter with a potato peeler, gave Perdita a curious look.

'So he's coming down from Shropshire to pick you up?' Lucas went on.

Perdita thought rapidly. If she just said yes, could she

be caught out in a lie? Could anyone – Lucas, for instance – be able to tell that a car driving into the village came from Cornwall, not Shropshire? 'Mmm.' She tried to sound noncommittal.

'Perhaps you'd like to bring him here for lunch?'

'Oh no, he'll be in a frightful hurry. We won't have time for lunch.'

Lucas's steely gaze narrowed frighteningly. 'I don't believe in this boyfriend of yours. I think you've just made him up.'

Perdita blushed furiously. 'How ridiculous! Why on earth would I do a thing like that?'

Lucas shrugged. 'To prove something to someone – to me perhaps.'

'I've never heard anything so silly in all my life.' Perdita was wearing outdoor clothes and the kitchen suddenly became unbearably hot. 'Why on earth would I bother to lie to *you*?' Oh, *why* had she?

'Then bring him here for lunch – a drink even.'

'No,' said Perdita firmly. 'I am not going to disrupt –' a moment's panic while she tried to remember if her mythical boyfriend had a name – 'his plans just to show you he's real!' She made a face. '"Sorry, darling, I know you're in a frightful hurry, but would you mind just coming to lunch so I can prove to –"' she almost bit her tongue as she realised how nearly she had referred to Lucas as 'my ex-husband' in front of Janey and Greg – '"someone I sell lettuce to,"' she hurried on, trying to sound scathing, '"that you really exist?" I don't think so.'

'Fair enough, but don't you forget, seeing is believing.'

Perdita, elated at having got herself out of trouble, smiled sweetly at him. 'And don't *you* forget that if you don't believe in Father Christmas he won't bring you any presents. And I don't suppose you've seen him lately.'

'True, but then, I don't hang up my stocking any more.'

This produced an 'oh' of compassion from Janey, and a tiny spark of it from Perdita. 'What are you doing for Christmas, then?' she asked.

'Like your boyfriend, I'm working, except on Christmas Day.'

'Oh.' Perdita's compassion warred with relief that she and Kitty were both going away, so she couldn't possibly feel guilty for not inviting him to spend Christmas Day with them. Or worse, with her on her own. 'But you'll have somewhere nice to go for the day, won't you?'

'Oh, no need to worry about me, Perdita. I expect I can conjure up a "girlfriend",' he said the word in inverted commas, 'from somewhere.'

'Oh, good. Happy Christmas then, Lucas. Janey, we must go for a drink together, or something. I'll see you before then, anyway.'

'Just a minute. I've got a card for you,' said Lucas. He handed her an impressively large envelope.

'Oh,' Perdita was horribly caught out. 'I'm afraid I only send them to people if they've sent me them, as they come in. And it's a bit late, now.'

'So I'm even cut off your Christmas card list? How sad,' he murmured softly, so Janey wouldn't hear.

'Oh God!' said Perdita. 'I'm leaving, before the violins start.'

When she got home and opened the card, inside it, as well as a beautiful Madonna, were neatly shredded strips of cheque.

Janey, whom Perdita ran into in the post office, was bubbling with Christmas spirit and enthusiasm. 'When I found out that Lucas was going to be on his own for Christmas, I invited him round.'

'To have Christmas with your family? How kind.' How brave, how foolhardy, she thought. And how surprising that he accepted.

'We'll all have Christmas lunch together, of course, but in the evening we usually go round to my auntie's. I thought me and Lucas could stay behind. He's not going to want to have tea with my Auntie Susan, is he?'

'Possibly not. But what will you do with him?'

Janey blushed. 'I thought we could watch the film on telly.'

'Really, Janey, don't you think Lucas is a bit old for you?'

'No. He's gorgeous. And I'm sure he's just grumpy because he's lonely. I mean, fancy being on your own at Christmas!'

Perdita did fancy that very thing, quite a lot, but knew Janey wouldn't believe her. 'You're so kind and generous, Janey, I just don't want you to get hurt.'

Janey sighed ecstatically. 'I wouldn't mind being hurt by Lucas. One night of passion would last me for years. I mean, I know he'd never look seriously at a girl like me, but he might just . . .'

At this moment, the queue shuffled on, but Perdita was horrified. Janey had no notion of what she was saying. A crush was one thing, but for Janey to sacrifice her body – quite possibly her virginity – to Lucas, was very much more serious. She was only eighteen, after all.

Perdita sacrificed her place in the queue, so she could keep talking to Janey. 'You wouldn't do anything silly, would you?'

'It's up to me what I do, Perdita. And anyway, what's all this about a boyfriend? You didn't tell me about him! And spending Christmas together! It must be serious! How dare you not tell me something so wonderful?'

Perdita took a deep breath. 'We really can't talk here,' she said. 'Let's meet for a drink, and I'll tell you all about it.'

'OK. White Horse, Thursday night, eight o'clock? We

can both walk there, and I'm not working then.'

'Sounds good, as long as I've got my Christmas shopping done by then.'

'But, Perdita! That's the day before Christmas Eve!'

'Is it? Oh, plenty of time then. Yes, that'll be great.'

Perdita retreated to the back of the queue to contemplate the evils of deception, and to speculate about whether she could trust Janey with the truth about her fictional boyfriend, or if there was a risk she might let something slip to Lucas.

As things turned out, Perdita was spared the decision. Geoff, her broken-hearted chauffeur, rang to ask if he could pick her up the night she had arranged to go for a drink with Janey. Perdita couldn't do anything but agree, and rang Janey to cancel.

'I wasn't expecting him before about midday on the Friday,' she explained. 'But he's managed to get away early, so I couldn't complain.'

'But where does he come from? I thought you said you never went on dates?'

'Honey, I really can't tell you all about it now. I've got to rush out and do some shopping, but I promise I'll give you a blow-by-blow when I come back. Now you won't do anything stupid with Lucas, will you? I mean, I know he's terribly sexy and everything—'

'How do you know?' Janey interrupted indignantly. 'I thought you hated him!'

'I do, I do! But I can tell you find him sexy, and I just don't want you seduced by a bastard, that's all.'

'It's really none of your business who I'm seduced by, Perdita.'

'Oh, Janey, I'm sorry. I don't mean to be bossy, but I'm just worried about you, that's all. You're so young and lovely, and Lucas is old—'

'And lovely.'

'Exactly, and you're worth so much more than him . . .'

Perdita sounded as desperate as she felt. 'So just be careful, OK?'

'OK, Agony Aunt. I won't do anything foolish. Well, I mean, I would if I thought Lucas was up for it, but I don't think he fancies me. Now you'd better run along to the supermarket, which will be the only shop left open, and do your Christmas shopping.'

Perdita was not reassured. After all, Lucas had fancied *her* once, and Janey did remind Perdita of her younger self. And why else would Lucas accept an invitation to spend Christmas Day with Janey's family? It seemed so out of character. Unless he'd changed one hell of a lot since she'd known him. And from what she'd seen, he'd got worse, not better. One good thing was that Janey would probably tell Lucas that Perdita had been picked up earlier than expected, which would, with luck, give her boyfriend story a bit of much lacking substance.

By about five o'clock on the day before Christmas Eve, Perdita had dispatched Kitty safely into the friendly hire car and driver who took her about if Perdita couldn't. Kitty, dressed in her best coat and skirt, made for her in the war by her husband's tailor, looked timeless and very fit.

'Goodbye, darling,' said Kitty, kissing Perdita. 'And have a lovely time. I do hope this Geoff turns out to be a dish.'

Perdita hugged as well as kissed the old lady. 'I don't suppose he will for a minute, but it'll be fun. And don't you run off with anyone without letting me check they don't just want you for your money.'

'Silly child. Now goodbye, and don't worry about me.'

'I won't,' said Perdita, knowing she would. Having waved the car out of sight, Perdita walked back to her own house and transferred some clothes into a sports bag. She put in a haphazard collection of garments, hoping they would do. Then she put on her best jeans and jumper, and waited for her lift.

Geoff knocked on her door an hour and a half after he had arranged to. He was full of apologies, but Perdita felt certain he blamed her directions. He was tall and stooping and had floppy brown hair, which would have been attractive had it been washed more recently.

'I'm so sorry you had such a dreadful time getting here,' said Perdita, pulling on her ancient sheepskin coat. 'How long will it take to get to Shropshire, I wonder?'

'Another couple of hours, I expect. Is this all your luggage? What about presents?'

'Um, they're all in the bag,' said Perdita, convinced by his question that it wasn't only her clothes which were totally inadequate. 'My boots and some bottles are in this cardboard box.'

'Right, we'd better get off, then.'

Geoff didn't seem inclined to chat, but as his car was warm and comfortable and Perdita was extremely tired, she prepared to just sit back and be driven. Just as they were moving out of the village, she noticed, to her absolute horror, Lucas, driving an extremely sleek convertible, as different from Geoff's Volvo as possible.

If she could have trusted Lucas not to pull over, and make them do the same and involve her in all sorts of complicated lying, she would have alerted Lucas to her presence in Geoff's car. Then he could have seen Geoff for himself, and believed that she had a boyfriend. But as Lucas was less predictable than one's chances of being struck by lightning, she slunk deeply down into the seat, so he couldn't possibly see her. Why wasn't he at Grantly House, cheffing, she wondered. She glanced at her watch. It was after ten; perhaps he'd finished early. She sighed. They wouldn't arrive at Lucy's until long after midnight.

'Does Lucy know we're going to be so late?' she asked.

'No. You'd better ring her. My mobile's on the back seat. The number's in the memory.'

Mobile phones were a wonderful invention, thought Perdita, for those who knew how to use them.

Chapter Seven

Lucy's face seemed to be wearing every one of the seven years since Perdita had last seen her. Then, she had been tanned and relaxed from living in the Caribbean, now, she had dark circles under her eyes and looked far too thin. She fell on Perdita as if she were her saviour, reminding Perdita of her school days, when Lucy always wanted Perdita to get her out of scrapes.

'Perdita! It's so lovely to see you! You haven't changed a bit, damn you. I'm so glad you could come. And you, Geoff, of course. We only got in the house yesterday, and hardly anything's unpacked. Mummy's arriving tomorrow, and we must get at least her room in some sort of order. It's her first Christmas since Daddy died, and I want it to be *perfect* for her.'

Perdita knew. 'But surely,' she said, as Lucy ushered her into the vast and echoing house, 'she'll understand you've just moved in. She won't want you to fuss too much over her?'

'No, of course not. But she always made Christmas so perfect for *us*, I want it to be right for *her*.' Lucy's voice was suspended for a moment, then she cleared her throat and swallowed hard.

Remembering how much she had cried on the phone, Perdita put a sympathetic hand on Lucy's arm. 'It must be quite upsetting for you, the first Christmas without your father.'

'Well, yes it is. But that's not why I'm crying. Not that I am crying, really. It's just a hormonal thing. Don't take any notice. Have you met Jake?'

'Only at your wedding. It's very kind of you to invite me,' said Perdita to the large, amiable man before her.

Jake's hand enveloped hers, and then he pulled her forward for a hug. 'The favour is all on your side. If you can stop Lucy getting thoroughly overwrought you can stay until spring. Come and have a drink.'

'But it's nearly two o'clock in the morning,' said Perdita, suddenly desperate for alcohol. 'Don't you want to go to bed?'

'The children are in our bed,' said Jake, leading the way into a vast sitting room, which would be wonderful with curtains, paint and floor covering and more than the few bits of furniture that were dotted about. 'Their cots are still dismantled, and so we can't go to bed until we've put them up. We slept on the floor last night. Geoff, I was hoping you might give us a hand. Whisky punch?' He handed Geoff a glass and looked questioningly at Perdita. 'We don't usually have this until Christmas Day, but we got desperate. It's guaranteed to kill off any cold bugs which may be lurking.'

'It's terribly important we don't give Mummy a cold,' explained Lucy. 'It goes to her chest. I really don't want her getting bronchitis.'

'Of course not,' agreed Perdita, suddenly wondering how Kitty was.

'The trouble is she will overdo things so. She lets the children exhaust her. She's a bit of a perfectionist.'

'It runs in the family,' said Jake, casting his wife a significant, reproachful glance.

'I'm not a perfectionist usually,' Lucy protested. 'It's just I want this Christmas to be right.'

'But you've just moved house,' said Perdita for what seemed like the tenth time. 'You can't possibly expect to be able to do everything you usually do.'

'Well, I haven't! I didn't make my own Christmas cards

this year. And Mummy made the cake and the pudding. I made the mincemeat while the people who bought our old house measured up for curtains. Far too late, really.'

'But you were up until after one making the pies.' Jake yawned. 'I hope you two don't mind sharing a bedroom,' he went on. 'There are only three habitable rooms upstairs, the roof leaks in all the others. Ma-in-Law's got the master bedroom with the dodgy en suite. Us and the children are crammed into the nursery, so that only leaves one room for you.'

'It's very big, though,' added Lucy. 'And it's got two beds. You don't mind sleeping bags, do you?'

Perdita felt that if she drank any more whisky punch she'd fall asleep where she sat. 'Er, not at all,' she said.

'Mummy's got to have the best room, and although the bathroom doesn't work terribly well, it is at least a bathroom. I'm afraid the rest of us have to use the downstairs shower and lav. Very bad feng shui, an en suite,' added Lucy. 'I hope she won't mind.'

'Your mother doesn't go in for feng shui, does she?' asked Geoff.

'I don't think so, but that's not the point, is it? It's either bad for you or it's not. You don't have to *believe*.'

'But, darling!' Jake seemed set to tear out what remained of his hair. 'I thought you were longing for an en suite! I thought that was one of the main reasons we bought the house!'

'Oh, *I* don't care about it. I just want it to be OK for Mummy.'

Jake sighed the sigh of a man who had given up hope of ever understanding his wife. 'Who's ready for another drink?'

'I think we're all just about ready for bed,' said Perdita, who had for some moments been longing for her own home, and her own bed, in which she would have been asleep for hours by this time.

'A night cap, then.' He drained the last of the punch into everyone's glasses, except Lucy's.

'I hope I don't disturb any of you in the night,' said Lucy apologetically. 'I have to get up to go to the loo rather a lot at the moment.' She paused, then shook her head and swallowed. 'I'm pregnant. Don't tell Mummy. That's why I'm so tearful. I'm perfectly all right if people don't draw attention to it.'

'The children are fascinated,' said Jake. 'They keep looking at Lucy and saying, "Mummy's crying again."'

'You're no better!' snapped Lucy. 'You keep saying, "'Ere we go, waterworks."' She laughed with an edge of hysteria to it. 'I suppose it is a bit bizarre. I just hope Mummy doesn't notice.'

Perdita thought that unless Lucy's mother was both blind and deaf she couldn't fail to notice, but didn't like to mention it.

'I don't suppose Perdita really wants to share a room with me,' said Geoff, getting up. 'Perhaps I'd better sleep down here.'

Lucy frowned. 'OK, but you'll have to promise to get rid of all your bedding before Mummy's up, when she gets here. It's so studenty, having people sleeping on the sofa.'

'I really don't mind sharing, Geoff, but if you'd feel happier sleeping down here . . .' Briefly, Perdita wondered how she'd have felt if she'd had to share a bedroom with Lucas. Not half so comfortable, she decided. But then, Geoff couldn't exactly be described as sex on a stick, not even by a frustrated divorcee like herself. She drained her drink. 'Well, let's go and get these cots organised. Lucy looks done in.'

As they went upstairs Perdita pondered that suddenly Christmases with Kitty seemed calm, comfortable, but a little dull. This was what many families had to cope with at Christmas – the hunt for perfection with no chance of finding it. She hoped she could cope.

Christmas Eve, with its own share of rituals, found Perdita in the kitchen, offering to cook a meal.

'Not that I'm much of a cook,' she said to Jake.

'Doesn't matter! I've got to go and assemble a bloody doll's house! And the instructions probably make perfect sense to a Japanese-speaking architect, but they make damn-all sense to me.'

'Geoff will help you. He seems like a man who reads instructions.'

'Why Lucy insists on giving them a doll's house, when there's no time to build it except when they're asleep, which hardly ever happens . . .'

'It's so they've got their own house to move into,' said Lucy, coming into the kitchen. 'It's like giving the first child a baby doll when the second one comes. Oh, Jake! I thought you agreed with me on this!'

'I'm going to cook supper,' said Perdita, quickly, before Lucy could burst into tears. 'I've explained to Jake. I'm not much of a cook, but I've had a lot of experience with less than perfect kitchens.'

Unlike the others, she was unfazed by the camping gas stove which was all there was until the solid fuel stove was persuaded to light. And the lack of any gadgets, except a rather unhygienic wooden spoon and a rusty knife with a loose handle, didn't faze her either. 'It's pretty much a home from home for me,' she explained.

Her long-neglected artistic skills were also called upon. The house was huge, filthy and empty, but it had beautiful proportions, and a garden full of wonderful evergreens. Once asked to 'do something about the sitting room, please!' by a potentially tearful Lucy, she let herself go.

Having sent Geoff to the nearest town to raid it for fairy lights, Perdita ripped ivy off the outside walls of the house, and sellotaped them above the picture rail. She sawed down an almost entire holly bush, which threatened to scar anyone foolish enough to come down the path, and stuck it into an enormous terracotta pot. She found a twisted willow in the garden, and made a designer Christmas tree out of it, decorated with the lights Geoff had brought back.

'It looks *stupendous*,' said Lucy, in tears again. 'It's a pity coloured lights are so "out".'

'It was all I could get,' said Geoff, defensively.

'And I'm sure I saw someone using coloured lights on *Changing Rooms*,' said Perdita.

'Did you?' This seemed to cheer Lucy up immensely, and Perdita was pleased she had lied. 'You've both been brill. Don't take any notice of me. I'm always like this when I'm pregnant.'

'Then how are you going to keep it from your mother?' Perdita felt that for everyone's sake it would be better if things were out in the open.

'Oh, I don't know, just keep a stiff upper lip, I suppose.'

'But why don't you want her to know?' asked Perdita, having dispatched Geoff to find dry wood for kindling so they could light a fire and take some of the chill off the room. 'Surely, a new grandchild to look forward to would cheer her up, wouldn't it?'

'Oh, I don't know. It just seems so selfish of us, having sex when she's in mourning and can never have sex again. Can you imagine that, never having sex again?'

Until recently, Perdita could have faced the prospect with equanimity, but just recently she had found herself wondering a bit about it.

'Well, I suppose it would be dreadful. But she can only be in her fifties, she might marry again.' Lucy's eyes filled up at the thought. 'And your mother would be horrified if she felt you weren't having a proper marriage because your father died,' Perdita added hurriedly.

Lucy sighed. 'I suppose that's true. But I really would rather not tell her about it just yet. She does worry about me when I'm pregnant.'

Perdita felt that Lucy's mother's fears were probably justified. Moving house, Christmas and pregnancy seemed a combination likely to bring on something dreadful – miscarriage, a nervous breakdown, or at the very least, chapped cheeks owing to Lucy's semi-permanent tears. 'So what else do you want to do in this room, then?'

'Well, in Scotland I always had a big garland of evergreens over the fireplace, and then hung the stockings from it. I made the family ones ages ago, but of course, this year I had to run up a couple for you and Geoff.'

Perdita was horrified. 'Lucy! How could you find the time? You must be mad! Making things like that with things as they are. Now don't cry! I mean, it's so sweet of you to go to so much trouble. But we would never have come if we knew we were going to cause so much extra work.'

'Nonsense! You're both doing far more work than you caused me! I don't know what I'd do without you!' Lucy sniffed, and then absently began to peel away a bit of wallpaper. 'So what about your love life, Perdita? No one since Lucas? Not that I was surprised you split up.'

'Oh?'

'Well, I mean, it was just too hot and passionate to survive, wasn't it? And you were so *young*, practically a child bride. Not that I'm implying it was your fault . . .'

'I did at least remain faithful for those few short months, but I had no idea how to handle him.' She wasn't exactly a dab hand at it now. She sighed.

'So, is there anyone in your life now? No? Oh well, I'm sure . . . I don't suppose you ever hear from Lucas?'

'Funnily enough, I do, sort of. He's become a chef at the local hotel and moved into the village. I sell him salads.'

'A chef? I thought he was something in the City?'

'He was. But he gave it up and became a chef. God knows why.'

'How bizarre! What on earth made him change direction like that?''

'I have no idea.'

'But is it awkward? Dealing with him?'

'Well . . .' Should she tell Lucy about Lucas's curiosity about her love life, and her pretending she was spending Christmas with her boyfriend? Perdita wasn't really accustomed to woman-to-woman chats, except with Kitty and Janey.

'Oh, go on, do tell,' pleaded Lucy, looking more cheerful than Perdita had yet seen her. 'I haven't had a good gossip for yonks.'

'He does keep asking me if I've got another man in my life and, of course, I haven't. So I pretended I was spending Christmas with my boyfriend.'

'You didn't want him to know you weren't attached?'

'No! He left me for another woman, an *older* woman. A girl has her pride.'

'But is he still with this woman?'

'No, but it's only a matter of time before he breaks some other poor schmuck's heart. He's spending Christmas Day with Janey, his sous-chef. She's got an almighty crush on him, and I'm really worried that she might do something silly, like sleep with him.'

'Oh dear. Men are such bastards – with a few notable exceptions, of course,' Lucy added quickly, as Geoff came in with an armful of twigs.

'Listen, Lucy, would you mind if I rang Kitty? I know I'll forget if I wait until after six, when your mother is here.'

'Oh no, please do. But I'll have to find Jake's mobile. We're not actually on the phone yet.'

Geoff sighed, reached behind him and produced his phone. 'If you've got the number, I'll punch it in for you. It'll take for ever, otherwise.'

Perdita felt herself go pink. 'I am sorry about erasing all those numbers. I'll just run up and find Kitty's.'

97

'I'm having a splendid time,' said Kitty, when Perdita finally got hold of her. 'They're looking after me so well. We've been playing bridge, and they don't think I play badly at all.'

'Well, I hope it's not for money, and don't play poker,' said Perdita, glad to hear Kitty sounding in such good form.

'And how are things with you? Did that Geoff turn out to be attractive?'

'Er, yes, I'm using his phone now.'

'Oh, and he's listening? I'd better shut up about him then. Still, it's very nice of you to ring.'

'I just wanted to make sure you were all right. But I'd better go now. Lucy's mother is arriving in a moment, and I must make sure her room's in order.'

'Really? I hope you're getting a rest, darling. You're supposed to be on holiday. But I mustn't keep you. Bye bye, darling. Speak to you soon.'

Perdita peered at the phone, eventually working out how to switch it off, and then went upstairs to the master bedroom with the dodgy en suite.

'How did you manage to get it so clean and tidy in here with no vacuum?' asked Lucy. 'And it smells wonderful.'

'Well, I found a stiff broom, which is all I have at home, after all.'

'Really? How extraordinary! Why haven't you got a vacuum?'

'Well, you know how it is, I have other priorities, and my house is tiny. I found an ancient tin of polish in the larder. That and the rosemary is responsible for the smell.' Perdita caught Lucy's little frown as she surveyed the bed. 'You want me to iron the sheet, don't you?'

'Mummy always irons sheets.'

'But do you know where the iron is?'

'Yes. It is a pity there isn't a plug in here. I don't know how they managed without even a bedside light. I've got a camping gas lamp for Mummy.'

Perdita realised that this meant she would have to heat up the iron in another room, and then run along the freezing passage to do the actual ironing. Not even for Lucy's mother was she going to unmake the bed and iron the whole sheet. The bit that turned over and the pillow case were more than enough, in her opinion.

'I do hope Jake gets the Aga going,' said Lucy. 'It's such a pity there's no central heating.'

'But a bit late to worry about now, don't you think?'

'Oh, don't!' Lucy's eyelids flickered. 'Do you think Mummy will freeze in here? She has an electric blanket at home.'

'Have you got a hot-water bottle?'

'Yes, but God knows where. Do you think we could buy one?'

In central London, possibly. In the middle of the Welsh Marches, at five o'clock on Christmas Eve, Perdita felt it was unlikely. 'I packed one, she can have mine,' she said, making the ultimate sacrifice.

'Oh, Perdita! You are a star!'

'Yes!' Jake's triumphant cry woke an infant who had been dozing on an old church pew. 'It's going! I've got the Aga going!'

'If it's an Aga,' said the child, who was six and frighteningly bright, 'why does it say R-A-Y-something on it?'

'That's because it's a Rayburn,' said her father. 'But don't tell Mummy. She's got her heart set on an Aga. It's a life-style thing.'

'Rayburn's are better space heaters,' said Geoff, who, with Perdita, was sitting at the table peeling potatoes. 'Which is a bloody good thing, if you ask me.'

Perdita was wearing all the clothes she had brought and

was still cold. As she worked outside most of the time and was therefore used to it, she wondered how the others were managing.

Lucy's mother finally arrived. She was a small, kindly, undemanding woman. Her little car was filled with baskets and boxes and suitcases. After the prolonged greetings, a relay of people unloaded it for her.

'I've brought ready-prepared sprouts,' Mrs Heptonstall confided to Perdita. 'Lucy's a dear, sweet girl, and so good to me, but she does tend to fuss, especially at Christmas.'

'I know she wants this Christmas to go well, for your sake,' said Perdita, from behind a huge cardboard box, en route to the kitchen.

'Oh dear! I knew this would happen. She's only just moved house and she's going to get upset if we can't find the cranberry sauce.'

'Oh no,' said Perdita. 'That'll be all right. She's made some from a special recipe. I know where it is.'

Mrs Heptonstall tutted. 'Honestly! And between you, me and the gatepost, I think she's pregnant. But don't say a word because I don't think she's realised it herself yet.'

Perdita put the box down on the kitchen table, panting slightly. 'How could she not know? I mean, she's got two children already. She must recognise the signs.'

'Her periods went funny when her father died. She probably thinks that's what's happening. But I think I'll let her get used to the new house before I say anything.'

Perdita opened her mouth, very tempted to tell Mrs Heptonstall about Lucy's reluctance to tell her mother about her condition, but decided against it. If she ever got Lucy on her own again, she would tell her instead.

Christmas Day passed far more calmly than Perdita would have predicted, thanks to Mrs Heptonstall eventually convincing Lucy that she really enjoyed feeling useful again, and that the world wouldn't end if not every detail was as it was in the magazines.

Everyone except Lucy, who was ordered to stay in bed, went for a long walk after the stockings had been opened and a chocolaty, boozy breakfast had been consumed. The turkey was timed to be cooked at three o'clock, so no one needed to rush, and after a light buffet lunch, which appeared, Mary Poppins-like, from Mrs Heptonstall's basket, they opened presents.

Perdita immediately draped herself in the huge, creamy white shawl her mother had sent her, and earmarked the cheque from her father to go towards a better van. Thus her pile was quickly dispensed with, as she hadn't brought Kitty's table lamp with her.

Her presents to other people were surprisingly successful. The green nail varnish was extremely popular with its six-year-old recipient, although less so with her parents. The four-year-old was thrilled with the huge plastic bubble filled with miniature chocolate footballs. Lucy genuinely liked the selection of herb vinegars which Perdita had made herself, and the lavender bags which she hadn't, and Jake looked at the wine, which had come from Kitty's husband's cellar, with quiet reverence. Geoff had a similar bottle and they exchanged glances which said, 'How did that rather scatty woman come up with such bloody good wine?' Perdita smiled, and said nothing.

'Do feel free to ring Kitty,' said Lucy, yawning. 'You must be worrying about her.'

Perdita, who hadn't been, suddenly did. 'That would be nice. Just to say Happy Christmas.'

'Jake, give Perdita your phone.'

'I'll do it,' said Geoff, resignedly.

Kitty was, as expected, perfectly fine, although annoyed to

be rung up when she had a very good hand. 'I was going to play five no trumps,' she said crossly. 'Now my partner, a very nice man, knew Lionel slightly, will take advantage of my absence and play it for me.'

'Oh? I am sorry. I wish I'd known.'

Kitty sighed. 'Oh, don't worry, dear. They said it was a difficult hand to make. I expect I'd have gone down horribly.'

Having no knowledge of bridge Perdita could make no comment. They chatted on about meals and presents and weather and eventually rang off.

'She's fine,' said Perdita. 'Now, should we be doing anything in the kitchen?'

She went in to see and found Lucy's mother searing the roast potatoes with a blowtorch.

On Boxing Day evening, Perdita had fallen asleep on the sofa in front of the fire, both children in her arms and a copy of *Magic Pony* open on her lap, when Lucy whispered sharply in her ear, 'Perdita? Wake up. Someone's at the door for you. I think it's Lucas.'

Perdita woke up with a start and for a moment thought she'd dreamt what Lucy had said. But Lucy was standing in front of her, looking highly agitated.

'Did you say it was Lucas?'

Lucy nodded. 'I only just recognised him. I only saw him at your wedding, and it's been years. But he's here, and he's asking for you.'

'What on earth is he doing here? And how did he find me?'

'I don't know! I only know he's asking for you!'

'Well, you'd better bring him in, then.'

'Who's Lucas?' asked the green-nailed six-year-old.

'He's – an old friend,' lied Perdita, guiltlessly.

'What's he doing here?' asked the four-year-old.

'I really have no idea.'

Lucas came in looking tired, with an air of unaccustomed concern.

'Lucas?' said Perdita, getting up. 'What is it?'

'I'm terribly sorry,' he said. 'It's Kitty.'

Chapter Eight

It seemed as if the floor was trying to pull Perdita downwards, specks of black danced around in front of her eyes until they joined together and everything went black. Then she felt a rough hand at the back of her neck, pushing her head between her knees. A thread of consciousness told her that you were not supposed to do that any more, that current thinking was that you should just let people faint. Then she came back to reality and panic.

'It's all right,' Lucas was saying. 'She's not very ill. She's not even in hospital, but the people she's staying with thought you should be informed.'

'Then why did you come in person?' asked Lucy.

Lucas gave her a look which could have provoked tears from a tougher soul than Lucy. 'Because Perdita didn't leave a telephone number.'

Fortunately Lucy remained unmoved. 'Oh,' she said, 'that would be because we're not on the phone.'

Lucas made a gesture with his hands which said, 'which was why I had to come in person, Dumbo.'

'So what's wrong with her?' Perdita's mouth was stiff and her voice sounded croaky, as if she'd been ill herself.

'She's had a TIA – transient ischaemic attack,' said Lucas.

'Well, what's that? It sounds dreadful.' Lucy glanced at Perdita, concerned.

'It's a very mild stroke, one which has left no after-effects. As I said, she's not even in hospital. There's really no need for you to panic.'

'But I must come now,' said Perdita. It wasn't a question.

He nodded.

'Do you feel better, dear?' asked Lucy's mother. 'You've had a nasty shock. Would you like a drink of water, or something.'

'No, I'm fine.' This wasn't quite true, but she didn't want to delay her departure by a second. She attempted a smile. 'I'll just go and pack.'

Lucy came up with her, leaving her mother to tend to Lucas. 'I'm so sorry, Perdita. I know what you must be going through. When Daddy died . . . It's a very growing up experience.'

And Lucy's daddy, Perdita couldn't help remembering, was much younger than Kitty. 'Well, Lucas says she's not that ill. If she's not even in hospital . . .'

Rather to her surprise, Lucy put her arms round Perdita and hugged her, very hard. 'You'll never get all this in that hold-all,' she said after a minute. 'I'll get you some carrier bags.'

Later, in the car, Perdita felt the need to talk. 'I know Kitty's very old. She's going to die sometime, and soon. I just don't want her to do it when I'm not there.'

'Of course not.' Lucas was driving fast. Perdita had been nervous at first but then got used to it. He'd always driven that way.

'She's been a lifeline to me, ever since I first went to boarding school.'

'I know.'

'And for her to die—'

'She's not going to die for a while, Perdita.'

'When I'm hundreds of miles away . . .'

'But she's not. And you're not. She's not going to die until you are by her side, and have probably been longing for her to die for some time.' He gave a little sigh of exasperation. 'You know what I mean. Old age can be very cruel, and you wouldn't want Kitty to suffer.'

'No, of course not.'

A little later she said, 'It was very kind of you to come and get me.'

'It seemed the least I could do, in the circumstances.'

'Which were?'

'A frantic phone call from the people Kitty is staying with. A Mrs Lettum-Havvit, or something.'

'Ledham-Gold,' Perdita sighed.

'Something like that. She'd got my number from Michael Grantly.'

'But how on earth . . . ? Why you?'

Lucas shrugged and changed gear to overtake the car in front. 'Apparently I was the only person Kitty could think of who might be able to get in touch with you.'

'So she wanted me to be with her, did she?' This did not bode well. Kitty hated causing anyone any trouble. Having Perdita shipped back from Shropshire on Boxing Day night was the last thing she would do unless she felt very ill and frightened.

'I don't think she did, particularly. But her hostess did.' He hesitated for a moment. 'I gather the doctor thought it was a good idea.'

Perdita digested this, trying to work out if it was good news or bad. 'It really was very, very kind of you to stop doing whatever you were doing . . .'

'Cooking.'

'To come and find me.'

'Bloody right it was kind. God knows what's happening in the kitchen. Those idiots have probably ruined my reputation by now.'

'What idiots?'

'Greg and Janey.'

'But it's Boxing Day. Surely you're not open on Boxing Day? Poor Greg, poor Janey.' At that moment Perdita remembered who Lucas had spent Christmas Day with and her anxieties concerning it. But not even present circumstances made it possible for her to ask Lucas if he had seduced Janey on the sofa while her family went for tea at Auntie Susan's.

'There aren't many in, just a few staying at the hotel for Christmas. Those two'll make a complete bollocks of it, but who cares? The guests have absolutely no appreciation of good food anyway.'

'They didn't ask for ketchup?' Perdita's horror was perhaps a little exaggerated.

'No.' He shot her a glance. 'They weren't keen on the cardoons, though.'

Perdita thought it best to ignore this. 'So what did they do about Christmas dinner? You had the day off, didn't you?'

'We gave them their meal in the evening. I was back to cook that.'

'So you spent the day with Janey's family?'

'You know I did.'

'Well, did you have a nice time?'

'It was very pleasant.' He sighed again. 'And no, I didn't seduce Janey, if that's what you're worrying about.'

'I don't know why you think the idea that you might have done any such thing had even crossed my mind,' she said. 'I'm sure you're far too professional to mix business with pleasure.'

'I am, and for your further information, sleeping with half-fledged ducklings does not come under the heading of pleasure.'

'It did at one time,' she said, blushing in the darkness.

'That was a long time ago, and that was you.'

Lucas filled the sudden silence with some rather complicated jazz which Perdita's tired and shocked brain found difficult to unravel. She closed her eyes and dozed.

'So,' asked Lucas, a little later, when she had woken up.

'Which one of those men was your boyfriend? The fat one or the one with dirty hair?'

With Kitty ill, perhaps dying, the lying and subterfuge just seemed silly. Perdita sighed. 'Neither of them. There is no boyfriend. Geoff, who gave me a lift up, is Jake's brother. I'd never met him before.'

Lucas nodded, but didn't look at her. 'And you told me a bundle of complete untruths. Why was that, I wonder?'

'Why the hell do you think? You and I were married once. You left me—'

'For an older woman.' He sounded bored.

'And I was on my own, years later. I didn't want you to think I was carrying a torch for you, that's all.'

'You mean, you're not carrying one? I'm devastated.'

'I would very much like to devastate you, Lucas, but I don't think the fact that my once-broken heart is very much mended is going to do it.'

'Oh, I don't know. It's not as hard as you think.'

'Of course, in some ways, you coming back has done me a favour. It made me aware that I didn't have a man, and made me wonder if perhaps there isn't something missing in my life.'

'Oh? What?'

'Well, you know. Sex, companionship, that sort of thing. Not that I have much time for it, of course,' she added. 'And I may be quite wrong. A lot of women are totally satisfied and happy being single these days. But I thought I might have a boyfriend for a while, and see if I liked it.'

'Unfortunately, as there's such a shortage of single, eligible men, and apparently none at all locally, it might be quite difficult for you to find a boyfriend.' He shot her a provocative glance. 'Maybe *I* should try my chances with you.'

Perdita continued to look straight ahead. 'Not if you ever want to be able to father children, no. And "eligible" is the operative word, Lucas.'

Lucas laughed in a way that Perdita hadn't heard for years.

'I need a cup of coffee,' he said. 'I'll stop at the next service station.'

'I wouldn't have thought you'd consider what they serve there as coffee.'

He laughed again. 'Beggars can't be choosers. I need something, or I'll fall asleep.'

Perdita let her breath out sharply, suddenly aware of what he had sacrificed to fetch her. It would amount to a drive of not less than three hundred miles. On Boxing Day.

'I really am so grateful to you for fetching me. I don't know how I can ever make it up to you.'

'Oh, that's quite easy. You can agree to make a television cookery programme. In your house. With a brand-new cooker. Provided by me. That's really not too much to ask, now is it?'

'That wasn't the reason you came for me, was it? So you could blackmail me into doing what you want?'

'Of course. The minute I got the phone call I didn't wonder why the fuck she didn't have a mobile phone, so she could be contacted, I thought, what a brilliant opportunity to get Perdita to be co-operative! I'll play on her anxieties over Kitty to manipulate her into giving me my way.'

Perdita blushed in the darkness and felt herself go hot. 'I'm terribly sorry. That was quite out of order.' She gulped. 'And of course I'll do the television programme.'

'Don't overdo the gratitude or I might be tempted to hold you to it. Here's the turn-off. Do you want to go to the loo? I'll meet you in the café. I want to look at the map so I can see where the Lettum-Havvits actually live.'

'It's going to be terribly late when we get there. It's past ten now,' said Perdita, when they were back on the road.

'Mrs—'

'Ledham-Gold,'

'—said she'd stay up for us. And we should be there soon after eleven.'

'It's still terribly late to be calling on people you've never met.'

'They sounded very kind, and very concerned about Kitty. Not because she's that ill,' he went on slightly impatiently, as Perdita frowned with anxiety, 'but because they're so fond of her.'

'How sweet.' Perdita sighed again, bracing herself for the effort of mentioning the cheque. 'Talking of kind,' she said, 'thank you for sending my cheque back, but I'm afraid I really can't accept it. I don't need your money . . .'

Lucas braked sharply and pulled onto the hard shoulder. 'If you ever mention that cheque again, or make any further attempts to give it to me, I will come and find you in whatever distant corner of the earth you've hidden yourself, and beat you. Do you understand?'

He sounded more genuinely angry than she had ever heard him. 'OK, OK.' Perdita hoped he couldn't hear the tremble in her voice. 'Don't get all worked up.'

'This is not worked up. This is simply telling you how it is.'

He paused a moment, to let his feelings on the matter sink in, then flicked the indicator, looked over his shoulder, and pulled back out onto the road. Perdita was shaking. If she wanted to touch that particular nerve again she must do it when she was in a position to escape.

After they came off the motorway they got lost three times. Rather unexpectedly, Lucas took responsibility for this himself. 'You can't map-read in the dark. There's no need to apologise for my taking the wrong turning. You're so unreasonable sometimes, Perdita. I'm pretty sure it's down here.'

A security light flashed on as they approached the gates

of the house, which were open. The front door also opened before they had time to knock, and they were ushered very kindly inside.

Perdita felt tears spring to her eyes as she saw Kitty, looking suddenly very small and old, lying in a vast double bed.

It was obviously the best bedroom, and Kitty was surrounded by colour co-ordinated floral fabric, little frilled table lamps, valances and mirrors. A kidney-shaped dressing table was wearing the same fabric as the multi-swagged curtains and the bed linen. Perdita saw a door to an en suite and glimpsed fluffy towels in matching pink. She knew the plumbing would work perfectly.

'Darling, how lovely to see you! I told them not to bother you.'

'I'm so glad they – you,' she glanced up at Kitty's hostess, whose name she suddenly couldn't remember, although she knew it wasn't Mrs Lettum-Havvit, 'did bother me. I couldn't have lived with myself if you'd been ill, and I hadn't known.'

'And did that nice man bring you down? The one who drove you to Shropshire?'

Perdita hesitated for a second. 'Lucas came and fetched me.'

Kitty frowned. 'Oh, my goodness. Why?'

Had Kitty really forgotten that she'd given Lucas's name as a contact? Perhaps she'd lost a bit of her memory. 'Because you – because he heard you were ill, and I hadn't left a telephone number.'

'Oh dear. I know I suggested they asked him how to get in touch with you, but I never dreamt he'd go all that way to fetch you. I hope it wasn't awkward for you.'

Relief that Kitty's memory was as sound as ever made Perdita lie gaily. 'Not at all. He was very kind. He's being given turkey sandwiches in the kitchen. He drives extremely fast.'

'Since he got you here safely, I won't grumble about that. They say I might have to give up my pipe.' Kitty frowned. 'I don't think it's worth it, at my age.'

'Oh, Kitty,' Perdita said helplessly. She wanted to order her old friend to give up her pipe, and do anything else which might prolong her life, but was it fair? 'We'll talk about that another time.'

'We've spoken to Kitty's doctor,' said Mrs Ledham-Gold. 'He wants to see her the minute she gets back home, and she's not to go home unless there's someone there.'

'I'll be there.'

'I thought you would be, though of course Kitty grumbled like anything . . .' Kitty made a sound confirming this. 'And he also wants to see you, to discuss Kitty's aftercare.'

'I'm perfectly capable of taking care of myself!' Kitty's firm assertion cheered Perdita, although she knew there would be lively arguments ahead.

'Now, my dear, would you like to stay the night? You must be tired after all that travelling?' Mrs Ledham-Gold was very solicitous. 'There's the little back bedroom free, though it's only got a three-quarter-size bed in it . . .'

'It's so kind of you to offer, Mrs—'

'Call me Veronica, dear.'

'—but I'm sure Lucas will want to get back. He has to work in the morning.'

Perdita eventually kissed Kitty good night, promising to collect her in a few days. She then spent a long time thanking the Ledham-Golds and Veronica's sister, who had spent a thoroughly enjoyable time with Lucas in the kitchen. Lucas had obviously decided to rustle up a little charm in the same way he might have rustled up a gourmet snack out of the contents of his fridge.

'You've looked after Kitty so well. I am so grateful to you.'

'She really needs someone living in, in case it happens again,' said Veronica. 'Has she got any relations who might oblige?'

'I'm all she's got and we're not related, but I'll live with Kitty.'

'But, my dear, haven't you got other commitments?' She glanced at Lucas.

'Only my business and I can run that just as well from Kitty's house as mine. We live very close.'

'Well, that is a weight off my mind, I must say. Because although it's perfectly possible to recover totally from a TIA there is always the danger of another one occurring. Or even a major stroke.' She smiled at Perdita's surprise at her technical knowledge. 'It's quite a common thing among people of our generation.'

Perdita kissed her firmly on the cheek. 'You've been wonderful.'

'Not at all. Kitty's very lucky to have a lovely girl like you to keep an eye on her.'

Lucas coughed in the background, obviously itching to leave. 'And I'm very lucky to have a friend like Lucas to fetch me,' said Perdita.

'Friend? Oh, I thought you were married.' Veronica sounded disappointed.

'That was years ago,' growled Lucas. 'Now, I don't want to hurry you, but could we please get on?'

'What time do you have to be at work in the morning?' They were in the village now, and Perdita tried not to sound as guilty as she felt.

'Eleven.'

'But if you've got people staying at the hotel, who cooks their breakfasts?'

'We've taken on a breakfast chef who supervises Greg and Janey doing the prep. And if they don't know how I like things done by now they can look elsewhere for a job.'

'That's terrible! Talking like that, when Janey had you for Christmas!'

'Janey did not "have" me for Christmas. Much as she might have liked to. But actually, Janey is shaping up very well.'

'I hope you tell her so. People do far better on praise than on criticism, you know.'

Lucas thought this highly amusing. 'That's not how things work in restaurant kitchens.'

'There's no earthly reason why they shouldn't.'

'I dare say. Now,' he slowed the car and drew up outside Perdita's house, 'do you want me to stay for what's left of the night, or will you be all right?' He pulled on the handbrake. 'I'm not inviting myself into your bed, Perdita, just offering to stay with you if you feel you need company.'

Perdita was shocked, mostly because she did need company, and the thought of sharing her bed with Lucas was far from unpleasant. 'No, no, I'll be fine. I'm perfectly used to living on my own, you know,' she added sharply.

'I hope you'll get just as used to living with Kitty, because someone's going to have to. If not now, sometime in the future.'

'Of course.'

'It will cramp your style a bit, won't it? If you're going to find yourself a lover?'

'You don't know Kitty very well if you think that.'

She opened the car door and clambered out. He got out his side and went round to the boot.

'You take the odd carrier bags, I'll take this,' he said. He waited while she found her key, and then followed her indoors. The house was very cold and smelt of wood ash. 'Are you sure you'll be all right on your own?'

'Oh yes. I'll have a hot-water bottle and some hot milk with brandy in it, and I'll be asleep in minutes.' He studied her carefully, obviously not convinced. 'Really, Lucas. I'll be fine.'

'Very well,' he said eventually. 'I'll take your word for it. Not because I believe you, but because I don't think you want me to stay.'

'No, really, really, I'll be fine.' And she did want him to stay, though she'd die before she'd admit it.

'I'll be off then.'

Perdita put down her carrier bags. 'I really can't thank you enough, Lucas . . .'

'And please don't thank me any more, or I'll die of boredom. Give me a hug instead.'

It wasn't hard to go to him and put her arms round his tall figure, made bulky by his overcoat. His arms round her were very strong, he held her very tightly for a very long time. She felt some of the stresses leach out of her body into the warmth of his. Eventually she dragged herself away.

He bent forward and kissed her on the cheek. 'Good night, Perdita. I'll be seeing you. And please, for everybody's sake, get a mobile phone.'

She watched him get into his car as she stood at her window, before drawing her curtains. The hug, she knew, had been for her benefit, not for his. And it had helped.

It took Perdita ages to get to sleep that night. She had left her hot-water bottle in Shropshire and there hadn't been any heat in the house for days, so she was very, very cold. And although she had long-life milk, she didn't have enough brandy to do more than give it a very slight taste.

She wrapped her feet in a mohair shawl and eventually warmed up, but it was the knowledge that she was by no means indifferent to Lucas that made it so difficult to drift off. Of course, she wasn't in love with him, she didn't even have a crush, like poor Janey, but she had been grateful for his presence, and his arms around her had been more than just comforting. They had felt right, as if no other arms would do.

Which of course was rubbish. It was only because she hadn't had a man for so long – she pushed the words 'since Lucas' firmly out of her thoughts – and because she had just been through a very worrying time, that she felt in need of companionship so badly. And although she did her best to avoid thinking about it, she was only too aware that although Kitty was better, she was very old, and would die, possibly quite soon.

She had always faced this, if not with equanimity, at least with acceptance. After all, there was nothing very much she could do about it. But having Lucas's arms around her showed her how very comforting a companion – a male companion, who you could hug and be hugged by at will – could be.

But she would no more give her heart to Lucas to shred, like her returned cheque, than she would spray weedkiller on her salads. She had done it at eighteen, and the heart had taken a long time to piece together – too long for her to do it again at twenty-nine. Lucas had indeed been very kind to fetch her from Shropshire, but he was basically cruel. Only a true masochist would let him ever get close again.

No, she wanted someone who would always be kind. She'd have to sacrifice things like looks, sex-appeal and dynamism, of course, but it was gentle companionship she wanted, not the nausea-inducing free fall of passion. Definitely not.

As sleep approached her mind escaped the confines of sense and she wondered about Lucas's provocative hints, his implication that he still wanted her. Why would he do that? Pure cruelty? Somehow, that no longer seemed so likely. Probably, she thought, a second before she slept, because he really wants Janey, knows he shouldn't, and I'm an older version.

These thoughts came back to her in the morning, while she was brushing her teeth. She blushed in the mirror at her complete idiocy. Lucas didn't want her or Janey, he just wanted three gold stars, or whatever it was, for his cooking. She chuckled, and then spat. Perhaps she should buy him a packet of them. They sold them in the post office.

Chapter Nine

Because Christmas fell at the weekend, the day after Boxing Day, when Perdita was foodless, hot-water bottle-less, and lonely, was a bank holiday. Fortunately her van got her to the nearest town, and after much searching of empty streets, she found an emergency chemist. She bought herself a new hot-water bottle, one with a furry cover, because it was Christmas, and she was alone.

Later she drove to Kitty's house, let herself in, then stole a bottle of brandy and had a rummage through the fridge. This was not only to save her from having to eat the pulses she intended to sprout and sell, but so she could throw away some of the more ancient packets and pots inhabiting Kitty's refrigerator. Kitty's cleaning lady wasn't allowed near it because of her justifiable objection to food so well past its sell-by date. Perdita was firmly on the side of the cleaning lady, but as Kitty had never had a stomach upset in her life, she wouldn't listen to their mutterings about salmonella, ptomaine or any other fell disease, and Perdita had to do good by stealth, removing the more elderly foodstuffs when she had the opportunity.

Then she checked the house plants and saw that Kitty's amaryllis was about to flower. She allowed herself a few seconds' sadness that Kitty might not be home in time to see it, and then went from room to room, checking the seed trays on the windowsills, thinking how empty the house was, and yet still so full of Kitty. Would it feel like that when Kitty was dead, and not just away? For how long would the essence of a person be trapped in their possessions? Kitty's death was no longer something Perdita could just put out of her mind. She must face it.

Worse than death, from Kitty's point of view, was becoming an invalid, dependent on others. And the ultimate misery would be an old people's home. Kitty had often told Perdita that if that fate seemed likely, Perdita was to obtain the necessary amount and type of drugs so Kitty could make her own arrangements. Perdita, knowing she could not possibly do this, usually changed the subject rapidly.

But there was another option. If Kitty were to become bedridden, there was nothing to stop her living at home. The drawing room would easily convert into an invalid's bedsit. Perdita might not be able to help Kitty commit suicide, but she could move heaven and earth and a lot of furniture to make sure Kitty could be in her own house, with her own things, her garden just beyond the window.

Perdita felt the soil round some orange-scented geraniums and decided they needed water. While she filled a jug she noted, as she always did, the china holder for hard squares of lavatory paper which hung above the more conventional roll for soft paper. It had been there ever since Perdita had first come into the house, apparently because Kitty's husband preferred it. Perdita always wondered whether in the unlikely event that the packet was ever emptied, it would be replaced. She must remember to ask Kitty when she got home, she thought, as she wrote her a note, telling her that her fridge and her drinks cupboard had been raided.

At home, Perdita lit her wood burner, waited until it could be safely left, and then went out to inspect her polythene tunnels. Once she was in the green-tinged, pungent atmosphere, life took on a more sensible perspective. Without Kitty, without a man, she still had her business, continually challenging, profitable (almost), infinitely satisfying, and giving her a sense of fulfilment nothing else could provide. She glanced towards the pot in which she had buried the crosnes Lucas had given her to grow. She had found a book which told her how to grow it, and was waiting until March to plant it. Until then, it had to be kept safe, not allowed to rot or dry up. She decided not to spoil her improved mood by inspecting it. Mice were fond of crosnes, and a lot could go wrong, before she'd even planted it, and if it had, it would seem symbolic. Why spoil her quasi-contentment by bringing Lucas into her day?

She picked a selection of salads to go with a baked potato and went back into the house to ring Janey. Telling Lucas she had lied about the boyfriend had been easy in the circumstances. With Kitty ill, a little sacrifice of pride seemed like nothing. But how could she explain it all to Janey? Janey knew that Lucas and Perdita had known each other many years before, but could that supposedly fleeting acquaintance reasonably be seen as a motive for such a lot of lying? It might have to.

Janey, extremely surprised to hear that Perdita was not still in Shropshire, was off duty unexpectedly, without plans, and more than willing to come and visit.

'Tell me everything,' she demanded, before the first glass of wine was even poured, let alone drunk. 'Why did you come back so early? Did you have a row with your boyfriend? I want to know everything.'

'You tell me about how you got on with Lucas first,' said Perdita cravenly. 'You know I've been worrying about it.'

'There's nothing to tell, really. He was very sweet to Mum and Dad, took over the carving because Dad had had one too many, but he didn't do anything when we were alone, watching telly.' Janey sighed with disappointment. 'He didn't even so much as put his arm round me, although that settee is small, and he had to rest his arm along the back of it.' She took a determined slug of her wine. 'But I'll get him somehow. I'll dazzle him with my cooking, and one day he'll look up and see what a jewel I am, and pounce.'

'Ooh. Very romantic.' Perdita was relieved. It didn't look as if Lucas was likely to take Janey up on what she offered.

'So? What about you then?' Janey looked expectantly at Perdita, hopeful that she could come up with a more salacious tale.

Perdita decided to just tell the truth – everything except the closeness of her relationship with Lucas. 'Well, to be honest with you, Janey, I haven't got a boyfriend. The man who took me up to stay with my friend at Christmas was just her brother-in-law. I came back early because Kitty was ill.' She blushed, although there was no reason why Janey should ask how Perdita got back.

'Oh. I'm really sorry about Kitty, of course.'

'She's not that bad, really. She should be home quite soon.'

Relieved that she could get back to the subject really of interest to her, Janey went on, 'But why did you – you know – pretend to have a boyfriend?'

'Well, it's terribly silly I know, but it's because of Lucas. You know we knew each other, years and years ago?'

'Yes?'

'Well, he always made me feel sort of inferior. I didn't want to seem on the shelf, or available or anything.'

'Oh.' Janey seemed more disappointed than shocked. 'And I was so thrilled for you. But I do understand. Lucas is so blissful he'd make anyone feel inferior. Though I'm a bit surprised he had that effect on you.'

'I'm sorry. It was sort of a fantasy, I suppose. You know, being whisked away to a glamorous location for Christmas, in a fast car.'

'And was it glamorous, where you went?'

'Not at all. It was very primitive. They'd only just moved in and nothing was unpacked, and it was freezing cold.'

'No opportunities to dress up, then?'

'Only in layers and layers of jumpers. Just as well I'd packed my thermal vest.'

'Thermal vest!' Janey was suddenly aware that Perdita was pushing thirty. 'Oh,' she sighed, 'I sort of pine for the sort of Christmas you read about in magazines, where everyone dresses for dinner and don't just put on their jumpers with reindeers on.'

Perdita chuckled. 'That was the sort of Christmas Lucy wanted – a perfect magazine one. I think she was suffering from that "addiction-to-make-Christmas-perfect" thing, when everything has to be home-made and decorated beautifully. It's a syndrome. I read about it. Poor old Lucy. It wasn't at all like that, but I think she had a nice time in the end. Her kids did, anyway.'

'Christmas is for children really.' Janey sighed. 'It's not quite the same when everyone's grown-up, is it?' Her moment of nostalgia lasted about a second before she went back to Perdita's love life, or lack of. 'So, what was the brother-in-law like, then? Still married?'

'Separated, but not fanciable, and too broken-hearted, even if he was.'

'Oh.' Janey drained her glass and helped them both to more wine. 'We're both a couple of silly cows – you for pretending you had a boyfriend, and me for having a crush on a man who'll never want me.' They clashed glasses. 'Cheers!'

'Cheers,' agreed Perdita glumly. Then came another tricky moment for her. Did Janey and Greg know why Lucas left them so suddenly on Boxing Day? Would Lucas have said that he was going to get her home because Kitty was ill? Or could she depend on him having a 'never apologise, never explain' philosophy? 'So did you have to work on Boxing Day or were you free then?'

'Had to work, which is why I'm off now. It was rather good actually. Lucas had to go flying off somewhere for some reason, which left me and Greg in charge. Well, me, really. Everyone was very pleased with what I did.'

'What, even Lucas?' Perdita could smile now she knew Lucas had been discreet.

'Well, no. He wasn't there, was he? But when I went into work this morning, Robert – the new head waiter? –' Perdita nodded, 'told him.' Janey sighed ecstatically. 'Well, Lucas looked down into my eyes, took hold of my chin, and sort of smiled. Oh God! I nearly wet myself. Then he said I could have today off because of having to take over yesterday. He can be really kind at times.'

Perdita, who knew this, took refuge in a gulp of wine. 'Let's go and see if the spuds are cooked. We need something solid like a baked potato to put our feet back on the ground. You especially.'

'He's just so gorgeous. I can't help being in love with him. Even if he never looks at me.'

'Come on, Janey!' said Perdita, not confident that Lucas's lack of interest in 'half-fledged ducklings' would last for ever. She led the way to the kitchen. 'Lovely girl like you should have a real man, not a fantasy. Leave that to the old birds like me.'

'You're not old!' Janey indignantly followed Perdita into the kitchen. 'Just mature – I mean, you're not even thirty yet, even if you do run a business and wear a thermal vest. And you'd be lovely if . . .'

Perdita turned round with a sigh. 'Don't tell me. If I did something about myself. Ronnie says something of the sort every time I see him.'

'And do you listen?' Janey's bright eyes were optimistic.

'Not very often. He's surrounded by people who are obsessed with their appearance, who make their living by making people cover themselves in volcanic mud or whatever. Just because I don't bother with things like that, he sees me as a potential victim.'

'You don't have to do the mud thing, but some of the

treatments are lovely, so my mum says. Dad bought her a weekend there once, as a present.'

'I'd hate it! I mean, I'd have to buy new underwear and everything. I can't lie there and be tortured in mauvy-grey knickers which won't stay up unless I'm wearing jeans.'

'What do you mean? Shall I take the butter?'

Perdita nodded. 'Oh, you know. Your underwear seems perfectly all right until the summer when you put on a skirt and don't wear tights. Then you realise you can't go anywhere in a hurry without your pants falling down.' Janey, who had settled herself by the stove, was looking bemused. 'Doesn't it happen to you, then?'

Janey shook her head. 'I buy new knickers every summer anyway.'

'Oh. Well. Perhaps I should. But that's one of the reasons I don't want to be made over.'

'I know!' said Janey. 'Promise that if this television thing comes off you'll get done up? That's fair enough, isn't it? After all, if you're going to be on television you might get fan mail, become a star. Especially if you don't wear a bra.'

'What?'

'Oh, never mind. Just promise me you'll have a makeover if you're on telly.'

Perdita sighed. 'OK. It's a very long shot, why not?'

Perdita and Mrs Welford, Kitty's favourite taxi driver, went up to collect Kitty from the Ledham-Golds. Perdita had already made up a bed for herself and was preparing to stay with Kitty until such time as the situation altered. It was only after Mrs Welford, having been given tea and teacakes, and discreetly paid was sent on her way that Kitty and Perdita had a row. It was, as usual, a ladylike row. No one shouted or hurled insults, both parties stated their separate cases with dignity, but Kitty flatly refused to let Perdita move back in with her.

'You cannot give up your life to look after me,' Kitty

said, after the battle had gone on for a while and she wanted a drink. 'It's not necessary and it would drive me mad, having you hovering round me all day looking to see if I was telling the truth when I said I was perfectly fine.'

Perdita, who did try and second-guess Kitty, was also tired. She wanted the best for Kitty, but was beginning to doubt that her own constant presence would help if Kitty was so against the idea. 'Veronica, your friend, with your best interests at heart, told me you wouldn't be able to live on your own. She asked me if you had any relatives.'

'Veronica is a fusser. She's never lived on her own in her life and doesn't understand that some people prefer it that way.'

'Supposing you had another TIA?'

'Don't talk to me in initials. It's a sloppy habit, and I don't understand what you mean.'

'Transient ischaemic attack. If you'd been alone when you had that one—'

'My dear Perdita, do let's have a drink. I don't think I can stand all this concern without one.'

Perdita didn't say a word about alcohol being bad for her, and nor did she protest when Kitty lit her pipe. 'Mrs Ledham-Gold distinctly told me that the doctor – your doctor, Dr Edwards – said you weren't to go home unless there was someone there.' He had also said he wanted to discuss Kitty's aftercare with her, but Perdita didn't mention this.

'Very well, if you insist on bullying me, you can stay here tonight, but tomorrow I'll ask Dr Edwards if he can come down and talk some sense into you. I am really not ready to be treated as a semi-competent invalid yet.'

'OK.' Perdita took a sip of whisky, which she only drank in emergencies. 'If he says I can go home, I'll go home. But if he doesn't, you're stuck with me, like it or not. Now I'll go and get us some supper.'

'That would be lovely,' said Kitty, as if she hadn't been showing Perdita the door only moments earlier.

Kitty arranged for Dr Edwards to visit the following afternoon. Perdita rushed through her jobs so she could be there, not daring to be a second late in case Kitty bullied the doctor into saying what she wanted him to.

Dr Edwards, a tall, well-set-up man in his forties, was courteous and pleasant, and Kitty was very fond of him. He didn't lie to her and he had the right accent: Kitty, for all her endearing ways, was a snob. She liked a doctor to speak the Queen's English.

He always asked after Kitty's garden, knowing she was more willing to talk about that than her health. Today, when he arrived, Kitty offered him sherry, although it was tea-time. It was, Perdita knew, to give Kitty a little Dutch courage; the thought of losing her independence reminded her of her old age. And her old age was something she'd managed to ignore up until now.

The doctor accepted the sherry gracefully and seated himself on the sofa.

'Have a cheese straw,' said Kitty. 'Not home-made, I'm afraid, but just about edible. Perdita, dear, help yourself to sherry and pour me one.' Kitty secretly despised sherry, Perdita knew well, but probably didn't want to scare the doctor by drinking neat whisky at half-past four in the afternoon.

When they all clutched cut-glass glasses, and the cheese straws had done the rounds, the doctor got down to the point. 'Mrs Anson, your . . .' he glanced at Perdita, unsure how to describe her.

'Perdita is nothing whatever to do with me, she just inflicted herself on me when she was a child. She's not related to me in anyway.' Kitty smiled lovingly at her.

'May I call you Perdita?' the doctor asked.

'Of course. She's just a child and knows nothing about

anything except growing mutant lettuces,' said Kitty.

Perdita laughed. 'Yes, do.'

The doctor looked at the two women, one of whom he had got to know over the years, and the other, much younger, whom he knew only by repute. 'Mrs Anson asked me to come here this afternoon to tell you, Perdita, that she can live perfectly well by herself.'

Perdita nodded, hoping fervently that he could see through Kitty's ability to put on a brave face, and appear much heartier than she really was.

'Well, at the moment, she can.'

'There you are!' Kitty was triumphant. 'I told you that you were fussing quite unnecessarily.'

He addressed Perdita. 'For her age,' he glanced at Kitty, apologetic for discussing her health in front of her, 'she's really in very good form. But she has had this TIA, and she could have another one.' Perdita wondered if Kitty was about to tick the doctor off for talking in initials. 'However,' Dr Edwards went on, 'I don't think there is any need for Perdita to move in with you at the moment.' Sunshine radiated from Kitty's wrinkled face. 'But you will have to make some compromises.' He turned sternly to her.

'Well, of course, anything within reason . . .'

'I'm not going to ask you to give up your pipe.'

Perdita bit her lip but said nothing.

The doctor answered her unspoken question. 'There's no point in doing things to prolong your life at your age, you're already prolonged.' He smiled and Kitty glowed under his charm. 'But you must have a personal alarm, a button you wear round your neck and can press if anything happens. The signal is picked up by the ambulance station who'll get in touch with Perdita, or whoever is nearest. If they can't they send an ambulance.'

'Really,' muttered Kitty, 'it sounds quite unnecessary to me. I can't bear new-fangled gadgetry.'

'It's that or contact a private nursing agency and have

127

carers in day and night,' said the doctor smoothly. 'Which would be very expensive and not really necessary at this stage.'

Kitty and the doctor locked eyes, both strong-minded and determined. Kitty backed down first. 'Oh, very well, I'll have your gadget then.'

'And I'll get a mobile phone. That way I can guarantee to be there if it goes off,' said Perdita. If Kitty was willing to take on 'gadgetry' it was only fair that Perdita should too.

The doctor raised his eyebrows, as if to wonder why she hadn't got one already. Perdita changed the subject. 'What happens if Kitty has another – transient ischaemic attack?'

'Then we have to consider the likelihood of her – you –' he smiled again at Kitty, 'having a full-blown stroke. If that happens—'

'I shall get Perdita to give me a lethal injection. I'm not going into a home.'

'Of course you're not,' said Perdita firmly. 'There's no question of it.'

'Besides, you haven't had the stroke yet,' said the doctor. 'You might get run over by a bus.'

Kitty snorted. 'Precious little chance of that around here! Do you know how infrequent the buses are in the village? You could die of exposure waiting for one.'

'But if you do have a stroke, and it's a possibility we must consider, you could stay here if Perdita lived with you, and you had proper nursing care.'

'It's a lot of nonsense about nothing,' said Kitty. 'Can I offer you another drink?'

Perdita showed the doctor out after Kitty had shown him the garden, proving to him just how fit and healthy she was. He was carrying several flowerpots with rooted cuttings in them from Kitty's greenhouse, and had a sprig of wintersweet in a bag to take home to his wife.

'She is remarkably fit for her age,' he said, even before Perdita could express her concern. 'And there's really no point in making her give up the things in life which give her pleasure. But there is a very real danger of stroke, which could make life very different for her. With the best will in the world, you could never look after her on your own, even if you didn't have a business to run. You'd have to have help, which would be very expensive. Could Mrs Anson afford private nursing care, do you know?'

'I'm afraid I don't know. She's always trying to give me money, but that doesn't mean she's got a lot of it. She's just generous.'

'I suggest you try and find out. Then you can both be prepared if the worst happens. I'd very much like to think of Mrs Anson dying peacefully and painlessly in the night, and I'm sure you do too,' he added firmly, 'but if that doesn't happen, it's a good idea to have a contingency plan. There are agencies who supply carers.'

Perdita sighed, more loudly than she realised.

'I don't suppose you go to the doctor very often, do you?'

'No. But there's no need, I'm never ill.'

'Even if you're not, you can always come and see me if you're worried about Mrs Anson, or anything.'

Perdita, who was already emotionally strung out, felt tears come into her eyes. 'That's very kind,' she said huskily.

When she went back, Kitty was in the sitting room, still wearing her gardening clogs, looking far more tired than she'd allowed the doctor to guess. Perdita cooked her an omelette and told her that she was staying the night, in spite of what the doctor had said.

Kitty accepted this without argument, an indication that the doctor hadn't been unnecessarily pessimistic. Kitty seemed to feel this too.

'To misquote dear Winston,' she said, 'it's not the

beginning of the end, but I have a feeling it's the end of the beginning.'

Perdita hugged Kitty very hard. 'I expect you're right. But although I can't promise to administer a lethal injection, I do promise you won't go into a home while I have breath in my body.'

Not usually much given to physical contact, Kitty returned the hug. 'Thank you for that. It would be important to me to stay here. Though, of course, the moment I thought I was becoming a burden, I'd . . .'

'Don't!'

'Well, if you're squeamish . . . But I have a little something for you.' Kitty went over to the mantelpiece in the kitchen and produced an envelope from behind the clock. 'To save you the trouble of opening it, it's the money for a new van. Don't argue. If all my money goes on private nurses, and I assure you I do have plenty of money, I want you to have something. Save on death duties.'

'Only if you live seven years.' Perdita refused to take the envelope.

'Darling, I can't guarantee to do that, but it would give me an incentive to look after myself, the thought of cheating the tax man.'

'That's very tax-man-ist. They're probably perfectly nice people.'

'I thought you were a perfectly nice person until you got so stubborn. Take the cheque and buy a van with it! Besides,' Kitty knew when she was winning, 'if I have one of these blasted bleepers, you'll have to keep running to my side, you'll need a reliable vehicle.'

'It doesn't have to be new-from-the-shop new,' said Perdita, when she had opened the envelope, and seen the vastness of the amount written.

'Yes it does. Buy the best and it will last you longer, that's what Lionel used to say. And he was right. Now do go to bed. You have to be up early, and Veronica lent me a book I've been wanting to read for ages.'

'Oh?' Kitty was a voracious and critical reader, devouring all the latest biographies and histories. 'Is that the book about Byron you were telling me about?'

'No, dear. It's the new Patricia Cornwell. Why didn't you tell me about her?'

Once New Year was over and the shops had reopened properly, Perdita used some of her father's cheque to buy a mobile phone. Completely at the mercy of the man in the shop, she did exactly what he told her, signed on for the arrangement he thought best, and generally put up no resistance. Nor did she make much effort to learn how to use it; she was much more excited about her new van.

She had to wait three weeks, and when it finally arrived, she found driving it such a different experience she hardly knew herself. She hadn't realised how heavy and difficult the old one had been until she didn't have to manage it any more.

Lucas must have been waiting for her the first time she took it to Grantly House, because he appeared as she opened the back doors.

'You've got a new van, then,' he said.

'Ten out of ten for observation,' she said glibly. 'Kitty paid for it,' she added more seriously.

'So how is Kitty, now she's home?' Lucas took a tray of salads from Perdita's hands.

'She seems fine. She wouldn't let me go and live with her, though. But at least she's got an alarm now.' She took another box out, and Lucas indicated she should put it on top of the one he was holding. 'I've got a mobile phone.'

'Welcome to the twentieth century. And is the alarm system working OK?' he asked.

'Well, yes. I was contacted a couple of times, and rushed over only to find Kitty in the garden, fit as a flea. She kept banging it on things and setting it off by mistake. She wears it tucked into her clothes now.' Perdita heaved out another box and made to follow Lucas.

'She does wear it, then?' he asked when they were through the kitchen.

'She did protest when I kept jumping up out of nowhere, as she put it. But I threatened her with twenty-four-hour care if she didn't persevere with it, so she agreed.' She watched Lucas reverse into the cold store, holding the door open for her to follow. 'It'll probably come to that, though.'

'Not necessarily. She might die in the night. People do.' Lucas peered into the first box, frowning. 'What is this muck you've brought me? We have our own compost heap, you know. We don't need contributions from yours.'

'There's absolutely nothing wrong with it!' she snapped, after a few moments' tense inspection. 'You're so bloody fussy.'

'I have standards I like to maintain, that's all.'

'Well, do you want the other boxes, or not?'

'I might find something salvageable in them, I suppose.'

As Perdita stormed back to her van she realised that Lucas had probably made her angry on purpose, to stop her feeling depressed about Kitty. If so, his plan had worked.

Chapter Ten

❧

'Hello, ducks. How's tricks?' asked Ronnie, as Perdita delivered a box of rocket and blanched dandelion leaves.

'OK. Why are you so cheerful all of a sudden?'

'Because you are going to get made over! And the thought of you getting rid of all that body hair fills me with spring fever.'

'What do you know about my body hair?' demanded Perdita, crossly.

'I don't need to know, I can use my imagination.'

'Obviously, otherwise you wouldn't be talking to me about being made over. It's not going to happen.'

'But the telly programme is going to be filmed soon. And you did say—'

'Did I? To you? I thought I told Janey—'

'And she told me. And between the two of us, we're going to make you keep your word.'

'OK. When I am told, officially, that I am going to be in Lucas's bloody television programme, I'll let you do your worst. But not until then.'

'He's very good-looking, your friend Lucas, isn't he?'

'My friend? Ronnie, your spies have let you down. We're not friends, we hate each other.'

'Oh? He didn't drive up to fetch you from Shropshire at Christmas then?'

Perdita was speechless. Should she deny everything, or, as she was longing to do, demand to know how the hell Ronnie had got hold of that story? She settled on the latter, as denying it would make life even more complicated.

'I can't reveal my sources, but it came via Mr Grantly.'

'Oh.'

'So, is it true, then?'

'Well, yes it is, but it doesn't mean we're friends, really. He heard that Kitty was ill and needed me, and he came up and fetched me. Of course, I am – was – terribly grateful, but that's as far as it goes.'

'Mmm.' Ronnie surveyed her doubtfully.

'Look, if there was anything between me and Lucas Gillespie, apart from mutual dislike and a bit of gratitude on my part, wouldn't I be in here begging your lot to do something about my hair?' She took hold of a handful of the offending substance and dangled it. 'I mean, would a girl go out with a man like Lucas Gillespie with hair like mine?'

Her ruse worked. Ronnie regarded the wild mass of curls (which even in Perdita's opinion needed a trim and some good conditioner) and accepted that a girl who cared so little for her appearance had no interest in any man.

'I thought you were quite keen on finding a boyfriend. What's changed?'

'Well, I was keen, but since Kitty's illness, and what with one thing and another, I can't really be bothered.'

'Fair enough,' said Ronnie, with the smugness of one who knows he'll get his own way eventually and can wait. 'But I don't know why you're so against having a few beauty treatments. Women queue up for them, you know.'

'Not this woman.'

Later, having escaped Ronnie and his threatened beauty treatments, Perdita went back to her tunnels. Lucas had ordered some Witloof chicory, and she wanted to check if it was doing something under its flowerpot. She also wanted to see if the crosnes had survived its hibernation, and would be ready to plant in March. William was digging in some alfalfa which had become tough, making room for a crop of elephant garlic.

'Hi, William. How's it going?'

'Work, or life in general?'

As his fork seemed to be working just fine, she said, 'Life in general.'

'OK, I suppose, but I'm meant to be going to a college reunion. Formal do.'

'That sounds fun. When is it? Do you need extra time off?'

'No, I need a partner. I don't suppose . . .' He looked questioningly at her.

'No, certainly not. What would all your college pals think if you turned up with an older woman on your arm?'

'That I'd got lucky.' He chuckled to hide his embarrassment.

'Why don't you ask Janey? I'm sure she'd love to go with you.'

'I don't know her well enough.'

'Of course you do! Tell you what, I'll ask her for you. She'll understand about you being shy because she's quite shy herself. Although really pretty, of course,' she added, checking his expression to see if he agreed with her.

'She's cool, but I don't suppose she'd want to go with me.'

'Rubbish! Of course she would. And she'd love an opportunity to dress up.' And she might look sufficiently gorgeous for you to make the effort to distract her from Lucas, she added silently. 'Where is it, and how will you get there?'

'We're all staying over in a guesthouse. Dad said I could take the car.'

'So it'll be a whole weekend thing?'

'Well, yes. You'll be all right here, won't you?'

'Oh yes, fine.' Even if she hadn't been fine, Perdita would have accommodated William's time off if it meant getting Janey away from Lucas. 'So you'd really like me to ask her?'

'Oh yes. I like Janey. She's dead pretty, and she makes me laugh.'

'But you don't want to ask her yourself?'

William blushed, undecided.

'Tell you what,' said Perdita, 'I'll tell her that you've got this lush ball to go to, and want to take someone with you, and are thinking about asking her. I'll see if she seems keen or not, and tell you. Then you don't have to worry about being turned down.'

'Really, Perdita? That'd be top.'

As Perdita had anticipated, Janey was enthusiastic about going to a ball with William. An excuse to really dress up, a weekend away, and if William wasn't the man of her dreams, he was at least available, and was quite nice-looking.

'After all, it doesn't look as if Lucas is ever going to ask me anywhere,' she added. 'Give William my number.'

Having made Janey promise to fill her in on every detail, Perdita rang William, telling him how keen Janey had seemed on the idea. William promised to ring immediately.

Feeling very pleased with herself, Perdita did a little cleaning while waiting to hear the results of her manipulations. Men always looked heavenly in dinner jackets. As long as she made absolutely sure that William was going to wear one, Janey was bound to feel attracted to him. She was delighted when Janey finally called back and told her she was all set to go to the ball.

Her satisfaction in playing fairy godmother to two people she was fond of was short-lived. Lucas was looking particularly grumpy when she delivered the next day. A glance at Janey told her she wasn't happy either, although that could just be coincidence.

'Hi, Lucas, I've got your Witloof chicory.' She didn't expect a bunch of flowers but would have liked a little more than the grunt she received. 'In the cold store? Or shall I leave it here?'

'Cold store,' said Lucas.

'So, how are you, Janey? Looking forward to your ball?'

'She's not going to any ball,' said Lucas. 'At least, not on that particular Saturday.'

'Come on! Surely someone could swap their days round to let you have it off?'

'No someone couldn't.' Lucas sounded as if he had said this before, and did not like repeating himself. 'We've got a very big event on. I need everyone I can lay my hands on. Especially Janey.'

'Surely you could get a sous-chef from an agency?' Perdita was as disappointed as Janey was and William would be.

'Why the hell should I? Janey's on the rota for that night. I need her and she can't have the time off. Is that really so difficult to understand? Unless she wants to look for another job, that is.'

Janey, and a new girl Perdita didn't know, quailed under his fury. He was obviously in a foul mood. Perdita decided she would ask him again when he was feeling happier. In the meantime, she would buy a local paper to see if there were any jobs in it for Janey. She was determined that Janey should go to the ball. The Demon King wasn't going to stop her.

'I tried asking him again, at the end of service,' said Janey, on the phone, 'but he flatly refused. He says he can't get anyone to replace me, and why should he pay an agency for inferior staff.' She paused. 'I suppose it is quite flattering that he feels like that about me.'

'But you did want to go to the ball?'

'Yes, but not if it means my losing my job.'

'Janey, run it by me what you *do*, exactly?'

'I'm a sous-chef. You know that.'

'But what does a sous-chef do? For Lucas?'

'Puddings, mostly. Lots of prep. I cook the veg some-times.'

'Well, I'm sure I could do that.'

'What do you *mean*? You can't cook to save your life.'

'I don't have to. All I have to do is stand in for you on the night of the ball. If I make it clear it's my fault I'm there and you're not, he won't blame you.'

'He'll *kill* you! And probably me too.'

Perdita couldn't tell if Janey was more horrified by the idea of Perdita trying to do her job, or the thought of her own fate at Lucas's hands.

'Honestly, Janey, I don't see why you're making so much fuss. I'll turn up in your place, and if Lucas breaks a few plates, he breaks a few plates. It's only one evening, and it can't be that important.'

'I can't do it, Perdita. It's not fair on Lucas. And I have my own professional pride.'

'Oh, stuff! It's one evening! You've got a whole lifetime to build up your reputation. And if Lucas is as shit-hot as everyone says he is, he'll be able to manage with me instead of you.'

'I'll think about it,' said Janey.

'Have you decided what to wear?'

'I've borrowed a gorgeous dress from a friend. Pale grey silk with velvet trimmings. It's very plain and makes me look a million dollars.' There was a hint of regret in Janey's voice.

Perdita acted on it. 'Then you must go to the ball! How often does a girl get an opportunity to wear a dress like that? Even I'd think about going!'

'Why don't you? I'm sure my friend would lend you the dress, if she'd lend it to me. You'd look wonderful in it. Better than me.'

'Oh no. I'm not going to a ball with William. No way. I'm afraid if you don't go with him, William won't go to his college reunion. And I know he was really looking forward to it.'

'Lucas will sack me.'

'No he won't, because if he does, I won't do his television programme.'

'That's blackmail!'

'I know.' Actually, it was worse than blackmail, as Perdita had already promised she'd do the programme. She'd have to rely on Lucas's sense of fair play – a very uncertain commodity – to stop him blaming Janey for something which wasn't at all her fault.

'OK,' Janey sighed, still very doubtful. 'But if I lose my job—'

'You won't! Anyway, there are lots of jobs.'

'I don't want to work in a pub, Perdita, cooking chicken and chips in a basket.'

'Pubs do lots of much more interesting food these days.' Perdita's perusal of the sits. vac. had told her that jobs in pubs were the only ones going in the area.

'I still don't want to cook in one.'

'You won't have to.' Perdita crossed her fingers. 'I promise!'

'What the hell are you doing here?' demanded Lucas, as Perdita entered the kitchen. 'We've got all the garnishes we need.'

She had got there a good half-hour early so she could familiarise herself with her surroundings, but although Janey had told her that Lucas wouldn't appear before six, here he was. 'I'm your sous-chef for the night.'

'What!'

For a moment, Perdita wanted to run out of the kitchen and never come back as his expression darkened from its habitual irascibility to incandescent rage. There was a terrible silence, when, if Janey had not been well out of reach, Perdita would have aborted the mission. Then Lucas spoke very slowly and softly, coming towards her.

'I don't believe even you could be so fucking silly! There's more to being a sous-chef than peeling fucking potatoes! Where's Janey?'

'On her way to a college reunion.' Perdita found herself backed up against the freezer. 'It's not her fault! It was all my idea. I'm here in her place. You won't even have to pay me.'

'Pay you? Pay you?' He was almost whispering. 'You'll be bloody lucky if I don't fucking murder you! Don't you know that we've got a dinner for thirty and a bloody Michelin inspector coming?'

Perdita didn't, and nor had Janey, or she would never have agreed to go to the ball. 'I thought that sort of thing was supposed to be secret.'

'It is! But I've heard a rumour.' He let out a loud, frustrated breath and then went on at normal volume. 'Of all the fucking evenings for this bloody game of soldiers! I didn't tell Janey she couldn't have the evening off to be awkward! I would have let her go if I could have! I've got a lot of agency staff coming. She's the only permanent staff member on tonight! I'm going to be left with a load of people who haven't worked for me before. Why the fuck did you have to interfere in things you know nothing about?'

Oh dear. 'I know about Janey and William.' Her voice seemed to have gone up a couple of octaves, and it was a real effort not to squeak. 'They wanted to go to this reunion very much. I know Janey wouldn't have gone if she'd known about the Michelin man.' Tension made her want to giggle as the picture of a large figure made of white car tyres appeared before her.

'Well, Janey had better start job hunting. I'm not keeping her on after this.'

'It wasn't her fault! I said – she would never have done this if she'd known about the inspector. It was my idea. You can't take it out on her!'

'But I can't sack you, can I? Because you don't fucking work for me, thank God for small mercies.'

'You can't sack Janey either.' Outrage at his injustice gave her courage. 'Because if you do, I won't let them use my house for the television programme.'

'Oh, really. So that's what your promises are worth, then? Never mind, I'm sure it won't be hard to find another – *suitable* – location.'

'I did promise, and I'll only take it back if you sack Janey.'

'I don't think the prospect of cooking in your kitchen is sufficiently alluring for me to keep on a member of staff who's proved so outstandingly disloyal.'

'She's *not* disloyal! She worships you! You can do anything you like to me, but don't take it out on Janey.'

'Anything I like? Really? I'm almost tempted, but then again I don't think there's anything I can do to you, or for that matter, anything you could do to me, that would make up for me not getting my Michelin star.'

She bit her lip and closed her eyes. 'Lucas!' she pleaded.

'Well, we'll have to see, won't we?' he said after minutes had become hours. 'If you do a good job, Janey can keep hers. But if you fuck up, Janey's out of here. Fair enough?'

Relief restored Perdita's powers of speech. 'It's not fair at all, Lucas. But that's not such a surprise, is it? Fairness never was your strong suit!'

'Then you'd better perform, sweetheart. Though what the hell I'll find you to do, God knows. If you weren't in your usual scruff order, I'd put you in the dining room, out of my way.'

Perdita had borrowed an apron from Kitty, and was wearing a clean white shirt and her newest jeans. Comparatively smart, she'd thought. 'I'm quite tidy!'

'No you're not! We could find you a chef's jacket but there aren't any plain black skirts around.'

'I could go home and get one!'

'Oh no you couldn't. For a start, I don't believe you possess one, and secondly, if you think you are leaving this place before you know exactly how hard it is to work in a professional kitchen, you are in for a very nasty surprise.' He looked up as the kitchen door opened, and other people began to drift in. 'I need a sous for tonight,' he said to the two men and two women who stood there warily. 'You!' he stabbed an accusing finger at a tall boy who looked very smart in his whites. 'What are your qualifications?' The boy mumbled something. 'You'll do. What's your name? What? Tom? You're sous.'

'Yes, Chef. Thank you, Chef.'

'The rest of you, familiarise yourself with the set-up. And, Perdita, keep your hair out of the food, please.' He stalked out of the kitchen to the fridge, and started pulling dishes out of it.

Feeling very surplus to requirements, and having put her hair into a painfully tight ponytail, Perdita followed him, hoping to get her orders out of earshot of the others. 'What shall I do? I could peel potatoes?'

'The potatoes were peeled this morning, and I very much doubt if there is anything you can do which is the slightest use to me. Which is a shame, because Janey was shaping up very well and I'll miss her.'

'You can't do this!'

'Oh yes I can. This is my kitchen, and I can do what the hell I like in it. Now get out of my way and wait for orders.

'Right! Listen, everybody. There's a party of thirty due in at eight. Nothing is pre-ordered. I want them dealt with as quickly and efficiently as possible. It's a party of hoteliers. They're not here on business, but they know about food and service, and I don't want any cockups with their orders. Understood?'

Everyone nodded.

'I have also heard a rumour, which might be quite unfounded, that there's a Michelin inspector coming in. You won't know which one he is, so I want everyone, but everyone, to receive first-class service. We're a member of staff short tonight,' he gave Perdita a glance which let her know she would never reach the status of 'staff', 'so we need to keep our minds on the job.' More nods. 'OK, let's party.'

Perdita went to the sink where a vacant young man with virulent acne was filling it with scalding hot water. 'Can I do that? I'm not trained, you see. You could do something more demanding.'

The boy looked at her anxiously.

Lucas put his hand on her shoulder and yanked her out of the way. 'That KP – kitchen porter to you – has learning difficulties. He can do the washing-up perfectly efficiently, but he can't do anything else. You, I wouldn't even trust with the washing-up.'

'I think you're taking this a bit far, Lucas,' she said under her breath. 'I'm not a complete idiot.'

'Would you let me loose in your poly-tunnels? No? Well, this is my work space, and I'd rather do without a pair of hands than have someone who's never even been in a kitchen under my feet! Now get out of my way!'

Perdita went and stood next to a boy who was boiling sliced potatoes in a pan. He was watching them anxiously, while darting glances at an aubergine which he was slicing into slivers you could almost see through. 'Can I help you? I couldn't possibly slice aubergines that thinly, but I could keep an eye on the spuds.'

'OK, but don't let them go too far. They've got to be sautéed.'

Perdita stood over them with a knife, poking at them occasionally. Then she heard a tiny scream in the corner and saw that a girl had dropped a cold poached egg on the floor, and a bowl of them teetered on the edge of the counter. Perdita ran to rescue the bowl and help her clean up before Lucas noticed. Even she knew where the huge roll of blue kitchen paper was, and she was back with her potatoes within moments. But not before Lucas.

'What are these?' he demanded.

It was obviously a trick question and Perdita had no idea what to answer.

He picked up the pan and a sieve and took them over to the sink. He tipped the potatoes into the sieve, his eyes never leaving Perdita's, then dumped the potatoes onto the floor. 'Clear that up,' he ordered her. 'It's complete mush. We are not running a pie shop here.'

Then he strode back to the boy whose potatoes they'd been. 'If I had time to fart about I'd make you eat those potatoes off the floor. They were your responsibility, you had no right to off-load it on to that girl, who knows jack-shit about cooking.'

'No, Chef, sorry, Chef.'

Perdita, having dealt with the potatoes, took a deep breath and went up to Lucas, who was scowling at a fillet of beef as if it were personally responsible for all his troubles.

'I think I'd better just go,' she said. 'I'm just getting in the way here.'

'You go, Janey goes,' he replied, not looking up.

'This is intolerable!'

'You put yourself here. If you don't like it, you can't blame me.' He sighed and looked up. 'Keep out of the bloody way. Go into the corner and chop parsley.'

It's nice to spend time with a friend, she thought, finding a bunch of parsley she'd grown herself, where she'd put it in the cold store. She took it as far away from Lucas as possible, found a board and a knife and started chopping.

A worried-looking waitress came in. 'The party of thirty

144

are starting to arrive. They're having drinks in the bar. Shall I take them menus now, or wait until they're all here?'

'Better wait. Now, are we ready, people?'

A hush fell over the usually noisy room. Tension and heat seemed to increase by the second. The newly promoted sous-chef wiped his brow, apart from that, no one moved.

Perdita shuffled deeper into her corner and crouched over her task.

Chapter Eleven

There was a stillness, while everyone stood at their places waiting to spring into action. No one could do anything until the first script came in, but the moment it did, they would be flying to get the order cooked, plated and garnished as quickly as possible.

Lucas, in the middle of the working area, was conductor, director, but also lead singer. The light shining down on him enhanced his jutting nose and strong chin, making him look devilish under the bandanna knotted into a rope and tied round his head, to catch the sweat. Perdita was glad Janey couldn't see him. Even to her jaded gaze he looked dangerous and extremely attractive in his double-fronted white jacket. Then she realised Janey must have seen him like this dozens of times, and hoped fervently that William looked half as good in his dinner jacket, otherwise this evening in Hell's Kitchen would have been for nothing.

Soon the waitress came in with the orders.

Perdita didn't allow herself to look over her shoulder often, but when she did, Lucas seemed to be everywhere, shaking pans, pulling lights down over plates, creating delicate towers of rösti, aubergines, puréed swede, which he heaped about with slices of crimson lamb or duck, and then drizzled with gravy. Every serving had to be as pleasing to the eye as it was to the palate, every detail of every plate had to be checked by Lucas.

He seemed to know what was going on in every pan and where each order had got to in its preparation. He

146

shouted commands in a voice which would have turned Perdita to jelly if she hadn't been jelly already. His temper, like the ovens, seemed to get hotter and hotter without ever actually exploding. His orders were loud and almost continuous.

'Get that fillet out of the pan, now! You're not at McDonald's now, and he wants it rare.' 'Table eight has been waiting ten minutes for their starters. Not good enough. Get it done.' 'Is that fingerprint on the plate edible? If not get it off!'

Perdita kept her head well down in her corner. She couldn't see properly and her knife wouldn't slice butter without an argument, but she was out of the way. Her survival instinct told her that if she made her presence felt, she would be on a plate, rare, with a beef and Madeira jus, roasted garlic and a garland of rosemary and pak choi before she could say Michelin Star.

Then the waitress who'd been dealing with the dining room and the dirty plates came into the kitchen. She was in her twenties and very experienced, but she cleared her throat nervously.

'The dishwasher's broken down!' she called, then stood well back and looked ready to duck. Up until that moment, Lucas hadn't used physical violence, but it felt like just a matter of time.

He took this news surprisingly coolly. 'Right, John, you stop doing pans and start doing plates. The glasses can wait. Perdita! Where the hell are you, when you're wanted? There's a number on the board. Ring the company and get them to come out right away.'

'There won't be anyone there at this time of night!'

'Don't argue. It's supposed to be a twenty-four-hour service. John, change the water, please.'

A few moments later, Perdita had to break the news that the dishwasher couldn't be mended until tomorrow, certain that this time Lucas would surely throw something, or somebody, probably her. But he didn't.

'Right, you keep the draining area clear for John, Perdita. Becky will give you drying-up cloths. Have you chopped that parsley, yet?'

'Yes, mountains of it.'

He swooped into her corner and picked up some parsley between finger and thumb and tossed it into his mouth. He spat it out. 'Gritty.' Then he swept the whole lot onto the floor with his hand. 'You didn't wash it, did you? Wash, dry, chop. Just as well we didn't need it until tomorrow. Clear it up and then help John.'

Perdita had spent a good fifteen minutes on that parsley, while the *Danse Macabre* on roller blades had been performed around her.

'You can't do that! You can't treat me or anyone like that! It's inhuman and barbaric!' she steamed, her rage just under the surface, but ready to erupt. 'I have spent hours chopping that parsley. You never told me to wash it! How was I supposed to know you had to?'

Lucas took a moment to consider this. 'Yes, I suppose it was unreasonable of me to assume you'd behave like any other human being. But I just forgot, for a moment, that you have your own rules about cleanliness, food and hygiene. Foolish of me. Still, it won't happen again. Could you dry the plates and stack them, that is, put one on top of the other, in the pantry? Thank you so much.'

This quiet sarcasm was so much worse than his shouting had been. If only Janey hadn't been so wedded to this job Perdita would have walked out. But she couldn't trust Lucas to play fair. He'd rather lose a good sous-chef than not carry out a threat.

Becky, the waitress, came in excitedly. 'I think I've spotted the inspector,' she said. 'He's balding, has got a French accent and is alone. Apart from the party, there are only three other tables occupied. Do you want to do his order first?'

Lucas turned on the poor woman. 'What the fucking hell are you thinking of? No way do we take orders out of sequence! Every service has to be as if there's an inspector out there and every customer has to be treated as if they are one! All the customers have paid good money to come here. I can't ask them to put up with crap service in case the man with his hair dragged over his bald spot doing Inspector Clouseau impressions really is an inspector! Now do the job you're being paid for!'

Becky scurried away, accustomed but not inured to such outbursts.

The evening went on, too fast for Perdita to follow. Becky brought in pile after pile of plates, so that it seemed that John washed and Perdita dried enough plates for each customer to have used ten of the things. When Becky finally came in and said, 'That's the last of the plates. It's just cups and glasses now,' Perdita's relief was enormous. She'd gone through dozens of tea-towels, and her feet, ankles and legs were aching badly.

The pace of the kitchen slowed. Now it was only coffee, various types of tea, and plates of hand-made chocolates which were going out, although there was a lot of cleaning-up going on.

'The party were very happy with their meal,' said Becky. 'They gave me a massive tip!'

'Well, don't feel obliged to include Perdita when you share it out,' said Lucas, knowing full well that Becky hadn't intended to share it at all. 'You and the other girl are the only members of staff they see, but not the only two involved.'

What seemed like hours passed, then at last, Lucas seemed satisfied with the state of the kitchen.

'OK, you lot, you can push off now. Bring me your time sheets. Good service. Tom?' He patted the boy's shoulder. 'Not bad at all. Work with you again. John, you go home now. You've done very well.'

Tom took this faint praise as the accolade it was, blushing and stammering his thanks. John just smiled. By this time Perdita was no longer surprised that Lucas didn't properly thank or congratulate his staff on doing so well under trying circumstances. The kitchen porter was the only member of the team he treated with any consideration at all. She limped to the passageway where she had hung her coat, pulling her hair free from its band.

'Where do you think you're going?' Lucas, hands on hips, made her feel like a cat burglar, stealing into the night.

'Home. Everyone else has gone.' Quickly, she took off her apron. 'I've done my night's work.'

'No you haven't. What about the pans? The glasses?'

'You said those could wait.'

'They have waited. Now you've got to wash them.'

'But the dishwasher's going to be fixed tomorrow! I'm shattered! I'm not going to stay here all night to do something a machine can do in the morning!'

'The machine can't do pans, and I'm not risking the man not coming. It's Sunday tomorrow: twenty-four-hour service or not, he may not turn up. Get back in here.'

Without bothering to replace her apron, Perdita hung her coat back on its hook and stormed back into the kitchen. There was no point in protesting further; he would only threaten Janey again. William would have to be showering her in diamonds, bathing her in asses' milk and giving her multiple orgasms to make this agony worth while.

Lucas stayed in the kitchen, tidying up, writing notes and cleaning the ovens, more, Perdita was sure, to make sure she didn't slacken than because there was work to do. But by the time she'd got to the glasses, he had finished, and was leaning against the worktop, watching her.

150

'These are smeary,' he said, picking up a glass from the side. 'And this one's got lipstick on it. Would you like to be given a glass with someone else's lipstick on it? Empty the sink and do them again. And this time, wash and rinse them in really hot water.'

Perdita didn't think her hands could stand any more exposure to boiling temperatures and detergent that may have been a virulent green, but was certainly not kind, either to the environment or to her skin. 'For God's sake, Lucas! The dishwasher'll be fixed tomorrow. Just put them all through it and stop nagging me!'

'I'm sure Janey wouldn't have put her job on the line if she'd known you couldn't even wash up competently.'

That was it. Perdita had kept a lid on her temper all evening, but now there were no witnesses she could let rip without inhibitions. 'Janey did *not* put her job on the line, you did! You are so fucking contrary, you'd rather lose a good and loyal member of staff than lose face! Well, I've had enough. You can wash the rest of the glasses yourself!'

She stood, still clutching a glass, waiting for the explosion. She was in the mood to throw things.

'Listen, you silly cow! If you play games with other people's lives, you've got to stick to the rules! You set up Janey and your friend to try and stop her having a crush on me! Well, Janey and I don't need your interference! If we choose to have an affair that's our business, and if I choose to sack her, that's mine. But we neither of us need you to poke your silly little nose into things about which you know nothing! Now get on and finish those glasses. Some of us have to work in the morning.'

The glass left her hand, sailed through the air, glanced off his shoulder and landed with a satisfying smash on the floor. 'You are such a bastard! I believe you'd seduce Janey, break her heart, just like you did mine, just to spite me! Well, I'm not going to stand by and let you!'

'So what are you going to do to stop me? Shower me with shards of glass which you're going to have to pick up off the floor? Somehow, I don't think that's going to do it. Janey's a very pretty girl, very like you were. I think I might like to have her, after all.'

His row of knives, neatly laid out by his chopping board caught her eye. One appeared in her hand without her knowing how it had got there. She rushed at him, not sure what she intended other than blood letting and violence, but he caught her wrist, causing the knife to join the broken glass with a clatter.

'Oh no you don't. You're not murdering me in a fit of pique.'

She kicked his shin as hard as she could, wishing that like him, she was wearing steel-capped boots, not just trainers.

'Bitch!' He grabbed her waist and pulled her to him. 'Don't you dare kick me!'

She kicked out again, but he was ready for her, hooked his leg behind the one she was standing on, making her lose her balance. She pulled him down on top of her as she fell, trying to roll so that he was underneath as they landed. Instead, she fell heavily on her shoulder, winding herself. Lucas lay on top of her. They were inches from the broken glass and both breathing hard. Perdita felt a deep, primitive satisfaction in grappling with him physically, releasing her anger by inflicting as much pain as possible. The thought that he might cause her an equal or greater amount of pain was irrelevant. Her anger would give her the strength to overpower him.

She tried to move but couldn't. Lucas was looking down into her eyes, not moving, not letting her move. She could see the knife out of the corner of her eye, it was quite near. With a huge effort she heaved upwards against Lucas so she could shift herself enough to put the knife within reach.

He saw her glance at it and adjusted his own position so she was totally immobile. 'Oh no. I'm not having my new jacket ruined because you can't keep your temper.'

'You,' she said, breathless from the weight of his body on hers, 'are the biggest, most bloody, most hateful bastard in all the world.'

'And you, in spite of being the most useless, irrational, temperamental woman I have ever had the misfortune to have in my kitchen, still drive me to distraction.'

She closed her eyes, not wanting to see if there was desire or just exasperation in his, but when she felt his breath come nearer, she said, 'If you try to kiss me, I shall bite you.' She looked up as she said this, defying him to take advantage of her.

His eyes widened as he met her challenge. 'Wait until you're asked! I have no intention of kissing you, wildcat, and if I did, you wouldn't be able to do a thing I didn't want you to do.'

She couldn't help it. She felt herself reach up to snap at him, like a terrier. Her teeth had dug into the soft tissue of his lip before he could pull out of reach.

'You bitch!'

He whispered the words, but she saw the fire in his eyes and wondered if he would bite her back, or knock her senseless with the back of his hand. She wasn't frightened, although she knew she should be. She just wanted to battle it out, tooth and nail, with the man she had hated for over ten years. She had never had a violent thought before, but now all her suppressed aggression came to the surface. The sight of his blood on his lip, the taste of it on her own, turned her into a savage.

She closed her eyes, fighting her feelings, trying to cling on to some remnant of civilisation. She felt dizzy, tumbling out of control. It was like the stage of drunkenness when you know you've had far too much to drink, but retain enough clarity of mind to bitterly regret it.

153

Somehow, she must get a grip, become a human being again, but the weight of him, holding her down, kept her hatred hot and powerful.

She looked up at him, bitterly resentful of his successful efforts to control her.

'Let me up, Lucas, or I'll report you!'

'Oh, yes? Who to? I wonder. And what will happen when I tell them that you bit me, drew blood, and probably left a scar?'

She got a leg free and kicked him.

It was a pathetic attempt, and he laughed. 'Don't you know when you're outclassed? And don't wriggle, or you'll find yourself lying on broken glass.'

'I'm not staying here all night!' she hissed. 'Let me up!'

'Not until I can be sure you won't try and savage me again.'

She still felt bursting with pent-up emotion. She wanted to take hold of his neck and shake it until his teeth rattled. She glared up at him, feeling like a tiger in a cage, infinitely powerful but declawed.

He seemed to sense her frustration. 'Now I warn you, I've had enough of being kicked and bitten, so from now on don't do anything to me you don't want me to do right back. I would have absolutely no qualms about slapping your face if you try to hurt me again.' He let this sink in. 'I'm going to help you up now.'

In spite of his warning, although she knew she'd gone so far beyond the norms of civilised behaviour it was unlikely she'd ever get back to them again, she couldn't stop herself. His soothing tone heightened her madness. The moment she was standing she flew at his neck, unable to bear his patronising attitude any more than she could tolerate the maelstrom of conflicting feelings which made her dizzy, wild, miserable, and yet elated.

This time he didn't spare her. He grabbed her wrists and lifted her so that she was half sitting, half lying on the worktop, then he stood over her legs so she couldn't hurt him, gathered her into his arms and kissed her, in a teeth-clashing, lip-bruising kiss that was as painful and passionate as it was arousing. Suddenly she found herself kissing him back, and she didn't want it to stop, ever. By some mysterious alchemy, all her hatred had turned to desire. She no longer wanted to kill him, she just wanted to make violent love to him, to have him make violent love to her.

He raised his head cautiously, not aware of her change of mood. 'You have to accept that I'm stronger than you and, however much you attack me, I'm always going to be able to fight back harder. I don't want to hurt you, but for God's sake, stop hurting me!'

She blinked up at him, not wanting him to know that he was no longer in danger, to reveal her vulnerability to him.

His voice sounded husky as he went on, 'I know I've probably just made you hate me more than ever, but I warn you, unless you're very careful, this could get way beyond kissing. I think I'd better take you home before this gets out of hand.'

There was no way she was going to let him leave her full of unsatisfied passion. Before he could stop them, her fingers flew at the buttons of his jacket, ripping them open, baring his chest. He hesitated only for a second before he returned the favour, tugging her shirt out of her jeans, undoing the buttons almost as fast as she was undoing his.

They kissed as if they hated each other, she bit and scratched and pulled at him, but she wouldn't let him go. He was less fierce, but just as passionate. When they stopped for breath his jacket hung open, exposing his naked chest, and Perdita's shirt was falling off her shoulders, joining her bra straps halfway down her arms.

'Not here,' he said. 'Not on the workbench, for God's sake. Come with me.'

As if not trusting her to follow him, he picked her up and carried her out of the kitchen, through the deserted foyer of the hotel and into the Ladies, kicking open the door. He rested her on the broad, mirror-backed Formica counter used as a dressing table, and, still holding her, swept everything off it. Potpourri, hand-towels, hand-cream and bottles of scent landed on the floor unheeded.

He slid her around and back so there was room for her legs. She didn't resist but her passion was beginning to fade. Cold air touched her bare flesh, cooling her. Back there, under the hot lights of the kitchen, where tempers and passions were heated beyond reason, the fieriness of her emotions seemed reasonable. Here, in the cool, soothing surroundings of a ladies' powder room, they seemed suddenly inappropriate.

And how did he know about the ladies' loo? How did he know there was a counter top suitable for making love on? Had he taken other members of staff there, for a little post-service fornication? There might have been a thousand innocent explanations for his familiarity with the Ladies, but none occurred to her. Sanity began to push through her dying passion, and leave her confused and full of doubts.

'Lucas – I really don't think we should be doing this.' Her voice seemed to separate her from her desires, reminding her of the sensible, down-to-earth person she usually was, disconnecting her from the wild, uncontrollable, passion-led woman Lucas had turned her into.

He was breathing audibly, not only because he'd carried her several yards. He swallowed. 'There's no should about it. Do you want to?'

She did want to. She wanted very much to make love to Lucas, to have him make love to her. She knew perfectly well that otherwise her sexual frustration would probably stop her sleeping for months, would haunt her now in a way that it hadn't for years. But she knew it would take her years to get back to being the contented, fulfilled person she had been, if they did make love. For her, lovemaking could never just be a simple release of sexual tension, and for Lucas she doubted if it would ever be anything else. She'd make herself vulnerable to him again, and this time she might not recover. But nor could she be anything but honest with him.

'I do want to, Lucas. You know I do. But not here, not like this – and I don't mean not in the ladies' lavatories, for God's sake! I'd have made love on the kitchen floor a moment ago . . .' She closed her eyes, briefly regretting that they hadn't done just that.

'But not now?'

She shook her head. 'I got very carried away. I did – want you. But I was angry with you. I wanted to hurt you, tear you apart, scratch and bite and leave bruises.' She noticed some marks on his torso. She reached out to touch them, but he stepped back sharply. 'I probably have left bruises,' she smiled, 'not that you didn't deserve it, but sex isn't about revenge. For me, it's about love.' He cleared his throat, watching as she buttoned up her shirt. 'I'm terribly sorry if I led you on,' she added.

He turned away from her and gave a brief laugh, starting to do up his own buttons. 'I suppose I've only myself to blame. As usual.'

'I don't usually mind contradicting you, Lucas, but I think I have to take my share of responsibility. Sad, isn't it?' She pushed her hair off her face, tucking it behind her ears. She watched him tidy himself in silence for a few moments. Then she said, 'What about this mess?' She indicated the potpourri, the towels and the bottles. 'Shall I get a dustpan and brush?'

'If I see you in close proximity to the floor, it's unlikely you'll get out of here with your virtue in tact. Wait here and I'll get your coat.'

157

When he came back he looked weary, and a little cynical. 'I think I should warn you that I wouldn't have made love to you for revenge, or to punish you – I've done enough of that this evening – but because I wanted you, very much. Now go away before I remember I'm the villain of the piece, and ravish you.'

When Perdita got home, although it was one o'clock in the morning, she had a very hot bath. Then she poured the remains of Kitty's brandy into a glass and took it up to bed with her. She gulped it down, feeling it tingle against her recently brushed teeth, hoping, but not believing, it would make her sleep.

'So,' asked Kitty, the following lunchtime, 'what was it like working for Lucas?' She had made Sunday lunch – roast beef and Yorkshire pudding – because, she said, she knew Perdita would need her strength building up.

'Hell. The sooner I get Janey out of there, the better.' Perdita drained her sherry glass and refilled it, in spite of the headache which nagged at her.

'I dare say Janey likes it. After all, she's trained.' Kitty stirred some flour into the meat juices.

'Shall I set the table?'

'Yes, just clear one end of it. That'll do.'

As Kitty's kitchen table had never been seen clear by anyone, this proviso was unnecessary. Perdita picked up the book which was open face down in front of Kitty's chair. 'Is this yours, or borrowed?'

'Borrowed.'

'I'll find something to keep your place, then.' Perdita found a leaflet offering cheap car insurance and slipped it between the pages. Then, to distract herself, she opened the book and looked inside. The name Lucas Gillespie, written in thick black ink, shouted at her. At first she thought she had imagined it.

'Kitty?' she demanded, having made sure she hadn't. 'Who lent you this?'

'Oh – I can't remember. Can you put some mats down for the vegetable dishes?'

Kitty wasn't usually vague, and Perdita had been putting mats down for the vegetable dishes since she was twelve.

'It was Lucas, wasn't it?'

'If you know the answer, why are you asking?'

'Why didn't you tell me he'd lent you a book? Why did you keep it from me?'

'Well, I would have told you, but he asked me not to, thought you might feel betrayed. And he was obviously right. You're getting all worked up. Now, pour some wine, there's a dear.'

'But I didn't know you knew him! Socially!'

'I didn't, but he came to see me shortly after I got back from the Ledham-Golds, to see how I was. Very polite, I thought. We got talking about books and he lent me some. Now, do start, or it'll get cold.'

Perdita sawed at her meat somewhat savagely, wondering if she was being totally unjust suspecting Lucas of having an ulterior motive for visiting Kitty.

'But why did he come?'

'I've told you, to see how I was. Of course, if you feel I've been disloyal, I'll ask him not to come again, but I do appreciate a little male company from time to time, and he has a very good mind.'

'I'm sure he has.' His body's not bad either, she added coarsely to herself. 'But when does he have the time to visit you?'

'It's just the odd afternoon. He rings to check you're not here, and not likely to be. He thought you wouldn't like it. I thought he was talking nonsense, but he obviously wasn't. I can see you're quite put out.'

Perdita got a grip on herself. 'I'm not put out at all. I

think it's very nice that he visits you, and it must be lovely to have someone to talk about books to. I'm just overtired from last night. It took me ages to get to sleep, I was so tired. My feet and legs are dreadfully stiff. Oh damn, I forgot the horseradish.'

Chapter Twelve

Janey rang Perdita on Sunday night. She was ecstatic, she had had a wonderful weekend, and was determined to give Perdita a drink-by-drink account of it. Somewhat unwillingly, Perdita agreed to meet Janey at the pub. Once they were established by the fire in the snug, each nursing a glass of cold red wine, Perdita said, 'Fire away then.'

She listened patiently, but it felt like a Pyrrhic victory. Soon, no doubt, she would revel in Janey's happiness, and not think her own peace of mind was too great a sacrifice. Just now, she felt too raw.

'. . . So William turned out to be a really nice person when he'd had a few beers. He's just really shy, isn't he?'

'Mmm.'

'He borrowed his dad's car to drive us down, and I was sort of dreading it. I mean it's dreadful being in a car with someone you don't know, and you don't know if they want you to chat or shut up.'

'Yes, I know that feeling.'

'Anyway, the journey was a bit awkward, but it turned out we both like Mogwai, and he had some tapes, so that helped. When we got there, I felt dreadfully shy, although William had warmed up a bit by then, and I must say, he was ace about introducing me to everyone. He seemed sort of – proud of me – know what I mean?'

Not from personal experience, thought Perdita, though she murmured agreement.

'So I met all his friends, and one of their girlfriends – a really nice girl called Carol – took me off to the B & B to get changed. Then we all went to the pub before we went to the ball. We were walking everywhere, so it didn't matter if we got a bit drunk . . .'

'Wasn't it a bit uncomfortable going into the pub in a ball dress?'

'Well, yes, we were all a bit overdressed, but the dress I borrowed wasn't exactly a ball gown, more just a long dress.'

Perdita suppressed a yawn, not so much because other people's accounts of splendid evenings are less entertaining than tales of disaster, but because she was very short of sleep. 'So did you get off with each other?' she asked, in an attempt to cut to the chase.

'Well, we didn't – you know . . .'

'Oh, come on, Janey! Spit it out! I'm on pins here!'

'We didn't go to bed. In fact – he didn't even suggest it, which I thought was rather sweet. And I must say he looked lush in his dinner jacket.'

This was good news, but it wasn't quite enough. For some reason she couldn't understand, Perdita very much needed Janey to have gone further along the road to destruction than she and Lucas had. 'But you did kiss?'

'Oh, yes. A lot. How about you?'

'What do you mean?' Perdita's voice was sharp with guilt.

'I mean, how did your evening in the kitchen go? What on earth did you think I meant?'

'Oh, nothing, it's just you were talking about kissing and then you said what about me.' She managed a laugh. 'I thought for a moment you were asking if me and Lucas had kissed.' Her laugh was more desperate this time. 'He is such a bastard! The dishwasher broke down and he made me wash all the pans and glasses.' In fact, she'd never finished the glasses. 'I don't know how you work with him, Janey, I really don't. He should be reported to the RSPCA, or something.'

162

Janey seemed to think she was joking. 'We're not animals!' she chuckled.

'Well, you'd never guess that from the way Lucas treats you all! The only person he was at all nice to was the washer-upper. Oh, and the person who did your job. But he didn't thank them properly, he just didn't kick them.'

'I hope you looked after him all right, Perdita. I mean, I know he is a bit of a pig, but he's so talented. And all the great chefs are—'

'Pigs?'

'Well – yes. But it's so exciting, isn't it? Watching everything happen, all that chaos, and then, beautiful plates go out as if there was all the time in the world to do it.'

'He threw my parsley on the floor. He said it was gritty.'

'I don't suppose you washed it in enough changes of water. I always wash the parsley the day before I use it, so it's really dry. Didn't Lucas tell you about the dry parsley? It's in the fridge, not the cold store.'

'He didn't say a word. He hated me being there, in fact I would have walked out—' Just in time Perdita stopped herself announcing that the reason she didn't was because Lucas had threatened to sack Janey; it wasn't fair to put that responsibility on her.

'Yes?'

'Except you're right. It is very exciting, and there was supposed to be a Michelin inspector in that night.'

'What! Oh, no! Oh God, I hope everything was all right. It's so important for Lucas to get his star.'

Perdita hadn't personally worried about stars since she was at primary school. 'Why?'

'A Michelin Star is such an accolade. I mean, they're really difficult to get and everything, and it'll give the hotel such kudos. Mr Grantly would have to put up Lucas's wages.'

'So it's just about money, is it?'

'No! It's about pride in your work. It's a public declaration that you're cooking to a certain, enormously high, standard.'

'Did Lucas tell you all this?'

'Of course.' She sighed. 'If he gets it, of course, he'll be all out for a second star. Men like him are never satisfied.'

'Well, I couldn't comment on that.'

Janey laughed. 'Really, Perdita.'

In spite of herself, Perdita began to feel twinges of guilt. It would be a shame if Lucas failed to get his star because of Janey having the night off. 'So, this star? Is it all or nothing? I mean, if you fail when the inspector comes, is that it?'

'Well, it's more like, if you succeed on one night, that isn't it. You have to prove you're consistent. The inspector will come several times. You don't know how many. Lucas was telling me. Some inspectors you get to know, although they only do it for two years, or they get too well known. And they do one visit they tell you about. But they could come five or six times and you'd never know. Why?' Janey paused. 'Nothing went wrong on Saturday, did it?'

'No, no, not that I know of.'

'That's all right. Only I'd never forgive myself if I've blown Lucas's chances.'

'Well, of course, we weren't sure there was an inspector, but you'd think they'd be easy to spot . . .'

'Why?'

'Oh, you know. All those white tyres round their tummies, and those goggly eyes.'

Janey didn't think this was funny. 'If I'd known there was the smallest chance of an inspector coming, I would never have skived off like that.'

'Oh well, can't be helped. When will you know, anyway?'

'Not until the beginning of January.'

'A whole year away? Oh that's all right, then.'

'No it's not!'

'Oh, come on, Janey. We can't be worrying about next January now. Forget the Michelin thing and tell me more about William. You're not sorry you went to the ball?'

'No, I had a lovely time. Quite romantic, really. We went for a walk along the river afterwards.'

'In January!'

'He gave me his coat.'

'Ah, sweet! And are you going to see him again?'

'I bloody well hope so! If he doesn't ring me—'

'I'll sack him. Now, I must go, Janey, my feet are still killing me from last night. I can walk for miles and dig all day, but standing about on those hard floors . . .'

'I'll let you take your ancient old bones back home to bed then. Night, night. And thanks again.'

It was when she was in bed that Perdita's troubles really began. It was worse than the night before because she wasn't so exhausted, and had no brandy to take the edge off her tension.

She couldn't concentrate on her book, and instead of being soothing, the radio irritated her. She lay in the darkness, trying to relax, mentally reorganising her poly-tunnels in an attempt to get to sleep.

All her strategies were useless. She couldn't stop thinking about Lucas, about whether she felt better about him now she had finally expressed her anger physically. But she couldn't decide, she couldn't get past speculating how it would have been if she hadn't come to her senses. She did know that if Lucas hadn't swept her into the Ladies she wouldn't have stopped, she would have willingly made love to him, in the kitchen, surrounded by the debris of the night's work. Thank goodness Lucas was too fastidious to do that. He had saved her from himself.

Then what would have happened? If they had made love? Would they have both gone back to their respective homes? Or would she have invited Lucas to come back here?

She suddenly objected to sleeping in a double bed alone, and regretted that because double beds folded in half and single ones didn't, it was only a double that could be got up her twisty stairs. She'd never minded before, but now it seemed to mock her single status.

She yearned for Lucas, not only for the passionate, red-hot sex she remembered, but for the comfort of hearing him breathing next to her – snoring, even. She yearned to put her head on his chest and hear the thump of his heart under her ear, to warm her feet against his calves, to be aware of the faint scent of his body, his after-shave, his shampoo.

Inevitably, her mind returned to their honeymoon, so many lifetimes ago. They had had a small, informal wedding, and then driven in Lucas's battered and noisy sports car up to Scotland, to where his family owned a shack on the shores of a loch.

It was very primitive. It had no electricity, running water came from the burn by the side of the building, and there was no loo. They had to put the two single beds together to make a double, but the cottage did have a wood-burning stove and the most beautiful setting one could wish for. It was May, and the surrounding woods were full of bluebells, scenting the air. The weather was wonderful, and Perdita and Lucas spent each day rowing on the loch, gathering wood for the fire, and boiling billycans, reading aloud to each other. They ate every meal they could outside, looking at the stars, smelling the bluebells, anticipating the night to come. And when it got too cold to stay outside, they raced back inside, built up the stove, lit candles, and then went to bed.

Because they spent so much of the night making love, they caught up on their sleep at odd times during the day. Perdita got used to washing her hair in rainwater, brushing her teeth in the burn and finding pretty, private spots to relieve herself. Lucas was so kind, teaching her to row, reading to her while she dozed, hunting among the stones for jewels for her.

He gave her a perfectly egg-shaped piece of rose quartz, which she still had, somewhere. She had found it impossible to throw away this symbol of love, although her wedding and engagement ring had been happily donated to a good cause. She had compromised by flinging the stone into one of the boxes of her parents' things, but not noting which one.

The honeymoon was a summer idyll which vanished when they got back to civilisation. They bought a small flat in London. Lucas had a high-powered job he was too inexperienced and young for. To keep on top of it, he worked long hours and when he came back to find Perdita had spent the day painting rather derivative watercolours, he grew angry. With hindsight, Perdita realised that her paintings really were awful, and that it was probably the job which made him angry, not her. But it was her he took his feelings out on. To please him, she got a part-time job in a bar, but he got jealous of the customers. He invited his high-powered colleagues home for meals, but Perdita couldn't cook, and her fey, romantic looks seemed childish and unsophisticated set against the sleek, well-paid women he mixed with. Perdita didn't even try to compete with them. She adored Lucas unrestrainedly, but even the sex, which had been so wonderful in Scotland, never worked for her again.

She never refused him, but she faked every orgasm, and though it was utterly devastating when it happened, she wasn't surprised when he found someone else.

When she eventually fell asleep her dreams were still full of the evening before, both the hectic, high-stress temperature of the kitchen, and what nearly happened afterwards.

'Bugger Lucas,' she said aloud when, heavy-headed and still tired, she got up the following morning. But she knew that the person she really held responsible was herself.

'Bugger Lucas,' she said again. 'If he'd been a gentleman, he'd have forced himself on me, and then he'd be feeling guilty and not me.'

The ambiguity made her smile, lifting her mood to a couple of degrees above deep depression, and she went downstairs for a cup of tea.

William was humming to himself when Perdita tracked him down later. While he wasn't actually grinning from ear to ear, his happiness was apparent.

'So, it went well then?' she asked him. 'You had a good time?'

'Oh yes. It was great.'

William was obviously not going to tell her in poetry how lovely Janey was, and how deeply in love with her he was, but Perdita could tell how delighted he was with his weekend away.

Jealous, in spite of herself, she decided he could spare her the embarrassment of seeing Lucas again so soon. 'Well, I'm glad it went so well. I want you to deliver to Grantly House today.'

'What? Why?' William didn't like dealing with customers. He was shy about going into people's work space, even when he was bringing them things they wanted, and Perdita, once she had discovered this, didn't ever ask him to do it.

Perdita felt she had no choice. The thought of breezing into the kitchen under Lucas's quizzical, questioning gaze, trying to pretend nothing had happened, was beyond her. She'd have to let her feelings revert to hatred, wait until they were no longer confused with lust, before she could carry on as normal.

'The thing is, William, Lucas and I got on really badly on Saturday night. I really don't want to face him until he's had time to calm down.' She was transferring her feelings to Lucas, she knew, but didn't mind maligning him. He had behaved badly long before she had. 'I mean, I really lost my temper. I threw a glass at him.'

'Really? I can't imagine you throwing things.'

'Well, nor can I, usually, but Lucas and I just rub each other up the wrong way. So would you please, please, deliver today? You'll see Janey.'

'I don't know what to do, or anything.'

'It's very straightforward. You drive the van round the back, go in through the kitchen entrance and bring the boxes with you. It'll be three loads today, I think. I've got some pea plants he ordered last week, but didn't get. He might as well have them today.'

'But supposing he doesn't want them?'

Perdita couldn't quite decide if William was afraid Lucas would throw them at him. 'Then he'll tell you, and you can take them back. It's no problem off-loading them, I can take them to Ronnie later. But Lucas will want them, I promise. Come on, William. You haven't had much opportunity to drive the new van.'

'Oh, OK.'

'Thank you, William. You're a star.'

William shot her an anxious look. Stardom was not what he wanted.

Perdita planned to catch up on her missed sleep in front of the television. Two bad nights and two days hard gardening had made her very tired and, with luck, the right kind of television programme would send her off in a way the World Service had been unable to. So she cursed when there was a knock at the door. Her feelings when she saw it was Lucas, in jeans and sweater, were not so much mixed, as homogenised. She couldn't tell if she was angry, pleased, irritated or plain terrified. She was definitely extremely wary, however.

'What do you want?' she demanded, standing in the opening of the door so he couldn't get past her.

'I need to speak to you.'

'My telephone's in working order and there's really no need to apologise. I know you behaved badly, but I did too, and the least said, soonest mended, don't you think?'

He scowled. 'I have no intention of apologising!' He was outraged by the notion. 'I bitterly regret what happened, but I'm bloody well not going to say I'm sorry!' He glared at her. 'Passions run high in professional kitchens, you know. People say and do things they don't mean. There's no need to take it personally.'

'Oh. So you'd've behaved like that with any of the people working there, or Janey, would you?' The thought was chilling, for lots of reasons.

'No! God, you do make a mountain out of a molehill! Janey wouldn't have driven me to distraction like you do, and nor would anyone else trained—'

'But any other woman – I take it you do restrict yourself to women – who was a novice, and made a few mistakes, would have received the same treatment as I did?'

He sighed. 'Perdita, you threw a glass at me, you tried to pull a knife on me, you bit me, you kicked me several times and I lost my temper – justifiably. You behaved extremely badly, and I wasn't much better, but as I said, these things happen in kitchens. Now, can I please come in!'

She held fast to the door. 'Why? You've said your piece, now go away.'

'Perdita! I've come about the cooker. You know? The one I'm having put in your kitchen so there's something half decent for me to cook on?'

'Oh God! I thought you'd forgotten about the cooker.' She meant that she'd forgotten all about it.

'How could I? And can I please come in? It's bloody cold out here.'

Perdita sighed and opened the door. It was strangely comforting to find Lucas the same ornery pig he always had been. And it had been nice of him not to refer to her shameless, uncharacteristic sexual passion. Compared to that, throwing the glass and trying to stab him seemed like mere irritability.

'I came because it's arriving today,' he said, having marched into the kitchen. 'I'll help you clear a space for it.'

'Hang on! Why didn't you warn me? You can't expect me to take delivery of a cooker without notice! And I'm not even sure I agreed to have one.'

He ignored her last sentence. 'I would have warned you this morning if you'd been brave enough to show up. But actually, I only knew about it myself on Friday.'

'I saw you on Saturday, why didn't you tell me then?'

He shot her a searing glance which reminded her only too well. 'Other things on my mind. But I've told you now, and I've come to clear a space for it.'

'Lucas, I'm sure I didn't agree to it. Why did you order it without telling me – asking me?'

'We did discuss it, you must remember. But I didn't mention it when I ordered it because I didn't know how long it would take to arrive. And I knew that you'd put up a lot of pathetic arguments against having it. Now can we please find room for it?'

Perdita, unclear if she had in fact told Lucas that he could put a new cooker in her kitchen, frowned. 'There's no need. There'll be space when they take the old one out.'

'The new one's a bit bigger than the old one.' Lucas knelt down and took out a tape measure from his back pocket. 'We may need to get rid of this shelving.'

'Well you can't!'

171

'Yes I can, easy. Look, it's rotten.'

'Lucas! Stop demolishing my kitchen! I know it's not much and that you hate it, but this is where I live! You can't just come storming in here and rip it apart!'

A piece of rotting melamine bent like cardboard before tearing. Woodlice and silverfish darted and dived, looking for cover, and a very large spider trotted indignantly across the floor. Perdita backed away unobtrusively. Being nervous of spiders didn't sit well with her independent-woman image.

Lucas rose to his feet. 'I'll get a carpenter to come and make good. And you'd have plenty of storage space if you didn't keep so much clutter. Here, take these.' He handed her a pile of Pyrex dishes, all opaque and edged with brown, from long-ago burnt pastry. 'I bet you never use half this stuff.'

Perdita put the pile in the sink, not because she intended to wash them, but because the sink was, for once, empty. 'I'll go and find a box to put these things in. But you'd better make sure I've got some cupboard space!'

'I'd put in a whole new fitted kitchen if I thought it would make you happy,' he said, without turning round.

Perdita stared down at his back, watching him pull out piles of jam jars, washed, but yet-to-be-recycled tins; polystyrene dishes which might be useful for seeds; a very beautiful but broken antique vegetable dish, and some yellowing paper plates of unknown origin. Was he teasing her? If so, why do it in a way she could so easily ignore?

'Are you going to get those boxes?' he asked.

She returned ten minutes later to find the entire contents of her kitchen in her sitting room.

'I thought you might as well have a clear-out,' said Lucas, 'while we wait for the cooker.'

Perdita felt strangely detached, and just watched as Lucas filled the boxes. After a few minutes she went back into the room previously known as her kitchen, and put the kettle on. By the time it had boiled, and she had made two cups of tea, Lucas had filled all the boxes, and had made a neat pile of the remaining crockery.

'You'll have much more space now you've got rid of that lot.'

'*You* got rid of it!'

'What do you want done with it? Charity shop? Jumble sale?'

'I think I'll just go through it all, if you don't mind, and check you haven't disposed of anything important.'

He sipped his tea. 'I haven't.'

Perdita surveyed the boxes. She was not attached to possessions for their own sake, but she did have a sentimental side to her. 'Kitty gave me most of those things. I may want to keep them to remember her by when she's gone.'

'If you need this junk to remember Kitty by, your memory must have deteriorated more than hers has. Besides, I imagine this house is full of things she gave you which you find useful. There's no point in hanging on to the tat.'

Knowing he was right, she decided to attack him on another issue. 'Well, you'd know all about Kitty's memory, seeing as you've been visiting her.' She just stopped herself adding, 'behind my back.'

'You found out about that, did you? I knew you'd be upset, but I wanted to see if she was better, and she seemed to enjoy my company. I think she gets a little bored of women gushing over her all the time.'

'I am not at all upset. Who Kitty chooses to see is none of my business. And I do not gush over her.'

'I didn't mean you, idiot, I meant all those visitors who treat her like a little old lady. I don't know why people believe that a woman of Kitty's age is likely to have less experience of life than they have.' He kicked the boxes

173

nearer the door with his foot. 'I'll put this lot in the car, to get them out of the way. You drink your tea. The men'll be here with the cooker in a minute.'

She perched on the window seat, watching Lucas putting boxes of her possessions into the boot of his car. She was unsure why she was allowing him to do it. There were probably a thousand, deeply significant, unconscious reasons, but the one she felt the most likely was that she didn't care enough about the things to fight him for them. Fighting Lucas could only be undertaken if you cared, passionately. She tutted at herself for her apathy. Really, she should block Lucas at every stand. Perhaps, she decided, if she wasn't so short of sleep she would have.

When she spotted a van driving up the road she set off for her poly-tunnels via the back door. Lucas could be on the receiving end of the inevitable unkind comments on the width of the cottage doors.

Only when she was certain that the delivery men had gone did she go back and see what Lucas had inflicted on her. It seemed to take up an entire wall.

'My God, it's big!' she declared.

'Thank you,' said Lucas. 'So is the cooker.'

She ignored him. 'It's taking up most of the kitchen. How am I to manage without any cupboard space or working surface? There's only the draining board left!'

'I've got a joiner friend of mine coming tomorrow. He's going to build you a counter with shelves underneath. For now, all the stuff you actually need is over there.' He indicated a neat pile of crockery. 'He's going to use recycled iroko and put a bit of slate next to the cooker to put hot pans on. It'll look very nice.'

'It sounds very expensive.'

'Actually, it's not. And I'm paying anyway.'

'Actually, you're not.'

'Yes I am. We agreed.'

'No we didn't.' In reality, she couldn't remember what they'd agreed, but it was irrelevant. She was not allowing Lucas to buy her a new kitchen.

'Perdita! Don't be silly! You can't afford all this! And you would never have bought a new cooker in a thousand years! I believe if the old one blew up, you'd manage on a camping gas stove.'

'You're probably right. But for whatever reason, I've got a new cooker, and I refuse to let anyone else pay for it. Anyway, how do you know I can't afford it?'

'Oh, stop playing games! I'm paying and that's that!'

'No.' She spoke quietly and calmly. 'I have my pride, Lucas, and if you think I can accept a very expensive cooker, and a new – some sort of wood—'

'Iroko.'

'—you're wrong. I don't need your charity.'

'It's not charity!'

'So if I have a new cooker, I pay for it.'

In the face of her obdurate calm, Lucas took himself in hand. 'Perdita, I perfectly appreciate how you feel. I left you in a very hurtful way, and it's very understandable if you hate me.' He frowned. 'Particularly after the way I behaved on Saturday. But think about it logically. I am doing a television cookery programme because I want to. To further my career, to get publicity for Grantly House, so eventually, I can ask Michael Grantly for mega amounts of money. You have nothing to gain from this—'

'That's not what you said when you tried to persuade me to do the programme in the first place.' Perdita was enjoying herself. For the first time in her life she had Lucas exactly where she wanted him, practically begging.

'You must see that it's only fair that I pay for the damn cooker!'

'Yes, I see it's fair, but you don't have the monopoly on being *unfair*, you know, Lucas. And either I pay for the cooker, and all the work needed to make the kitchen habitable, or there isn't going to be a television programme, and you will have paid for a kitchen you'll never get to use. OK?'

Chapter Thirteen

Perdita's delight in getting her own way with Lucas was a little spoilt by the fact that Lucas had paid for the cooker already and he wouldn't tell her how much it cost. But having found out from the supplier, she was eventually able to give him an envelope full of used tenners – far harder to give back or destroy than a cheque. The joiner, who had come the next day, had been easier to deal with; she told him he couldn't leave the house until he'd been paid.

But Perdita was angry on her own account. Lucas had reduced what had happened after the night in the restaurant to the sordid scufflings of two people enraged with each other. And while Perdita wouldn't have admitted, even to herself, that it was anything more, she knew she wouldn't have scuffled like that with anyone else, however angry she had been.

With a new cooker and kitchen confronting her every day, she could no longer keep the TV programme at the back of her mind and she was hoping Lucas would mention it when she next delivered. It has caused her so much trouble, they might as well get on with the bloody thing. But he just glanced up at her when she came in with the first boxes and said, 'Janey, give Perdita a hand.'

'That's a turn-up for the books!' said Perdita, while she and Janey unloaded the van. 'Fancy Lucas letting you escape, even for a few seconds.'

Janey scowled. 'Yes, and it's not very convenient, I've got some crème brûlées due out of the oven in a tick.'

'Well, don't worry. I'll be fine. But what's got into Lucas?'

'He's been making a real effort to be nice lately. You must have said something to him when you worked here that evening. Either that or he's practising being nice for the television cameras.'

Perdita laughed. 'I wish Lucas would tell me when it's all happening.'

'Why don't you ask him?' said Janey.

Perdita shook her head. '"Never trouble trouble, till trouble troubles you," as my house mistress used to say. Now just hold the door open, there's a dear.'

She was reorganising the cold store, so it was no longer necessary to climb over several pints of cream and a brie the size of a cartwheel to reach the lettuce, when a persistent ringing penetrated her consciousness. Unfortunately it took her a few moments to realise it was her phone, and by the time she had worked out how to answer it, it had stopped ringing. She took it through to the kitchen and sidled up to Greg.

'My phone's just gone and I didn't answer it in time. What do I do?' she murmured to him, hoping Lucas, who had his head in the oven, wouldn't notice.

Greg took hold of the phone and frowned at it. 'I haven't got a mobile,' he said.

Lucas strode over and snatched it out of Greg's hands. 'You should be able to see who rung you. Don't you know how to work this thing yet?'

'No one ever rings me on it. It's probably a wrong number.'

He pressed buttons, producing little beeps and squeaks. 'There you are. Missed call – it shows the number.' He handed back the phone to Perdita.

The number on it meant nothing to her. 'It's probably a client. I'll go home and ring them back.'

Lucas tutted in exasperation. 'Why don't you ring them

from here? That's the point of a mobile, you know. You don't have to be at your desk to make calls.'

'I need to have my order books with me, though,' she said sharply.

He ignored this. 'Are you going to be at home this afternoon? I need to have a word.'

'Can't you have a word now? That's the point of having people you want to speak to right in front of you, it saves you having to make appointments.'

'Are you going to be in, or aren't you?'

'I'm going to see Kitty for lunch, but I'll be back early afternoon.'

'I'll call round then.'

Perdita stalked out, forgetting that she had left the cold-store floor covered with boxes of salad and tubs of cream.

After she had dealt with her missed call, she went round to see Kitty, and wasn't at all surprised to find the house empty. It was a chilly day, but the sky was bright and shot through with sunshine. Kitty, she knew, would be inspecting the progress of the bulbs she had put in the previous autumn.

Kitty was lying on her back in a lake of crocuses. Perdita hardly had time to react before she spoke.

'Hello, darling. You're late.' The words were understandable, but slow, and only one side of Kitty's mouth moved.

Perdita swallowed hard, trying not to show how upset she was. 'Kitty, what are you doing here?'

'Fell.' Kitty tried to smile.

'I think I'd better phone an ambulance. Good thing I've got my mobile with me, isn't it? Why didn't you press your alarm? Then you wouldn't have had to stay lying out here, squashing your beloved tommasinianas?'

'Don't want ambulance. Ring doctor.'

Perdita looked at Kitty, so still among the flowers. She knew she should call 999 immediately. Kitty had obviously had a stroke, and should be got into hospital straight away.

'Please,' said Kitty.

Her sudden vulnerability caught at Perdita. She couldn't ignore Kitty's wishes; her being ill automatically robbed Perdita of choice. 'I'll have to go into the house and find the number.' It was in her phone memory, she knew, but it would take her too long to retrieve it. 'Will you be all right out here?'

Kitty did her best to nod. 'Pleasant. Listen to birds.'

Perdita ran into the house, found the number, and pressed it into her mobile phone. Then, while she waited to be connected, she ran upstairs to the airing cupboard, gathered up a pile of blankets, and went back to Kitty. She had just dropped them on top of her friend when the phone was answered.

'Hello, it's Perdita Dylan. Kitty Anson has had a stroke. She doesn't want me to call an ambulance, but I must, mustn't I?' This was a compromise between doing what Kitty wanted and what Perdita knew was right.

The receptionist was wonderful. Having checked the address, she said, 'Hang on. I know Dr Edwards has been visiting near there. I'll beep him.'

Perdita tried to appear cheerful as she arranged the blankets over Kitty, and folded one to put under her head. 'They're going to ring Dr Edwards, probably on his mobile. I hope he's better with it than I am with mine. It rang today for the first time and I couldn't remember how to answer it.'

Half of Kitty's mouth moved. 'Gadget.'

'I know. But it would have been useful if you'd pressed your alarm. I could have been here ages ago. How long have you been here?'

Kitty shook her head.

Now the initial shock was over, Perdita tried hard not to feel angry with Kitty for not summoning the ambulance.

Before, if she'd been asked, she would have said that she wouldn't want Kitty to live if she wasn't in control of her life. Now, she would have kept Kitty alive in any circumstances.

'Are you cold?' she asked her friend. Kitty was in her winter gardening uniform of several layers of coats, ending with an ex-army body warmer. Now she was covered with blankets, too. 'No? Well, at least you're well wrapped up, or you'd have died of hypothermia.'

'Good thing if I had.'

'Rubbish. If you are going to die, you want a good deathbed scene, with all the family round you, and some golden-haired children weeping.' Kitty acknowledged the joke with a small nod. 'Though I suppose we'd have to hire them specially,' Perdita went on. 'Do you think the doctor will know to come out here to find us?'

Perdita kept up the chatter, managing to sound light-hearted until the doctor arrived. Then she had to turn away while he examined Kitty. He was so gentle and kind. He didn't ask her what she was doing outside on such a chilly day, or why she hadn't used her alarm, he just moved his hands over her body calmly and efficiently.

'I'm afraid you're going to have to have a spell in hospital,' he said.

'Damn,' said Kitty.

Dr Edwards took out his mobile phone and moved a little way away to make his call.

Perdita went back to her friend. 'Don't worry about hospital, Kitty. I'll bring you in food parcels, and things to read. You might quite enjoy it, plenty of medical students to flirt with.'

It seemed to Perdita that Kitty was finding it harder to speak now than she had done earlier. And her eyes, which had been tranquil, had taken on a look of anxiety.

Dr Edwards came back. 'Listen, I think we are going to have to move Mrs Anson. I was hoping that if the ambulance came straight away, they could do it, but it's going to be a good thirty minutes. Is there anyone you could ask to give us a hand? A neighbour, or something?'

Perdita thought. Kitty's immediate neighbours were elderly themselves, although there was a young mother across the road and it was just possible her husband came home for lunch. 'I'll go and see who I can round up,' she said.

No one was in. She banged on every door, willing some-one to come, even if they could only support the blankets while she and the doctor carried Kitty. But that wouldn't do. Kitty was – had been – a strong woman. She was no frail old bundle of bones which anyone could carry.

When she got back to the house, breathless and begin-ning to panic, she saw Lucas's car in the drive. Lucas himself was standing outside the back door as if about to enter.

'Oh, hi,' he said to Perdita. 'I came to see you, but when you weren't there, I assumed I'd find you here. Do you suppose Kitty's in the garden?'

'Oh, Lucas! Thank God! Yes, she is. She's had a stroke and we need to move her, but I can't find anyone to help.'

'Have you called the doctor?' he said, following her as she ran round the house into the orchard.

'Of course!'

'Oh, well done,' said the doctor, seeing Lucas.

Kitty opened her eyes. 'Lucas. How nice.'

'Well, now we've got a half-decent stretcher party, let's get you into the house, Mrs Anson.'

Kitty turned out to be surprisingly heavy. Lucas got hold of her head end, and the doctor took the other. Perdita tried to take some of the weight in the middle, but it was awkward.

'There's an old table under the apple tree. Perhaps we could rest her on there for a moment,' she suggested, panting slightly. 'You wouldn't mind lying there for a second,' she said to Kitty, 'if I took the apples off it?'

Perdita sprinted ahead and tipped up the table of rotting apples, left there for the birds.

'Should have just let me stay there,' said Kitty, when she was lowered onto the table. 'Just died quietly. Much better.'

'Oh no,' said Perdita. 'I want to see you in a bed jacket, with a purple and pink crocheted blanket over your knees.'

Kitty's twinkle reassured Perdita, but she was finding her glib, cheerful exterior hard to keep up. She'd been preparing for this moment, finding Kitty inert in the garden, for years, but none of it was of the least use now it had actually happened.

When they had finally got Kitty into the house and onto the sofa, Perdita went to Kitty's bedroom to pack a few things.

She knew it was possible that Kitty would not see her bedroom again. For however well she recovered from this stroke, and Perdita was determined she would recover, the stairs might remain beyond her.

Now she was alone, she let herself weep as she moved about the room, hunting in drawers for a clean nightdress, underwear, pills and reading matter. She hurried, but while her hands were busy, emotionally she could hardly face rejoining the party downstairs. She didn't want to see Kitty, lying awkwardly on the sofa, with the doctor being kind and manly, and Lucas equally, unnaturally, so. While she was alone up here she could pretend the stroke had never happened, that Kitty was downstairs making tea, her pipe in her teeth, a pile of gardening catalogues on the kitchen table.

She found an ancient holdall and piled things into it. Would Kitty's thick, thermal nighties, essential for her chilly house, not be far too hot for hospital? Also, Kitty's knickers were long-legged and woolly; she would die of heat if nothing else. Where did Kitty keep her summer things? Probably in a black plastic sack, in the attic. In which case Perdita would never find it, among all the other black plastic sacks. She started to make a list of things to buy on the notepad by Kitty's bed – nightdresses, pants, proper tissues.

Eventually, she rejoined the others, and the reality of Kitty's illness confronted her again.

'I'll make some tea,' she said. 'While we wait for the ambulance.'

The kitchen was still the same as ever – the gardening catalogues covered one end of the table, and the remains of Kitty's breakfast egg stood on the drainer. A pipe lay in a chunky glass ashtray, purloined from some French station café many years ago. Tears came again as Perdita cleared up what could be the last meal Kitty would ever make for herself.

She bit her lip sharply as she found a tray for the selection of mugs. 'You don't know that's the last meal,' she muttered, trying to hold herself together. 'She might make a full recovery. She might be cooking Christmas dinner for you again next year.' But she knew it was more likely that she and Kitty had had their last cosy, restful Christmas together, the year before.

The doctor came into the kitchen to see how she was getting on. He caught her with tears in her eyes. Perdita hoped he wouldn't comment, but he put a hand on her arm.

'Mrs Anson is very old. She might make a full recovery, but she might not. You will have to think about how to go on from here. Unless we're very lucky she won't be able to live alone again.'

'But she will survive?'

'Of course I can't make promises. But the signs are good. It seems to be only the left side of her body which is affected, which means the right side of her brain is OK.

Her speech is slow, but she isn't suffering from dysphasia – when speech and comprehension are damaged. Whether she'll ever come home again is another matter.'

'I want her here. Even if she has to have twenty-four-hour nursing. I don't want her in a nursing home.'

'Perdita, my dear, that is a major commitment. Even if Kitty can afford it, the organisation involved is a nightmare.'

'I can move back here. My business is only over the other side of the garden. I can just shut up my house and come here.'

'I can't imagine Kitty allowing that. And she asked me to call her that, by the way.'

Perdita smiled faintly. 'Well, obviously. You wouldn't dare use her Christian name otherwise. But as far as me moving in goes, I don't think she'd mind.'

'It may not be necessary, but from my point of view it's very reassuring to know Kitty has you batting for her. Now, is that tea ready? I'm gasping.'

Kitty was propped up to sip her tepid tea. She didn't complain, but Perdita wondered if Kitty, who liked her food and fluid scalding hot, would now have to have everything lukewarm. Some of the liquid dribbled down the side of her mouth.

Perdita made a deliberate effort to smile as she produced a tissue, to hide another lot of tears. Kitty was not a milky-tea person.

Kitty had made it quite clear that she didn't want Perdita to travel in the ambulance, and while Kitty was being manoeuvred onto a stretcher, Lucas offered to drive Perdita to the hospital.

'No, don't be silly! You've got a restaurant to run, and I'll be fine. I don't need to be driven!'

Lucas frowned, torn between the desire to disagree with her, and the knowledge that she was right, he had got a restaurant to run.

Perdita put a hand on his sleeve. 'Really, Lucas. You don't need to worry about us. You've been marvellous; we never could have got Kitty indoors without you. But you've got your own life to lead.'

He grunted. 'I'll ring you later, then. And promise to call me if you need me. For anything. I'm very fond of Kitty.'

'I know you are. And she's very fond of you too.'

'Yes. Now, have you worked out how to use your phone yet? So you can ring if necessary?'

She grimaced. 'If I have a problem, I'll find an ordinary phone. People did manage before mobile phones were invented, you know.'

'Are you sure you'll be all right, driving yourself to the hospital?' asked Dr Edwards, when Lucas had gone, and Kitty and the ambulance were safely dispatched.

'Absolutely. I've been driving myself about for years.' The doctor looked disbelieving. 'I'm nearly thirty, you know!'

'Oh, sorry. I thought you were younger.'

Perdita glanced in the rather spotted hall mirror to see why. 'I look like an anxious adolescent!' she complained. 'No wonder everyone keeps treating me like a child.'

'Hardly that. But however old you are, it's still a big responsibility, caring for an elderly relative.'

'I know. But I really want to do it, and I'm sure I can.' She gave him a rueful smile. 'Now I think I'd better lock up and chase after Kitty's ambulance. She'll need me when she arrives.'

Chapter Fourteen

Four hours, a thousand questions and answers and a million forms later, Perdita drove her van into the gateway of her house and turned off the ignition. She was exhausted. She had left Kitty lying on a high, narrow hospital bed, looking small and frail and light years older than she had when Perdita had seen her just the day before. It occurred to Perdita that life would now always be divided into pre-stroke and post-stroke. Pre-stroke already seemed a long time ago.

She let herself into her house, planning what to say to her parents on the phone. It was ten o'clock at night, and she ought to work out what time it was in their part of the world. But on the other hand, it was an emergency and they probably wouldn't object to being woken.

She had her address book open and was ready to dial when there was a very quiet knock on the door. For the first time in her life Perdita wished she had a dog so she could hold on to its collar and pretend it was vicious.

'Who is it?' she called through the door.

'It's me, Lucas.' She opened the door. 'I came to see if everything was all right,' he explained. He sounded almost apologetic.

'You'd better come in. I've just got to ring my parents. If you listen, then I won't have to say it all twice.' Perdita swayed with fatigue, and Lucas steadied her elbow.

'When did you last eat?'

Perdita had answered enough questions. She flapped her hand at him, went to the phone and started dialling.

Her mother, who had never accepted that Perdita was grown up, wanted to drop everything and fly over to be there for Perdita and Kitty. Perdita, who would have liked that in many ways, knew her mother drove Kitty mad.

'I really don't think that's necessary.'

'But, darling,' her mother persisted, 'it's a lot for you to cope with on your own. Old people can be so difficult!'

Perdita didn't like Kitty being lumped together with her mother's idea of 'old people'. 'Honestly, Mum, I can manage. Kitty and I get on very well, you know that. We'll be fine. There's no need for you to come rushing over here.'

'Well, we were going trekking in the Andes again, but—'

'You go trekking. I can cope. I'd rather keep you for when I can't than have you coming over now.'

'Well, if you're sure . . . I've never got on with Kitty in the way that you seem to. But she could turn into a really dotty old lady, love. You've got to promise to tell me if she gets difficult, and we'll find a nice home for her.'

Perdita managed not to say that Kitty had a nice home, and that Kitty would stay in it while she and Perdita had breath in their bodies. 'We hope it won't come to that,' she said instead.

'And Kitty told me that Lucas Gillespie is in the area. I do hope it's not awkward for you.'

'No, not at all.' Lucas was in the kitchen, so wouldn't overhear. 'He's been very helpful with Kitty, actually.'

'So she said in her letter. I thought she must be going senile. But you're not going to let yourself get tangled up with him again, are you?'

'Of course not! I'm not a complete idiot!' Lucas came back into the room with a plate of sandwiches. Perdita gave him a rather hysterical smile. 'But, Mum, I must go. I'm completely exhausted. I'll give you a ring tomorrow with a progress report.'

'OK, love. But don't do anything foolish, will you? After all, Kitty has been very good to you, but you don't have to sacrifice your life to looking after her. She's not actually a relation, after all. I'm sure there must be a distant cousin or other who could be made to take responsibility.'

Perdita put the phone down before she could express her feelings on this matter, and utter phrases like blood not necessarily being thicker than water, or generally causing upset.

There was cocoa to go with the sandwiches. Lucas handed her a mug and the plate without speaking. Too tired to do more than murmur her thanks, Perdita sank into the armchair and started eating.

'Right, now I know you've at least eaten something, I'll get back. I'd offer to stay, but I know you'd refuse. Let me know how Kitty is when you've seen her. When are you going in?'

'Tomorrow afternoon. But they say it'll be about a week before they can do a full assessment. They can do a lot with physio and stuff these days.' She repeated the words that had been said to reassure her. Somehow they didn't seem very reassuring.

'But she's unlikely to do her garden again.'

Perdita nodded. In fact, the nurse had told her that it was perfectly possible that Kitty would be able to work on waist-high beds, even if she was in a wheelchair. But Perdita was very tired, and felt that if she tried to explain all this to Lucas, she'd start to cry. She didn't want Lucas feeling obliged to put his arms round her or anything, and she certainly didn't want to appear as if she wasn't coping.

'Well, I'll go. Ring me if you need me.'

She nodded again. 'Thank you for the sandwiches.'

'That's OK. I see the kitchen's reverted to being a potting shed again.'

This time, when Perdita nodded, she felt less desolate. If

Lucas was still sniping at her, the world hadn't completely fallen off its axis.

The next morning, after a night of confusing dreams, most of them about Kitty, Perdita rushed through her jobs as quickly as possible, telling William what had happened as she worked.

'You'll have to do more delivering than you did, because people must get their stuff. I can always catch up on the afternoon chores in the evening if necessary.'

'Well, of course. Anything I can do to help.' William looked doubtful. Although his romance with Janey had given him confidence, he was still shy.

'So, you deliver in the morning, and then I can have the van in the afternoon, while you get on with what I've prepared for you.' Perdita did a lot of the more menial jobs herself, as she didn't have to pay herself wages.

'Fine. It's going to be difficult for you, though, isn't it? With the old lady in hospital?'

'Well, a bit, but not as difficult as it is for her. She hates being surrounded by people who call her "dear", I could tell yesterday. I do hope they won't use her Christian name, either. She's dreadfully old-fashioned about that sort of thing.'

William shuddered at the thought of anyone daring to call Mrs Anson anything but that.

Perdita smiled gently. 'Nurses aren't always as sensitive as you are.'

William made himself scarce. Being labelled 'sensitive' was almost insulting.

When Perdita got to hospital she found Kitty, in a ward of three other women, lying propped up in bed. Her left hand rested on the sheet, looking as if it was no longer part of Kitty. Her long hair was in a plait over her shoulder and she looked tiny and very frail. The other women, all wearing pastel shades of brushed nylon and crocheted bed shawls, seemed equally fragile. Perdita wished she hadn't made jokes about the garments that society dressed its female elderly in; none of it seemed at all funny now.

'Darling,' Kitty's voice was croaky, as if she hadn't yet spoken that day. Her expression brightened when she saw Perdita, relief at seeing someone familiar. 'Lovely to see you,' she said slowly.

Perdita gulped back the tears. 'Lovely to see you too. How are you?'

Kitty smiled with half her mouth. 'Don't know. Won't tell me. You find out.'

'I will in a minute. Let me check you over myself first. Here, I've got the regulation bag of grapes. You don't have to eat them if you don't want. Do you want me to peel one for you?'

Perdita chatted and joked, fighting her desire to weep at the sight of Kitty and her ward-mates, looking inches away from death, wondering if any of them would ever look after themselves, let alone anyone else, ever again. They were women who had probably spent all their lives caring for other people to a greater or lesser extent, forced by illness into utter dependence.

When Kitty seemed to tire, she went in search of information. The nurse she asked told her to wait while she fetched Sister. When the sister finally appeared, looking younger than Perdita and four times as tired, she couldn't give her much information.

'It's very early days yet. Mrs Anson had quite a severe stroke. It'll be the end of the week before we have much idea of the prognosis.'

'But she's not going to die, or anything, is she?'

The sister smiled wanly. 'We're all going to die – sorry, who are you again?'

'A friend – it's a long story. Mrs Anson is my nearest relative, in a way, though we're not actually related.'

'Oh. I'm not sure I should be telling you about her condition. Who is her next of kin?'

'Kin doesn't come into it. Kitty – Mrs Anson – hasn't got any living relatives that we know about. She's my mother's godmother, and she looked after me during the school holidays. We look after each other, now.' Perdita bit her lip, nearly crying at the thought that because they shared no actual blood she might be prevented from looking after Kitty. 'You could talk to her GP about it if you like, for a reference. Dr Edwards, at the Edwards, Spring and Chapman Practice?'

'Oh well, if she's got no actual family – she's lucky she's got you, isn't she?'

'Actually, I'm lucky I've got her. And I would like to keep her as long as possible – or at least, get her home.'

The sister shook her head. 'I'm afraid it's far too early to be thinking about that. We'll want to be doing a great deal of physio, and she'll need to get accustomed to her disability.'

Perdita left the hospital feeling tired and depressed. All she was able to do for Kitty was wash her nighties, otherwise she was in the hands of strangers, who, however well meaning, might not understand her needs, and wouldn't have time to offer her stimulating companionship.

She drove her van home, heated a tin of soup and tried to have an early night. She was extremely tired, but couldn't sleep. Usually her physical outdoor life meant she slept like a log, but spending the afternoon in the hospital had depressed her deeply. Partly because it brought home to her so strongly what she had always known, that Kitty was a very old lady and would die soon. And partly because she realised that without Kitty she would have no focus for her love and affection.

Lying there in the dark, she realised that although she was no more alone now than she had been for years, it was the first time she'd felt alone. The difference between solitude and loneliness, she said into the blackness, was that solitude was voluntary, and could be ended at will. 'Therefore,' she went on bracingly, 'I am not lonely, because tomorrow I can go and talk to William, or deliver something to someone.' Perhaps I should get a cat, she thought as she turned her pillow and curled onto her side.

The next day, Perdita decided to go to Grantly House first, in theory so she could bring Lucas up to date, but also so she could have some contact with the young and fit.

'So, how is she? Why didn't you ring?' Lucas demanded.

Perdita found herself smiling at him. His abruptness was such a relief after the hushed voices of the hospital. 'They won't commit themselves, they just keep saying, "It's very early days." Of course it is early days, but I can't help feeling that she'll give up and die if she doesn't get home soon.'

'Is she eating?'

'I don't know. I shouldn't think she has much of an appetite. I don't know what the hospital food is like, or whether she can feed herself, or anything.'

'I expect her appetite needs tempting. They're probably offering her slop.'

'You don't know that. I don't know when you were last in hospital, but I expect the meals are lovely.'

He looked at her dubiously. 'I know you, too well bred and ladylike to find out whether the food is edible. I'll go in this afternoon and ask her.'

'Oh, I was going to go in this afternoon.'

'Couldn't we both go?'

Perdita shook her head. 'Only one at a time at the moment.' She thought for a moment. It would be nice for Kitty to have more than one visitor. 'I suppose I could go this evening. I've got a lot to do this afternoon.'

'Fine, when are visiting hours?'

'I think you can go more or less any time. I'll give you the number, you can ring up.'

He gave her a teasing smile. 'Got it in your mobile, have you?'

'As a matter of fact, I have.' Hugely smug, glad that an evening in front of the telly, when she needed added entertainment, had paid off, she tapped the keys until she came up with the number of the hospital. 'There you are. Do tell Kitty I'm coming this evening, though. I don't want her to think I've deserted her.'

When Perdita arrived at the hospital that evening, armed with clean clothes, she found her elderly friend looking much better. The reason, she soon found out, was Lucas.

'He told the sister he was my long-lost nephew,' Kitty explained slowly, but highly amused.

'But why?'

'Sister said I could only have family members to visit. Lucas said he *was* family.' Kitty chuckled laboriously. 'Sister said, couldn't be. You'd said I had no relatives.' The chuckles became so strong Perdita feared her old friend might actually die laughing. 'He said you didn't know about him, he was a black sheep denied by all family members.'

'But how did he find out you were ill, I mean, if he really was a black sheep?'

'Telepathy!' Kitty would have been speechless with mirth even if she hadn't just had a major stroke.

Perdita was laughing too. 'So what happened? Sister surely didn't just let Lucas find you? I mean, if you hadn't seen him for nearly forty years, or whatever, she wouldn't have let him just bowl up to you and say, "Hi, Auntie, long time, no see!"'

'No, she led him by the arm and brought him to my bed. Then she said, "Bit of a surprise for you, Kitty – I mean, Mrs Anson."' Kitty paused for breath. '"Lucas has come all the way from Scotland to visit you."' Kitty's giggles again became life-threatening. '"He heard you were ill in a dream, and he's come to visit you. You remember Lucas? Matilda's youngest son?" Had to disguise my laughter as emotion.'

Perdita could appreciate the funny side of the situation, but was more pleased with Kitty's upturn in spirits. But how was *she* supposed to react? Would the sister spare her the knowledge of Lucas's appearance? Or would she draw her tactfully to one side and explain about the long-lost nephew with second sight?

'He brought food,' Kitty went on, still delighted.

'Well, I don't suppose a clean nightie can really compete,' she said, fishing about in Kitty's locker for dirty washing. 'Though I did bring "a wee dram". If Dr Edwards approves it, you might be allowed an occasional sniff of the cork.'

'How kind, dear,' said Kitty, suddenly tired after all her laughter. 'Do you know, I'm not missing my pipe at all. Do you think that means I'm getting old?'

When she got home later that evening, having discussed the miracles of ESP with the ward sister, Perdita found an array of little pots and a note on her kitchen worktop.

You must make your house more secure and give me a key. It's far too easy to break in. Eat this for your supper, I know you won't have anything decent otherwise. Love, your friendly neighbourhood house-breaker and counterfeit nephew to the stars.

Smiling in spite of herself, Perdita inspected the pots. There was a little ramekin of some very strong-smelling pâté, a pile of matchstick carrots with threads of courgettes sprinkled with herbs and blobbed with mayonnaise, and some soup. The soup had 'Heat in the microwave if you can find it' written on it. There was a pot of chocolate mousse with a large dollop of cream on it.

Perdita ate the chocolate mousse and then glanced at the clock: half past ten. The kitchen would be quiet now. It would just be clearing up and serving coffee time. She rang the number. Lucas answered.

'Hi. Thanks for the food.'

'Have you eaten it? What did you think of the soup?'

'I've only had the mousse so far. It was yummy.'

'How did you get on at the hospital?'

'Kitty was delighted with your performance. She could hardly speak for laughing. The sister was fairly gaga about you too.'

'It must come from working with all those old ladies,' he said blankly.

Perdita chuckled. 'Will you be able to get in and see her again, do you think?'

'Of course! You don't think I'd miss an opportunity to mix with all those lovely, desperate nurses, in uniform, do you?'

'The sister's on to you, by the way. She worried in case you're after Kitty's money.'

'So how did you react to that?'

'Oh, I was very noncommittal. I said it didn't matter who you were as long as you cheered up Kitty.'

'Very noble of you.'

'Noble yourself. It was kind of you to visit Kitty and bring her nice things to eat. And me too,' she added, with an effort. 'It was kind of you to leave me a midnight feast.'

'I know you don't eat properly, and you'll need your strength.'

Perdita did need her strength. It was hard work keeping her business going and keeping Kitty well visited, cheerful and in clean clothes. And then one evening, after a particularly hard day, there was a man sitting by Kitty's bedside as she arrived.

It could only be a doctor, and Perdita's heart sank. She approached him carefully, preparing herself for bad news.

'Hello, are you the specialist?' She tried to smile as he got up. 'I'm Perdita Dylan. I'm not actually related to Mrs Anson, but I look after her.'

He put out his hand. He was a pleasant-looking man, probably in his early thirties, smartly dressed with a tie and shiny shoes. Just as Perdita decided that Kitty would like him, she noticed the camelhair coat over the back of a chair.

'No, no. I'm not a doctor,' he said, smiling. 'I'm Roger Owen. Unlike you, I am related to Aunt Kitty, although only very distantly. Do sit down, I'll get another chair. We can chat while Aunt Kitty dozes.'

Perdita did as she was told, wondering simultaneously why on earth she'd never heard of him before, and how the nursing staff had coped with a second long-lost relative.

Kitty continued to sleep, offering no information on either count.

Roger Owen came back with another plastic chair. 'How do you do? I don't suppose you've ever heard of me. I'm the son of a distant cousin of Aunt Kitty's, but they didn't speak. After my mother died I found some correspondence relating to Aunt Kitty, and I was just thinking about looking her up when a Mrs Dylan – would that be your mother, I wonder? – rang me and told me about Aunt Kitty being ill.'

'It probably was my mother, but how did she know about you?' And why did she get in touch with you without telling me? Perdita wanted to add, furious that her mother had obviously gone on a relative hunt without consulting her.

'I don't know, but she told me you were dealing with the situation all on your own.' He smiled. 'You're probably not at all pleased to see me, and have everything in hand.'

Because this was what she was thinking, she found herself smiling. 'No, no, it's very nice to meet you, and I expect Kitty was pleased you came.'

He smiled back. 'She was rather surprised, and the nurses insisted I produced documentary evidence of our relationship. Fortunately I'd brought some, for Aunt Kitty, but apparently there's another nephew who's been visiting.'

'Yes, it's complicated. But how long can you stay? I'm sure we could wake Kitty if you've got to get off somewhere.'

'Actually, I'm hoping to do a little work while I'm around, so I've booked in at a hotel here in town. It's not the Ritz, but it's comfortable and not too expensive.'

'Oh.' Perdita was just struggling to think of something to say when Kitty stirred.

'Oh, hello, Perdita, darling. How nice to see you. Have you met . . . ?'

'Roger – Roger Owen.'

'Yes,' said Perdita. 'We've just been introducing ourselves.'

'Poor Roger,' said Kitty. 'I'd forgotten all about him. I never got on with his grandmother, and so lost touch.'

'Apparently Mummy got in touch with him,' said Perdita.

'Clever of her, wasn't it? I expect she thought it was too much for you, looking after me all by yourself. Quite right too. You're looking dreadfully tired. I keep telling you, you don't need to visit every day.'

'But, darling, you need some contact from the outside world, or you'll go mad.'

'Lucas can come and see me on the days you don't. One visitor a day is more than most of these poor old things get.'

'And now I'm here, I can visit too,' Roger added.

Both women regarded him thoughtfully, unable to decide, without conferring, whether this was good news or bad.

'You're probably far too busy,' they said, more or less together.

'Not at all,' he said with another smile. 'I'd be delighted. But I must go now. I'll leave you two ladies to have a chat.'

They watched him make his way through the ward in silence.

'He's a nice man,' said Kitty, 'but I do hate being referred to as a public convenience.'

'He could hardly have said "women", although I do agree with you. So, tell me all. Who is he? Or are you too tired?'

'His grandmother was a vicious old woman who kept changing her will depending on which relative she'd taken against. Apparently poor Roger got nothing.' She paused. 'I know you've got a lot on your plate, but do try to be nice to him while he's here.'

'Of course.'

A couple of days later, Kitty had progressed to a wheel-chair, and now spent her days in the day room, where the television watched itself, and the old ladies watched each other slip further down in their seats. Kitty had taken it upon herself to be in charge of the bell. The moment any-one looked remotely uncomfortable, she would demand, 'Shall I ring for the nurse?' Few patients ever said no.

Perdita privately asked the sister if Kitty was driving them mad.

'Oh no, if she's in there, we don't have to go and check up on them. We know Mrs Anson will let us know immediately anyone wants a bedpan, even if they don't when the time comes.'

'She's doing well, isn't she?'

'She certainly is. She grumbles about the physio, but she's very determined to improve, and works really hard at her exercises. You'd better think about how you're going to manage when she comes home.'

Dr Edwards summoned Perdita to discuss this. 'She's done extremely well. She's absolutely determined to get home. But what she doesn't quite realise is that she'll never be able to cope on her own again.'

'I can look after her . . .'

'I'm afraid you're not going to be able to manage on your own either. You'll have to have a professional carer full time.' He paused. 'It might, of course, be cheaper to put her in a home. A lot easier for you, too.'

Perdita took a deep breath. 'Not while—'

'I knew you'd say that,' said Dr Edwards, before Perdita had time to finish. 'Kitty seems confident that her finances are fairly healthy. You'll need to organise enduring power of attorney. You are her next of kin, aren't you?'

'I'm not sure. I'm not kin at all, really, and now she's got Roger – Roger Owen. He's some distant cousin, and visiting regularly.'

'I'd heard about a couple of long-lost nephews. Why two?'

Perdita grinned. 'One's genuine, and the other's Lucas, the chef at Grantly House. You remember? He helped us carry Kitty into the house when she had her stroke. He told them he was a nephew so he could visit.'

'Well, if he's the one bringing her all those delicious titbits it doesn't matter who he is. Eating well has greatly improved her recovery. Now,' he became more business-like, 'Kitty's going to be able to come home in about a month. Here's a list of numbers, the district nurse, et cetera. And here's a couple of numbers of nursing agencies. It's not going to be easy for you, but if you're determined, we'll give you all the support we can.'

The agencies were less helpful. Most of them, it appeared, catered for people, who, it seemed to Perdita, were fit enough not to need carers. No one incontinent, unable to use the lavatory unsupported, or who woke in the night was acceptable.

Eventually Perdita found herself speaking to a very aristocratic-sounding woman who, Perdita felt, would refuse to provide carers unless the caree was guaranteed to be a lady. Perdita dropped every name she could think of, dragging into the conversation all of Kitty's well-connected friends. At last a bargain was struck, and Perdita could prepare for Kitty to come home.

Chapter Fifteen

Perdita decided to ask Ronnie for help in transforming Kitty's elegant drawing room into a bedroom fit for an invalid, or, as Ronnie remarked when he saw the task before them, turning it into 'a cross between *Casualty* and *The Antiques Roadshow*'.

'Well,' he said. 'That sofa's got to go. It's huge, probably not very comfortable, and without it, we could put the bed along here.'

'She and her husband first made love on that sofa,' Perdita informed him.

'Well, if she wants to make love now, she'll have to use the bed, like everyone else. You said the bed had to be by a wall?'

'So the lifting gear can be fixed to it.' She gave the wall an experimental knock. 'It has to be a good wall, too. A lot of the walls in this house are held together by plaster.'

Ronnie gave the wall a thump. 'Solid as a rock. The bed goes here, the sofa goes to the tip – if there isn't room for it anywhere else.'

'There must be somewhere we can put it. I can't just get rid of Kitty's past—'

'So we've got room for her future life.'

Perdita sighed. Ronnie was right. It was no good trying to hang on to the things as they were. Everything was different now.

Once she'd got into the swing of it, and found a corner in the spare room in the attic which would take a large chesterfield with the stuffing coming out of it, she began to enjoy herself.

'It's quite like *Changing Rooms*, isn't it?' she said to Ronnie, 'only without the redecorating.'

'Mind you, you'll have to redecorate a bit when they put the grab handles in. Now, where is the nearest bathroom?'

'Upstairs. There's a cloakroom down here. I'm going to knock through that alcove,' she pointed to where several shelves of china were tastefully displayed, 'so you can get straight into the downstairs loo, which will become a bathroom.'

'Wow!' Ronnie was impressed. 'I bet that took a bit of persuading, to get the old lady to agree to that.'

'It was hell. Fortunately I had support from Roger – did I tell you about him? Long-lost nephew?'

'You did mention it. Nice-looking, is he?'

'All right, I suppose. Anyway, he turned up just at the right moment.' She looked at her watch. 'Hell! We must get on, he's coming for lunch in a minute. I promised Kitty I'd be nice to him.'

'So where are you going to put all the china?' Ronnie nodded towards it. 'That looks like Meissen to me.'

'It is. There's a cupboard upstairs that's full of the cups and saucers Kitty used for when the garden was open to the public. I told her it would all fit in there.' She sighed. 'I felt awful having to bully her. It's such a dreadful up-heaval for her – mentally more than anything. Eventually I said if she didn't agree to pay the builders, I'd sell my own furniture and pay for them myself.'

'It's horrid having to take charge of someone's life when they've always taken charge of yours. I felt just the same when my mother died.'

They were sharing a consoling hug when they heard a car draw up outside.

'That'll be Roger.'

'Well, I'll have a quick butcher's at him, and then leave you to it. He's single, is he?'

'As far as I know.'

Ronnie gave her a knowing look. 'And he's going to help you sort out the furniture?'

'Well, he said he would.'

Perdita offered Roger a glass of sherry. He accepted with a pleasant smile. 'I never knew Aunt Kitty when she was well, but I imagine she liked a glass of sherry.'

Perdita returned the smile. 'Well, she really preferred whisky, but she did drink sherry at lunchtime, sometimes.'

Roger frowned slightly. 'Whisky? I would have thought she was too much of a lady to drink spirits.'

Perdita laughed, bringing a bowl of salad to the table. 'She wouldn't care about things like that.' Perdita found room for the bowl in between a pile of post and a pot of African violets. 'She smoked a pipe, after all.'

Roger appeared disconcerted by this information. 'Um – is there anything I can do to help?'

'If you'd just bring the breadboard over . . . I'll get the butter. Do sit down. Just shove those catalogues on that spare chair . . . Well done. Damn, the butter's rock hard. I'll just pop it in the microwave for a second.'

Having managed to rescue the butter before it turned to liquid, Perdita turned round and found that Roger had shuffled all the papers into a neat pile. She felt a pang of something she identified as jealousy, as if she was the only one entitled to mess with Kitty's things. It probably comes from being an only child, she thought. I don't want to share Kitty with Roger. She summoned an especially charming smile to make up for the meanness of her thoughts. 'Do tuck in. It's only tinned soup, I'm afraid, but I've dolled it up a bit with sherry and cream, à la Kitty.'

Roger picked up his spoon. 'It's really very nice,' he said after trying it.

Perdita decided that he was, too. 'Have some butter on your bread.'

He shook his head. 'Better not. I have to watch the waistline, I'm afraid.'

'It looks fine to me,' said Perdita, having checked.

'Only because I watch what I eat and work out.'

'Oh.' Perdita scanned him for evidence of this. Perhaps a perfect six-pack might mean he was more exciting than he first appeared, but nothing was visible under his crisp cotton shirt. 'Have some salad. It hasn't got dressing on it. I never add it to the whole bowl unless I can guarantee it's all going to get eaten.'

He poured a dribble of dressing on his leaves. 'I can tell you either watch what you eat very carefully, or you take lots of exercise. What do you do? Jog?'

'No, dig,' said Perdita, chuckling. 'I'm a market gardener, don't forget.'

'Of course. And do you do that nearby?'

'Oh yes. Just over the fence, really. You must come and have a look after lunch.'

'I must say I would like to see Aunt Kitty's garden. I gather it was all she really cared about.'

'She still does care about it.'

Roger put out his hand to cover Perdita's. 'Of course she does, and I hope she will do for a very long time.'

Perdita put her hand back in her lap. 'It's easy to talk about her in the past tense because she's not here. Would you like some more soup? There's a bit left, and it would only be wasted.'

'I think I've had enough, thank you. Now,' he got up briskly, 'shall we tackle the washing-up?'

'Oh no. Let's not waste a lovely afternoon. Let's go and see the garden.'

*

Roger was regarding the orchard at the bottom of the plot with narrowed eyes, and Perdita felt Kitty's reputation as a great gardener was on the line. 'It's nothing like as good now as it was years ago, when Kitty was really well, but it's jolly good considering.'

'Oh no, it's fine. And an absolute haven for wildlife, of course. How big is it, do you think?'

'I'm not sure. About an acre, I suppose. There was more before she gave me a chunk. Those are my poly-tunnels, over there.'

'I see. I expect she let the undergrowth develop to screen them.'

'I suppose they are rather an eyesore, now you point it out. I don't come to this bit of the garden much.'

'I'm sure Aunt Kitty wouldn't have minded them being there. After all, she gave you the land, didn't she? Or did she just suggest you use it?'

Perdita bit her lip. 'I don't know. Is there a difference?'

'Only technically. You may need to get the boundaries sorted out. Later.' He smiled. 'I know we've agreed not to talk about Aunt Kitty as if she was already dead, but when the time comes, do call on me if you need help sorting out those sort of details.'

Perdita opened her mouth to say that it didn't matter about the boundaries because she would probably inherit it all anyway, but stopped herself. She had no real right to make such a presumption. 'Thank you, that's a kind offer.'

'Sometimes it's useful to have someone who's accustomed to these things handy. Someone who understands, that is.' His gaze lingered on her for a second before he went on briskly, 'Now, do show me where you grow your salads.'

'Of course.' Perdita had meant to ask him what he did for a living, but now had lost her chance.

'Aunt Kitty tells me that you and Lucas Gillespie used to be married,' he said, as they walked to the gap in the fence.

'It must be difficult for you, with him hanging round Aunt Kitty all the time.' He opened the gate for her.

'Oh no, not at all. They get on really well.'

'That's all right then.' He waited for her to go through before closing the gate carefully behind him. 'I wasn't sure if there was anything – you know – still between you,' he added diffidently.

'Oh, no.' She crossed her fingers in her coat pocket to expunge a certain evening on his restaurant floor. 'He's a local chef I supply salads to, and he and Kitty talk about books. There's nothing more to it than that.'

'Oh, good.' He smiled, and brushed his hair back from his forehead. 'I'm glad you're not spoken for.'

Perdita blushed. She wasn't used to people making gallant remarks.

After they'd inspected Bonyhayes Salads, Roger offered to go back with Perdita to Kitty's, to advise on the shifting of furniture. While he was very strong, and had lots of useful suggestions, Perdita couldn't help wishing it had been Ronnie helping her instead. Roger didn't seem to understand sentimental value in the way Ronnie did.

It was Ronnie, however, who was with her to greet the carer as Roger, who had offered, was away on business. Perdita and Ronnie were peering out of the upstairs window, watching for her car, speculating wildly what she might be like – they'd decided on a modern Mary Poppins – when she arrived.

She was of the school of nursing which Perdita would have assumed would have gone out of fashion before Florence Nightingale's time. She appeared to be in late middle age, but had probably looked the same since her twenties. She cast Ronnie a brisk, reptilian flicker from the corner of her eye, which consigned him to the outer darkness.

'As the agency will have told you,' she addressed Perdita coldly, 'I am a qualified nurse, unlike most of those on our books.' There was a disapproving pause. 'Miss Argent likes to send me to new clients, especially if they need physiotherapy, which I understand Mrs Anson does.'

'That's right.' Miss Argent had also explained that Nurse Stritch was a lot more expensive than the other carers, but until a routine was established, it was a good idea to have a fully qualified nurse. 'Do come into the kitchen. We can have a cup of tea.'

Nurse Stritch followed Perdita cautiously. 'I am also here to ensure that the circumstances are suitable for unqualified staff, and that nothing untoward is expected of carers.' She scanned the kitchen through narrowed eyes, looking for mousetraps and coal buckets.

While she was inspecting the pantry, which housed the washing machine and freezer, and just a touch of damp, Ronnie whispered in Perdita's ear, 'Sorry to bail on you, love, but I'm a coward. You'll be better on your own.'

The sensible, grown-up side of Perdita, which had shrunk to minute proportions since Nurse Stritch's arrival, hoped that Kitty would take to this anachronistic woman, a Mrs Gamp unsoftened by the humanity of her gin bottle. The child in Perdita, which had swelled almost over-whelmingly, hoped Kitty would send the martinet packing.

'Would you like to come upstairs? Let me help you with your bags.'

Nurse Stritch inspected the bedroom which Perdita and Miriam, Kitty's cleaner, had prepared for her. It had its own washbasin, was pleasantly furnished, and had an excellent view of the garden. Perdita had washed and ironed the curtains, provided a lace mat for the dressing table as well as a huge selection of towels – bath, hand and a linen one for her face – and a carefully arranged vase of flowers.

Nurse Stritch's lack of comment offended her.

'I hope you'll be comfortable here,' said Perdita stiffly, hoping the room was haunted, and that the bed turned out to be hugely uncomfortable.

'There isn't a television. Could you please arrange to have one installed?'

'Of course,' Perdita replied, kicking herself for not having thought of this, knowing she would have to bring her own television from home. Kitty, if applied to for funds for a television for the carer, would just say, 'Nonsense,' which might make Nurse Stritch hate her.

Fortunately, William was still working when Perdita flew into one of the poly-tunnels, needing his immediate assistance.

'Can you be a love and put my telly into the carer's room at Kitty's? I should have thought of it, really, but I didn't and I'm hopeless with aerials and things.'

William fortunately was brilliant with them. He not only carried the television over, but managed to connect its aerial to Kitty's, so the picture was good.

'What will you do without a telly?' he asked her, as they walked back together, so Perdita could pay him for the overtime. He knew she quite often did her pricking out in the sitting room, in front of the afternoon chat shows, spilling compost onto the oriental rug.

'Oh, I'll manage. I'll just prick out in the shed, like a grown-up, and listen to the radio.'

'I'm seeing Janey tonight.'

'Are you?' Since Kitty's stroke, Perdita had almost forgotten about setting up Janey and William. 'I haven't seen much of her lately. Tell her when Kitty's settled that we must go out for a drink, or something.'

'I will. She's been asking after you. So's her boss,' he added, sounding wary.

'Has he? I expect he wants to find out about Kitty. She told me he hadn't visited her lately. I wonder why not.'

'Been busy, he says.'

'Oh.' Perdita found an emergency ten-pound note in a teapot, and gave it to William. 'Thank you so much for sorting the telly.'

'Tell you what, we've got an old portable I got at a car boot. I'll fix that up for you. It's not brilliant, but it's better than nothing.'

Nurse Stritch was peering into the fridge when Perdita rejoined her, determined to make an effort to be pleasant.

'Shall I cook us something nice for supper?' Perdita said, wondering why she'd said 'nice', when 'edible' was almost beyond her.

'I don't know what you'll find to cook with,' said Nurse Stritch. 'This refrigerator is full of all sorts of things which need throwing out. Did you make them?'

Her accusing tone made Perdita deny all knowledge. 'Oh no. Kitty – Mrs Anson – has a friend who's a local chef. He's been bringing her things from the restaurant to eat in hospital. He must 've brought anything left back here.' Oh dear, if Lucas hadn't seen Kitty lately the leftovers would be rather old.

'None of this is remotely suitable for an invalid, all highly indigestible.'

'But she's been getting on very well. At the hospital they said, "A little of what you fancy does you good." ' Kitty had been maddened by the cliché, but had enjoyed the food.

'Good ingredients, simply cooked is what invalids require.'

'Oh well, I'm sure the chef would agree with you about the ingredients.' She hesitated. 'What about some scrambled eggs on toast?'

'That would be adequate, but I would prefer to make it myself. Apart from anything else, there's nowhere for me to sit.'

Perdita could have made some fairly graphic suggestions

but, in the interests of concord, didn't make them out loud. Instead, she cleared one end of the kitchen table and got out a bottle of wine. Nurse Stritch was bound to disapprove of the wine, but Perdita felt she couldn't go another second without alcohol. It was wine or whisky, and from Nurse Stritch's point of view, wine had to be better.

While Perdita was washing up, and Nurse Stritch was glancing through a copy of the *Lady* (probably looking for a better job, thought Perdita), Perdita said, 'Would you like me to stay with you tonight? Or are you happy about being alone in the house?'

Happy was, in this case, a relative term. Nurse Stritch looked appalled. 'Leave me alone in the house? I'm afraid that's quite out of the question. There's no alarm system, or even a guard dog. I couldn't possibly stay here by myself.'

'I'm glad I asked then.' Perdita had been longing to go home and relax. 'It'll be no trouble for me to stay.'

'Thank you.'

For a second, Perdita spotted a little vulnerability in Nurse Stritch. It heartened her. Perhaps there was a human being in there somewhere.

Kitty's arrival home lacked a fanfare and bunting, but it had all the other trappings of a state visit. To begin with, much to everyone's disapproval, she insisted on being carried round the upper garden on a stretcher, the wheelchair not being up to it.

Fortunately, Perdita had removed some of the weeds which had appeared with the spring sunshine, and once Kitty'd caught up with everything accessible in the garden, she consented to be brought inside.

'These young men can't go on carrying me about on my litter for ever. Give them something, darling, do.'

'Not necessary,' said their leader, as Perdita, much embarrassed, tried to press on them the ten-pound note she knew Kitty meant as 'something'. 'She's a lovely old duck.'

Kitty was appalled at the sight of her drawing room, although the builders had made a very attractive arch round the door to the new bathroom, and Perdita had arranged the mantelpiece with Kitty's favourite bits of china.

'It's not that it's unattractive, dear,' she said, almost apologetically, 'but it's just not mine.'

'I think you should be getting into bed now, Mrs Anson,' said Nurse Stritch. 'If you get overtired, you won't be up to your physiotherapy later.'

'I'm going to put the kettle on. I'm sure we could all do with a cuppa,' said Perdita, wanting to be well clear of any flak which might start to fly.

'Very well.' Kitty sounded tired. 'It will be a pleasure to have a proper cup of tea out of a proper china cup, I must say.'

While Perdita was making the tea, Roger arrived. She let him in through the back door.

'Hi, just come to say hello to Aunt Kitty. It's so wonderful that you've managed to get her home. I never thought she'd leave that hospital alive.' He smiled sympathetically.

Perdita, who had been feeling quite cheerful, suddenly found herself depressed. It was the anticlimax, she decided. 'Well, she's very much alive. Go and say hello before the scary nurse puts her to bed.'

Roger seemed to get on very well with Nurse Stritch. Unlike Perdita, he seemed able to make her smile. He even coaxed her to eat a biscuit. Perdita wouldn't have bothered.

When Perdita went back in later with more hot water for the teapot, Kitty said, 'Perdita, my love, Roger's just been telling us that the hotel where he's been staying have asked him to leave.'

Perdita looked at him with new interest. Had he been thrown out for rowdy behaviour?

'Yes,' he said. 'They've got a big wedding coming up which they told me about, and as I didn't expect to be here this long, I said it was fine. Now I've got to find somewhere else.'

Disappointing, thought Perdita. 'But there are lots of good little hotels in town. I'm sure it wouldn't be difficult to find somewhere comfortable.'

'I've asked Roger if he'd like to stay here,' said Kitty, 'if that's all right with you, darling?'

Kitty looked small and old, and Perdita's heart lurched, saddened by Kitty feeling obliged to ask permission to have people to stay.

'Of course he can stay, if you want him to,' she said brightly. 'He could have the room I've been sleeping in. Then I can go home, and Nurse Stritch will have company.'

Nurse Stritch, who had been looking quite cheerful, shook her head. 'I can't possibly look after house guests. My duties are clearly laid down.'

'But you wouldn't have to look after me,' said Roger. 'I'll just make myself at home and look after myself. I'll soon find out where everything is.'

Perdita suddenly felt uncomfortable, and Kitty's expression became anguished. 'I can't have you to stay if you're not properly looked after,' Kitty said. 'Who'd give you your breakfast?'

Perdita smiled. 'Don't worry, Kitty. I'll make up another room, and I'll give him breakfast. I don't do other meals,' she said, turning her gaze to Roger. 'But I can put a packet of cereal on the table.'

Why do I feel strange about him? she asked herself. He's perfectly nice and pleasant, Kitty obviously likes him. Why aren't I thrilled that he's turned up to cheer Kitty's last years?

'Well, I for one will be very pleased to have a man about the place,' said Nurse Stritch.

'Yes,' said Perdita, sweetly. 'They are handy for changing the high light bulbs, aren't they?'

'To think I was feeling lonely,' she said to herself, sorting through her drawer for knickers. 'I thought it was time-consuming having Kitty in hospital. I'm obviously going to be a lot busier now.'

She looked out of the window at the little patch of garden which bordered the poly-tunnels. Suddenly, the sight of some crocus foliage reminded her of something. 'I never planted the crosnes thingy that Lucas gave me. It said I had to in March.'

Pleased to be doing something horticultural which didn't involve sorting out, or throwing away, or generally saying goodbye to a way of life, Perdita ran downstairs, picking up her book on how to grow oriental vegetables on the way.

'Now, crosnes. Rich soil, plenty of water, gross feeders. Where did I put you?' She found the pot with the tuber in it and carefully unburied it. It seemed perfect. It hadn't rotted, it still looked like a very fat brown caterpillar. Feeling this was a good omen, she spent a happy ten minutes planting it, referring to her book and muttering endearments.

When she got back to Kitty's house, Nurse Stritch looked pointedly at Perdita's fingernails. Perdita went to the new bathroom to scrub them, before she could be told to.

Roger fitted surprisingly easily into the household. Once Perdita had tracked down the low-sugar muesli he liked for breakfast, arranged to have a pint of skimmed milk delivered every couple of days, she found him no trouble. He was out most of the day, wiped his feet when he came in, was tidy in the bathroom, and never left the seat up in the loo. Nurse Stritch thought he was perfect, mostly because of the loo seat.

Nurse Stritch, although less easy as a member of the household than Roger, was excellent at her job. She was gentle but firm with Kitty, making sure she did her physiotherapy every day, and by the end of the week, when Nurse Stritch was due to leave Kitty to a lesser mortal, Kitty had improved a lot. In a strange way, Perdita was quite sorry to see her leave.

'She wasn't exactly entertaining,' said Kitty, while Nurse Stritch was giving Eileen, her South African replacement, a handover session, 'but she was a natural at nursing, and you have to respect that.'

'Yes, and we'll miss the physio, although she has shown me what you should be doing, so I'll be able to bully you now.'

Kitty sighed. Perdita had meant it as a joke, and Kitty knew that, but she had not yet settled into her role as patient.

'Where's Lucas?' she said, changing the subject. 'I haven't seen him for ages. Roger very sweetly plays backgammon with me, but of course he has to go off and do his surveying, or whatever it is he does—'

'And you miss having a man to flirt with?'

'Not at all, Roger's far too respectful to flirt.'

'Well, I don't know what's happened to Lucas. I haven't seen him either. He's sent messages, but I gather he's away. William isn't very communicative, and he only gets his information from Janey, so I'm not really sure. But I do think he'd have called round or telephoned if he was here.'

'Oh. Perhaps he's sorting out that television programme business. He did say something about it.'

Perdita shrugged. 'You know more about it than I do, then. And I'm supposed to be in it!'

'I know, it's so exciting. By the way, darling, did Roger mention to you that he's got to go away for a few days?'

'Yes he did. You've enjoyed having him around, haven't you?'

'I have, rather. And with him here to fuss over me, you do get a bit more time to yourself.'

Perdita was about to protest when Nurse Stritch came in with Eileen to say goodbye. Kitty thanked her warmly and sincerely, but the two women kept up their formality, even after a week of living together.

Eileen promised to be much more fun. Although only just twenty, she had nursed a dear and sick aunt through a terminal illness, and had a maturity which offset her youth. She was also reluctant to sleep in the house with only a bedridden old lady for protection, so Perdita decided to cut her losses and went home and fetched her house plants.

'So, do you like her?' Perdita asked Kitty while they had a pre-prandial drink together. Eileen was cooking chicken supreme from a packet. It was a relief to be free of Nurse Stritch's strictures about natural ingredients and Roger's obsession with his weight. Both Kitty and Perdita missed the occasional shot of E numbers.

'Well, she's a child. But she took me to the lav and was perfectly competent. Pretty little thing. Nurse Stritch was a wonderful nurse, no doubt about it, but she did make one feel the grim reaper had his good points.'

The doctor came to make sure Kitty had settled in well at home.

'I've been here a week, dear boy,' said Kitty. 'A bit late to come now.'

'Ah, but I knew you had terrifying Nurse Stritch looking after you. Nothing untoward could happen if she was in charge.'

'This little girl is very good too. And much more cheerful company for Perdita. She's had to move in, you know, because although my great-nephew's been staying, he can't be here all the time, and so far everyone's been too nervous to stay in the house with only me for protection. Utter rubbish, but what can one do?'

'Actually, Perdita, now I've seen that Kitty's right as ninepence, I need to have a word with you.' Dr Edwards was making eloquent remarks with his eyebrows which told Perdita he wanted to talk about Kitty.

'Of course. Shall we go into the study?'

'Right, m'dear. How are you? Not too exhausted yet?' he asked when Perdita had closed the door.

'Oh no, why should I be?'

'Because you've got a business to run as well as a house with an invalid. It takes energy.'

'Well, yes, but I'm sure now we've settled into a routine, things will be less hectic.'

'Kitty told me you've been working quite late in the evenings.'

'I have to a bit, because Kitty likes me to watch *Countdown* and stuff with her in the afternoon, while the carer has a couple of hours off.'

'I know you want to look after her, and do the best for her, but you need to look after yourself as well. She'll understand if you're too busy to be with her in the afternoon.'

'I suppose so. But I don't like to leave her alone in the house, and it's not fair for the carer to be on call constantly. Eileen's only young. She needs to get out to the shops and things, if there were any.'

'We might have to think about getting a rota of people to sit with her in the afternoons. You need some time to yourself, as much as the carer does.'

'I'll talk to Kitty about it. She certainly has plenty of friends, it's just, how many of them could she stand to have with her for so long? It'd be tiring for them too. Kitty and I don't have to make polite conversation all the time.'

'Mmm. What you need is a mature student, who could study in another room, in here, perhaps, but be within easy earshot. I'll ask around. My wife may know someone.'

'That would be good. I can never get everything done in the morning, what with the deliveries and stuff, and I get careless at night, when I'm tired.'

The doctor nodded. 'And have you done anything about getting enduring power of attorney?'

Dr Edwards had mentioned this before, but Perdita hadn't been able to bring herself to ask Kitty if she'd mind letting her write cheques for her. 'No.'

'Then I'll talk to her about it. It's probably a lot easier for me. I don't want to be depressing when Kitty's getting on so well, but she could have another stroke at any time. If she did, you could need funding for fully trained nurses day and night, if you still couldn't bring yourself to let her go into a home. You will need to be able to write cheques.' He frowned at her. 'You ought to have some idea of how much money she's got, too. You don't want to run up huge bills there isn't the money to settle them.'

'Well, no. I just hate intruding on her privacy.'

'Better that than get into a financial muddle.'

'I suppose so, but it seems such a dreadful intrusion.'

The doctor put a hand on her shoulder, gave it a little shake, and then left.

Chapter Sixteen

A routine was soon established. Various friends of Kitty's, and the granddaughter of one of them, doing A levels, arranged between them when they could be either at Kitty's side, or within easy earshot, so Perdita could work in the afternoons. When Roger was with them, he took on the early evenings so she could work later. If Kitty was asleep by the time she got back, he would wait up for her in the kitchen and chat.

Although she knew she should be grateful, she really preferred it when he was away, so she could rush home early and have some time alone with Kitty. Now, to Perdita's secret relief, Roger had a contract somewhere the other side of the country, leaving Perdita to establish a relationship with the carers.

They worked for a week, or at most, a fortnight at a stretch to give everyone a break. After a couple of less-than-successful carers, who wanted to see Kitty again even less than she wanted to see them, a group of three regulars established a rota which suited everyone.

There was Eileen, very young, but experienced, who got on well with Perdita. She and Perdita shared the cooking, which they were both very bad at, and played three-handed bridge with Kitty, at which they were worse.

There was Thomas, an ex-Merchant Navy steward, whose first appearance had Kitty and Perdita in a froth of indignation. Neither of them liked the idea of Kitty being nursed by a man, Kitty because she was old-fashioned, and Perdita because she was shy. Fortuitously, Kitty needed the bathroom quite urgently while Eileen was collecting her clean washing from the tumble drier and Perdita was making tea. Thomas, possibly aware of Kitty's uncertainty, wheeled her to the lavatory before she could protest. His masculine strength made the transfer from chair to loo much easier than usual, and Kitty forgot about nursing being 'women's work' and very quickly learnt to value him.

The last in the trio was Beverley. Beverley had never married, but had nursed first her mother, and then her sister. She had a rather coy manner, which irritated Kitty, but she was so good-natured that it was impossible not to love her.

'Perfectly possible if she stayed longer than a week,' retorted Kitty, when Perdita said this, 'but she does like gardening. She's been taking cuttings for me, really quite efficiently.'

Only Thomas was happy to sleep alone in the house with Kitty, but by this time Perdita felt it was hardly worth going back home.

She mentioned this to Kitty while they had a drink together. Perdita was tired, and trying not to show it. Kitty was observing her keenly, but not making any comment. Thomas was cooking a vegetable and chicken breast stir-fry and liked to have the kitchen to himself.

'I could sleep at home tonight,' said Perdita, feeling she could sleep on a rail right now, if given the chance. 'But I don't think I'll bother. I always leave something I really want over here. I might as well just stay put for the time being.'

'That's what I said to Lucas.'

'Lucas?' Perdita hadn't seen him for ages now William was doing all the deliveries.

'I didn't mention it because we hardly have a moment alone, but he does visit me in the afternoons, quite often.'

'Oh – well, that's nice of him.'

'It is. Which is why it seems a good idea for him to sleep in your house.'

'What!' Perdita was outraged.

'Don't get all worked up, darling. His flat is being treated for woodworm.'

'But how dare he suggest such a thing?'

'He didn't. It was my idea. But he said he couldn't possibly sleep in your house without your permission.'

Partially mollified, Perdita said, 'Oh.'

Kitty frowned. 'You don't mind, do you?'

Perdita did mind, very much, but it was hard to say why. But she didn't want to let on to Kitty, or Kitty would feel guilty for making the offer. Kitty so rarely interfered in Perdita's life in a negative way, but she'd done it this time. 'I don't know, really . . .'

'Perhaps he'll pop round one evening and talk to you about it.'

'I doubt it, he's working in the evening, remember.'

'Not every evening. Janey does a night on her own now, and then he always has Monday off.'

'Janey never said anything about it.' Perdita was glad to get off the subject of Lucas and on to someone she had no ambivalence about.

'When did you last see Janey?' demanded Kitty. 'Since I've been a cripple what little social life you had has stopped completely. You must get out more. Ring her up and arrange to go to the pub, or something. You never get to mix with people your own age, now Roger's not here so much.'

'Roger is a lot older than me. At least thirty-five. Anyway, he's coming back in a day or two, isn't he?'

'Is he? Anyway, I still think you should get out. I'm quite happy reading, especially if I've had to make polite conversation all afternoon.'

'Poor Kitty, it must be a dreadful strain, having to be sociable.' Perdita certainly found Roger's attentive conversation quite tiring.

'Oh, it's not too bad. If I get fed up I just pretend to fall asleep until whoever it is tiptoes out of the room.'

'Do you do that with Lucas?'

'Oh, no. He doesn't bore me, although he reads to me, and that sometimes really does send me off. He has turned out to be a nice man, you know.'

'So nice, in fact, that you've offered him my house.' She smiled to disguise the snap in her tone.

'Only for a short time. And it's not as if you're in it. I wouldn't want him sleeping there if it wasn't empty.'

'There'd hardly be room for two of us,' said Perdita. 'Only one bedroom, with only one bed.'

Kitty regarded Perdita over her glasses. 'I'm sorry, I shouldn't have offered a house that's not mine to offer.' I would have invited him to stay here, only I feel the carers and Miriam have enough to do without having Lucas to look after. Which is why I rather rashly offered him the use of your house. I shouldn't have, of course. It's not mine to offer.'

Perdita smiled tightly, feeling petty for minding about Lucas when he was so marvellous with Kitty.

The garden seemed to be the only place she could be on her own these days, and she made the excuse of picking some purple-sprouting broccoli to get away. On the way to the vegetable patch, which was still full of plants Kitty had grown, she worked out why she didn't want Lucas in her house. There were two reasons really. One was that it represented a bolt hole from the carers and Roger, and the stream of visitors, but mainly it was because that house, cottage really, represented her life post-Lucas. When he had left her she was nothing but a lachrymose heap of despair. Now, the only thing she lacked was a nice cosy boyfriend to take her out for a drink and make love to her on Saturday nights.

Roger flitted into her thoughts. He would probably take on this role like a shot, he'd made that clear with his intimate little chats. She might be out of practice, but she could still read the signs and could tell he was interested in her. But she found the prospect unappealing. There was nothing wrong with Roger, exactly, he was just rather dull, and not at all sexy.

Lucas was different altogether, and what she didn't want was Lucas sleeping, living, in the space where she had wept so much she had to keep drinking glasses of water to stop herself dehydrating. She didn't want him waking in her bed, hearing her blackbird singing in the tree outside. She didn't want him padding in his bare feet to her bathroom, leaving the seat up on the loo, or putting smears of toothpaste in her washbasin, where she left them herself.

Picking away she asked herself why she was reacting like this to the thought of Lucas sleeping in her house without her, when the thought of him sleeping there *with* her didn't have the same effect at all.

'But that's lust,' she said, apologising to the cluster of aphids she squashed as she picked. 'It's not the same. It's perfectly all right wanting Lucas for his body, providing he never knows about it, of course. And when Kitty was in hospital and I felt lonely, it was perfectly understandable to want a man to cuddle. I just chose Lucas because there aren't any other men in the area. And as I didn't cuddle him, only hugged him that time he brought me home after Christmas, and didn't actually let him rape me in the ladies' powder room at Grantly House, I must have pretty much got Lucas out of my system. But I'm still not having him in my bedroom. Not without me there.'

When she got back to the kitchen with her colander, she was greeted with the news that while she'd been communing with the purple-sprouting broccoli, Lucas had rung to say he'd be over to see her that evening, at about eight.

'He probably wants to talk about living in your house,'

said Kitty, regarding Perdita as if trying to read her mind.

Perdita smiled blandly. She didn't want to discuss her feelings for Lucas just now.

'Take her for a drink, Lucas!' demanded Kitty, the moment he arrived. 'She never goes out. She'll go green and fall over if she doesn't see daylight occasionally.'

'I get plenty of daylight, Kitty,' said Perdita, unusually annoyed with her. 'I'm not one of those poor plants you put in the garage and forget about all winter.'

Lucas eyed Perdita. 'I think we should go out. We can't have a good row here.'

Not wanting to be seen to agree with him, especially when she didn't want Kitty to realise that a row was in the air, she almost smiled. 'Let's go somewhere far away. I don't want to be seen with you in public.'

'Perdita!' Kitty was horrified at this apparent lapse of manners.

'You know what people are like round here. If we're seen together their imaginations will run riot. We'll never hear the last of it.'

'She's right, you know, Kitty. Then it might get out that we'd once been married.'

'Which would be so bad for Lucas's reputation,' Perdita finished silkily. 'I'll go and brush my hair and put on some lippy.'

As she left the room she heard Kitty muttering about slang and young people. It made Perdita feel adolescent and rebellious.

'I expect you know why I want to talk to you,' said Lucas, having given Perdita half a pint of cider.

'You want to move into my house,' she said, trying to sound noncommittal, but not managing it. 'Kitty told me.'

'I'm already moving into your kitchen—'

'And I was fine about that, was I?'

'You know you kicked up like hell about it. And you obviously feel the same about me using the rest of your space.'

'I'm not thrilled by the idea, no.'

Lucas narrowed his gaze over his pint of Old Snout. 'Why not? Kitty tells me you're not living there yourself.'

'Yes I am. I'm just not sleeping there. I still use the house for my pea plants and things. I'm in there most days.'

'But not at night? My presence wouldn't really make any difference to you.'

'That's not really the point. I don't like the idea of my bolt hole being occupied. Kitty's house is full of people, and I'm used to living on my own. It's nothing personal.' Pleased to have thought of a reason which he wouldn't connect with himself, Perdita took a gulp of cider which was a little too home-spun and vinegary for her liking.

'Yes, it is. If it was Janey, or her bloke, the one that works for you, who needed somewhere to live, you'd say yes like a shot. It's me you don't want there.'

Perdita contemplated continuing with the lie but decided not to. Lucas was too good at seeing through her. 'Well, can you blame me?'

'Tell me, then I'll tell you if I blame you or not.'

Perdita took a deep breath. 'You don't need reminding of the circumstances we parted in, and I'm sure you're aware of how completely and utterly devastated I was.' He nodded. 'Well, that house represents my recovery. By the time I was in it, I was better, I'd got up off the floor, I'd made a new life for myself, I'd bought somewhere to live and I was OK. If you lived there, to me it would be like winning a prize and having to give the cup to my opponent.'

He considered this for some time. Perdita tried another sip of her drink.

'That's OK, then,' said Lucas. 'I'll find somewhere else

to stay. Do you want to finish that, or would you prefer something else?'

Perversely, because Lucas wouldn't argue with her, she had to argue with herself. 'Where else would you go? There's not room at Kitty's with me, the carer and Roger there most of the time. She's got so much furniture, not many of the rooms are habitable.'

'Roger? Oh, the real long-lost nephew? I met him a couple of times at the hospital. Not exactly a ball of fire, is he? What's he hanging around for?'

'He's working in the area and Kitty asked him to stay. He's not "hanging around".'

'I expect he's after Kitty's money.'

'You don't really think so, do you? Anyway, why shouldn't he be? He's Kitty's only remaining blood relative.'

Lucas didn't speak for a moment. 'I'm sure he's fine. Now, what about a gin and tonic? Have a grown-up drink, for a change.'

Perdita let him exchange her cider for a gin and tonic. She didn't want to pursue the matter of Roger, but she couldn't abandon the subject of where Lucas was to stay so easily. 'There may be somewhere at the health farm. A staff flat, or something. I could ask Ronnie.'

'You don't have to worry about me, Perdita. I can find somewhere to stay. It's only for a couple of weeks, three at the most. I could have a suite at the hotel if all else failed.'

'Only if all else fails? It sounds lovely to me. The rooms are really nice at Grantly House, aren't they?'

'Lovely for a night, but you wouldn't want to live there.'

Perdita's drink was strong and surprisingly pleasant. It enhanced her tiredness and made her feel weak. 'You probably think I'm pathetic, not wanting you to stay in my house.'

He stared into his pint to avoid agreeing that he did.

'I know it's the logical solution. In fact, it would prob-ably be good for someone to be there. Keep burglars away.'

He put down his glass and cleared his throat. 'Listen, Peri— Perdita . . .'

He corrected himself hastily and Perdita started at the sound of his pet name for her, a name that no one else used.

'I do know how much I hurt you,' he went on. 'And there hasn't been a day since I did it that I haven't felt terrible remorse.'

This admission made Perdita feel even worse about not wanting him in her house. He'd done wrong, but he'd regretted it. She shouldn't hold it against him.

'Also anger,' he added.

'*Anger?*' She felt angry now. 'How have you felt anger about me? You were the one—'

'Yes, I know all that, but while I actually ended the marriage, you have to accept that the fact it went wrong wasn't only my fault.'

Perdita had not accepted that, and, as a concept, this was actually entirely new to her.

'I don't know what you mean. How can I possibly have had anything to do with it? I loved you, I was faithful to you. How can it have been my fault, in any way?'

'You didn't fight back, Perdita. You didn't demand that I was faithful, you didn't curse me for bringing colleagues home unexpectedly. You let me get away with murder.'

'But you can't blame me for any of that! I was only eighteen, for God's sake!'

'If you hadn't put up with so much bad behaviour, I might have stopped behaving badly. You should have thrown me out when I came home smelling of other women, made me see what I stood to lose by abusing our relationship.'

'That's so unfair! I can't believe you're blaming me for all that!'

'I'm not blaming you for my bad behaviour, I'm blaming you for not reacting to it.'

'But how was I supposed to react? Hit you over the head with a rolling pin?'

'That's what you'd do now. You wouldn't be so bloody passive.'

'This is absolutely outrageous! You were a complete bastard, you were a bully, you slept around! I was lucky I didn't get some foul disease! And you're holding *me* responsible!'

'Not responsible, *partly* responsible.' He looked at her with something which could have been respect. 'You've changed so much, Perdita.'

'Just as well! I never thought that even you could be so unfair as to blame me—'

'I said, I didn't blame you, but that you being so passive didn't help.'

'I didn't know how to be anything but passive. I was so young – and young for my age. I didn't realise I had any control over my own destiny until after you left me.' She glared at him as a thought occurred to her. 'I suppose you'd say I should be grateful.'

He smiled back. 'Too right! If I hadn't left you, I'd have bullied you to death, and I expect our six children would have bullied you too. You had a lucky escape.'

'Not so lucky that I didn't avoid meeting you in the first place. That would have been really lucky.'

He met her gaze with an expression which was both rueful and challenging, a little amused. 'You owe me your independence, everything about you that makes you the successful businesswoman you are – *if* you are. But I don't want you to feel obliged to let me sleep in your empty house. And thinking about it, I don't want to sleep in a bed that you've watered with a million tears, because of me. I don't suppose I *could* sleep.'

Perdita finished her gin. 'That's all right then. That's us both happy.'

'I wouldn't go as far as that. I still need somewhere to stay.'

Suddenly Perdita decided the whole thing was silly. She was silly to mind about Lucas being in her space. If she was over him, she was over him, and if him leaving her had turned her from a mouse into a mover and shaker, perhaps she did owe him something. She chewed on the lemon, which was all that was left of her drink. 'It's all right, Lucas. At first I couldn't hack it, but I realise now that nothing you can do to me can hurt me any more. Do have my bed, Lucas. Feel free.'

Lucas frowned. 'I don't know if that makes me feel better, or profoundly depressed. Do you want another drink?'

Perdita shook her head. 'I don't think I should. I feel sleepy enough as it is.'

His frown cleared. 'There's a lot going for you, Perdita.'

'I know. I'm probably in line for a Business Woman of the Year award, or something.'

'No you're not. You probably have to make money to get one of those. But you are a wonderfully cheap drunk. Two sips of cider and a gin and tonic, and you're anybody's.'

'Except yours, Lucas. I'll never be yours again. Now, could you please take me home?'

As usual, Perdita went in to say good night to Kitty.

'So, is he going to stay in your house?' she asked, looking very small and childlike, with her hair freshly plaited.

'I can't remember how we left it,' said Perdita, feeling foolish. 'Kitty, do you think it was in any way my fault that our marriage failed?'

'Why do you ask, dear?'

Perdita took this as a yes. Kitty would never chide her about it, but the fact that she called her 'dear' in that particular way told Perdita that yes, she was in some way responsible.

'Lucas said if I hadn't been so passive, he wouldn't have behaved so badly. I think that's really unfair.' This was directed at Kitty, as well as Lucas.

'But it's probably true. If you'd been more mature, more sophisticated, you might have been able to handle him better. If you married him now, you wouldn't let him get away—'

'The difference is,' Perdita interrupted, all trace of the gin and tonic gone, 'I would not marry him now. Not for anything. Which I suppose answers my question – I was too naïve not to marry him, and too naïve to keep him. Therefore, it was partly my responsibility too.'

'Your personality might have been very suppressed when you were eighteen,' said Kitty, 'but when there are two people in a relationship, however dominant one of them is, the other still has some part to play.'

Perdita sighed. 'Perhaps it's nice not to think of myself as just a victim. Perhaps being a failure is marginally better.' She suddenly laughed.

The following Saturday Roger was due to return from his business trip, and Perdita wondered if she should take Lucas's comments about Roger being after Kitty's money seriously. She decided not to and as she had a lot to do in her tunnels, she put it out of her mind. It was also change-over day.

Thomas was leaving, and Beverley was taking over. Now they knew each other's ways, the handover was almost nonexistent, according to Kitty, amounting to little more than an exchange of gossip. Having signed Thomas's form, Perdita left them to it and went across to the poly-tunnels. When she came back she was exhausted, and longed to sink into a bath with a bad book and a glass of whisky, which had been promoted from 'only in emergencies' to 'drink of choice'. But Roger was there, so she felt obliged to drink sherry with him and Kitty. She made Beverley join them so she wouldn't have to talk.

'While you were out,' said Beverley, 'someone called Ronnie phoned. He was very insistent that you had agreed to have your hair cut. This evening, at about half-seven? Before dinner? Is that right? Did you have that arrangement?'

'No! Honestly, that Ronnie, he's so bossy.'

'He said he'd cut my hair too, if I wanted him too.'

'Well, what about mine?' said Kitty. 'Will he leave me out?'

They all laughed. The thought of Kitty having her hair in any way different from two plaits round her head was totally unthinkable.

'You couldn't do that, Aunt Kitty,' said Roger. 'What would people think?'

Kitty didn't answer this question.

'And surely,' went on Perdita, thinking aloud, 'Lucas would have said something if the television show was that imminent? I mean, I know he believes in keeping people in ignorance, but surely he'd mention that. I'll have to get the kitchen sorted out a bit and things.'

'Well, let's have our hair cut anyway,' said Beverley. 'As I said to that Ronnie, I haven't had a chance to get mine done for ages. I would appreciate the opportunity.'

'Don't you have the chance to get it cut when you're not with us?' asked Perdita, trying to be tactful.

'No, my other lady lives in an even more remote place than this is.'

'You mean, you have another client? You don't have time off when you're not looking after me?' asked Kitty, who obviously thought Beverley worked one week in three.

'Oh, I do have a couple of days, but I need the money.'

Kitty and Perdita exchanged guilty glances. 'Of course,' said Perdita.

'And although you're very conscientious about making sure I get my two hours in the afternoon, not like some people, there isn't time to get my hair done. I said as much to Ronnie on the phone.'

'Ah.' Perdita realised that the television programme was probably months away, but Beverley really needed a haircut, and Ronnie was sympathetic. She glanced at her watch. It was nearly seven now. 'Well, I must have a quick bath first. I'm covered in grime and probably stink. Let me grab a sandwich, I'm starving.'

'You're surely not going to eat a sandwich in the bath?' protested Roger.

Perdita nodded, heaving herself to her feet. 'If I fall asleep, Ronnie can start on you.'

'When are *we* going to eat?' asked Roger, plaintively.

When Perdita got downstairs, nearly an hour later, she found Ronnie in the sitting room. Roger was nowhere to be seen, but Beverley was sitting on a stool with a cape round her neck. Kitty was sitting in her wheelchair watching with apparent interest as Ronnie wielded the scissors. Something about her was different. Then Perdita gasped.

'Kitty! You've had your hair cut!'

'I thought it was time for a new look,' she explained, somewhat smug. 'Do you like it?'

Perdita looked. Kitty had had her hair in a plaited coronet about her head ever since she'd known her. Now it curved softly round her face with a short, feathery fringe. It looked wonderful.

'It's amazing! What on earth made you decide to get Ronnie to cut it?'

'I told you, I thought it was time for a new style. And it saves the carers and you having to plait it all the time. Thomas,' she explained for Beverley's benefit, 'has never really got the hang of plaiting. It means Perdita has to do it, and she's got enough on her plate.'

'I hope you didn't do it because of that,' said Perdita. Beverley was looking concerned too.

'She did it because she wanted a new look,' said Ronnie. 'She's told you. I think she looks ten years younger.'

Perdita smiled. 'He's right, Kitty. You don't look a day over seventy-nine.'

'Which means Perdita will look eighteen again,' said Kitty, 'when Ronnie's had a go at her.'

Perdita shuddered at the thought. 'Oh, please not! I was awfully young and silly at eighteen. Make me look thirty and sophisticated.'

Ronnie, was carefully levelling up the back of Beverley's hair and biting his lip in concentration. 'I'll see what I can do.'

When Perdita's turn came, Beverley took Kitty to the bathroom to get her ready for bed.

'You'll be done by the time we get back,' said Kitty, 'the amount of washing Beverley makes me do.'

'So, Perdita. What do you want? Something young and sexy to attract that man you were going to get yourself?'

'To be honest, I can't be bothered to think about men just now. Kitty takes all my spare time. I can hardly remember what life was like before she had her stroke.'

Ronnie tugged a wide-toothed comb through Perdita's curls. 'You were going to find a man and let the girls give you a makeover.'

'Was I really? Would you mind terribly if I ducked out of that particular agreement? I just don't have the energy.'

Ronnie hissed. 'Honestly, you young women. No stamina. And what about the dating agency?'

She bit her lip. 'Getting to know someone new is just so much effort.' She was thinking of Roger.

'Especially when Mr Wonderful is on your doorstep in the shape of Mr Michelin Star.'

'*What?*'

'So, take to an inch all over? An urchin cut would really suit you.'

'Ronnie! What are you thinking about? If you take off more than an inch, I'll sue you! And as for Mr Michelin Star being Mr Wonderful, I don't think you know him very well!'

'Calm down, love. I was only joking. Two inches should do it.'

She closed her eyes while he combed her hair. It felt very soothing. 'That feels wonderful. Would you mind if I had a little nap while you worked?'

'Go ahead. It'll give me a free hand. But keep your head up.'

Chapter Seventeen

In spite of her fears, Perdita was pleased with her new hairstyle. It was a bit shorter, so it bounced round her face in a way which was at once youthful and sophisticated, but she could still tie it back so she could lean over her work without it getting in the way.

Roger had been very complimentary, but if she had been hoping for admiring comments from Lucas, she was disappointed.

'The television people are going to start next week,' he said when she delivered to Grantly House the following Monday. 'Can you be ready?'

'What do I have to do?'

'I'll give you a list of veg I'll need, so you'll need to supply that.'

'Well, don't go setting your heart on anything out of season, or that I haven't got. I'm not a miracle-worker. There's not much I could grow by next week, apart from a few cresses.'

He scowled at her. 'I pretty much know what's available and when, but I would like a chance to go and have a look.'

'Oh, well. Come this afternoon then. You can have a tour.'

'I like your hair,' whispered Janey, as Perdita walked out of the door. 'It suits you shorter.'

'Thanks. Seen William lately? He's not very good at keeping me informed about his love life.'

'Well, I go to his mum's for Sunday dinner quite often. And my mum thinks he's wonderful.'

'So he is. And—'

'Janey! You're not here to gossip with Perdita! Get on with your work!'

'There's no need to be so rude, Lucas. How are you going to cope with all those television people if you can't even be civil to your own staff?' muttered Perdita.

Lucas sighed. 'God knows!'

The sight of Perdita's poly-tunnels, filled with such delights as chrysanthemum greens, Chinese box thorn, edible burdock, purple-flowering pak choi, as well as more conventional crops, made Lucas glance at Perdita in admiration as he took notes, walking along tasting as he went.

'Look,' she said, picking a sprig of tiny flowers encircled by the leaf. 'I think they look like little fairy ballet dancers.'

'You don't really talk to your plants, do you?' It wasn't entirely a question.

'Well, I do, but not necessarily politely.'

He laughed, remembering his first visit to her poly-tunnels when she had cooed at them nauseatingly. 'This lot is quite inspiring, I must say. I'll make up a list.' He sighed. 'Although I dare say they'll only let me use bog-standard ingredients you can buy at the supermarket.'

'Then they won't want me involved. You can buy your lollo rosso in town.'

'Oh no, they definitely want you involved. The producer was on the phone again the other night. They've slightly changed their original idea.'

'Oh? Do you want to tell me over a cup of tea?' Perdita didn't eat much these days, but she drank a lot of tea. 'Come into the house, and I'll make you one.'

'You haven't been in your house lately, have you, Perdita?' he asked, as they walked back together.

'No. I don't have much time to be in it, what with one thing and another.' Then she remembered that Lucas was going to stay in it while his flat was de-loused. 'Why? Do you know something I don't, like, my kettle's gone missing?'

'Oh, your kettle's still there. I think. If it was a battered, antique copper one.'

Alerted by his tone, Perdita hurried along the walkway to her back door and opened it.

Perdita's kitchen looked like something out of a magazine. Everything in it that she ever used had vanished. There was now a three-tiered wooden plate rack attached to the wall, next to a bar from which butcher's hooks supported a selection of copper cooking implements. There were ladles, tiny frying pans, a conical colander, a nutmeg grater and a box grater, a cream-skimmer and a set of cream measures. A wire egg basket in the shape of a chicken hung next to upside-down bunches of dried flowers. The worktops were mostly obscured with similarly beautiful but useless ephemera. There were sets of jelly moulds, milk jugs, an old, enormous oil lamp, copper bowls with rounded bottoms, salt-glazed pots filled with wooden cooking utensils and a set of storage jars. Nothing in it, with the exception of the wooden spoons, looked as if it were any use at all.

'Oh my God!' she breathed. 'It's gone all *Country Living*.'

'I know you hate it. I couldn't stop them. They are set on having it look all antiquified, and when they heard you weren't living in the house, a set designer came down and went mad.'

Perdita looked about her. 'Well, it does look pretty, I must admit. But can you work in among all this clutter?'

He laughed. 'You don't usually have a problem with clutter.'

'No, but I'm me. You're – you.'

'I shall do my best. I did try and get them to tone down the tastefulness a bit, but as I had messed them around rather a lot already—'

'Had you? How did you do that?'

'Oh – well, I had to postpone the show once. If they hadn't been so keen they'd have given up the idea.'

'I didn't know you'd had to postpone it. Why was that?'

'Nothing to do with you. Now, while you're getting used to your new-improved kitchen, I'll hunt out your kettle and make a cup of tea. Don't go in the sitting room.'

She needed no other invitation. It was as transformed as the kitchen. It was as if the pages of a magazine had settled over her old house like a mantle. Looking carefully, she spotted a few of her own possessions, hidden under kilims and throws and log baskets, but her papers, her clutter, and all signs of her personality had been waxed, polished and dusted out of sight. The floor looked spectacular with a sheen to shame the most over-the-top advertisement.

She went back into the kitchen. 'Where's all my stuff? You didn't let them throw it away?'

'Of course not. It's all neatly packed into that container at the end of the drive. I don't suppose you saw it, coming from the back.'

A little groan escaped her. 'And what about upstairs? Did they trash that too, or did you?'

He seemed offended. 'Go and see.'

Upstairs was as she'd left it. She clattered back downstairs, almost disappointed. 'They haven't done anything. I was expecting a lit-bateau draped with antique French linen and lace, at the very least.'

'I wouldn't let them go upstairs. I said I had to live here and couldn't have it messed with.'

'Oh. Are you living here? I didn't notice any of your stuff around.'

'Some of us manage not to go through life scattering litter as we pass, although it must seem strange to you.'

'It's a really good thing we didn't stay married, Lucas. We'd have made each other so miserable.'

'I'm glad I no longer have the monopoly on causing

misery. Now, come and have your tea and I'll tell you what's going on. By the way, whatever else happens, and it probably will, I think we both agree that we mustn't let them find out we were once married. They'd have a field day.'

'As much as I hate to agree with you, ever, I think I have to this time.'

They perched on some wobbly but rustic stools and he opened a battered antique tin which, according to the advertising on the outside, had once contained short-bread. Now it was full of florentines.

'Have one. I'm trying them out as a base for fruit and ice cream, but they may be too dominant.'

'If this is dominant, I like it,' said Perdita, biting into a wafer of flaked almonds, glacé cherries, and other dried fruits coated on one side with chocolate.

'Hmm. I'm not sure the nuts aren't too overpowering. I might be better with just the brandy snap base. Now,' he went on briskly. 'Don't distract me. Filming starts this Friday. It's only a half-hour programme at the moment, but it'll take three days to shoot, at the least. Will you be able to manage that, with Kitty?'

'Oh, yes. All her sitters are primed to be on call whenever they're needed. And Kitty is really looking forward to hearing all about the television.'

'They want this show to be more real, with a few failures on view. And they want interaction between us.'

'But I thought I just had to totter on with a few decorative vegetables in a trug and give them to the star chef.' She paused. 'I hope you get it, by the way.'

He made a face. 'We won't know until the end of January next year. But no, they want me to talk to you about the veg, say what it's used for and what it tastes like.'

'Hell! I know what it tastes like, but I don't know what to do with the bloody stuff! I just grow it!'

'That's what I told them, but they wouldn't believe that

a gardener didn't know or care what happened to her produce after she'd sold it.'

'I didn't say I didn't care, I just don't know! Did you manage to convince them?'

'They'll give you a script, which I will help write. They said, "Never mind, she could have fewer brain cells than her pak choi and we'd still want her for her looks." '

Perdita found herself blushing. Whether it was because of the slur on her intelligence, or the reference to her appearance, she didn't know.

'Don't take it out on me,' added Lucas. 'I didn't say it.'

'Just as well. How soon will you know what you want?'

'Go and play in the garden for ten minutes, and I'll give you a list now.'

Perdita took another couple of florentines and her mug of tea, and went out into her shed. When she came back for more, he was ready. She read through it.

'I'm afraid you can't have purslane until the end of next month, claytonia's fine—'

'I know. I saw it in flower just now.'

'As long as you appreciate the flowers, they are so divinely pretty. Ditto sorrel, *mâche* and mizuna. You can have sprouted lentils if I start now, and you can have celery leaf, but not a lot, so you'll have to be careful. You won't be able to mess it up and start again.'

He looked affronted, and she patted his knee placatingly. 'I mean,' she went on, 'they won't be able to get endless shots. I do have other customers, after all.'

'I'm sure they'd all understand if you make the show the priority. They'll be getting mentions, I expect, as businesses that use you. Certainly in any publicity the press gives us.' He saw her frown. 'I'll deal with the local paper, don't worry – and any nationals that show interest.'

'Thanks. Normally it would be fine – I like talking about my veg – but just now, with Kitty, I can't cope with anything extra.'

'Perdita, if you want to change your mind about this show—' He sounded disconcertingly sympathetic.

'Oh, no. I want to do it. And Kitty would never speak to me again if I backed out. Ronnie wouldn't forgive me either. I'm already in his bad books. He desperately wanted me to have a makeover before the show and I said I couldn't face it.' She smiled brightly. She didn't mention Roger, because she didn't want to bring up Lucas's opinions as to his motives. That way she could avoid thinking about them. 'Good to think it's so soon. It means I won't have time to be tortured.'

'What would a makeover involve, do you think?'

'I don't know, being submerged in mud possibly, having one's body hairs ripped out, one by one, by a girl in an overall covered in badges. Could I have another biscuit?'

He handed her the tin. 'Just as well I didn't want to use these. Do you eat proper meals, ever?'

'Of course. Whatever the carer puts in front of me.'

'What about lunch?'

'I have a sandwich, or something.'

'Liar.'

'What?'

'If you came in here to make yourself sandwiches, you'd have known about the kitchen.'

Caught out, she said, 'I make sandwiches at Kitty's, and take them with me.'

'Nonsense. I know you, you just fly out of the house with nothing more than a cup of tea inside you. You probably don't even have toast.'

'I do sometimes.' When she stole half a ready-buttered and marmaladed piece from the carer's plate. 'Anyway, what are my eating habits to do with you?'

'I don't want you fainting on set, or anything. The lights will be quite powerful, you know.'

'Well, I promise to eat more when we start.'

'Do it now! You can't do what you're doing, living two

lives, and not have proper nourishment! From now on you'll have a proper breakfast every time you make a delivery to Grantly House. It won't take long,' he added, 'so don't go saying you haven't time.'

'Well, that would be very kind. But I won't be making any deliveries between now and the show. I'm going to be working flat out making sure everything's perfect.'

'Then I'll send William back with breakfast on a plate! But after the show, if you don't turn up, I'll come and find you and feed you myself!'

Perdita opened her mouth to make some scathing remark, but didn't. Lucas's form of caring was nannyish and overbearing, but it was also strangely welcome.

'Hi! Lucas!'

'Hello, Perdita. What have you got in your basket for us? Anything nice?'

Perdita felt that if she had to come in through her own back door, smiling, with a trug of now somewhat wilting vegetables on her arm again, she would tell the world she had slugs and snails and puppydogs' tails, and see what the star chef made of that.

'Well, I've got some mizuna, which is a sort of mustard leaf, some cress, some nettle tops and some Good King Henry. And over there—' she gestured to a copper bowl – 'I have some sprouted lentils.'

'And did you sprout these yourself?' asked Lucas.

'No, the fairies did it,' she muttered, she thought, inaudibly.

'Heard that!' said the sound man. He was a taciturn young man in black, who held his endearingly fluffy mike like a fishing rod.

'Cut!' called George, the producer. He had replaced the charming, floppy-haired David Winter, who had called Perdita 'Capodimonte in jeans', and was a lot brusquer and more businesslike.

'For God's sake, Perdita,' snapped Lucas, 'stick to the script! We'll be here all night.'

'Well, it's such a stupid question!' said Perdita defensively. 'Who else would have come into my kitchen and sprouted lentils!'

Lucas groaned. 'Just say what's on the script. We're getting tired!'

Perdita had opened her back door, smiled, and said hello to Lucas possibly twenty times. Something was wrong every time. Her patience had suffered more than her vegetables. 'But it's so artificial! Lucas asks me if I've got anything nice, as if I'm likely to say, no, I was on my way to the compost heap with this lot! It's silly!'

'There does seem to be a bit of an edge between you two,' said George. 'Or is it just the script?'

'It's just the script,' said Lucas.

'We hate each other,' snapped Perdita. 'We told you that ages ago.'

'Doesn't look like hate to me. Let's try again.'

A girl came up and powdered Perdita's nose. 'Getting a bit of shine, there,' she said,

'It's called sweat,' said Perdita. 'It happens in kitchens.'

'Actually,' said George, who had been looking at Perdita through narrowed eyes. 'I think she's got too much make-up on. I think the natural, dryad look would be better.'

Perdita, who had never worn so much make-up at one time in her life, had been rather pleased with the effect. She'd never realised how long and curly her lashes could look, or how kohl could increase the size of her eyes. She didn't want to take it all off, like a schoolgirl being made to scrub her face. 'We spent hours putting it all on, and I like it. Can't we just leave it as it is?'

'Just do as you're told, Perdita! You're a natural beauty, you don't need all that crap,' said Lucas.

The producer flashed a glance at him. 'He's right, love. Let's see how you look without it.'

Perdita and Sukie, the make-up girl, who'd had plenty of time to become friends, railed against the unreasonableness of the male sex together. They were in Perdita's bedroom, which had been turned into a dressing room.

'So, do you and Lucas know each other well?' Sukie asked, scrubbing at Perdita's lips with a tissue. 'There seems to be, like George said, a bit of an edge.'

'Oh, there's an edge, all right. We fight all the time. But there's nothing whatever romantic, if that's what you're hinting at.'

'Hmm.' The make-up girl regarded her through the narrowed gaze of a professional. Whether her comment referred to Perdita's relationship with Lucas, or the effect a lot of make-up remover had had on Perdita's face, Perdita couldn't tell. 'You know, you do look lovely. Especially with just the traces of make-up. You know how it is, your make-up always looks best first thing in the morning, when you've been too drunk or tired to take it off properly the night before.'

Perdita sighed. She could dimly remember this phenomenon.

'And no woman could avoid fancying Lucas.'

'I think I've got a hormone missing,' she lied. 'He does nothing for me.'

'Really! What a waste, when he so obviously wants you!'

'How on earth can you tell? I mean – you're wrong. But what makes you think he wants me?'

'Oh, you know! The way he snarls and smoulders at you all the time. He's charm itself to me. There,' she flicked Perdita's face with a brush. 'That should please them, now we'd better get back or they'll go mad.'

'There's been a change of plan,' said George. 'We're abandoning the script. Perdita will come in and show Lucas her basket. He'll say something spontaneous – like, "What's this load of rubbish?"—'

'And I hit him?' asked Perdita, hopefully.

'No. You tell him what you've got, but in a light-hearted way, and he'll take a bit of each thing and tell us what it tastes like. And you can make a joke about the dandelions being called *pissenlit* in France.'

'So do we need to practise this spontaneity?' asked Lucas. 'Or can we just make it up?'

A girl with a clipboard murmured something in George's ear. 'Make it up, but quickly, it's nearly time to break for lunch.'

The lighting was altered, the microphone lowered, and everyone got out of the kitchen and squeezed themselves into the passage, several of them crouching down behind the table.

'Action!'

'Five, four, three, two, one—'

'Well, Perdita, what have you got in that trug of yours? Anything edible? Or do they all just have indigestible names, but no flavour?'

Perdita smiled sweetly. She had nipped back to her tunnels to fetch something Lucas hadn't asked for. 'Well, here's something which could have been grown with you in mind, Lucas.'

His brows narrowed suspiciously. 'What is it? It looks a bit like spinach.'

'It's really more like sorrel.'

'So what is it?'

'Something you really, really need, Lucas . . .' Perdita could feel the heat of the lights on her face, she knew the camera was trained on her face. She gave a brilliant smile. 'Herb patience.'

Perdita left Lucas and the crew at four o'clock. He was cooking trout fry, which were like whitebait and looked enchanting peeping from the crust of miniature star-gazy pies. Perdita felt sorry for the tiny fish, though she agreed with everyone, they were extremely decorative.

Almost as decorative were the people who crammed her sitting room, alongside the bygones. There was a producer, an assistant, a sound man, a camera man, his assistant, and, to Lucas's chagrin, two home economists, who had done all the preparation, and had previously cooked all the food, to every possible stage, so Lucas's genius fingers were shown doing comparatively little.

Perdita was completely exhausted and her face was stiff from smiling. She couldn't wait to get out. She walked over her land, climbed over the fence and into Kitty's, grateful that at least it wasn't her responsibility to clear up. It would be her responsibility to produce all the vegetables again tomorrow that hadn't made it into shot today, but she could think about that later. Now, she collapsed into the chair by Kitty's wheelchair, grateful that the ubiquitous Roger seemed to be absent.

'I need a very large drink, then I'll tell you all about it.'

Beverly came in with the whisky bottle, two glasses and a slightly disapproving expression. She didn't think women should drink neat spirits. Perdita remembered that she hadn't liked whisky very much herself, once, but it seemed a long time ago.

'I told you about my house being turned into something out of a magazine, all bunches of flowers in inconvenient places, and piles of packing cases where they catch your shins as you turn round the corner? Well, at first the script was just as artificial, but then we asked if we couldn't just say what we were meant to say, and not use the words they'd given us. That worked quite well for a while, but I can't see Lucas putting up with it all for long. He upset everyone by using an antique copper bowl to whisk egg whites in. He couldn't understand why they were so cross. He said there was a chemical reaction between the little bits of copper which get scraped off and the egg whites, which increases their volume. Apparently they'd got it on loan from an antique shop and it wasn't supposed to be used.'

'Don't say any more until I've got the supper!' said Beverley. 'Roger's not coming back tonight, so we can have it on our laps, and I don't want to miss a word.'

Perdita took advantage of her absence to close her eyes for a few moments, wondering why they ate formally for Roger, when they didn't want to. She failed to push away her uncharitable thoughts about him. She didn't believe he was after Kitty's money, but he was boring.

'Well,' said Beverley, putting a plate of cod-in-sauce, green beans and new potatoes on Kitty's table, and handing one for Perdita to eat on her lap. She put her own on a little side table. 'Did they make you wear make-up?'

'To begin with, I had the works. The make-up girl, Sukie, was lovely. I really liked how I looked – not a bit like me, of course, but quite a nice-looking woman. But then they made me take it all off. Fortunately, what was left looked quite nice too. Look, can't you see it?' Perdita batted her eyelashes at Beverley and Kitty, who peered, but didn't comment.

Perdita took a forkful of cod-in-sauce and had a moment of longing for the duck which had been cooking on and off all day, in a way that meant they couldn't eat it. It had ended up being sprayed with glycerine, to give it the shine it had lost since nine o'clock that morning. Shine on for the food, shine off for Lucas and Perdita.

'What about Lucas? He didn't wear make-up, did he?' Kitty sounded horrified.

'I'm not sure,' said Perdita, not wanting to spoil Kitty's image of macho Lucas being above such frivolities. 'What he does have is women, home economists who do the food – all the preparation, the producer's assistant—'

'What do the home economists do?' asked Kitty. 'If they want Lucas to cook, why do they need them?'

'To save Lucas's valuable time. They prepare every-

247

thing, chop the onions and put them into little bowls – you should see the little bowls: none of their Pyrex crap, like on *Blue Peter*, for this they've used little pottery bowls with little handles. Very cute. Apparently some home ec. women will even devise the recipes, but Lucas balked at that. The producer's assistant, Karen, told me. Anyway, the home economists cook everything to every different stage, so you might have a shot of him putting a bit of duck into a pan, but then he won't go on cooking it. Or you might have him slicing it into slivers about a centimetre thick, really small, anyway, and practically raw, or putting the sauce on, or whatever. Everyone faffs around Lucas like anything, because he's the star, and the more they do the more he smoulders, and the more he smoulders the more they seem to like it.' She look a large sip of the small whisky which Beverley had poured her. 'It's quite funny, really. Only everything takes so long to set up, my poor veg keep wilting under the lights.'

'It sounds terrific fun, darling. Did you eat all Lucas's delicious cooking?'

'No, because it had all been kept hanging around too long. His women wouldn't let us eat it. They said it had probably picked up all sorts of bugs.'

She sighed. Now the excitement of telling Kitty and Beverley about it all had worn off, she felt exhausted. She had lost her appetite and the whisky had made her very sleepy. She pushed her food around her plate until it looked as if she'd eaten some of it, and then excused herself.

'Would you think I was an awful spoilsport if I had a bath and a really early night? I've got to be up God knows when tomorrow, to get the day's veg organised. And I ought to send a few things to Ronnie. It's not fair to forget all about him. The other customers can manage because I told them I couldn't give them anything. But I think Ronnie should have his stuff.'

She was up at four the next morning, stealing downstairs in the dark, putting on her boots and going across Kitty's land to her own. She felt better after her long night's sleep, but she wanted to spend time in her tunnels, not only to pick salads, but to remind herself what real life was like before spending another day in front of hot lights, people, and Lucas.

On the final day of filming, her energy, and therefore her temper, were running out. She found Lucas infuriating. He was being such a bully, shouting at one of his women for cutting something up into too small cubes, just as if she were Janey, and throwing a batch of alfalfa into the sink because it had gone brown. It would have been easy if he'd just said it was brown, someone would have taken it away and given him some more. As it was, it had to be picked out of the sink, which took ages and eroded everybody's patience still further.

'He's so brilliant,' said Karen, the assistant producer, and one of Lucas's biggest fans. 'He really cares about the food, which is what makes him temperamental.'

'You can care about food without having tantrums,' said Perdita, who was sorting out more corn salad, originally earmarked for Ronnie. 'I mean, I care about my salads all dying under the lights, but I don't stamp my foot and shout about it.'

'He's an artist. More to the point, he's eye candy. The women will love this programme. It's the ultimate safe sex.'

'Huh! What about the men?'

'Oh, they've got you.'

Perdita muttered a rude word.

It was when 'Eye Candy' reduced one of his women to tears that Perdita lost her temper completely.

'For crying out loud, Lucas! You are such a bastard! She's trying her best, doing her job, chopping and slicing her socks off, but it's never good enough, is it? Oh no, His

Highness wanted the cucumbers in one and a half centimetre chunks, and got them in two centimetre chunks, so he has a tantrum about that! And now you're shouting at her for something which isn't her fault at all! If you're not used to cooking with sorrel, you don't know it loses its acidity if it hangs around too long. You can't blame her for not knowing! You were always fucking arrogant, but now you're so up yourself, it's not true!'

Everyone was silent. Perdita was suddenly aware she hadn't used language like that, or spoken to Lucas in that way, in front of the entire crew before. They may have been snippy with each other, but she hadn't really let rip until now.

Lucas didn't seem to notice the effect Perdita's outburst had had, he just went right on and had his own.

'Will you butt out? This is none of your business. She doesn't need Saint Perdita to rush to her rescue, saving every woman within fifty miles from Wicked Lucas, just because he once broke your heart! She happens to be a professional, not like you, playing about with your mustard and cress farm!'

'Playing about, am I? Well, where would you be without my mustard and cress farm? You can't get what I produce from the supermarket, you know. But from now on, you'll have to. After this programme, I'm not supplying you with anything else! You can whistle for your hairy melons from now on!'

'Children, children, what is going on?'

George rose from behind the table like a jack-in-the-box. He was staring in amazement. 'I mean, I know you two know each other, but this is looking very like a domestic!' He'd worked on several episodes of *The Bill*, and knew the jargon.

'Well, that's hardly surprising,' said Lucas. 'Considering—'

Their eyes locked. At the same moment they realised

250

that Lucas had nearly announced to the world via television that which they most wanted to keep secret.
Laughter sparkled in his eyes and his mouth twitched
convulsively.

'Considering what, Lucas?' asked Perdita, her expression solemn with the effort of trying not to laugh.

'Considering what a very – very – exasperating woman
you can be!'

Chapter Eighteen

Perdita got herself out of the way as quickly as possible. She didn't want to confront Lucas until the memory of that shared moment had been forgotten. For that instant, they had been united – them against the world. For a mad, idiotic moment, she allowed herself to imagine what it would be like if their union was for real, and not just a split second of airtime.

Beverley wasn't in the kitchen and was unaware of Perdita's arrival, and for the first time ever, Perdita didn't immediately go in to see Kitty. She slipped upstairs to one of the attics, from which she knew the view was both magnificent and calming. She needed to see the sun gild the trees and hills turning the fields to a green velvet bedspread, and get a sense of perspective.

She was more shocked than annoyed to find Roger. He had a notebook and pen and was sorting through a cupboard of china.

'Hello,' she asked, somewhat breathlessly. 'What are you doing?'

He turned. 'Oh, Perdita. Back already? I was going to make you a nice cup of tea.'

'That's a kind thought, but what are you doing up here? Has Kitty persuaded you to look for something?'

He hesitated for the merest second. 'Er, yes – I mean, in a way. She did mention some photographs the other day, and I thought I'd see if I could find them for her.' He sensed her unease. 'There'll be a lot of sorting to be done when the time comes.'

'What do you mean? What time?'

'When Kitty dies. This'll all have to be itemised and a proper inventory made.'

'I expect you're right, but she hasn't died yet.'

'But, Perdy,' Perdita hated this contraction of her name, 'it won't be long now, will it? She's very frail.' He put a hand on her arm. She moved to the window, partly to remove it.

'She's not particularly frail. She's made a brilliant recovery from her stroke. She may last for years.'

He exhaled sharply. 'Oh, come on! I don't want to seem harsh, but she's going to die soon! You have to face it!'

'I know, but I don't have to face it until it happens.'

'You need to make some preparation,' he persisted gently. 'Because I don't think things'll be quite as you expect them when she does die.'

'What are you talking about?'

'I think I should warn you – so it doesn't come as a shock – that Aunt Kitty has made it clear to me I'm going to feature in her will. With a substantial legacy.'

'But why should I need to prepare myself just because Kitty wants to leave you something?'

'You still don't get it, do you? I'm not talking a nominal hundred pounds, or whatever old ladies think is generous these days, I'm talking about most, if not all, the estate going to me.'

Perdita's mouth had gone dry. She was appalled, not because he might be Kitty's sole heir, but because he was thinking about it now, before she was even in her grave, let alone cold in it. 'What?' Her voice came out as a croak, as if the dust in the attic had got into her throat.

'I am her only living relation, you know,' Roger said gently. 'She'll have to leave everything to me now she knows about me. It's only right, only what she'll feel is right.' Perdita got her arm out of reach quickly, before he could pat it. 'But don't worry, I'll let you have the land you use for agricultural rates, although –' he gave a rueful shake of the head as if things were out of his hands – 'I'm sure I could get planning permission for it.'

Perdita moistened her lips and perched on a tea chest. Her mouth had gone stiff with shock and her heart had begun to pound in her chest. She knew her knees would have failed her if she'd tried to stand. 'Roger—'

'I know she's led you to believe you're entitled to everything, but I'm her own flesh and blood, you're not even her goddaughter.' He let this sink in. 'And she already feels bad about the way my grandmother's family treated my mother.'

Perdita still felt weak. How could anyone be so mercenary? 'Oh, I know,' she said, trying to sound normal. 'She told me.'

'What did she tell you?'

'That she felt bad about the way your family had been treated, and that she meant to put things right.'

He nodded. 'She does have a strong sense of justice. But will it convert to reality?'

'How do you mean, exactly?'

He made a small, impatient gesture. 'I mean, will she get round to changing her will? She could have had no idea of my existence when she made it.'

'If she wants to change it, she will. She's not gaga, you know.' Perdita tried to conceal her shock and confusion which was heavily overlaid with outrage.

'I know this is a bolt from the blue for you, but I will see you're all right. I know it's disappointing for you, when you must have felt for years that she didn't have anyone else to leave her money to . . .' This time he got hold of her wrist and held it between caressing fingers. 'Do you know where she keeps it, by the way? Her will?'

Perdita pulled her hand away and shook her head. She had a fair idea, but she wasn't sure, and she certainly didn't want him getting his hands on it. How dare he assume that she'd spent her life with Kitty looking forward to her money? 'I'm afraid I haven't a clue. It's probably in the bank, or something. But what makes you think she didn't know about you before? If my mother knew about you, why shouldn't Kitty?'

'It's possible, but I'm afraid I can't take the risk.' He brushed the dust off his hands. 'We don't want Aunt Kitty's wishes ignored because we couldn't find the will.'

Perdita clenched her teeth to stop herself shouting that if Roger referred to Kitty as Aunt once more, she wouldn't be answerable for the consequences.

'I know you'll want to do what's right, and if you help me, I'll let you have anything that's of sentimental value. I'm not greedy, I just want what's mine by right.' He reached out and squeezed her upper arm.

'Let's go downstairs,' said Perdita hoarsely. 'I need a drink.'

Somehow she got through the evening with an appearance of normality. She almost found herself telling Beverley and Kitty how Lucas had nearly announced to the world that they had been married. But all the time her brain was chewing over Roger's revelations about himself and his motives. Should she tell Kitty what had happened? If Kitty had been fit and able, she would have like a shot. But she wasn't fit and able, and if she wanted to leave everything to Roger, that was her right. After all, Roger was a blood relation, and Perdita certainly didn't feel she was entitled to anything just because she and Kitty loved each other.

Eventually she decided she'd have to think long and hard to decide what to do, and made an excuse to go to bed early. It was a huge relief to discover a note from Roger on the kitchen table saying he'd been called away. Perdita mean-spiritedly checked that he hadn't taken the silver with him. It was only later that she realised he might have gone off to arrange a new will for Kitty, or something equally underhand, but even if he had, there was nothing she could do about it.

The filming, scheduled for three days, went on for five. Perdita began to find it difficult to keep her business going. Ronnie and Lucas had both agreed to have whatever she wanted to give them, so she was able to cut swathes through anything which threatened to bolt, and dispatch William with a vanload. But when, on the third day of filming, she went to one of her seed tins, and discovered that the little bag of silica gel had gone pink, indicating dampness, she began to worry. She saved a lot of seed from year to year, but if she was to keep producing new salads to tempt the jaded palates of chef and bon viveur, she had to buy in expensive seed from other sources.

Most of the seeds seemed to be still in good condition, but the bag turning pink was an indication of her losing her grip as well as of dampness. Her anxiety about Roger didn't help. She got up the moment it was light, did as much as she could in the poly-tunnels, and then came home to check that the Kitty-sitters were arranged for the afternoon. Then it was back to her cottage, to have her make-up put on and taken off again. After the day's filming, she rushed back to Kitty, to regale her and Beverley with amusing tales about Lucas's tantrums, and the enormity of the producer's demands. On the final day she asked Sukie if she could paint on a smile for her, to save her face muscles.

Sukie laughed. 'You are looking tired, I must say. Fortunately we have the technology to deal with those little rucksacks forming under your eyes.'

'Good. Apart from anything else, I don't want Kitty thinking I'm tired.'

'It will be better when we've all gone.'

'Yes, but I have enjoyed it. Really. It was a completely different experience. And Kitty and Beverley have loved hearing about it all. In fact, Kitty wants to invite everyone back for a drink before you all go home. I told her I thought you'd probably all want to push off, but that I'd see.' Perdita was dubious about mixing Kitty with the world of television, but at least Roger was still away, although a postcard had arrived for Kitty saying he would be back soon. Perhaps by that time Perdita would have thought of how to handle him.

'If we finish early – and God knows, we've overrun by two days, so we might – I'm sure the crew would be delighted. They've all heard so much about Kitty, from you and Lucas, it would be lovely to actually meet her.'

So, after a successful day of Lucas and Perdita fencing with words and (almost) cooking utensils, with just enough warning for Beverley to find Kitty's hoarded bottles of champagne and put them in the freezer, the entire crew, except Lucas, who had to go back to Grantly House, trooped into Kitty's sitting room.

She enchanted them. She found something pertinent to say to each one, she made everyone feel flattered and talented, and by the time they all left to go home, the producer was begging Kitty to let him make a documentary about her.

Perdita, who was delighted to see Kitty so happy, was also anxious about her. Her colour was heightened, which could just have meant she was having a lovely time, and had had a glass of champagne too many. Or it could mean she was running a fever, and knowing Kitty's capacity for alcohol, Perdita feared the latter. Oh please, God, she prayed silently, don't let Kitty die until I've found how she wants things left!

Perdita didn't press her hand against Kitty's head, for fear of having it bitten in annoyance, but she did kiss her cheek, placing her own against Kitty's. As she had done

257

this every day since her stroke, she knew that Kitty felt the same as she had that morning. But something was wrong.

'Are you feeling all right? Not overtired by those media types?'

'No, they were all delightful. I thoroughly enjoyed myself.' Kitty sounded a little cross. 'What a pity Lucas couldn't come. I haven't seen him for ages.'

'He's been dreadfully busy – filming all day and then rushing back to cook at night. He says you can lose your star if you appear on too many television programmes and seem to have dropped the ball.'

'He hasn't got his star yet, has he?' Kitty frowned. 'He didn't tell me if he has.'

'No – the book doesn't come out until January. But if he does get it, and the telly thing's a success, and they want to make a series with him, he wants to be able to do both.'

'Would you do a series, if they asked you?'

'Oh, I don't know.' Perdita didn't want to commit herself. She was worried about Kitty but couldn't say why. 'It was huge fun, but terribly time-consuming. They probably won't ask me to do another one.'

'You and Lucas are good friends now, anyway.'

'Are we? First I heard about it. I threw a bowl of sprouted lentils at him yesterday.'

'My dear child! I don't know how he puts up with you. Still, when you're in love, you're in love.'

Perdita felt the blood rush to her face; suddenly she felt she must be the one running a temperature. 'What on earth are you talking about?'

'Oh dear, have I said something I shouldn't? I thought you must know. It's so obvious to everyone else.'

Perdita wiped her forehead on her sleeve. 'Kitty darling, I hate to be rude to an old lady, but you're talking complete rubbish. Lucas and I barely manage to be civil to each other. But he is extremely fond of you, which is why he's kind to me sometimes.' Although that morning he had made some very unflattering remarks about her delivery of the lines, 'This really is delicious, Chef' in a very public way.

'I've spoken out of turn, and I shouldn't have. It's not as if Lucas has actually said anything to me, after all. It's just the way he talks about you.'

'Oh, Kitty, I'm sure you've got your wires crossed.'

'I'm sure I haven't. It will give me great satisfaction to see you remarried from whatever cloud they allocate me.'

'You're very sure of yourself! How do you know it won't be a red-hot tufa rock?'

'Don't change the subject. I know it's too much to hope to see you married while I'm still alive, but I'll be there in spirit.'

'Oh, Kitty!'

'But if you can't behave decently, I'll be content with a torrid affair.'

Should she choose this moment to talk about Roger? She decided not to spoil the moment; memories of such times might be all she had of Kitty soon. She laughed instead. 'You're a wicked, interfering old woman, as I've told you before. Now, do you want supper in bed?'

'No, no. I'm hungry! If I have to wait until I've gone through all that palaver, I'll starve to death.'

As Perdita went through to the kitchen to see how the frozen fish pie was coming along, it occurred to her what an effort life must be for Kitty. Even the most simple procedure took ten times as long as it would have once, and none of it could be done on her own.

If I was less selfish, or less dependent, she thought, as she and Beverley washed up glasses later, I'd let Kitty die. As it is I can't contemplate life without her, even in a wheelchair. 'What was that you said?'

Beverley put down her tea towel and put the last

champagne flute on the tray. 'I said I was going to do Mrs Anson's Horlicks now, and would you like a cup?'

'No, I don't think I do, thanks, Beverley. I'll just say good night to Kitty, and go up. I'm shattered.'

The following morning Kitty couldn't be got out of bed. Dr Edwards, visiting before morning surgery, told all three of them, Kitty in bed, and Beverley and Perdita hovering anxiously round, 'It's another stroke, I'm afraid.'

Kitty groaned, Beverley tutted and Perdita said, 'How bad?'

'It's hard to say at this early stage and, as you know, physiotherapy can do a lot to help. But it might be a while before Kitty's able to get into her chair again. I'll arrange for the district nurse to come and see her later this morning, if I can. And we might need a special mattress to help prevent bed sores, things like that.'

'You don't sound very optimistic.' Perdita, who was feeling near despair herself, had been hoping for something a little more bracing.

'We'll do everything we can, Perdita, but we've got to be realistic. Kitty is a very old lady. She's had one major stroke, another was almost inevitable. Be grateful that her mind seems to be as good as ever.'

'My mind is but a shadow of its former self,' Kitty mumbled from the bed.

It was hard for Perdita not to feel very depressed. The amount of time spent in either nursing Kitty herself, or arranging for others to do it, was inordinate. She decided to tell Roger he wouldn't be able to stay with them when he came back from his trip. It was only partly an excuse to keep him out of the house.

'I'm terribly sorry, but I'm sure you understand,' she said into his mobile phone. 'We might have to have two carers, and what with one thing and another . . .' She hoped he'd be able to finish this sentence for himself.

'Well, I can't say I'm surprised,' he said. 'It was bound to happen. Have you told Aunt Kitty?'

'No. I thought I'd better tell you first.'

'Then tell her I can go back to the hotel where I was before, and that I'll still be able to come and see her often, probably every day.'

Perdita subdued the suspicion that the message was really for her, not Kitty. 'I'm sure she'll be very pleased.'

'Oh, she will be. She did like having me around, you know.'

Perhaps this was true. 'I'm sure she did.'

'I'll call in to collect my stuff, then.'

'Oh no, don't worry about that! Just give me the address of the hotel and I'll send everything on. Then it'll be there for you when you arrive.'

She wrote it down as he dictated it. 'You're such a tidy person,' she went on, elated with relief that she could avoid seeing him for a bit longer. 'It will be no trouble to post your things.'

'I do like to be organised, yes. Which is why I'm going to be hiring several skips when Aunt Kitty pops her clogs. She must have spent the past seventy years surrounding herself with clutter.'

Perdita decided to take this as a compliment.

Kitty wasn't greatly put out that Roger was no longer going to be living with them.

'You must do whatever you think is right, my dear. I'm causing you all quite enough trouble as it is.'

Perdita, who'd been bracing herself to mention Roger's expectations with regard to Kitty's estate, decided she couldn't. She didn't want to worry her with it. After all, if it was Kitty's wish that Roger should have everything, she didn't want Kitty thinking that she, Perdita, felt at all put out. And if she brought the subject up, that was what Kitty would think.

The summer rushed past in a blur of ever-changing visitors for Kitty. The professionals: health visitors, nurses, doctors, and various carers; and then there were the social visits. Roger visited mostly when Perdita was out of the way. Whether this was tact or serendipity, she didn't know, but it did mean she could avoid confrontation when it would have been very inconvenient. Then there were the old friends who hadn't seen Kitty for years and wanted to come and stay. There were neighbours continually popping round with flowers from the garden, home-made jam, magazines. Perdita never knew who was going to greet her when she came home for lunch, or after a day in her tunnels. If she and Roger did coincide, he treated her with unpleasant familiarity. She almost expected him to give her an exaggerated wink and tell her 'he'd see her right'. She knew if Kitty had been herself, she wouldn't have been able to stand him either.

Although she rarely saw him herself, Lucas was one of the most frequent visitors. He brought food: morsels of duck breast, truffle mashed potato, buttered spinach, all in tiny portions, beautifully presented. Kitty, whose appetite was poor, ate every mouthful.

Caring for Kitty became more difficult. Bathing her took two people, and she became incontinent. The doctor told Perdita Kitty really needed two nurses now, as all the kindly neighbours in the world couldn't put her on a bedpan, and Kitty often woke in the night.

A baby alarm was rigged up between Kitty and Perdita, so at night, Perdita would hear if Kitty needed anything. Perdita became accustomed to running down to Kitty before she was even properly awake. Roger called almost every day, sending Perdita fleeing to her tunnels for sanctuary.

One morning Janey came to visit her there.

'Hi!' Perdita was thrilled to see someone from life outside the world of bedpans, social chitchat or smarmy Roger. 'I haven't seen you for ages and ages! Has Lucas let you out?'

Janey nodded. 'Since William's been doing the deliveries I never see you.'

Perdita stuck her fork into the ground. 'I know. I never see anybody these days except carers, health professionals, and Kitty and her mates. And Roger.' She shuddered. 'Sorry!'

'It's all right. I know how busy you've been. Lucas says you're never in when he goes. I've just come to ask you a favour.'

Perdita sighed. 'As long as it doesn't require any of my time, the answer's probably yes. What is it?'

'It's about your house. You're not living there at the moment, are you?'

'Well, no. I'm at Kitty's. I only use it to make coffee and tea in. Talking of which, would you like one?'

'If you're not too busy, I'd love it.'

Perdita's kitchen and sitting room had been shorn of their borrowed finery, all of which had gone back to the various antique shops from which it came, but Perdita's own, familiar clutter, had not yet replaced it. The kitchen still had its new cooker and worktop, and a bowl of peas soaking in the sink, and there were various bowls of lentils sprouting, but there was nothing more personal there. The sitting room was still unnaturally empty.

The two women came in through the back door. 'I've got some nice biscuits that Lucas left for me,' said Perdita. 'I expect you made them.'

Janey peered into the shortbread tin, which had somehow stayed behind. 'No, they must be Lucas's. I wonder what they were going to be?'

Perdita put the kettle on. 'So, what about my house?'

She had a fair idea what Janey was going to say, and wasn't sure how she felt about it.

'It's me and William,' said Janey. 'We want to live together.'

'Oh.' It was hard to believe that they had reached this stage so soon, but then she realised that half the summer had gone without her noticing, and they had got together in the winter. 'I had no idea my matchmaking had been that successful. I'm really pleased. He's so nice, it would be an awful shame to let him go to waste.'

Janey laughed. 'The trouble is, although our parents are fairly happy about our moving in together, there aren't many places round here to rent. Not that we can afford, anyway.'

'So you want to rent my house?'

Janey nodded. 'But you could go on using it during the day. I wouldn't want to cut off your bolt hole.' Janey nibbled her biscuit. 'I was talking to Lucas about it, and he explained about you needing somewhere during the day, somewhere you could get away from everybody, if you needed to.'

She was silent for a moment. Lucas was surprisingly perceptive, for a bully. He probably also remembered how much fuss she had made when he needed the house for a little while. 'But, Janey, look at all this stuff.' She waved a hand towards the plastic bowls, filled with water and sprouting pulses. 'There's nowhere else I could do it, especially not when it starts to get colder. They need a bit of warmth.'

'We wouldn't care about that. We wouldn't mind if you used the kitchen – or any of the house if you wanted to.'

Perdita poured boiling water onto coffee powder. Should she accept money from Janey and William so she could buy back the land Kitty had given her from Roger? No, it wouldn't be enough, and it might not be necessary.

She stirred the coffee. 'No, it wouldn't be fair to take money from you when I'm still cluttering up the place. I tell you what, you can borrow the house, while you save up for somewhere else.'

'Oh, I couldn't possibly do that!'

Perdita silenced Janey's protests. 'I feel guilty leaving my little house unlived in. As long as you remember I start work early, and you don't mind the kitchen full of peas, I would like to think of you and William having it as a love nest.' Actually, at that moment, she felt overcome with jealousy. She wanted a love nest of her own, complete with someone to nest with, and she knew which someone. She smiled. 'So, when would you like to move in?'

The next evening, Perdita was tossing up between having an early bath, and joining Kitty and whatever visitor it was for a drink, when Lucas appeared. She hadn't seen him since the television programme, though he'd visited Kitty almost every afternoon.

'Oh, hi!' said Perdita, her foot on the stairs. 'How are you?'

'Better than you are, obviously. You look dreadful. Janey told me you did.'

She didn't feel strong enough to discuss her looks, so she attacked him on another front. 'Oh. Was that why you let her have time off in the morning, so she could spy on me and report back?'

'It was her morning off, but I didn't come here to argue, just to take you out for a meal.' His raised hand shut her up before she'd opened her mouth. 'You never go out, you live a punishing routine of work and caring, and you have no fun at all.'

The corner of her mouth twitched. 'And going out with you is supposed to be fun, is it?'

He saw the twitch and answered it with one of his own

which would have sent most of the film crew into a hot sweat. 'It is. Go and have a quick shower while I see Kitty. Be ready in half an hour. OK?'

As Perdita stood under Kitty's shower, which didn't know the meaning of the word 'quick', preferring to distribute its water droplets slowly, on only carefully selected parts of the body, she realised it was quite nice to be bullied occasionally. Not in a slap-'em-around James Bond sort of way, but in a way that meant she didn't have to make a single decision. She could just take what he said as what he meant. She didn't have to second-guess him to see if he really wanted to take her out, to try to ascertain if he *really* felt well, or whether he was just saying that, or if he did feel put upon by the extra people, but didn't want to say.

When her entire body had been at least cursorily washed, she stepped out of the shower and blotted herself, wondering if she should take the opportunity to unburden to Lucas about Roger. What would Lucas do? If he knew about the way Roger kept trying surreptitiously to fondle her, probably commit a criminal assault, which would be satisfying, but not useful. No, she'd keep Lucas as a backstop if she couldn't take care of Roger herself. Now, she'd stop worrying about things which might not happen and prepare to go out with Lucas. With him, she could be as rude as she liked, and know she didn't have to face any unpleasant consequences in the morning. As she smeared her face with a bit of moisturiser, she wondered for a giddy moment what the recriminations would be if she seduced him. Supposing they staggered down to breakfast together. What would Beverley think?

Beverley was a fan of Lucas's – all the carers were. But would she continue to admire him if he came down having obviously spent the night with Perdita in his arms? She sighed and chuckled and rubbed her legs. It

266

was a hypothetical question. You don't seduce decision makers. You just decide if you want to be seduced. Besides, she looked dreadful. He wouldn't want her on toast, layered with ratatouille and a black olive dressing.

She pulled on the first summer dress she found which didn't need ironing, and went to join Lucas and Kitty.

'Darling, you look lovely, doesn't she, Lucas?'

'Much better. Clean, even.'

'Isn't he kind? Lucas is going to take you out for a nice meal so you can get away from the sick room for a bit. Now, do you want a drink first? So much cheaper than paying those ridiculous prices in restaurants.'

'Well, the poor little orphan girl would hate to cost the kind gentleman a penny more than absolutely necessary, so perhaps she'd better have a drink with her kindly benefactress.'

'Nonsense,' said Lucas. 'If you and Kitty start gossiping we'll never get away. I want to check out a colleague's place over towards Oxford, so we have to leave now.'

'It's only six thirty!' protested Perdita. 'I haven't said hello to Kitty yet.'

'Oh, do what the man says,' said Kitty. 'I've spent all day being sociable, I really don't have the energy to talk to you.' She smiled fondly, making the words into a caress.

'Very well, you grumpy old woman.' Perdita kissed Kitty's cheek. 'But I've got my mobile. If you need me, get Beverley to give me a ring, and I'll come straight back.'

Once in Lucas's leather-seated car, Perdita knew she should lay into him on the matter of his overbearing nature, or some such, but she didn't have the energy.

'I hope you're not expecting scintillating conversation, or anything, Lucas,' she said, with her head back and her eyes closed.

'Well, I was rather hoping for an evening of wit and insight, followed by exotic sex on a tiger-skin rug, but she was out, so I asked you.'

Perdita chuckled, her eyes still closed. 'Wake me up when we get there.'

She woke up of her own accord before they got there, feeling refreshed after her nap. One of the advantages of getting so little sleep during the night was that she could sleep almost instantly if any other opportunity to nap presented itself.

'So, where are we going? Our local restaurants not good enough for you, then?'

'Not good enough for *you*, my sweet.' He laughed at her surprise. 'Don't worry, I just want to call on an old colleague of mine who's just taken over a little place in the Cotswolds.' He frowned. 'Actually, he took it over months ago, but I haven't had a chance to go and visit him before now.'

'Oh. Well, I hope I don't embarrass you with my plebeian habits, asking for ketchup and stuff.'

'Don't worry, I won't let you do that.'

He took her to a market town which didn't look as if it could support anything too way out and gourmet in the way of restaurants. L'Escargot was tucked between an antique shop and a shop which sold gingham napkins, rope angels and shaker-style hatboxes. From the outside the restaurant looked small, hardly bigger than a tea shop, but inside it was much bigger, and although it was a weekday, the place was nearly full.

Lucas murmured to the beautiful woman who came to greet them. She hurried away and came back with an elegantly dressed man who greeted Lucas with hugs and back slapping and a lot of language inappropriate for the surroundings.

'You've made it at last, you old bastard! About bloody

time! And who's this lovely woman you've brought with you?'

'This is Perdita. She co-starred with me on the TV programme. This is Bruce.'

Bruce grinned. 'Actually, it's Anthony, but they call me Bruce because I come from Australia. Names always get changed in kitchens. It's lovely to meet you, Perdita.'

'And you, Anthony.' Perdita stopped worrying about her faded cotton dress and gave him a warm smile.

Bruce, or Anthony, took this as an invitation. He embraced her warmly, ending with several firm kisses on the cheek and one on the lips.

'Put her down, Bruce, she's spoken for.'

By this time, two other couples had arrived, and the small reception area was filling up.

'Pity,' said Bruce, 'I suppose I'd better find you guys a table. Follow me.'

'Well, he seems like a nice man,' said Perdita, twinkling and feeling girlish for the first time in months.

'He's married. Or doesn't that put you off?'

'Oh, it puts me right off, Lucas. Is he going to bring us some menus?'

'I doubt it. I expect he'll bring us some aperitifs and some canapés, and then whatever they've got that's best. Bruce and I used to cook together years ago, but he got fed up with the hours, and decided he'd rather run a restaurant than cook in one. I wonder who he's got cooking for him?'

'You mean, I won't get to choose what I eat? Supposing they give me something disgusting, like sweetbreads, or brains?'

'You must learn to educate your palate. After all, you might become a cooking celebrity.'

'Might I? Why? It was just a pilot.'

'Wait until you see the programme. They're seriously considering doing a series, with us both.'

'I shall demand a huge increase in salary, then.'

'But you'd do it?'

'Oh, I'll do anything for money.' She laughed, knowing he would think she was joking, and realising how serious she was. If she had to buy her poly-tunnel land, she'd need every penny she could get. 'Ah, here come the drinks.'

Chapter Nineteen

Although certainly not a gourmet, and not usually very interested in food, Perdita thoroughly enjoyed herself. Eating with Lucas brought out her wickedest streak, a streak she'd almost forgotten she had.

Lucas had been right when he'd told her the L'Escargot people would just bring what they thought were their best dishes. After the tiny squares of Welsh rarebit which came with their pre-dinner drinks, they moved to the table. Once seated and draped in enormous scarlet napkins, their gin and tonic glasses were whisked away and the feast began.

Perdita never thought she'd manage to eat it all. Starting with hand-dived scallops and finishing with an assiette of puddings, there were about seven courses in all. They were all tiny, beautifully presented, and in Perdita's opinion, with the exception of the salad which she pronounced unimaginative, it was all delicious.

Bruce brought each dish to Lucas, and stood over him while he tasted it. Lucas chewed each first mouthful with the concentration of a man who was reading something it was imperative that he understood and remembered. Bruce stopped his wisecracking until he had received the verdict. After he had worked out what all the ingredients were, and decided if they were good combinations or not, Lucas was surprisingly generous with his praise. Perdita had expected him to be critical for the sake of it, but while he didn't hold back if he felt something would have gone better with something else, on the whole he was very appreciative.

After the first time, when Bruce had gone away, smiling broadly, Perdita said, 'I'm surprised you were so polite about that. I thought you'd be really picky. You're so bloody fussy in your own kitchen, and dead snooty on the cookery programme if they suggested anything you didn't like.'

'Because I have high standards, it doesn't mean I don't appreciate other people's good cooking when I come across it.'

'Glad to hear it. Although personally, I think these scallops are a bit chewy.'

He narrowed his eyes over his wine glass. 'Oh really? Well, don't tell the chef, he'd be heartbroken.'

She chuckled, enjoying herself more and more. Bruce joined them whenever he could and his presence took away any awkwardness Perdita could have felt about being alone with Lucas. Their relationship was so strange nowadays. They weren't quite 'just friends', although 'friends' most nearly described their relationship, and they certainly weren't anything else.

For tonight, Perdita put all such complications, all other concerns, aside. Both men flirted with her shamelessly, making her feel witty and attractive, she enjoyed the food, and the attractive surroundings. She forgot all about the many responsibilities she had left behind her. Just for tonight she could be young and frivolous, and carefree. She ate langoustines, truffles, and home-made pasta, chocolate fondant, pistachio parfait and glazed passion fruit tart, and a whole lot of other things.

While they were toying with the cheese, finishing up the last of a very good red wine, Lucas pronounced himself impressed with the meal.

'All in all it was very good, although I thought the veal was a little overwhelmed by the tomato vinaigrette.'

As Bruce was momentarily absent, Perdita felt free to protest. 'Veal! You didn't make me eat veal! I'm morally opposed to it!'

'Don't worry. I know Bruce gets all his meat from a farm which guarantees everything is humanely reared. If more people ate kind veal, there'd be no need to export the calves to places where they keep them in the dark and feed them nothing but milk.'

'Oh.' Perdita had, by this time, had rather a lot to drink. Each course had been accompanied by a different wine, and as Lucas was driving, he only took one critical, crunching, swilling sip from each one. She had happily consumed a full glass each time. Now she gathered up a few biscuit crumbs with her finger, suddenly melancholy, aware that her freedom from responsibility was nearly over. 'It was so kind of you to bring me, Lucas. I've had a lovely time.'

'Kind! Not at all. I wanted you to come.'

Perdita shook her head. 'Let me tell you how it was. You said to Kitty, "It's my evening off. I'm thinking of visiting the restaurant of an old friend of mine in the Cotswolds." She said, "Do take Perdita. All she gets to see nowadays is the sick room and those damn polythene tunnels of hers." '

She watched him closely. She didn't resent him for taking her out, out of kindness; she had enjoyed herself, and his company, but she wanted to know the truth.

'Nearly right. I said to Kitty that I had the evening off and had a good mind to take you to visit the restaurant belonging to an old friend of mine, in the Cotswolds, and did she think you'd come, or would you be too tired?'

'And what did she say?'

'She said you'd probably jump at the chance because anything would be better than eating fish in sauce in front of the television again. Needless to say, I was flattered.'

Perdita laughed. 'I don't know whether or not to believe you, but thank you anyway.'

'Why shouldn't you believe me? Why wouldn't I want to take an attractive woman with me to see an old friend? It does me credit.'

'After the telly programme is out, you won't need the likes of me. You'll have women after you in droves.'

'Then I'll beat them off with a big stick. I don't want women after me in droves.'

'Of course you do. All men do.'

He shook his head. 'No. Some of us just want a lifetime of commitment with the right woman.'

The sudden seriousness of his tone unsettled her. She took refuge in sarcasm. 'Oh, really?'

'Yes, really. People do change, you know. Years pass, stuff happens, people want different things.' He looked at her intently and frowned. 'Don't look so anxious. I'm not about to make any embarrassing declarations.'

'I'm not looking anxious,' she lied. 'I've just got indigestion. I've had more to eat this evening than in the last fortnight put together.' This was probably true.

'I know you never eat. That was one of the reasons I wanted you to come. Here, Bruce!' When Bruce came over he said, 'Perdita needs a *digestif*. Do you have any mint tea? Or just some mint you could make it with?'

'Too much to eat, eh?' said Bruce. 'Well, a spot of mint tea, followed by a crème de menthe, should sort that out. Go on through to the lounge and I'll bring coffee for Lucky Lucas, and some mint tea for you.'

'Lucky Lucas, eh? Why does he call you that?'

'It's a long story. Come on through to the lounge. You've got home-made petits fours to eat now.'

'I couldn't!'

'You must.'

With the tea and coffee came a young man in checked trousers and a tomato-spattered chef's jacket. 'Thought you'd like to meet the lad,' said Bruce. 'This is Oliver, Olly, so we call him Stan.'

'Of course you do,' said Perdita. 'But whatever your name is, that was the most fantastic meal I've ever eaten in the whole of my whole life.'

Stan flushed and stuttered. Lucas murmured that Perdita had had rather a lot to drink.

Bruce raised his eyebrows. 'Lucky Lucas lost his touch, then. He was a mean chef when I knew him.'

'He's still a mean chef,' said Perdita quickly, resenting Lucas's comment about how much she'd had to drink. 'I haven't eaten at Grantly House since he's been there.'

'No,' said Lucas, 'but you've worked in the kitchen. Word of advice – however stuck you are for staff, don't let Perdita into your kitchen. She throws things.'

'All the best chefs throw things,' said Bruce. 'Isn't that right, Lucky?'

'So, why do you call him Lucky?' Perdita asked. Bruce might tell her what Lucas wouldn't.

Bruce shot Lucas a glance. 'Haven't you told her? He once threw a cleaver at the kitchen door, just as someone came in. They weren't killed, but they bloody nearly might have been. He didn't even get the sack. He's been called Lucky ever since.'

'Enough of this reminiscing,' said Lucas. 'Stan, that really was a very good meal. If ever you can't stand working for Bruce any longer, or want a slightly bigger operation, let me know.'

'Steal my staff, would you? Bastard,' said Bruce good-naturedly. 'Now, do you want a liqueur, on the house? Or Perdita could stay here and talk to Stan while he chills out, and I'll give Luke a guided tour.'

Perdita sat with Stan while he drank his coffee. As he had made them, and wanted her opinion of each one, she had to try the petits fours. She nibbled home-made fudge and drank mint tea while Stan told her of his hopes and dreams.

'Of course, I want a star of my own. This place has got its star, but they'll test it again while I'm cooking to make sure the standard hasn't slipped.'

'Lucas was tested quite recently.'

'Oh, he'll get a star, no problem. Bruce tells me he's one of the best. If he'd gone into it as a boy, he'd be very famous by now.'

'The television programme will probably make him famous.'

Stan looked doubtful. 'I'm not sure about all these television chefs. Sometimes they forget how to cook for themselves, and you can lose your star, you know. If they think you're spending too much time being a celebrity, and the food isn't of the standard, they'll take it away.'

'Lucas said something of the sort.'

'But I'm sure he'd never let that happen. From what Kangaroo Kate tells me . . . Bruce?'

'Oh, you mean, Anthony?'

Stan nodded. 'Lucas is very good. He'll be after his second star the moment he's got his first.'

Perdita laughed. 'I expect you're right there. He's very ambitious.'

'So, how did you get to know him? It's hard for chefs to have a social life, unless they get together with someone they work with. The hours are so long, and not many women can take staying in on their own almost every evening.' He said this with feeling.

'I can see it would be hard, but Lucas and I met years and years ago, before he was a chef, and – well, we're not going out together or anything. We're just friends. We don't see each other that much.'

'I didn't think you looked like the sort of woman to go to clubs, which is where I meet my girlfriends.'

'You go clubbing after a night in the kitchen? You must be very fit.' She had been shattered after her one experience, although that might not just have been tiredness.

'Oh, I'm fit. You have to be, or you couldn't do the work.' He grinned at her, his teeth very white in the stubble which was emerging from his chin.

Perdita was just coming to the conclusion that there was definitely something about chefs when Bruce and Lucas came back.

'Just as well Lucas doesn't want to take me clubbing,' said Perdita. 'I'd never have the stamina.'

Lucas's look of horror earned him a beatific smile.

Perdita slept all the way home. When she got out of the car, and they were both standing by the gate, she forgot it was Lucas, forgot all the many complicated strands of their relationship, gave him a hug and kissed him on the cheek.

'Thank you, that was absolutely wonderful. I had a brilliant time.'

Although his arms came round her, he didn't hold on when she pulled away. 'So did I, Perdita.'

He sounded wistful, as if he had been dismissed.

'You don't want coffee, or anything? I mean, it's two o'clock in the morning.'

'No. I don't want anything, Perdita. Just you go in and try to sleep well for what's left of the night.'

She tiptoed in to check on Kitty and found her awake.

'Not waiting up for me, I hope?' said Perdita.

'Of course not. You're old enough to stay out as long as you like. I just want a bedpan.'

While she was dealing with Kitty, Perdita realised that her skin felt warmer than usual.

'Do you feel all right?' Perdita hoped she'd get her head bitten off, and be told off for fussing.

'No, I'm fine,' said Kitty, unconvincingly.

'Let's take your temperature.'

Kitty made token grumbling noises while Perdita searched for the thermometer, but she didn't protest when Perdita stuck it under her tongue.

'Now, while it cooks, I'll tell you about this evening. The

277

food was superb! I think I could get into this gourmet life style.' She chatted on, fetching the bedpan, lifting Kitty onto it and afterwards straightening the bed and plumping up the pillows. When she came to look at it, the thermometer told her she was right, Kitty's temperature was up.

'OK,' she told Kitty. 'I can either wake Beverley, who'll know if I can safely give you a couple of paracetamol with all the stuff you have to take anyway, or I can just pop you a couple of pills, and see how you are in the morning. What do you think?'

Perdita was extremely tired, but that wasn't the reason she didn't want to wake Beverley. Beverley would probably want to call the doctor, which would upset Kitty dreadfully. She didn't like the doctor being called during ordinary hours, and the thought of him being rung in the middle of the night would horrify her, and convince her that she had but moments left on earth.

'Beverley will want the doctor, and I'm not having him disturbed in the night, poor man. Just give me the pills. I'm sure I'll be fine in the morning. And you must be exhausted.'

'Do you want me to stay with you?'

'Of course not! I've got the bell. I'll ring if I need you. I'll be fine now I've been to the lav.'

Perdita was woken by Beverley banging on her door. It had taken her a little time to drop off after seeing to Kitty, and so was in the depths of sleep at seven o'clock, an hour later than she usually woke up.

'I think it's time you were up, dear,' called Beverley. 'I've made tea. It's downstairs. Mrs Anson isn't well, I'm afraid. The doctor's on his way.'

Perdita was overcome with guilt. If she'd woken Beverley, or even called the doctor herself, Kitty's chest infection might not have got so bad. If she hadn't gone out she would have been aware of Kitty becoming ill during the evening, and the antibiotics could have been started immediately. The chest infection might not have got a hold.

Dr Edwards spent precious minutes reassuring Perdita that Kitty was probably perfectly well at bedtime, and only developed the infection later.

'Beverley's very efficient. If she'd been aware that Kitty was ill at bedtime, she would have called me.'

'I suppose so, but I came back at two o'clock in the morning. I knew she was ill and I just gave her a couple of paracetamol. If I'd called you, or even woken Beverley, the antibiotics could have been started much sooner.'

'Not much sooner, and you getting her temp down so quickly was a very good thing. Now, I'll pop in after surgery to see how she's getting on. Don't worry about it more than you can help, and for God's sake don't feel guilty about going out for an evening. You have to have some time off, Perdita, or you'll get ill yourself.'

Perdita worked hard on suppressing the guilt, but she knew her low spirits were partly because she'd had such a good time. 'I'm like a child who got overexcited at a party,' she muttered, as she cleared a bed ready for autumn sowings. 'Now I'm having the tears before bedtime. Only it's after, and there hasn't been enough sleep in between.'

She rang Lucas. 'Hi, it's me. Thank you so much for last night. It was brilliant.'

'Thank you.'

'But I'm afraid Kitty's got a chest infection.'

'Oh, I am sorry. Is she going to be all right?'

'The doctor says so. But I thought I'd let you know in case you were going to call this afternoon. She won't be up to seeing you for long.'

'I'll pop over anyway. I've got some news for her.'

'Oh? What?'

279

'We've got a date for the transmission of the telly programme. A couple of weeks from now.'

'Really? I thought we'd have to wait ages and ages.'

'We would, normally, but we were the last programme in a series of one-offs, and they turned us around really fast.'

'I can't wait to see it. Or can I? It might be desperately embarrassing.'

'Not a bit of it. You'll look lovely, I assure you.'

Kitty's chest infection got better, but she didn't seem to improve with it. Her appetite disappeared and she had to be tempted into eating every mouthful. And having stayed in bed for a few days, she no longer railed against it, and seemed reluctant to make the effort to get up. She woke more often in the night – so often that Perdita made up a bed on the floor in Kitty's room, to save having to drag herself awake and almost fall downstairs. If she was in the room with Kitty, the whole matter could be dealt with much more quickly.

Going to the bathroom in the wheelchair seemed more effort than Kitty was prepared to go to, and more often than not, she had a bed-bath. Perdita and the doctor discussed her prognosis.

'You're not going to be able to manage with her like this for long, Perdita. You're going to have to think about either employing more nurses – and I mean nurses, not just carers – or a home.'

'It'll have to be nurses. I won't let her go into a home.'

'It'll cost an absolute fortune. I assume Kitty does have some money, but home care, day and night, could run into thousands.'

Should she voice her concerns about Roger to the doctor? She sighed. There wasn't anything he could do about it. 'Not if she doesn't live very long.'

'There's no reason why she shouldn't go on for months,

280

even years like this. You, on the other hand, can't. Not when you've got your business to run.'

She opened her mouth to say that the business could go hang, but didn't. Some of her customers – Ronnie and Lucas – would probably come back to her if she took time off while Kitty was so ill. But what about the others? They'd find other suppliers, do without the more specialist salads she provided, and she'd be less financially viable than ever.

'I don't know what to do. I wish I had someone I could ask.'

'What about your parents?'

'My parents don't understand Kitty. My mother would have her in a home before you could say Jack Robinson, and I don't think I could cope with them coming over here, looking into Kitty's affairs, and then insisting we sell all her furniture to raise money.' She looked at the doctor. 'Of course, I'd sell anything to keep Kitty going – it's not that I'm overly attached to her possessions – but my parents, my mother particularly, does tend to rush in.'

'Kitty wouldn't mind if you looked at her papers. You could ask her solicitor.'

'So I could.' That might be the answer. If she knew what was in Kitty's will, she could prepare herself.

'Did you ever arrange enduring power of attorney, like I suggested?'

'No.' She sighed. 'I know it's silly, but at the moment Kitty still has all her wits. I don't want to treat her like a dependent relative, incapable of making her own decisions.'

'That's very admirable, Perdita, and I'm sure Kitty appreciates your discretion, but Kitty could have another stroke tomorrow, be unable to speak, or write, or communicate in any way. What are you going to do then?'

'Whatever I have to, I suppose.'

'You won't be able to access her money, you know.

You'd have to go to the Court of Protection for permission. She could be a millionaire, and have to moulder away in a mental hospital for months, before you could get permission to put her somewhere more comfortable. Or, you could put her in a good home and pay for it yourself. Do you have lots of money?'

'No.'

'Then sort out the enduring power of attorney. I'm sorry to be so harsh, Perdita, especially at a time like this, but really, you have to face facts.'

Perdita did get as far as finding out who Kitty's solicitor was but he was on holiday. As she didn't want to speak to anyone else about Kitty's affairs, it still wasn't organised before the television programme was broadcast.

The morning it was due to be shown, Roger rang. He wanted to check what time the programme was so he could see it with Kitty. When Perdita got the message she bit back a cry of rage and frustration and sighed instead. There was no point in wishing she and Kitty could just watch the programme on their own because they couldn't. Not amount of hysterics would alter that.

Thomas was the carer at the time, which was somewhat of a relief. If Roger's attentions went too far and she had to scream, Thomas could probably man-handle Roger if it came to it. Beverley had done two weeks, and although she was pure gold, and an excellent nurse, she got on Perdita's nerves, rather. Perdita suspected she got on Kitty's too, but Kitty wouldn't confess it. At one time they would have shared a few catty moments of, 'if she says "upsy-daisy" again, I'll scream!' But Kitty complained less the iller she became. She was sinking into herself, perfectly lucid, polite and charming to her visitors, yet somehow, diminished.

But the thought of seeing the television programme she had heard so much about cheered her immensely. She greeted Roger quite warmly, told him where to sit, and then turned to Thomas. 'Be a kind man and go and look in the cellar and root about for some champagne. We drank some of it when the film crew came, but there should be some left. Put a couple of bottles in the freezer, we'll have them while we watch the show.'

Perdita saw Roger dispatched to the wrong end of an uncomfortable settee and wondered if it was just coincidence that Kitty had consigned him to a seat in a draught, or if she had her own doubts about her long-lost nephew.

They all sat together in Kitty's room, Kitty's bed and the television arranged so everyone could see. Thomas distributed glasses of champagne and packets of crisps, and they settled back to watch.

First of all came some of the sort of classical music which Perdita loved, and music buffs despised, then the credits, and finally, a long shot of Perdita's cottage. It looked more fairy tale than ever, and she could see why they had been determined to use it. Even she, who knew about the damp patches, felt it was a little gem.

Then up came the titles: *A Gourmet and a Gardener*.

'I had no idea they were going to call it that,' said Perdita. 'How embarrassing!'

'Shush, dear. Have some more champagne.'

Kitty was sitting up in bed, concentrating hard, more attentive than she had been for a long time. Thomas was clutching a can of lager, preferring that to champagne. Roger, perched uncomfortably on the edge of his seat, didn't comment. Perdita decided to stop being embarrassed, and just enjoy the show.

It was magical. Her house, full of collectables which didn't belong to her, shone with a gloss it had never had in real life. Her kitchen looked compact and bijou, rather than cramped and overcrowded. And Lucas looked sensational.

When Perdita had told him that he'd have to beat women off with a stick, she hadn't realised how photogenic he would turn out to be. He not only looked extremely handsome, but charming, too. His smouldering bad temper was punctuated with dazzling smiles. No wonder all the female crew had idolised him.

Lucas gave a short spiel about what he was going to cook, and then Perdita watched herself come in through her own back door – except it wasn't herself, or her back door, it was this dreamy, girl-woman, and her back door was the entrance to a quaint old cottage, bursting with character and charm. How did they know it was all going to look so wonderful on television? How did they make it look so wonderful?

'I look quite pretty, don't I?' she said, sipping champagne, staring at the screen.

But it was when they started to speak to each other that the show really took off. They sparkled and sparred, responding to each other's off-hand remarks, throwing out challenges. And the food looked just as wonderful. Everything he cooked, or appeared to cook, shone with the same brilliance. Her vegetables were fresh and pretty and appetising.

'Wow,' said Thomas, when the show was over. 'I think you girls should have another glass of champagne.'

'It was marvellous, darling. You look so beautiful and Lucas looks so handsome. You really are a lovely couple.'

'Yes, they are, or were,' said Roger, producing something from his pocket. 'Look what I found.' He laughed. 'I wonder if I could sell it to the tabloids and make my fortune.'

His laugh implied he was joking, but he gave Perdita a leer which told her he wasn't.

'What have you got there, dear?' asked Kitty innocently.

'It's a picture of Perdita and Lucas, outside a register office – proof that they were once married. It might cause

quite a scandal if I let that cat out of the bag, mightn't it?'
Again he laughed, but this time it didn't look as if he was
joking.

Thomas said nothing. Perdita tensed. She no longer
cared who knew about her marriage – it was an irrele-
vance – but she didn't want Kitty to be exposed to a lot of
unpleasantness, which if Roger got in touch with the
papers, she would be.

'Show me,' demanded Kitty.

Roger handed over the picture. 'Mmm,' Kitty said
thoughtfully. 'You were a pretty girl then, but much
better-looking now. Thank you, Roger, I enjoyed seeing
that again. Where did you find the picture?'

Roger was a little thrown by this reaction. He'd
expected a scene and hadn't had one. 'Oh, in the attic, in a
box marked "Perdita".'

'And what made you want to go up to the attic? Did you
have business there?'

'Perhaps he went up to look at the sunset,' suggested
Perdita, a little drily.

'That was it. I met Perdita on the same errand.' He
smirked at her, implying an assignation. 'And I found
some other interesting things too.' He plucked the
photograph from off the bed and tucked it back into his
wallet.

Perdita, who was watching his every move, noticed, as
he dealt with the photograph, a business card with the
name of Kitty's solicitors on it.

He saw her spot it and gave her a glance which
encouraged her to think the worst.

'Now, Roger, dear,' said Kitty, still in that same calm,
nannyish tone, 'I think you'd better go now. I'm really
quite tired. Thomas, would you be so kind as to show
Roger out?'

When they were alone Kitty said, 'That side of the
family were always frightfully common.'

Perdita drew breath to tell Kitty that being common wasn't their only fault, but then she saw that Kitty had fallen asleep.

Chapter Twenty

Something told Perdita that Kitty was dead even before she opened her eyes. She had not got Perdita up in the night at all, and unlike with many of the dying, Kitty's breathing had not become laboured. But it might have been the silence which woke Perdita. She wriggled out of her sleeping bag to check the time. It was a quarter past five in the morning.

When she saw Kitty she was quite sure. Although she felt for a pulse, and then fetched a hand mirror to make sure that no breath was coming from between Kitty's lips, it was unnecessary. Kitty just wasn't there any more.

Perdita waited to cry, to feel a rush of tragic emotion, but none came. She felt perfectly calm, and relieved for Kitty. From her point of view, being totally dead was better than being mostly dead, full of drips and tubes and medicine which would keep her alive, but not well, for another few weeks. Perdita and Kitty had discussed this, if not often, enough times for Perdita to be sure of her feelings.

It was also wonderful that she'd been spared the transfer to a home, and all that that entailed. If Kitty had been less unwell, there would have been a lot about a home which she would have enjoyed – grumbling about the other residents, rebelling against the staff and dis-obeying the rules would have delighted her. But latterly, she had been too ill for rebellion and petty gossip.

It was lovely that Kitty had seen the television pro-gramme. She had thoroughly enjoyed watching Perdita and Lucas setting sparks off each other, noticing every time the show had been cut to avoid offending the viewers with violence and bad language.

And now she was dead.

Perdita sat on the chair where she had sat to feed Kitty, to read to her, to gossip with her, and silently, to pray for her. Now she wanted to enjoy these moments of quiet before the rest of the world discovered that Kitty had died.

Perdita had been dreading Kitty dying, both consciously and subconsciously, for years. Now it had happened and she was alone in the world. She had her parents, of course, and they would support her and be kind to her, provided she was willing to go and live in whatever part of the world they finally settled, but Kitty had always been *here*, constant, static, reliable. This was where Perdita's life was. She wouldn't move away – unless the land she used for Bonyhayes Salads was taken from her.

Still perfectly calm, Perdita wondered which aspect of Kitty she would miss most: the supportive sage, advisor and comforter, or the witty, interesting friend. Instantly, she decided it was her friendship that would leave the biggest gap. Now Kitty was actually dead, Perdita would probably become fully adult and independent. But who could she share jokes with, make cutting little remarks to, remarks she would be ashamed to let anyone else hear? Now she would have to depend on books for gardening advice, and do without knowing the scandals caused by the great-grandparents of the latest It girl. None of it was important, really, but it was the sort of detail which added colour to life.

Lucas came into her mind, probably put there by Kitty, whose spirit seemed to hover around, trying not to interfere, but doing it anyway. That was an area where Perdita was bound to disappoint Kitty. Her romantic old heart, heavily disguised by a crust of cynicism, had wanted them to put aside their differences, fall in love and get married. That would be nice for Lucas, whom Kitty loved and respected, because he had a fine mind and had been very kind to her, Kitty. And it would solve the problem about who was to look after Perdita now that Kitty was gone. Not, she would no doubt hasten to add, that Perdita needed anyone to look after her precisely, but everyone needed someone to keep them warm in bed at night. But Lucas had broken Perdita's heart once, and once was enough, thank you very much.

It was true that Lucas was infinitely warmer and more cuddly than her lettuces, but in the same way that a tiger was – by being a hot-blooded mammal – furry in places. But Kitty wouldn't want Perdita driving to Longleat and flinging her arms round the neck of the nearest half-ton of fur and fang, and to Perdita, loving Lucas was just as potentially fatal.

Besides, Lucas had spent most of his spare time in the house looking after Kitty. Now she was gone, he would turn his attention back to his restaurant, his Michelin Star, and possibly, a television series, with another, more biddable, co-star.

Perdita found herself smiling wryly, longing to point out the irony of the situation to Kitty. Lucas had hated Kitty when he and Perdita were married, calling her 'that old witch'. And Kitty had hated Lucas when he had behaved so appallingly to Perdita, and in the years since had referred to him in a manner which was even less complimentary. But they had come to love each other, and he would miss Kitty nearly as much as she would herself.

She wondered if she should warn him about the photograph that Roger hinted he would sell to the tabloids but decided against it. It was probably just an empty threat, Lucas was quite big enough to look after himself if he got doorstepped – in fact, he'd probably enjoy the ruckus.

Perdita sat with Kitty until six o'clock, when Thomas

289

came in. 'Morning,' he said in a low voice. 'How's the patient? Oh.' He, too, saw the absence of life. He looked anxiously at Perdita, who felt oddly detached and calm, faintly irritated with Kitty for not being there to share the moment, but otherwise tranquil. 'I'll make us a cuppa. Have you been up long?'

Perdita shook her head. She didn't feel in the least like crying but she didn't trust her voice. Thomas, to her enormous gratitude, seemed to understand. 'Back in a tick.'

Perdita sighed. She would have to ring her parents, and they would come flying back, her mother trying hard to take over. She felt ambivalent about both parents. It would be nice to have someone to comfort her, to call her 'darling', and 'my little Perdi-werdi' for about five minutes. Then they would fill the house with funeral etiquette, they would panic about the amount of books and furniture to sort out, and try to get Perdita to call in a house-clearance firm, all before poor Kitty was buried.

Should she tell them about Roger, too, and how the house-clearance might yet turn out to be his responsibility? Her mother would be overcome with remorse; she was bound to feel responsible for losing her daughter what might be a massive inheritance. Perdita shuddered, knowing she couldn't face her mother's self-recriminations, not now.

It's not, she told herself, nearly out loud to make it more convincing, that I don't love Mum and Dad, because I do, very dearly. But this had been Kitty's space, and her own, and she didn't want them moving in on it, tidying Kitty's personality away.

She should try to arrange to visit them for a holiday, after everything was sorted out, so she could let herself be spoilt and bullied and generally looked after. But getting away would be no easier now than before. She still had a business to run, plants to tend and harvest and sell.

When her parents came, she would have to combine her usual role of dependent and dippy daughter with that of businesswoman, head of the household and decision maker. The split required in her personality would probably be as stressful for them as for her. Perhaps she should just abandon her daughter role, and carry on here as usual.

And then there was Lucas. She'd never persuade Lucas, even if she dared to ask him, to behave as if he was not an intimate of the household. When her mother saw this was the case, she would descend into paroxysms of maternal anxiety.

Luckily for Lucas, Perdita's mother was unlikely to say anything to him about the unsuitability of his presence, but Perdita would not be spared. Lecture on lecture would be muttered out of the corner of her mouth while they counted teacups and bemoaned the fact that half the saucers didn't match.

For a moment, Perdita contemplated having the funeral tea at the local pub. They'd put on a 'good spread' and it would save so much upheaval. But she knew she couldn't. Kitty was such a sociable person and her house was so important to her. It would have to be held here, where she had enjoyed giving parties, in the summer, when the guests could spill out of the French windows into the garden.

The funeral feast would have to be lavish and delicious, and probably, now it was September, and the weather less reliable, would have to take place in the drawing room, which would have to look like a drawing room, and not like the bedroom of an invalid. Perdita looked about her, seeing the room as a room for the first time in ages. There were signs of Kitty's illness everywhere. There was the lift for getting her in and out of bed, there were the grab rails on the wall, there was the hospital bed itself, high, narrow and efficient, top and bottom easily raised or lowered.

There was no way she could block up the door through to the shower room, replace the alcove and all Kitty's china collection. But she and Thomas could shift the furniture, perhaps put a china cupboard in front of the door, and make it look like a room Kitty would be proud of. She hadn't liked her drawing room becoming 'a side ward', as she had said scathingly. They could bring back the blue sofa, and make the room beautiful again.

Lucas drifted into Perdita's thoughts again. She remembered that cold spring afternoon when she'd been searching the neighbourhood for someone to help with Kitty. Lucas had appeared. She closed her eyes. She had known then that life would never be the same again. Kitty's death was another watershed, one which would be far more definitive, one which would affect her life for ever.

Lucas still in her mind, it occurred to her to ask him to arrange the food for the funeral. He would understand the need for celebratory canapés, elegant little *bouchées* along with more substantial quiches and samosas, things for those who'd travelled far to pay their last respects to Kitty. She'd ask him to do that, she could pay the hotel, and she would be spared endless discussions with her mother about the suitability of serving champagne at a funeral, or whether smoked salmon was really necessary. She'd let her mother make a fruit cake. She was very good at those, and it would give her something to do.

Perdita got up and stretched. She seemed to have been sitting a long time. She went to the window, looking out across the lawn, newly cut by Thomas, and dew-spangled. The garden looked lovely, although Perdita always felt a little sad when summer began to turn to autumn. She never quite knew why this should be; as she always told Kitty, it wasn't as if she minded winter. It was just the turn of the year which made her melancholy, while summer optimistically clung on as if perhaps this year the swallows wouldn't desert, the leaves wouldn't turn, and the roses would flower all winter. The tiny purple and white cyclamen, which Kitty and Perdita both loved, were a sign that summer was over. The first appearance of the little mauve and white lanterns always caused Perdita's heart to sink a little.

Thomas came in with tea and shortbread biscuits. Kitty always had a shortbread with her early morning tea and it seemed right that Thomas and Perdita should have them now.

'You'll have to start ringing people. The doctor, and then your parents.' He was quite firm about this, as if he knew she would have preferred to get the arrangements underway before telling them. 'If they're halfway across the world, it'll take them a few days to get here. You will have got it all sorted before they arrive.'

She nodded. 'I'll make a list.'

'And Roger. Otherwise he'll turn up as usual. Talk about an ambulance chaser!'

'He didn't bother Kitty, did he? He didn't make her last days miserable?'

Thomas shook his head. 'Oh no. She made him read Anthony Trollope to her. Tiny print, lines really close together. She used to doze off.' He chuckled. 'I felt quite sorry for him, struggling with the long words.'

Perdita chuckled gently. 'OK, I'll ring him.' She shook her head as she reached for a pad and pen from Kitty's bedside table. 'Now, who else should I write down? Doctor, undertaker, newspapers for an announcement—'

'Lucas,' he interrupted firmly. 'You must tell Lucas immediately. He loved Kitty. You can't let him hear it from anyone else.'

Perdita sighed. 'You're right.' She reached for the bedside phone. 'I'll ring him now.'

Thomas raised an eyebrow. 'Or you could wait until eight o'clock. There's no point in waking him with the news. Unless you want him to rush round and comfort you immediately.' He paused. 'He will come round, you know.'

'I'd lost track of time. I thought it was later. I don't need him to comfort me.'

On the dot of eight, Perdita rang Lucas. She didn't need to say anything. The moment he heard her voice he knew what had happened. 'Are you all right? I'll be there as soon as I've got some clothes on.'

Still Perdita couldn't cry.

By the time Lucas got there, the doctor and the undertaker had been telephoned. While it had seemed macabre at the time, Perdita was now grateful that one of Kitty's friends, recently widowed, had recommended an undertaker. 'You don't want to be going through the Yellow Pages at a time like that,' she had said. 'Believe me, I know. But they were very good and efficient and – sensitive.'

Lucas stood on the back doorstep, with his arms half opened, ready to receive a sobbing Perdita. Only Perdita wasn't sobbing, didn't want to start, and felt that being hugged might release a lot of emotion she didn't have time to indulge in.

'Hello, Lucas. Do you want to see her? Or would you rather not?'

'No, I'd like to, otherwise I'll never believe it's really happened. Come with me.'

Together they stood and looked at the woman they had both loved and both cared for.

'You know,' said Perdita, 'of all the things I admired her for, and there were a lot of them, one of the things I thought was bravest was having her hair cut. She hadn't changed her hairstyle for about seventy years. To do it when she did was so brave, and positive.'

'It suits her,' said Lucas.

'She wants – wanted – you to have her books, you know.

As many of them as you have room for, at least. She didn't want to burden you with them.'

'Of course I don't have room for many, but there are some I'd treasure. Is it in her will?'

Perdita shook her head. 'I shouldn't think so. I don't know what's in her will, to be honest.' She frowned.

'But surely, she'll leave everything to you, won't she?'

'Not according to Roger. He was very intent on getting her to leave it all to him, as a blood relative, you understand.'

'Bastard!' he whispered. 'But surely you'd have known if she'd changed it?'

Perdita shrugged. 'He was here a lot, and I was out a lot. I wouldn't necessarily know about it.'

'And you never asked Kitty?'

'No. The moment was never right, and by the time it was, she'd gone to sleep. That was last night.'

'I see.'

'I don't care about Kitty's money, although I do care a little about this house; it was home for such a long time. But what really bothers me is that Roger knows that Kitty never gave me my land officially. I just use it, but I'm pretty sure she won't have had the deeds altered, or anything.'

'And he'd take that land away from you?'

'With the utmost pleasure. He'd put houses on it.'

Lucas bit his lip, struggling to keep back his anger. 'Jesus, Peri, I wish you'd told me about this before, when I could have done something about it!'

'I probably would have told you sooner or later, but I didn't expect her to die so soon.'

He put his hand on her shoulder. 'No. We none of us did. Her death was expected, but still a shock. Is the doctor coming to do the death certificate?'

'Before morning surgery. The undertaker's coming later.'

'Are you going to leave her here for a bit?'

'I don't know. What do you think?'

Lucas looked at Kitty, lying with her mouth slightly ajar, her new haircut bent out of shape, her eyes closed. 'I think it's up to you. But somehow I don't think Kitty would like people looking at her when she's not at her best. You could get out lots of photographs of when she was alive and well, instead.'

'That's what I'll do. I'll let the undertakers take her away, and get out photos. There are some lovely ones. She was very photogenic, though she'd never admit it.' She sighed. 'I'll go and find a clean nightie for her.'

'They will provide a robe, you know.'

Perdita shook her head. 'No, that would be wasteful. She would want a clean, but old nightdress, one that's not quite fit for dusters, but that hasn't much more life in it.' She almost smiled. Lucas almost smiled back.

Perdita sent Lucas away when the doctor and the undertaker had been. Like the doctor, the undertaker had looked at her dry eyes suspiciously. Perdita, painfully aware that she was not behaving as expected, hoped she didn't appear hard-hearted. She said as much to Thomas.

'I know I should cry, I know people must think I don't care, that I'm glad Kitty's gone so I don't have to look after her, or because I'm supposed to inherit her money. But I just can't.'

'No one who's known you for more than five seconds could think you were hard-hearted, love. You just do what you feel you need to, and don't worry about what people think. Have you rung your parents?'

The corner of Perdita's mouth lifted. 'I don't feel I need to do that.'

'If I ring them, they'll think you've lost it. They don't know me – imagine how they'd feel hearing a rough old cockney voice telling them that Kitty's dead. They'll worry themselves sick that you've got involved with a bad boy.'

Perdita smiled. 'Again.'

Thomas chuckled. 'That was a bit of a surprise, although, in a way it wasn't. You seem to suit each other.'

Perdita shuddered. 'Not really, it was a dreadful marriage.' She changed the subject. 'Thomas, would you be willing to stay on? Just until after the funeral? I know you're being paid to look after Kitty, but could you look after me too? I'll never get the house organised on my own.'

'I wouldn't leave you now, Perdita, love. As long as you don't think Lucas will mind us being alone in the house together.'

Perdita frowned. 'Lucas? What on earth has he got to do with it? I'll ring Roger and get that over, and then I'll call my parents.'

Roger was very nauseatingly sentimental about it, referring to Kitty's 'passing over', and then he mentioned the funeral. 'Just a few sandwiches and cups of tea for anyone who comes back to the house, but I don't think we should encourage it. After all, it is a bit of a mess, and most of Aunt Kitty's close chums will be dead already. No point in spending money unnecessarily.'

Perdita drew a deep breath. 'Roger, I don't care if Kitty's left you every penny in her will, but she is going to have the sort of funeral I know she would have wanted. You may be her closest relative but I was her friend for nearly twenty years. If you think we're going to fob people off with tea and sandwiches, you don't know me or Kitty very well. The very idea would have her turning in her grave before she's even in it!'

Elated by this outburst, she felt more than able to handle her mother.

Perdita's mother was very good on the phone. She checked that Perdita was all right, was glad she wasn't sobbing hysterically, and said she and Perdita's father would be over within three days. 'Will you be OK on your own until then?'

'Oh, yes. I've got Thomas, the carer. I thought he might as well stay and help me get ready for the funeral next Thursday. We won't get a rebate on him now.'

'No, of course not. But what about Roger? Couldn't he do all that?'

'He's got a bad back,' Perdita lied. 'And he's a bit – well, you know, gropey. Thomas is a mate and strong as a horse.'

'Well, I'm sure you know best,' she said, meaning just the opposite.

'I do. Thomas is brilliant and we've got lots of furniture to move before the funeral.'

'Now, Perdita, dear, you must be sensible about the furniture. I'm sure none of it's as valuable as Kitty thought. Just get a house-clearance man in and get him to give you a good price.'

Should she break it to her mother about Roger now? No, it was a long-distance phone call and not worth the uproar the news would cause. 'It's OK, Mum. When the time comes to sort out the house, I will be sensible. But Kitty's only just died. I won't be getting in the removers for a while yet.' Although Roger had mentioned skips, he'd probably insist on trying to sell every last jam jar and plastic flowerpot.

'There's no point in being sentimental about things. It's people who matter.'

'I know you're right. And I will be sensible. But not just now.'

'Oh, darling, how tactless of me. Now you go and have a good cry, and I'll ring you tonight to tell you our arrangements.'

Perdita didn't have a good cry, she dashed across to her poly-tunnels and did some work. She sorted out the deliveries, and when William arrived, told him about Kitty.

'Of course, it is sad, but it would have been sadder if

she'd lingered too much longer. Her quality of life was going every day. It's a relief, really.'

William nodded. His relief was at the fact that Perdita wasn't sobbing and he didn't have to feel obliged to comfort her. He was very fond of Perdita, and putting his arms round her wouldn't have been a hardship, precisely, but he was too young to handle a weeping woman he couldn't take to bed.

'I will have to depend on you rather a lot, I'm afraid, as I will be a bit frantic until after the funeral, but you've been so great already. I think you actually like making deliveries.'

William nodded. 'It's all right when you get used to it. Janey always checks the order for Lucas now, and Ronnie's OK when you get to know him.'

'I'd be grateful if you'd go to Ronnie first today, and tell him about Kitty. He'll want to know, but I'm a bit tired of telling people over the phone.'

'He'll be sad. She was much loved, your – Kitty.'

Perdita nodded. 'She was. Now, I must get on. Is Janey in the kitchen, or has she gone?'

'No, she's there. She'll make you a nice cup of tea.'

Perdita reflected that no one offered to make anyone a nasty cup of tea, although other people's tea frequently was.

She shared breakfast with Janey, but got away as quickly as she could. While she was working, Perdita could forget that Kitty had died, and all that that entailed. But she couldn't stop thinking about Kitty as a person: Kitty when Perdita had first met her; Kitty in the garden, pipe between her teeth, muttering curses on the aphids; Kitty with a glass of whisky in her hand, looking at the sunset, a smudge of earth on her cheek. Kitty reading intently, pencil in hand, annotating the books in her old-fashioned, slightly untidy writing. That was the real Kitty. The sick, invalid Kitty had died, and left these vibrant memories behind.

Perdita's positive attitude lasted until she went back to Kitty's house. Thomas had cooked her lunch.

'You're taking your duties as my carer too seriously,' she said, seeing the sausages, mashed potato, peas and green beans set out on a plate for her. 'I don't need to be cooked for, you know.'

'Yes you do. If I didn't cook for you, I'd have Lucas after me. He's always saying you don't eat enough, which is why he sends meals over. Now, get that down you. Will you have a glass of red wine with it?'

'At lunchtime? Thomas, what a suggestion!'

'It's what Mrs A would have wanted. You know she would.'

'You're right, of course, but I still won't have it. I must think about the funeral service. I want it to be really Kitty-ish. I don't want the dearly beloved gathering round to mourn a sweet old lady. Kitty was so much more than that.'

'Have you arranged to see the vicar?'

Perdita nodded. 'I'm a bit nervous about it. Kitty wasn't religious in a conventional way. And although she did used to open the garden for church fêtes, that was before this vicar's time. He's popping over at tea-time.' She looked at her watch. 'Which means I must finish this and be off.'

Thomas tutted. 'You eat your lunch. You'll do yourself no good gulping it down. You'll get a hiatus hernia, and you don't want that at your age.'

'I'm sure I don't want that at any age,' she said with her mouth full.

'I did meet Mrs Anson,' said the vicar, who was young, untidy, and asked Perdita to call him John. 'It was at a coffee morning in the village. She was wonderful – absolutely charming.'

'Her beliefs weren't exactly conventional, I'm afraid.'

'Don't be afraid. We had a long talk about her beliefs,

and I must say I enjoyed the conversation, even if she did challenge me on rather a lot of my best points.'

Perdita chuckled. 'I hope she didn't offend you. She thought about spiritual matters a lot, but her ideas didn't really fit in with the good old C of E.'

'No, but they were near enough for me to be able to bury her without too many qualms. She's got a plot, you say?'

'Yes. When her husband died she bought a doubler, as she put it. I could show you it, if you like.'

He shook his head. 'Not necessary, I can look it up. Now, have you thought about hymns, music, readings, stuff like that? You may have talked about it with her.'

'I did try, but she didn't really want to think about it. I think she felt that funerals were for those left behind, and it was up to them to decide what they wanted.' She sighed. 'It's a pity, really. It would have saved me so much trouble.'

'Would you like to read something? Or say something? You could write a bit about her life, tell those who only knew her as old what she did when she was younger. I bet it was interesting.'

'It was, of course, and I wouldn't mind writing something, but there's no way I could read it out loud in church. I'd sob hysterically, and Kitty would be so disappointed. She'd say – she would have said – that it would have been better to get someone else to read it.'

'That's OK. Get someone else to read it.'

'But who? Would you do it?'

'Of course, but it would be better if someone else did, someone who knew her well. Why don't we talk about music, and perhaps you'll think of someone, or someone will volunteer?'

'I must say, you are making this as painless as possible, but I'm not sure . . .' Then she brightened. 'She was very fond of "I know that my redeemer liveth".'

'Very appropriate. Did she have a favourite recording you'd like to use? Or, if you like, there's a member of the choir with a lovely soprano voice, who did the *Messiah* with another choir last year. I'm sure she'd be thrilled to do it.'

'That would be lovely. I'm not keen on recorded music in church. What about hymns? Let's not have, "Eternal Father . . ."'

The vicar left Perdita with the task of writing an essay on Kitty, and worse, of finding someone to read it. Should she find someone of Kitty's generation to do it? Or should she ask Lucas, who would be audible in church, would be unlikely to break down in tears, and of whom Kitty was very, very fond?

'I don't suppose you'd do it, Thomas?' she asked him at supper.

He shook his head. 'Ask Lucas. He's the obvious choice.'

'I know, but he's doing the food. I don't want to pile too much on him.'

'He'll be supervising the food, love, not making each vol-au-vent by hand. I'm sure he'll be well chuffed to be asked.'

Perdita shook her head. 'I'll think about it.' She took a sip of the wine which Thomas insisted she drank. 'I think I'll move out of Kitty's room now, and into somewhere smaller. Then we could put a couple in her room. We're bound to have to put lots of people up.'

'Would you put your parents in there?'

The thought of her parents in among Kitty's plethora of books, chests of drawers and unusable dressing-table sets almost made her laugh. There was not a square inch spare in any of the many drawers, and her mother liked to unpack. 'No. I thought I'd put them in my house.'

'But aren't Janey and William living there?'

'Oh my God! I'd completely forgotten! And I can't face having my parents here.'

'Well, don't worry. Give Janey a ring and tell her. I'm sure it won't be a problem for them to move back home for a week or so.'

'Do you think so? It seems a bit mean, somehow.'

'You're not charging them rent, are you? Give them a ring.'

Janey was just as understanding as Thomas said she would be. 'Of *course* I understand, Perdita! And I'll make sure we leave the place absolutely gleaming. No condom wrappers on the floor, or anything.'

Perdita was chuckling as she put the phone down.

'Janey promises she'll leave everything tidy, but I will go and check.'

'You could just let your parents cope with things as they are,' said Thomas. 'If they're always going on these adventure holidays, living in tents, they should be able to cope with a bit of dust.'

Perdita shook her head. 'If I don't appear to be in control of everything, my mother will just take over.'

Thomas frowned. 'Well, in her absence, I'll tell you it's time for bed. I'll clear up. No arguing. You're paying for a carer, just be cared for! OK?'

Chapter Twenty-one

Perdita felt impossibly tired. She fell into Kitty's bed upstairs, in spite of her intention to make herself a space somewhere else. She could do that tomorrow. Tomorrow she could sort out how many beds she could provide, for how many people. Now, she just needed to sleep.

She fell asleep the moment she put out the light, and woke again four hours later. She lay, listening to the World Service until six, when she got up, left a note to Thomas, and went to her poly-tunnels.

Over the next few days, Perdita divided her life into two halves. In the early mornings, when she woke, she went to work, switching on the fluorescent tube and the anglepoise lamp and staying among her seed trays, sacks of compost, and jars of seed until nine. When she'd sorted out the day's deliveries for William, she went back to the house and organised furniture, telephoned people, received condolences and burrowed in the airing cupboard, searching for sheets and pillowcases and duvet covers.

Between them, she and Thomas cleared Kitty's mahogany kitchen table for the first time in years. Off came the seed catalogues, the newspapers, the correspondence, the shopping lists, the gardening hints cut out of magazines and newspapers, and the obituaries and death notices of her friends and acquaintances. Most of it Thomas threw away.

'Keep it clear at least until after the funeral,' said Thomas, lovingly rubbing the table with polish. 'We'll need somewhere to give people meals.'

Perdita nodded. 'Kitty's cleaner will be delighted. She's been polishing it in sections for years, and Kitty always just put the junk back on it. Now it can be admired properly.'

'So, don't open the post anywhere near it,' said Thomas firmly, 'otherwise the junk mail will just creep back.'

Perdita went to Kitty's desk, found her address book and her Christmas card list and looked at them. There were a lot of names. Starting with people she actually knew, she rang the Ledham-Golds first.

Whoever answered the phone, either Mrs Ledham-Gold or her sister was silent for a moment or two, and then swallowed.

'Well, I am sorry. It's hard to believe that anyone with so much strength of character and vitality could die, but I suppose she was very old.'

'Eighty-seven. And her vitality had faded a lot lately.'

There was another silence, and then the almost audible indication of someone 'pulling themselves together'. 'So, how are you coping, Perdita, dear?'

'All right. I'm very busy, of course. I expect it'll hit me when the funeral is over.'

'Yes. One is sort of borne up by busyness at first. I remember that when my dear husband died.'

It must be the sister, then, thought Perdita, after a moment's panic that somehow Mr Ledham-Gold had died, and she hadn't known about it.

'But Kitty wouldn't have wanted to go on if she was bedridden. We talked about death, you know, when she was here at Christmas, and the only thing she minded about dying was leaving you. She worried about you, you know. Didn't want you to be alone for the rest of your life. Highly unlikely, or course, pretty girl like you.'

'Mmm.' It was difficult to answer this without sounding conceited.

'There's nothing we can do to help you, is there? One of the worst jobs is telling people.'

'I know. It's people who aren't in the address book, but that I don't know knew her I'm worrying about.'

'You're putting notices in the papers?'

'Of course, but not everyone reads them.'

'And people hate not knowing. So you're going to ring everyone up?'

'Or write. I haven't got telephone numbers for everyone.'

'It'll take you for ever. I dare say Kitty's been saying that everyone's dropping off the perch for years, but you'll be surprised how many people are left. All those old friends had children, after all.'

Perdita wondered where this was leading to.

'Why don't you pop the address book in the post, and let us go through it? We'll know lots of the people, after all.'

'And I might have to explain who I am to some of them,' agreed Perdita, her heart lightening at this generous offer.

'Exactly. You must have so much to do. Let us take this chore off your hands.'

'Well, that's really kind. I'll post the stuff to you, or deliver it, or something.'

'Excellent. Now, what about flowers?'

Perdita hadn't thought about it until now, but she knew immediately. 'Home-grown flowers only, please. Kitty would have hated people wasting their money on shop-bought flowers, and she'd die if anyone gave her a wreath. Oh. Sorry.'

'Don't worry, my dear, these sort of puns come out all the time. You mustn't worry about them. So, home-grown flowers only.'

'Yes, nothing formal or expensive.'

'Fine. It'll be sad making up a bouquet for dear Kitty now she's dead, but you know, the thought of her as a bedridden vegetable is even more sad.'

In the end Thomas volunteered to take the address book

and the Christmas card list over to the Ledham-Golds.

'It'll be a nice little run out for me,' he said. 'And give you a chance to have a good cry on your own.'

'I've got a million things to do, Thomas. If I want to cry, I'll have to do it while I work.'

On Friday evening, the day before her parents were due to arrive, Perdita went across to her own house to sort out her bedroom for them. In spite of Thomas telling her it was fine to leave it to Janey, she had to make sure for herself that everything was in order. It would be the first time she'd been upstairs in her own home since Kitty's death.

Her kitchen, which she'd been using to soak and sort her pea plants, and for all the chores which required water, looked empty and strange. Janey had removed all traces of her and William's domestic bliss.

The sitting room was also unnaturally empty, and she dumped her armful of clean bed linen on the back of a chair. She was rummaging in the cupboard under the stairs for a duster and some polish when the back door opened. She jumped as Lucas appeared.

'Sorry, did I give you a fright?'

'Yes you did! What on earth are you doing here?'

He didn't answer immediately. 'I just came to pick up my sleeping bag.'

It seemed insufficient excuse. 'Is that all? You don't need it, do you?'

'Not really. Actually I came to make sure Janey and William had left the place reasonably tidy. Janey told me your parents were going to stay here.'

Perdita relaxed. 'How kind. I was on the same errand.'

'I was coming to see you afterwards. How are you?'

Perdita was becoming accustomed to this question. It was always followed by the sort of peering look which at normal times would be considered rude. 'I'm fine. I just wanted to put clean sheets on the bed and stuff. Janey said she'd do it, but I have only one set of things, so I brought some things from Kitty's.'

'How do you usually manage?'

'Oh, I choose a fine day and wash them and dry them and put them straight back on the bed.' She made a face. 'Don't tell my mother; she'd be horrified.'

'Don't worry, I don't expect she'll ask me. I never was her favourite person, was I?'

'You're still not.'

He was silent for a moment. 'Do you want a hand with the bed?'

'Probably.' Oddly, Perdita was in no hurry to rush upstairs and prepare her room for her parents. She knew when they came Kitty's death would become much more real. And they would never be able to accept that Lucas was now a friend and ally, not a wicked adventurer. She and Lucas had worked hard to get over their old relationship, and to develop a different one; having to explain how much had changed to her parents would be depressing. She didn't want to hear their recriminations, to be reminded of the pain he had put her through.

She sighed and picked up the bedding. 'Come on. It might be a dreadful mess up there.' She bit her lip. 'I never checked it before you had it. Was it OK?'

'I don't know. I never went upstairs. I just slept down here, on a camping mat. I thought you'd have known that.'

'You must have been dreadfully uncomfortable! Why didn't you stay at Grantly Manor?'

'Because I'd already told them I didn't want a room, then there was nothing left for me. But I was fine, really.'

'And I never even knew. I'm sorry. I've been so preoccupied lately.'

He smiled ruefully, biting his lip. 'There was me, going to so much trouble to be sensitive, not to intrude on your space, and you didn't even notice.'

She smiled back. 'And there was me, making such a fuss

when Kitty offered you this house, and I wasn't even aware of you being here.'

There was a moment's silence. All their quarrels suddenly seemed childish. I expect I've joined the grown-ups now, she thought. 'Come on. Let's get this done.'

Before Kitty's death, she would have felt awkward, going into her bedroom with Lucas. Now she felt perfectly matter of fact about him catching the opposite side of the sheet and lowering it onto the bed.

'Lucas, I wonder if I could ask you a favour?'

'Anything. I'm yours to command, Perdita.'

She smiled. 'No, you're not. I know I've asked you about the food—'

'Yes, and it's all in hand. What else do you want me for?'

'This is for Kitty, really.'

'What is?'

'The vicar suggested I wrote about her, so that people who didn't know her when she was young would know something of her. I couldn't possibly read it myself. I was wondering if you would.'

'Shouldn't you ask someone like your father?'

Perdita shook her head as she stuffed a pillow into a clean case. 'He and Kitty never really got on. I think it should be someone who knew her well, and who loved her.' There was a tiny pause. 'Also, someone who Kitty loved.'

Lucas didn't answer immediately. He pulled off the duvet cover and started to put on the new one.

'You're making a complete horlicks of that, Lucas.'

'I know.'

'Shall I do it?'

'No. I don't want to be defeated.'

She watched him struggle. It wasn't the end of the world if he didn't read what she wrote, when she finally wrote it. The doctor would probably do it, if she asked him, but she really wanted Lucas. 'So, will you read that thing about Kitty, or not?'

Lucas emerged from inside the cover of the duvet. 'If you want me to.'

'I said, it's not for me, it's for Kitty.'

'But do you want me to read it, Perdita?'

There was a moment's silence in which something intangible and unspecific hung. Perdita wanted to tell him that yes, she did want him to. But for the first time she felt her throat clog with tears and she couldn't speak. Instead, she nodded, and put her hand on his wrist. 'Mmm.'

He put his hand on top of hers but still hesitated. 'Then I'm flattered to be asked. After all, although Kitty was fond of me, I don't expect I'm your favourite person any more than I am your parents'.'

Perdita cleared her throat. 'Oh, I expect you are. In a way. Now tuck in your side of the sheet, and I'll sort out towels. And I'll have to empty at least one drawer. My mother thinks it's slutty to live out of suitcases, which is weird, considering how much travelling they do.'

Later, when Lucas had walked her back through the garden, and shared a nightcap with her and Thomas in the kitchen, Perdita wondered if Lucas had noticed what she'd said about him being her favourite person. She hadn't meant to say anything like that. With luck, he'd put it down to Kitty's death, and not think too much about it.

She snuggled down into her bed and tried to sleep. Hot milk and whisky had become a habit since Kitty had died, but tonight they didn't work. She began to fret. Why had she said that to Lucas? It wasn't even true! Oh, she'd acknowledged she wanted his body. What red-blooded, sexually deprived female wouldn't? Especially when she knew perfectly well what that body could do in conjunction with hers. But her favourite person? Kitty was her favourite person, and her being dead didn't stop that. But was Lucas favourite in a different way?

Finding these thoughts were waking her up rather than sending her to sleep, Perdita concentrated on trying to remember the words of the hymns she had chosen on Kitty's behalf. And when she'd done that, she started mentally writing Lucas's speech.

Perdita was a little light-headed when her parents arrived at lunchtime the following day. After her usual chores, she'd spent the morning emptying drawers in her bedroom for her mother and pushing her horticultural activities to one end of the kitchen so her parents would have room to make themselves breakfast. When she'd done that, she'd made a start on the speech. She was still working on the second sentence when she heard their taxi arrive.

She rushed out to greet them.

'*Darling!*'

Her mother's familiar-smelling kiss nearly undid Perdita. She hugged her hard, clinging in a way she hadn't clung since boarding school days.

'Are you all right? You look exhausted! And what have you done to your hair? It suits you.'

Her father hugged her just as hard. 'How's my brave girl?'

'Not very brave at the moment, but coping. Come into the kitchen and meet Thomas. I don't suppose you've had lunch.'

'Only a stale baguette on the train down,' said her father.

'Then come on through and see what Thomas has got for us. I'll organise a drink.'

On the table was a whole poached salmon, potato salad, green salad, and a salad of fine green beans and salted almonds.

'Oh, Thomas!' said Perdita, who'd been expecting bread and cheese, and with luck, soup. 'You've excelled yourself.'

'No I haven't. Lucas sent this over.'

'Lucas!' said her parents, practically in unison.

Perdita debated for a second if she should have warned Thomas not to mention Lucas in front of her parents, but it might have been awkward for him.

'He's been wonderful since Kitty died,' said Perdita.

'He was pretty wonderful when she was alive,' said Thomas. 'Reading to her, sitting with her during my time off, taking her to the lav and everything.'

Lucas assisting an old lady to the lavatory was hard to imagine, even for Perdita, who'd seen it happen. Her parents visibly struggled with the idea and regarded her accusingly.

'Didn't I mention how good he'd been?' she said. 'Well, never mind. He's been fab. And this is Thomas, Thomas Hallam, just as fab but not as awkward. Thomas, my parents, Mr and Mrs Dylan.'

'How do?' said Thomas. 'Now, wine everybody? Or there's sherry? Unless anyone wants anything stronger?'

Perdita's mother looked a little askance at the paid help making free with Kitty's drinks cupboard, but when her husband said, 'I must say, I could murder a gin and tonic,' she agreed that so could she.

'I'll do it,' said Perdita. 'Thomas showed me how to make them like they do at sea.'

'I'll just go up and wash my hands,' said Perdita's mother. 'Come up and talk to me when you've mixed the drinks.'

Knowing her mother wanted to disapprove of Thomas and Lucas *in absentia,* Perdita took her time sorting out ice and lemon, and found her father some cashew nuts to keep him going until he'd be allowed at the salmon.

'Well, this is very nice,' said her father, settled on the sofa in the sitting room. 'Tell your mother not to be too long. I'm hungry.'

Perdita had brought drinks up for them both when she

joined her mother in Kitty's bedroom. Her mother was crouched in front of the dressing table, trying to see her reflection in the mirror.

'Here you are, Mum. This'll make you feel better.' She took a fortifying sip of her drink which was strong, even by Thomas's standards. 'By the way, I thought you and Daddy would be happier in my house. It's going to be a bit chaotic here, as we'll have to offer beds to the other two carers, at least, possibly the Ledham-Golds, and I'm not sure who else. You'll have a bit of peace and quiet over there.'

'I think it would be much better if you had the peace and quiet, and we were on the spot to organise things. You really don't have to have everyone to stay, you know. People don't expect it.'

Another sip of gin and tonic and Perdita said, 'No, I really need to be on hand to keep an eye on things. There's a lot to organise.'

Felicity Dylan sat on the bed and took a sip of her drink. She raised her eyebrows as the gin hit her, and peered at Perdita. 'But, darling, we've come to do all that.'

Perdita shook her head. 'It's lovely of you, really, but I've started this, and it's easier for me to finish it. And don't get too comfortable up here. Daddy says he's starving.'

'He can't be. Besides, I must have a few words with you alone. How are you? I suppose you've closed down the business for a bit? People will understand.'

'Oh, no. I can't do that. I get up early and sort it out for the day, and go over again in the evening if I've got the chance.'

'No wonder you're looking so exhausted.' She opened her mouth to say something else, but changed her mind. 'Tell me about Thomas. He seems quite one of the family.'

'Oh, he is,' said Perdita firmly. 'He was with me when

313

Kitty died and is staying on as long as I feel I need him. Probably just till after the funeral.'

'And you're paying him?'

'Of course! He cancelled one of his regular clients for me. He's great. He cooks all the meals, answers the telephone and has helped me move all the furniture back as it was. Come and see.' She stood up, hoping her mother would do the same.

'Just one minute, darling. What about Kitty's nephew, Roger? Is he coming to the funeral?'

Perdita gripped her glass. 'I've no idea. I can't stop him, I suppose, but he certainly won't be particularly welcome.'

'Why on earth not? He seemed perfectly pleasant on the phone.'

Perdita couldn't take any more of Roger's so-called pleasantness. 'Oh, he's pleasant, all right, it's just that he's after Kitty's money and property, including the bit I've got my tunnels on.'

It was a moment before Perdita's mother took in what her daughter had said. 'Oh my God! Oh, darling! What have I done? I never would have found him if I'd known.'

'It's all right, Mummy! There's no need to panic! We don't know he's got Kitty to change her will, and if he has, well, it's too late to worry about it now.'

'We could contest the will – do something!'

'Only when we know what the will says. Until then, I'd really rather not talk about it.'

Perdita's mother took some time to be persuaded that this was the best course, but eventually she said, 'Very well, darling. If that's the way you feel, but I must say I wouldn't have thought—'

'Mum, please!'

'OK, tell me about Lucas. I mean, I know you did the television thing together – and I do hope you videoed it – but it must have been awkward for you, to have him insinuate himself into the household, bringing meals and things.' She frowned. 'Looking after Kitty.'

Perdita shut her eyes briefly, trying not to let the gin reveal her anger. 'Lucas does not insinuate,' she said tensely. 'He loved Kitty. He used to read to her, and talk about books to her, books that I've never got round to reading. When she was in hospital he made special meals for her, so she wouldn't have to eat hospital food. He did the same when we had carers who couldn't cook. He's been so supportive, and brilliant.'

Perdita's mother regarded her daughter, a little startled. 'He must have changed an awful lot since I last saw him, then.'

Perdita was suddenly aghast at her outburst. 'I'm sorry. I was forgetting that you hadn't seen him since—'

'Your wedding.'

'And he has changed. A lot, really. I didn't notice at first, because superficially he's just the same. Bad-tempered and difficult. But underneath that, he's kindness itself. At least, he was to Kitty.'

'And what about you?'

She sighed, and drank some more gin. 'He's been pretty kind to me too.'

Her mother's mouth crinkled with anxiety. 'Darling, he's not – you know . . .' She struggled for the right words. 'Coming on to you, is he?'

Perdita laughed. 'Don't worry. I've no intention in getting involved with him again. He's just been a kind friend, that's all.' Realising she'd been a little economical with the truth, she finished her drink.

Felicity Dylan delicately rubbed the corner of her mouth with a fingertip. 'You've grown up such a lot since I last saw you, darling.'

'I'm sure I have. Death is a very growing-up experience. And I needed to grow up.'

Her mother got to her feet and patted her daughter's hand. 'You've turned into a woman, all of a sudden.'

'About time too, Mum! I'm nearly thirty! And I'm sorry if I seemed a bit snappy. I am a bit preoccupied with everything.'

'Don't worry about it, darling, and don't forget, we're here now.' She hesitated. 'We'll help you with anything you want.'

Perdita kissed her mother's cheek. 'Thank you for being so understanding.'

'I can be, you know,' said her mother. 'Now, let's go down before your father's low blood sugar makes him bad-tempered.'

After lunch, for which Perdita insisted Thomas sat and joined them, she took her parents over to her cottage to settle in and have a little lie-down. She wandered back to Kitty's house, aware that she was swaying a bit.

'I must have had too much to drink. Those G and Ts were a bit strong.'

Thomas took a quick look at her, removed the crystal glass she was drying from her hand and sent her upstairs for a nap, ignoring her protests that she couldn't possibly sleep. 'Just go up and listen to *The Archers* with your eyes shut. When it's over, you can come down again. Here, I'll make you a hot-water bottle.'

As she was hustled up the stairs, bottle under her arm, she realised why Thomas made such a good carer. He could tell what was wrong with people better than they could themselves.

When she came down again, it was tea-time, and her parents were in the sitting room. Sitting with them was Lucas.

'Oh. Hi, everyone,' said Perdita, scanning faces for signs of disharmony. 'Sorry, I've been asleep.'

Lucas, who had got up, came over to her. 'We can tell: you're hair's sticking up at the back.' He smoothed it down for her.

316

'I'd better go and brush it,' said Perdita, wanting a chance to interpret this tender gesture, and to ask Thomas if everyone was getting on OK, or had she walked into a scene of battle. Reluctantly, Lucas allowed her to leave, and she fled to the kitchen.

'What's Lucas doing here?' she demanded from Thomas. 'And are they getting on?'

'I think so,' said Thomas, who'd found cups with matching saucers and was putting them on a tray. 'Why shouldn't they?'

Perdita exhaled loudly. 'They didn't like him while we were married, and hated him afterwards. I did tell you Lucas and I were once married? They think he's the arch enemy, and to be fair to them, so did I until I got to know him again.'

'I see. Did he hit you, or anything?'

'No. He just ran off with an older woman.'

He closed his hand round a cup and it broke into pieces. 'Perdita! I'm so sorry! Whatever made me do that?'

'I don't know. But don't worry about it. We've got plenty more cups.'

'Not of that particular tea set.'

'I still don't mind. Don't cry over anything that can't cry over you.' Suddenly Perdita was reminded that she hadn't yet managed to cry over Kitty. Perhaps she never would, perhaps she had used up all her tears crying at processions, the Deaths column in the newspaper, and vet programmes on television.

'So you don't think you and Lucas will get back together again?'

'No. We separated on very bad terms. We couldn't possibly get together again.' It was only later she noticed that for the first time, she hadn't put all the blame on Lucas.

'But he so obviously—'

'Who does what obviously?' asked Lucas, who

317

wandered into the kitchen. 'Where's the tea? I can't go on making polite conversation any longer.'

'Never mind, I'm sure my parents will have been impressed by just a couple of minutes,' said Perdita.

'It's been twenty at least, and you still haven't brushed your hair.'

Perdita made a face. 'Take the tray, and I'll go and do it. Are you joining us, Thomas?'

'Not likely. I'm going to get this larder sorted before your mother finds the tins of bully beef, left over from the war.'

Perdita stopped on her way to the cloakroom. 'Not really? Oh, you're joking.'

Chapter Twenty-two

'I just came over to check the details of the food,' said Lucas. He handed Perdita a menu. 'Is there anything else you think we should have?'

'Looks fine to me.' Perdita passed the menu to her mother, who produced her reading glasses from her bag and examined the card.

Perdita's mother frowned. 'It seems very lavish for a funeral. What's wrong with sandwiches and fruitcake?'

'One of your fruitcakes would be nice,' said Perdita, 'if you had time to make one. But Kitty was always very sniffy about the food at funerals. She said she wanted proper party food. But substantial, so people don't have to drive miles back home after only a couple of bits of soggy bread and butter wrapped round tinned asparagus.'

'I can hear her saying it,' said Perdita's father. 'I dare say you'll have to serve whisky, as well.'

'And champagne,' acknowledged Perdita. 'She didn't tell me much about what she wanted, but did want decent champagne and whisky.'

'And tea, I hope,' said her mother. 'With the funeral at two, people will be wanting tea, not alcohol.'

'We're having tea, too. Thomas and I have sorted out dozens of cups and saucers. Kitty used to get them from jumble sales to use when she opened the garden to the public.'

'What about the flowers? Have you got a decent florist around here?'

'Well,' Perdita braced herself. 'I put "Home-grown

319

flowers only" in the announcement, because that was another thing Kitty felt strongly about – people spending money on things no one really gets to appreciate. I'm doing the flowers for the coffin, and the vicar's best church flower lady – can't remember her name just now – is going to do the ones in the church.'

'Darling, I don't want to be unkind, but the flowers are rather important. You don't want it to look amateurish.'

'Oh, I know,' said Perdita. 'But I'm still going to do them. Apparently flowers for a coffin cost about seventy-five pounds. Kitty would hate that.'

Perdita's mother sighed deeply and opened her mouth to protest some more.

'Well, I think that menu will be fine,' said Lucas, quickly, before she could. 'But a good home-made fruit-cake would just finish it off, for people who want something more traditional. Would you have time to make one, Mrs Dylan?'

Perdita's mother turned to him. 'Well of course, if you think it would go down well,' she said, 'I'd be only too happy.'

'That would be brilliant, Mum,' said Perdita. 'At school your fruitcakes were what kept me alive. The food was terrible.'

'Which explains your lack of interest in it today?' said Lucas.

'Probably,' said Perdita, whose mind had moved on. 'For fruitcake, Mum, does it matter if the fruit is a bit old? It's just that Kitty's had cupboards of it for years. Does it go off?'

A couple of pained seconds later, Lucas answered.

'I'll bring you round some dried fruit, Mrs Dylan. Perdita, give Kitty's old fruit to the birds. They'll appreciate it, and won't sue if it gives them food poisoning.'

'Thank you, Lucas,' said Perdita's mother, who hadn't

been able to stand Kitty's notions of economy when she was alive, and wasn't sure she could do so now she was dead.

'For someone who hated waste, Kitty was a dreadful stockpiler,' said Lucas.

Perdita's parents waited for their daughter to fly at Lucas for daring to criticise her beloved Kitty.

She didn't. 'It must have been something to do with the war. She always wanted to be able to feed an army if she had to.'

'I'd still be grateful if I didn't have to use ten-year-old fruit for my cake,' said Perdita's mother somewhat tensely.

Perdita still hadn't cried by the morning of the funeral. She got up at five to finish the flower arrangement for the coffin. When she finally came in from the old stable where she was doing the flowers, partly so they would be out of the way and cool, and partly so her mother wouldn't discover that Perdita had been using all Kitty's crumbling old oasis and bits of chicken wire as a base, she found her parents in the kitchen. They looked smart and businesslike in their funeral clothes.

'We thought we'd come over early to give you a hand,' said her mother. 'What are you going to wear?'

She said this with a defiant anxiety, prepared for battle if Perdita announced she would merely put on clean jeans for the occasion.

'There's a lovely old black dress of Kitty's,' said Perdita. 'I thought I'd wear that.'

'I know Kitty was keen on recycling,' said her mother, implying that Kitty was in fact just stingy, 'but don't you think that's taking economy too far? There's time for us to go into town together and buy something suitable. A nice suit, perhaps. Or a dress and jacket if you want something a little less formal.'

321

Perdita had known her mother wouldn't like her choice of clothes, and had prepared her argument. 'When would I ever wear a suit, or a dress and jacket again? Especially a black one?'

'It doesn't have to be black, darling, not these days. I'll pay for it, if it's money you're worrying about.'

Still Perdita shook her head. 'I couldn't possibly. I haven't time, apart from anything else. And I really want to wear this dress of Kitty's.' It wasn't only because she didn't want to spend a lot of money on something she'd never wear again, but because she wanted to have a bit of Kitty with her at her funeral. 'Come up and see.'

Her mother swished up the stairs behind Perdita, which reminded her that while she might persuade her mother to let her wear a recycled dress, her tights would have to be perfect, and she might even have to search among Kitty's things for a slip, not owning one herself.

The dress was on a hanger in a cupboard in one of the rooms she had prepared for guests. 'There it is. I've always liked it, but when I tried to get her to give it to me, she said I could wear it at her funeral if I liked, but otherwise it was too gothic for words. I think it looks rather good on me.'

Her mother sighed. 'Well, put it on, and let's have a look.'

'You wouldn't be very kind and see if Thomas is up? I'm longing for a cup of tea.'

Mrs Dylan bustled out saying that she would bring one up immediately, why hadn't she said earlier? While her mother was safely out of the room, Perdita quickly got undressed and put on the dress before she could see, and therefore comment on, the state of her underwear.

Her mother came up with a mug of tea, saw Perdita in the dress and said nothing. The dress was made of some extremely fine material and was lined with satin. It was high-waisted and fell in handkerchief points to just above Perdita's ankles. It had a boat neck and the sleeves were fitted until the elbow where they widened out into a trumpet shape.

'Darling, it is rather wonderful. I wonder when Kitty wore it,' she said at last.

'She wouldn't ever tell me, so I suspect she did something highly improper in it.' Perdita moved about in front of the mirror. 'That's partly why I want to wear it. I want a bit of Kitty's young and wicked past there, not just the little old lady.'

'It does look stunning, I must say. But is it suitable for a funeral?'

'Whyever shouldn't it be? It's black, smart and I'm sure it was wildly expensive.'

'Come downstairs and show your father. I still think a suit would be better.'

Her father was reading the paper. 'Edward, don't you think this dress is quite unsuitable for a funeral? I mean, Perdita does look heavenly in it, but don't you think it's a bit – well – over the top?'

Edward Dylan looked up. 'She looks sensational. In fact, I don't think I've seen her look so lovely since her wedding day.'

Perdita smiled. 'I'm obviously destined to look good only on tragic occasions.'

Perdita, hatless and chilly in her unaccustomed clothes, detached herself from the occasion by admiring the flowers. The church flower lady had done two huge arrangements, which seemed to incorporate whole trees and certainly included giant hemlock. They were unrestrained, impressive and just a little bit excessive, but as all the flowers were either wild, or grown in a garden, Kitty would have loved them. None of that mealy-mouthed subtlety for her.

Her own arrangement on the coffin gave Perdita a certain amount of satisfaction. Whatever artistic talent she might have once had was in those flowers. Even her mother had been impressed. 'You could always take up floral art if you get bored with vegetables,' she had said. Her *pièce de résistance* was the miniature cabbages on wires which looked like tiny green roses. Kitty would have said they were too young to die, and it was wasteful to put edible plants into arrangements which weren't going to get eaten. Well, too bad, Kitty, thought Perdita. If you feel that strongly about it, you shouldn't have gone and died.

When Lucas got up to speak, Perdita felt overcome with nerves. Not just for him, but because she had let him down dreadfully in the matter of writing what he was to say.

After struggling with the speech for ages, Perdita had finally given up. She just gave Lucas her many failed attempts, as many facts about Kitty's life as she could remember, and told him a few anecdotes. The rest was up to him.

In spite of such poor material it was a wonderful eulogy. He captured Kitty's rebellious spirit, her charm, her wit and her great wisdom. Much of it was from his own knowledge of her, Perdita realised, as he told stories which she had never heard.

He managed to recreate the spirit of Kitty, letting everyone know that she had achieved far more in life than just a great age. He even made people laugh, which pleased Perdita. She had wanted people to remember the fit, healthy and alive Kitty, and not think too much about the one who had died. She didn't think about it herself. She was aware that people were watching her, expecting her to cry. She found her father and Lucas, one on either side, as they walked out of the church to the churchyard. At least if I keel over backwards, I'll be caught, she thought. Then she spotted Roger, wearing a black arm-band as well as a black tie. Perdita had insisted the other men wore attractive, bright ties, that Kitty would have loved. How like Roger to be conventional, and in this case, wrong.

Still the tears wouldn't come. She seemed to have lost the mechanism. People will think I'm so hard, she thought. They'll think I don't care, that I'm glad she's dead so I can inherit her money. Perhaps I should borrow Dad's hanky, and blow my nose. But she couldn't pretend to cry, either. She did utter a sharp intake of breath when she spotted a wreath of acid yellow chrysanthemums. She peered at the card. It said, 'For my dear Aunt Kitty, with fond memories, from her loving nephew Roger.' The resulting shudder had a bracing effect – she knew perfectly well she'd told him Kitty didn't want wreaths.

Afterwards, at the house, she was a charming hostess. The sitting room, full of more flowers, (Perdita and the church flowers lady had got very matey and carried away), looked magnificent. Food, whisky and champagne did their magic, and soon everyone was talking hard. Perdita spotted Roger looking disapprovingly into his champagne glass, obviously wondering if he was going to have to pay for it. It made Perdita wish she'd asked Lucas to provide oysters and caviar, vintage champagne instead of ordinary, and malt whisky instead of blended. What a wasted opportunity to take her revenge on Roger!

It was lovely to see Beverley and Eileen and Thomas gassing away to each other. They were all staying the night, and Perdita knew she'd have plenty of help with the clearing up.

'Is Mrs Anson's solicitor here?' asked Beverley.

'I don't think so,' said Perdita. 'He wasn't a personal friend, or anything.'

Beverley frowned. 'Oh. It's just that he called on her while she was ill, I thought he must be. And Roger was asking if he was here.'

Perdita's heart dipped violently. 'He called on her while I wasn't here? Why didn't you tell me?'

'Oh, sorry.' Beverley was aghast. 'I just forgot to mention it. It was the day Ronnie came to cut our hair.'

Panic affected Perdita's memory. 'And was Roger staying with us at the time?'

'Oh, yes. He was with Mrs Anson while the solicitor was there. Did I do something wrong?'

Perdita forced a smile. 'No, of course not. Now, do eat up, everyone. Lucas has gone to so much trouble with the food.'

She moved away. There was no point in having a fit: what was done was done. Roger had either got Kitty to change her will or he hadn't. She would find out soon enough. She would have asked Roger then if she could have relied on him giving her an honest answer.

The Ledham-Gold trio spent a long time talking to Perdita's parents, looking at her so often that Perdita knew she was being talked about. The vicar and the doctor were obviously old friends and, between them, knew almost everyone. Lucas was putting himself out to be pleasant, and accepting a lot of compliments on the food and the television programme with equal grace. Roger smiled blandly at everyone, doing his devoted nephew impression, and Perdita wondered how many people he convinced.

Janey and William were there, so much a couple that Perdita wondered if they would have got together without her machinations, they were so clearly destined for each other.

But the person who seemed to Perdita to be having the most fun was Kitty. She could almost see her moving among the people, offering more drinks, more to eat, introducing her friends to each other. She's so nearly here, she thought. It's as if she's in the kitchen, or showing someone something in the garden, or finding a book to check a reference. She's only just *not* here. It's only just a trick of the light that I can't see her. Perhaps that's why I can't cry. I don't believe she's dead.

*

326

'Now, are you sure you'll be all right? I really think I should stay and help you sort out the house.' Her mother took her duties seriously, and if Perdita hadn't been telling her ever since she arrived for the funeral that she did not want to be looked after, she would never have left.

'Yes, Mum. I've got to get used to living on my own. Only I can sort out Kitty's things. You've had this—' Just then, she couldn't remember which exotic location her parents were off to, or what it should be described as. Safari? Walking tour? Expedition? – 'holiday booked for ages.'

'I'd never forgive myself if anything happened to you. What about that dreadful Roger?'

'I can deal with him, and what's going to happen to me here? You're far more likely to get kidnapped by terrorists. In fact, I think you should cancel and go to Skegness instead.'

This was supposed to be a joke, but her mother didn't see it. 'Do you want us to cancel and look after you?'

'No! Really! I want to get on and sort out my life. When it's all over and we – know how Kitty's left things, and got probate and everything, I'll come and have a long holiday with you. But for now, I must get on with it.' Whoever Kitty had left her money to, Perdita wasn't going to have her friend's personal possessions sorted by anyone but herself.

Her mother was still torn between duty and pleasure. 'I'm just a little bit worried about unsuitable men, darling. When one is vulnerable, one does fall in love with inappropriate people.'

'But not twice, Mummy! I'm hardly going to fall in love with Lucas again and if I did, he wouldn't with me. Besides, you said yourself he did a wonderful job with the funeral.'

Perdita's mother's face turned ashen. 'Who said anything about Lucas?'

Perdita realised she had made the most ghastly mistake. Horror caused beads of sweat to form in her hair as she fought to think of what she could say to put her mother's mind to rest, and stop her leaping to all the right conclusions.

'Only joking, Mummy. Really. Gosh, we fight more than we did before. Besides, he'd never look at me, not now he's the nation's heartthrob.'

Her mother, who had seen Lucas watching Perdita in Kitty's dress at the funeral, went away not at all reassured.

Getting Thomas to leave was harder because in some ways, in spite of her longing to be alone, Perdita would have liked him to stay. He was quietly supportive but not bossy. He was also worried about leaving Perdita.

'I just don't want you turning into a dotty old lady, never going out, never seeing anybody.'

'For goodness' sake! Because I looked like a character out of Dickens for the funeral, it doesn't mean I'm going to turn into one permanently. I'm fine, and I promise I won't get any dottier than I am already.'

Thomas was still doubtful. 'And there's that Roger. Always on the phone hassling you about getting things sorted . . .'

'I told him last time if he mentioned the house or its contents again, I'd burn it to the ground. I think I managed to convince him I'm loopy enough to do it. I don't think he'll bother me again.'

'Supposing he does?'

'If I get stuck without you, I promise I'll summon you back, as long as I can afford to pay you.' She raised a hand to silence his protest. 'You know you can't afford to work for nothing, and I know you lied to the agency about how long you stayed, telling them you went home the day after Kitty died.' She pressed an envelope of bank notes into his hand. 'I'm an heiress, I can afford it,' she said, although she knew that until Kitty's estate was settled, one way or the other, that she couldn't.

In spite of her promise to Thomas not to become dotty, Perdita did realise that she was not quite normal. For a start she found it quite impossible to ring the solicitors to find out what was in Kitty's will. She knew it was irrational, but she didn't feel she could face the possibility of having to lose her poly-tunnels. While she was in ignorance, she could cope.

She had boundless energy, she hardly slept, and when she wasn't working, she sorted Kitty's things.

She was in the attic reading through a file of newspaper cuttings when Lucas found her.

'What the hell are you doing up here?' he demanded.

'Sorting through Kitty's papers. And how did you get in?'

'Through the front door, like any self-respecting burglar. Haven't you heard of opportunist crime, or do you just think no one's going to break in because you're a woman on your own?' He was angry and, unusually, was trying to conceal it. 'I've brought you an answering machine. I'm fed up with you never being in when I ring you.'

'Oh, sorry. I should of course be waiting by the phone night and day in case you phone me. Why would you want to phone me, anyway?'

'To find out how you are! Hell and damnation, Perdita! You're recently bereaved, no one ever sees you, even William says you mostly just leave notes, and you wonder why I'm worried! Have you resigned your membership of the human race?'

'Of course not! I've just got a lot of sorting out to do. Kitty was a terribly hoarder.'

'I know. And she was constantly cutting bits out of newspapers to read again later. But you don't need to read them all too. Either keep them, or throw them away.'

'But I can't, they might be important.'

'You're in no fit state to decide that.'

'What do you mean? I can read, can't I?'

'Well, I suppose so, but Janey told me that William said you threw away all the good peas and sprouted the damaged ones the other day. And she also said that William is having to watch you like a hawk in case you pull up the good lettuce and try to sell the stuff that's bolted.'

'Oh. Well, perhaps I am a little tired. I probably just need a few early nights to sort me out.'

'What time do you go to bed now?'

'Oh, about midnight. Not that late, really.'

'But do you sleep?'

'Of course. You always sleep more than you think you do, anyway. When they test people who say they don't sleep well, they always find they've slept better than they said.'

Lucas scowled at her. 'You're protesting a bit too much, lady.' He removed a cobweb from her hair. 'I daren't ask when you last ate. You look awful, you've got shadows under your eyes, although that could be dust, and your clothes are hanging off you. And I don't know what Ronnie would say if he saw your hair.'

Perdita smiled weakly. 'I expect I can guess.'

'He's worried sick about you. He wants to book you in at the health farm, for a fortnight's rest cure.'

'And how does he think I'm going to pay for it?'

'He thinks you're an heiress. Everyone does. Janey, William, the whole village.'

She almost told him that the whole village might be horribly mistaken, and that far from being an heiress, she might have to sell her business; Bonyhayes Salads barely made a profit as it was now; without Kitty's land it wouldn't be viable. But she didn't want to voice her fears out loud. If she told Lucas, she could no longer live in that happy place called denial.

Instead, she said, 'And do *you* think I'm an heiress?'

'I have better things to do with my time than speculate on other people's money. And for your personal interest, I don't give a fuck if Kitty didn't leave you a red cent.'

'Oh.' This was strangely consoling.

'So come downstairs and have something to eat while I fix up the answerphone.'

Later, when she'd eaten the scrambled eggs that Lucas made her, she pondered on everyone's interest in her financial status. Her parents certainly shared it. She supposed it was natural, but as long as the land was hers, she felt very much as Lucas did: she didn't care if Kitty hadn't left her anything. But the thought of losing her livelihood was terrible.

The following week Perdita had had three messages from the surgery on her answerphone, the last one from Dr Edwards personally, before she finally rang back.

'It's Dr Edwards,' said the receptionist. 'He says he wants to see you. It's urgent.'

'Oh? I don't think that can be right. I haven't had any tests or anything. He can't be about to tell me I'm pregnant, or anything.'

The receptionist didn't respond to this light-hearted remark. 'He's very insistent. He said I wasn't to take no for an answer.'

She made an appointment, feeling bullied and complained about it to William.

'I think you should go, Perdita,' he said seriously. 'We've all been worried about you. Lucas especially.'

'Oh? What makes you say that?'

'He keeps nagging Janey about you, that's what.'

'If he's worried, he could come and see for himself that

331

I'm all right. He doesn't need to bother Janey about it.'

William gave her a rather odd look. She was used to odd looks – they were all she got these days, from the few people she saw – but this was a different kind of odd.

'I expect he's frightened of gossip.'

'Gossip! When has Lucas ever given a damn about what people say about him?'

William took on the expression of a messenger, about to be killed. 'Since they started saying that now you're an heiress, he's going to marry you and open his own restaurant with the money.'

'*What?*'

'Since the telly programme. People reckoned there was something going on between you, and that now that the old lady was dead, and everyone knew you were due to inherit millions, he was bound to marry you so he could open his own place.' William obviously gave this a small amount of credence himself.

How would people react if and when they discovered she was anything but an heiress? 'Oh God! I can't cope with all this nonsense as well as everything else.'

'Do you want me to run you to the doctor's then?'

Chapter Twenty-three

The doctor started off with easy questions she could answer, like, when did Kitty die. That date was engraved on her heart, she'd had to put it on so many forms.

She suspected he was gentling her, like a horse-whisperer, steadily gaining her confidence until she no longer felt like running away. He knew she would never have stepped foot in the surgery if she hadn't been summoned, and probably not then if William hadn't physically delivered her. Then, as she knew they would, the questions got a lot more difficult.

'So, are your parents at home at the moment?'

'My parents? No. They're walking somewhere. With rucksacks and sherpas and stuff.'

'It must be quite a long trip.'

'Oh, it is. A couple of months, I think.'

'And when are they due back?'

'I really don't know. They travel a lot. I can't keep track.'

'Have you got anyone else you could go and stay with? Some friends your own age, perhaps?'

After some moments reading the eye chart on the wall, Perdita remembered Lucy. Lucy seemed to belong to another time, as did anything that happened before Kitty was ill. 'Umm, well, there is the friend I spent Christmas with, but she cried a lot, because she was pregnant. She's probably had the baby by now.'

'Haven't you heard?'

'No.' Perdita didn't mention that she'd stopped opening letters, and there might well be a picture of a stork carrying a nappy somewhere in the pile of envelopes on the hall table.

'Is she the sort of person you could go and stay with, and sleep a lot?'

She cast her mind back to the neurotic, dependent woman addicted to perfect Christmases. 'Not going on what she was like when I last saw her, and the house was in need of a very major makeover. I suppose Kitty's is, too.'

'It's your house now, Perdita.'

'Not necessarily. Kitty had a nephew – or he may be a great-nephew.'

'But she always told me she was leaving everything to you.'

'Yes, but that was before Roger turned up. I'm not actually related to her.'

'What makes you think she may have changed her will?'

Perdita sighed. She hadn't voiced these anxieties to anyone else and she wasn't sure it was wise to do it now. 'Beverley, one of the carers—'

'I remember. Very efficient.'

'—told me that Kitty had had a solicitor round, while Roger – that's the nephew – was staying.'

'And you haven't rung the solicitor to ask what's in the will?'

'Why should he tell me? Supposing I'm not mentioned? He'd just ask me what the hell it was to do with me.'

The doctor frowned.

'I'd rather not know, anyway. If Kitty has left everything to Roger, I might lose the land my tunnels are on. She gave them to me years ago, but I bet she didn't get round to changing the deeds of the property, or anything. I can't cope with the thought of winding up my business, and trying to find some other way of earning a living just now.' She smiled weakly. 'Please don't ask me to take a reality check.'

The doctor sat in silence, regarding her in that respectful, listening sort of way which always made Perdita feel very stupid. 'How are you sleeping, Perdita?'

She gazed at a print of Monet's *Water Lilies* for a few moments. 'Oh, the usual way, on a bed, with a duvet.'

He didn't laugh. 'I'm going to give you something to help you sleep.'

'I never said I couldn't sleep!'

'You didn't need to. Now, these are very mild, they're not addictive, and you can stop taking them the minute you sleep eight hours.'

'I don't need eight hours' sleep. I can manage on very little. Like Margaret Thatcher.'

'I'm going to ring through to the desk to make you another appointment next week.'

'Oh, I can do that on my way out.' She was already on her feet.

'You could, but you won't. Just sit back down.'

She looked back to the eye chart while he made the call and realised that the bottom row was moving. She decided not to comment in case it wasn't a wonderful new invention but something to do with her eyes.

'You can go now,' said the doctor. 'Now don't forget to take this to the chemist. The receptionist will give you a card with your appointment time on it.' He gave her a look she'd seen him use on Kitty. 'And if you don't turn up, I'll have to make a house call.'

Perdita was delivered back home by William, who was going on to make some deliveries. She made herself a cup of tea and stared at the pile of post which Miriam, the cleaner, had moved from the hall to the kitchen table. It was her way of saying it was time she did something about it.

Miriam was right, no doubt about it. Perdita ought to check there were no final demands, or letters from bailiffs lurking like land mines in among the letters of condolence, and those addressed to Kitty from official organisations who didn't know she was dead.

But on the other hand, it seemed unwise to add to the vast amounts of paper already in the house and Miriam was very good at squaring up the piles of envelopes.

Perdita got up a little stiffly. Nothing about her seemed to work quite as well as it used to. She glanced at her watch. She should go and work in the poly-tunnels but William would be back by now. She had avoided discussing how she had got on at the doctor's while they drove back, but he might not spare her now. She decided to go and clean the windows in the old stables.

She had the cleaning stuff and some rags in her hand, but somehow she found herself in among the lettuces with William.

'What did the doctor say? Janey was furious with me for not asking before.'

'You can tell Janey that the doctor didn't say anything much, except I've got to go back next week.'

'Have you made an appointment?' From William's expression, this was the last thing he expected her to have done.

'Yes! Look!' She pulled the appointment card out of her jeans and waved it at him. With it came the prescription. He picked it up.

'Do you want me to get this filled out for you?'

'No, it's OK. I've got to go into town soon. I'll do it then.'

William gave her the strange look everyone gave her these days and went back to his digging. 'I've got a friend who needs a job,' he said.

'Oh?'

'Yes. He's done an agricultural course. Just qualified. You wouldn't need to pay him much.'

It took Perdita some moments to grasp that William wasn't just passing on chitchat about his mate, but wanted her to offer him a job. It was probably because she had got so batty, he was scared to be alone with her. She gave him what she hoped was a reassuring smile. 'I don't want to think about taking on any extra staff at the moment, William. I've got too much on my mind. We're managing, aren't we?' She picked a leaf at random.

'Not really. I need some help.' William addressed some bolted lettuces.

She frowned. 'We've always managed before. I know I've been busy at the house, but I still put in the hours here. And much as I'd like to help your friend out, I just don't think I can justify taking on any more staff at the moment.'

'It's not to help my friend out,' he muttered. 'It's to help me.' Then, a bit louder, he said, 'You've inherited all Mrs Anson's money, haven't you?'

'I don't know, William. Possibly not. But even if I have, it'll be a while before I get probate. I can't just hire staff on a whim.' She didn't like to tell him what might happen to her existing staff if she didn't inherit.

'But really—' said William to her retreating back.

Perdita fell asleep on the sofa, and woke up at midnight. She didn't feel tired then, so instead of going to bed properly, she got out another box of papers and started to sort them. At about four o'clock in the morning, she realised they were familiar to her, and that she'd already sorted them, and now they were in heaps over the attic floor. She swore for a few moments and scooped them up and stuffed them back in the box. A ghost in her head said, just burn the lot, but another, more insistent voice told her she must read every paper Kitty had ever kept, even if it took her years.

William came to her door at five to ten in the morning, and told her it was time to go to the doctor's, and she should get dressed first. She was wrapped in Kitty's dressing gown and did realise that she'd have to put on something more conventional, or he'd look at her even more sympathetically. William waited in the kitchen while she found jeans and a sweatshirt, and then drove her to the surgery.

'I'll see you get home OK,' he said, 'so just wait, if you come out early.'

Perdita was a little surprised when she came out of the surgery to see Lucas's car in the car park. Strange, she thought, he was never ill.

He got out when she walked across to the car park, looking for the van.

'I've come to pick you up,' he said.

She shook her head. She knew William had said he would come for her. 'It's all right, Lucas. I've got a lift.'

'William is busy. I've told him I'm going to take you away for a while. He's going to hold the fort while you're gone. Now, jump in.'

She stood there, confused. Lucas wasn't exactly a strange man, in fact, she knew him quite well, but she was certain she shouldn't just get in his car and run away from all her responsibilities. 'I don't think so.'

'It's either that or drive you to the nearest loony bin so you can have a nervous breakdown.'

'That's nonsense!'

'I'm only quoting Dr Edwards, though I do agree with him. He said if you don't get away you'll have a break-down. So I'm taking you away. Now do get in, people are watching us.'

Perdita looked behind her and was aware of a couple of faces looking at her. Lucas waved and nodded at the faces and held the door open impatiently.

Perdita got in. 'Where are we going? I don't think I could face a hotel or anything like that.' Just pulling on her jeans and sweater had become enough of a chore. The thought of dressing up for breakfast made her want to weep.

'The bothy. Now go to sleep. I'll wake you up when we stop for lunch.'

Obeying him was frighteningly easy. She was so tired, a long, built-up tiredness which had become part of her. She had no energy to fight or protest, she just felt grateful that the decision was made for her. She closed her eyes and fell into unconsciousness.

It was slightly unnerving, sleeping so deeply in a car, for every now and then, she woke up and found herself apparently going at full speed into the back of a lorry. For a split second Perdita always thought she was driving, had fallen asleep at the wheel, and was speeding to her death. Seeing Lucas, calm and controlled at the wheel, driving slightly too fast for safety, reassured her, and she allowed herself to slip away again.

When he woke her, they were parked in a motorway service station. 'Pee break, also I need food and fuel. Come along.'

She was so reluctant to be disturbed she pleaded to be left in the car to sleep. 'I'll be fine. I'll just doze off again.'

'No, or you'll need to stop when I don't need to. Come and have something. God knows what time we'll get there, and if there'll be any food.'

She found herself biting into a hamburger with all the trimmings. It was surprisingly tasty, though after a few mouthfuls she was full. Lucas finished her fries and then steered her to the Ladies. She felt so dazed she probably couldn't have found it by herself. There were so many people, the service station felt like an airport, and everyone seemed to know where to go, except her.

'I'll wait for you outside,' said Lucas, seeing her try to open the door the wrong way.

She was asleep again before he'd finished filling the tank.

They stopped again, just before the motorway ended,

and had tea and fruitcake. This time she was awake enough to ask a few questions.

'Surely you can't take time off just now, Lucas? Isn't it your busy time?'

'I've got minions. Janey's very good, and there's another young chef I'm training up, Tom. The lad who was sous for me that time you – worked in the kitchen.'

Perdita decided to ignore this reference. 'Well, I'm not at all sure I can take time off.'

'Yes you can. I've given William permission to take on that friend of his, and anyone else he needs. And he's got Janey to tell him what people need.'

'Yes, but Lucas, I may not inherit Kitty's money! I may not be able to afford staff!'

'Nonsense! You don't need to inherit from Kitty to employ an extra bloke.'

She sighed and decided she couldn't face explaining about the land and if she was going to be making people redundant, it might as well be two as one. 'I still don't think William can run the business without me.'

'Yes he can. Apparently you haven't been a lot of use, lately. Pulling up the wrong things, cutting weeds instead of salads – you won't have a business soon, unless you take some time out. The doctor made no bones about it.'

Perdita tried to make a joke about a doctor and bones but couldn't think of one. 'When did you speak to him?'

'Last week. I rang him and told him – well, never mind what I told him just now – and he said you were cracking up. He put it more politely, of course.'

'Well, I probably am cracking up, but I'm not happy about William hiring extra people. The business won't stand it.'

'It won't stand without it. Besides, you can afford the wages.'

She sighed. 'Not someone else assuming I'm a heiress! I'd have thought you'd know better!'

He was silent for a few moments. 'But I do. Know better, that is. I know that you are an heiress, quite a considerable one.'

'What? How do you know? I might not inherit anything! I might even lose the land Kitty gave me!'

He shook his head. 'You inherited almost all Kitty's worldly goods.'

'Have I? But what about Roger?'

'I don't know about the odd individual bequest, but you get the bulk.'

This was an enormous relief. 'That's so amazing, and I've been so worried. I was sure she never changed the deeds and I'd have to sell up.'

'She didn't change the deeds, but it doesn't matter.'

'Hang on. How do you know all this?'

'Because Kitty showed me her will. She wanted me to be an executor, but I refused.'

'But when was this? Roger got the solicitor to visit one day when I wasn't there. Just before we made the television programme.'

'Really?' Lucas took time to think this over.

'Yes! And Roger had told me he was going to get Kitty to change her will in his favour. I didn't think he'd done it until Beverley told me about the solicitor at the funeral.'

Lucas looked up. 'And you've been carrying this anxiety around on your own?'

Perdita chewed her lip. 'The anxiety wasn't on its own, it had plenty of company.'

'But why didn't you tell me about Roger? If I had that little shit here now, I'd—'

'Commit grievous bodily harm and get thrown in prison?'

It was his turn to look rueful. 'Probably.'

'Kitty told him he was common. He wouldn't have liked that. Oh, and he was going to tell the tabloids we were once married. I meant to warn you, but then Kitty died and I forgot all about it.'

'Bastard! Not that it would have mattered, really.' Lucas leaned forward and put a large warm hand on her chilly ones. 'And I wouldn't worry about Kitty changing her will. She may have fiddled with it, but I'm sure she won't have changed her mind about the bulk of it.'

Perdita, feeling better than she had for ages, chuckled. 'Bulk might not be the right word. She bought me a van at Christmas, don't forget, and then we had carers for ages.'

'That won't have even dented it.'

'You can't possibly know that! Even if you saw the will, you couldn't have known what the estate was worth.'

'She told me. As I said, she wanted me to be an executor, but I refused.'

'But why?'

'First, because I have so little time.'

'And secondly?'

He rearranged his teacup, teapot and milk jug, apparently equally keen to avoid eye contact. 'I felt bloody awkward about it.'

'Because Kitty asked you to be an executor? She loved and respected you, Lucas. I'm not at all surprised she asked you, or that you refused, come to that. Sorting out her things would be a nightmare.'

'That wasn't why I felt awkward.'

'Then why?'

He looked up at her, for the first time in ages, it seemed. 'Can I take a rain check on answering that?'

Perdita rubbed her forehead. 'I suppose so. Can you tell me how you've got time to suddenly shoot off?'

'Would you have preferred it to be your parents? I did wonder if I should try to get in touch with them.'

'No! But I don't think it's fair that you should have to let everything go hang because I need a little break. I could have got in touch with Lucy in Shropshire, or the Ledham-Golds would have had me.'

'Would you have asked either of them?'

She put off answering for as long as possible. 'Probably not.'

He humphed. 'I knew kidnapping was the only answer.'

Perdita persisted, 'But it still doesn't seem fair that you should just drop everything, to take me away . . .'

'Oh God, Perdita, don't be so dense! I love you! If you need me to take you away, of course I'll drop everything!'

'What?' She felt she was watching a film and had fallen asleep, missing a vital bit of plot.

Lucas was unsympathetic. 'Oh, for God's sake, Peri! Why are you the only person in the whole village, the whole viewing public of *A Gourmet and a Gardener*, who doesn't know how I feel about you?'

She blinked at him in confusion. 'Possibly because you never said anything about it.'

'The others didn't need to be told, and how could I come near you when Kitty had just died, and the whole village are assuming I'm going to muscle in on you so I can open my own restaurant?'

She took a moment to think about this. 'No one knows if I'm going to inherit enough to open a restaurant . . .'

'Except me. I know. I knew that all the rumours about your great wealth were true. God, how I wish I didn't.'

'Lucas . . .'

'Never mind, don't think about it now. Let's get back on the road. You can do some more sleeping.'

Perdita, bewildered, and feeling as if an ant could push her over if it had a mind to, agreed that this was the best course. When she next woke up, Lucas was opening the gate to the track which led down to the bothy. She rubbed her eyes and shook herself awake as they passed through the woods to the loch-side. It was ten o'clock at night.

'Welcome back.' Lucas pulled on the handbrake and

smiled. 'It'll be freezing cold and possibly damp, but once I've got the stove going and the kettle on, we'll be fine. You can wait in the car while I light the fire, if you like.'

'No, I'll come in.' She was still very tired, and a totally different person from the innocent young bride she had been when he'd first brought her here, but she felt the same bubble of excitement at having arrived as she had all those years ago.

She followed him into the little wooden building. It was pitch-dark outside. He struck a match and lit a camping gas lamp.

'Now, is there any kindling left?' He rummaged in an old fishing creel which hung on the wall of the shack. 'No, damn it. Never mind, I've a secret supply somewhere. You wait here.'

While she waited for him, she looked around, wondering how much was different from the last time she had been here. Very little, she decided. There was a patch of damp which hadn't been there, and there seemed to be more hooks. The little two-burner camping stove looked identical, but now, she noted, there was a fridge under the table. On their honeymoon they had kept their milk outside, in a hole covered with large stones. As a system it worked well as long as they regularly bought packets of frozen peas.

Lucas came back with a box of kindling. 'The trouble with a family property is that not all members of the family are as good at leaving the place as you'd wish to find it as others. That's why I always leave some kindling and some whisky well hidden.'

'Oh.'

'So – whisky or fire first?'

'Fire, then we can drink the whisky watching it burn.'

'Fair enough.'

In no time the stove was crackling with flame, and

although no heat came from it as yet, it was a wonderfully welcoming sound.

'Oh.' He regarded the two single beds which had been pushed together to make a double. 'I'll sort them out in a minute. It takes a bit of shifting about, but I can soon separate them. I'll see if there's a can of soup, or something. Or aren't you hungry?'

'I'm not hungry, and please don't bother about the beds now. It's awfully late, and you've been driving for hours. Let's leave it until morning.'

He looked doubtful. 'If you're sure. It does make the bedding situation a bit easier, actually. I just grabbed what was handy and it turned out to be a double sleeping bag and a double duvet. Like this we can sleep on one and have the other over us. If you'd be all right with that.'

She nodded. 'I know I've slept most of the way up here, but now I've started to sleep, I don't think I'll ever stop.'

'Fine. Er – you remember about the loo situation, don't you?'

'Like, there isn't one?'

He nodded. 'You need a torch, a spade and some loo paper. Luckily the ground's very soft. Go now, before you get comfortable and can't face it.' He handed her a torch and a roll of paper, slightly damp. 'I'll just find the spade.'

Perdita groped her way round the back of the bothy, shone the torch for stinging nettles, and found, rather to her surprise, a strange pleasure in sitting under the stars. Back in the bothy, she found that Lucas had boiled a kettle, and there was a bowl of hot water for her to wash in. He had also brought in most of the bags from the car, including a cold bag.

'Now, whisky? Or shall I make a hot toddy?'

'You haven't got lemons, you can't make a toddy.'

'That's what you think, Miss Know-it-all.' He dug into his pockets and produced a lemon from each one. 'I grabbed them just as I left the flat.'

Perdita chuckled, and realised that it was the first time she had laughed for ages, although a polite smile had been pinned to her face seemingly for ever. 'I'll still make do with whisky. I haven't the energy to wait for you to faff around.'

He made a face at her. 'Get into bed while I go to the loo, then. Your clothes, those I could find, are in that bag. I bought you a toothbrush and some toothpaste, because they weren't in your washbag, and what do you sleep in? I could only find a T-shirt.'

'A T-shirt is what I sleep in,' she said. 'Usually.'

'It won't be enough up here.' He plunged his hand into a small sports bag. 'I packed some pyjamas, you'd better wear them.'

'What about you?'

'I never wear them. They were a present from my sister. I've told her a dozen times I don't wear pyjamas, but she still buys them. She's trying to reform me.' He frowned. 'But if you'd feel more comfortable with me covered up, I'll put them on and find something else for you.'

'It's all right. One pair of pyjamas between two of us is fine.'

'You get ready for bed. I'll be back in a moment.'

She brushed her teeth standing on the wooden veranda and spat over the rail into the undergrowth beyond. In the morning, she would wash away the toothpaste; now, it was too chilly to worry about. Back inside, she fumbled her way into the pyjamas, found a smear of face cream which, fortunately, was in her sponge bag, and got into bed. She was huddled under the duvet, shivering violently, when he returned. She was freezing cold and longed for her vest. The pyjamas were stiff and new and didn't cling to her in a cosy way.

'I'll get you a hot-water bottle,' he said, seeing her teeth chatter. He opened a cupboard. 'It won't take long to bring the kettle to the boil. The fire's going really well now and will have heated the kettle quite a lot.'

Perdita remembered the routine. You kept the kettle full and on the wood-burner, and when you wanted to boil it, you put it on the gas. He filled her a hot-water bottle, and handed it to her.

'Actually, you couldn't wrap it in something could you?' she asked. 'It's far too hot.'

He found a scarf which hung, with a lot of miscellaneous waterproofs, on some hooks by the stove. 'Here.'

It was wonderfully soothing, but she couldn't decide if it was her feet or her stomach which needed it more. In the end she had pushed it down to her feet and put her head on the pillow, which smelt of woodsmoke and the musty damp of summerhouse cushions. When the whisky kicked in and she was drowsy once more, she snuggled down deep under the duvet, heard him turn out the gaslight and felt him clamber into bed.

She didn't have the energy to think about what he'd said about loving her. It was too complicated. But it was also a little golden casket, something to be taken out and dreamt over, in private.

Chapter Twenty-four

Two single beds pushed together were not the same as a double bed. Perdita felt no awkwardness sharing it with Lucas, although she had noticed that he'd gone to bed in his boxers and a T-shirt.

It was very quiet. Only the sound of the burn and the wind in the trees broke the silence of the deep countryside. She felt relaxed, and was starting to warm up. She was nearly very happy. Then suddenly, unexpectedly, she started to cry. She was appalled. It was so embarrassing. She hadn't cried since before Kitty died, and had no idea why she was doing it now. She tried to keep quiet. Lucas had been wonderful, looking after her so well, she didn't want to keep him from his well-deserved sleep with her stupid tears. It wasn't as if she was sad, or anything, she was fine. It was just that she was crying.

She managed not to sniff or sob as the tears ran wetly down her face, over her nose and into the pillow, but she couldn't stop shaking.

In spite of there being separate mattresses, Lucas felt it. He lay still for a moment, and then he put out an arm and pulled her towards him. 'Come on.'

He heaved her over the join so she was sharing his bed. He put his arm round her and her body remembered what her mind had long forgotten, how to lie alongside him. She laid her head on his shoulder and her arm across his chest, one leg slid between his, and, like the last piece of a jigsaw puzzle, she settled comfortably into position.

'That's better,' he said, whether because she had

stopped shaking, or because he liked having her in his arms she didn't find out, because she fell asleep.

She awoke some time later, boiling hot. She kicked at the hot-water bottle until it landed on the floor with a thump. She had felt she would never get warm, and now she was sweating. The pyjama bottoms had tangled themselves round her legs, tying them together. Could she sort out the situation without waking Lucas?

He was lying on his back, on the join between the two beds, snoring. It wasn't very loud and she found the sound comforting. She eased herself from under his arm, and, trying not to disturb him, slithered out of bed and out of the pyjama bottoms. She watched him in the shaft of moonlight which came through the gap in the curtains. She remembered, on their honeymoon, in high summer, how they had cursed that gap in the curtains, which woke them so early. They had usually managed to go back to sleep again, after making love.

Now, she wondered if she should get out and get in the other side, to give them both more room, but as she cooled down she decided just to get back in.

His arm came round her, and she turned onto her right side, so it was on her waist. Another position which seemed so natural and so familiar. It was funny, she thought, as she settled herself, I couldn't have told anyone how we used to lie together, I wouldn't have known. But my body knows. Which is a good thing, she added prosaically, because it means we can both get some much-needed sleep.

The next time she woke his hand wasn't on her waist, in a chaste, companionable way, it was on her breast.

'Lucas,' she whispered, hoping he was still asleep, and she could move without him knowing his hand had strayed.

There was no answer, but his fingers began circling her

nipple. It was difficult to believe he was really asleep. She decided to give the matter a little thought. Should she stop him, or should she do what she'd been wanting to do for ever?

She moved away half an inch. His hand continued its task.

'Lucas,' she spoke out loud. 'Your hand. It's on my breast.'

Still no answer, but there was no possibility of him being asleep, he was just pretending to be so he could take her past the point of no return. He knew just how to do it, he was nearly there already. Perdita sighed. Why not just go along with it? A fling wouldn't hurt, a little Highland Fling. But she had to clear her decks while she could still think.

'Lucas, you're not taking advantage of a recently bereaved woman, are you?'

'Peri, if you don't know how much I love you by now, I don't know what I can do to convince you.'

Again his special name for her, because, he said all those years ago, she was like a fairy. She smiled. Both his hands were working hard now, but she still had her back to him. 'You could try telling me.'

'I love you more than life itself. I love you more than I want sex with you. Here,' he shuffled backwards, abandoning her breasts. 'I'll get up and go and swim in the loch to prove it.'

This was taking it all too far. 'There's no need to do that.'

He laughed. 'No, I think I should prove to you that I just don't just want you for your body, that I want a lifetime's commitment.' He moved onto his mattress, and it seemed a long way off.

'What if *I* just want you for your body?' demanded Perdita, beginning to enjoy herself. 'Are you denying me a single girl's right to a sex life?'

She turned to peer at him in the dim light, propping

herself up on her elbow. He made an attractive silhouette, with his hair ruffled up at the back, moonlight catching his shoulder and upper arm.

'Yes I am. I don't think you should be a single girl with a sex life. I think you should be a married woman with one. Married to me.'

Perdita sighed. 'Oh. Do you really think that's a good idea, after last time?'

'Yes I do!'

He reared up and leant over her so she collapsed backwards. She felt the warmth of him as he supported his weight on his arms.

'Supposing I don't agree with you?'

'You know me. I'll either torture you, or bully you until you submit.' He freed a hand to start unbuttoning her pyjama jacket. 'You'll soon give in.' Her chest was bare now, and he looked down longingly at where the moonlight lit her breasts.

Perdita didn't think she could put up with much in the way of torture, if it involved being thoroughly aroused and then left unsatisfied. She felt her chances of holding out against the merest fingertip on her collarbone were nil.

'Does it have to be marriage? Couldn't we just have an affair?' she countered. After all she didn't want him to think she was desperate for him, even if she was.

'No we can't. We have to get married properly, preferably in church. I'm not risking losing you again.'

'You didn't lose me last time, you threw me away.'

'I was such a bloody fool. Why didn't I realise that you were the one, and always would be?'

'Because you were young, and I was even younger, and very silly. We've both changed; it's like having a relationship with a totally different person.'

'Except that some things are wonderfully the same.' He ran his thumb down from her collarbone to the top of her ribcage. 'Do you still like that?'

'Mmm.' She nodded.

'So, will you marry me?'

Perdita turned her head to one side. 'Make love to me first, I'll decide afterwards. After all, you may not be as—'

He roared and leapt on her, taking her in his arms and rolling with her so she lay on top of him. 'If you agree to marry me,' he said, 'we can go into Perth and buy a double mattress.'

She gave an ecstatic sigh. 'Oh, all right then . . .'

In the morning, when, sated at last, Lucas got up to rekindle the embers in the wood-burner, and make a cup of tea, Perdita sat up in bed and pulled the pyjama jacket back on.

Lucas was crouching naked on the hearth, breaking sticks and posting them into the fire. He looked very primitive, and beautiful. For the first time in many years, she wished she had a piece of charcoal and a pad, so she could draw him.

'I think we should talk,' he said, concentrating on his task, unaware of how the lines of his body, the movement of muscle under skin affected both the artistic and a baser side of Perdita. She looked away, so she wouldn't be distracted.

'If that's all you can think of to do on a fine morning like today.'

He got up. 'It's raining, and although I want to get back into bed and make love just as much as you do, there are a few things I think you should know.' He picked up his clothes and started to dress.

'Oh.'

'Nothing to look worried about, little one. Just some things I need to get off my chest.'

'Can I suggest you start with that rather startling lumber jack's shirt you've just put on?'

He frowned at her. 'No. Now, stop thinking about sex

and listen to me! I want you to know everything, so you can trust me. This time.' He hesitated. 'I can always get undressed again.'

She didn't think she'd have a problem trusting him, this time, but then she'd trusted him before. 'Then speak.'

'I'm going to tell you about Kitty's money and everything in a minute, but first I want to tell you all the stuff which happened before.'

'Before when?'

'Before I came to Grantly Manor. It wasn't coincidence. I knew you lived nearby.'

'Oh?'

'I came back to find you.'

'That sounds very romantic.' But she knew it wasn't.

'I wish I could say, now, that I came back because I knew I still loved you and wanted to claim you as my own. But it wasn't quite like that.'

'So, what was it like?' He needed to tell her, but did she need to know? At the moment she felt their love was enough. But he was probably right. It was better for them to be completely open with each other.

'I wanted to make sure I hadn't made a mistake, leaving you. I wanted to find out that you'd turned into someone I wouldn't want to be married to in a thousand years. But I didn't.' He poured water from the kettle on the wood-burner into the kettle on the gas stove, and lit it. 'You came into my kitchen, and either I fell in love with you all over again, or I was still in love with you from before. I don't know which it was, but it was bloody inconvenient, I can tell you.'

'I suppose you're going to tell me I was always "bloody inconvenient".'

'Well, you were – are! First of all, we meet when we're both far too young to know how to handle a relationship. Then you crop up again, a beautiful, successful, confident, irresistible woman, just when I'm starting to succeed in a new career.'

'It's hardly my fault you chose to succeed in the village where I live! Where you knew I lived! You could have fallen in love with another – of those women.'

'There aren't any more of those women. There's only you.' He squatted down to the fridge and took out a packet of bacon. 'And I do know it's my fault I came back, like everything is my fault.' He ripped open the packet with his teeth and started peeling rashers from it, laying them carefully in a frying pan.

'Not everything,' said Perdita. 'Though, God knows, I blamed you for everything for years. I always thought you broke up our marriage single-handed. Then something, or someone – you or Kitty, probably – made me realise there are always two sides to a relationship.'

'There was more to you than just a victim, even then.'

She shuddered, troubled by the ghost of failure. 'Do you think we'll make it, if we get married again?'

'There's no "if" about it! We're getting married again, that's definite.'

'But supposing it doesn't work? I don't think I could go through that again . . .'

'Without Kitty?'

She put her arms round her hunched-up knees. 'No. Kitty has nothing to do with this. I don't need her any longer.' She bit her lip. 'Oh, I *want* her, I miss her terribly, but I don't *need* her. I know I can't have any more of her encouragement and support, but what I've had – and I had years and years of it – I've still got. It doesn't go away because the person who gave it to you does. I've come to realise that these last weeks.'

'I'm glad. Really glad. Kitty would be so proud to hear you talk like that.'

Perdita cleared the tears from her throat and wiped her eyes.

354

'And I'm glad to see you crying, allowing yourself to let go.'

She sniffed unromantically. 'You were in the middle of a confession, Lucas.'

'Not really a confession – more a short talk on why I think our marriage would work this time when it failed so spectacularly before.'

Perdita was smiling now. 'Let's have it then, but don't burn the bacon.'

'As if I would!' He turned down the gas under the pan. 'When we got married before, we were all sex and no substance. We've both grown up a hell of a lot, and been through a lot together. I've learnt so much from that, so much about you I might never have known.'

'Like what?'

'Fishing for compliments? Well, I guess you're owed them. I've learnt that in spite of your dreamy expression, you're enormously competent, brave, loyal, and loving.' He stirred at the bacon. 'Although you were those last two things before.'

'And I've learnt that under your grumpy exterior, you're extremely kind, but you don't want people to know it. You disguise it as self-interest. You were wonderful to Kitty.'

He looked up. 'Actually, when I first called on Kitty, it *was* self-interest. I called on her so I could either get closer to you, or discover if Kitty was a witch, making you one too.'

'But when you got to know her, you loved her for her own sake.' It wasn't a question.

'Yes.' He frowned over the bacon for a few seconds. 'And we'll make our marriage work this time because we're both too stubborn to let it fail. Would you like an egg, or just a tomato?'

'Egg, please.' She hesitated for a second, but then decided to ask her question; if their marriage was to work, there must be no doubts between them. 'Lucas, why were you unfaithful to me? The first time? And how did you get to be a chef?'

Lucas pushed his hand through his hair, making it stick up. He thought for a few moments, trying to work out what to say. 'I was frightened. I was in a marriage I couldn't make work, a job I couldn't do, and wasn't suited for. Celia wanted me. She was senior to me, older than me and her attention was flattering. She came on to me when she'd summoned me into her office to give me a bollocking.'

'Instead she gave you a rollicking?'

He frowned. 'She took off all her clothes and then started on mine. I'm not saying I shouldn't have resisted, but I'd stopped giving you orgasms—'

'It's all right, you've started again.'

'Don't interrupt. Celia wanted me so blatantly. It seemed easier to abandon you and carry on with her. God! I was such a shit! I don't know how I lived with myself!'

'What about Celia? Did you live with her?'

'For a bit, until she got bored with me. Then she kicked me out.'

'I thought you said you left her!'

'I did, my possessions followed rapidly behind.'

Perdita chuckled. 'Go on.'

He added butter to the pan, and put in the halved tomatoes. 'I bummed around the City for a while, making money, sleeping with older women, collecting some extravagant presents on the way. Then I saw a girl I thought was you. It brought me up short. Some mates had hired a house in France, asked me to go with them.' He paused to add the eggs to the pan.

'Go on. How did you get to be a chef?'

'We got talking to one, one night. Strangely, he was English. He came through into the bar for a coffee. We'd had a bloody good meal, and told him so. I asked him a couple of questions, he saw I was interested, and said if I wanted to learn more, I could sign up at the hotel down the road.' He looked at Perdita, his expression rueful and self-deprecating. 'I don't know if the chef was a sadist or a genius or both. But he taught me about food – after he'd taught me about cockroaches and maggots and working fifteen-hour shifts with no break, in the blistering heat.'

'So when you got to be a chef, you modelled yourself on him?'

He shook his head. 'You think I'm a bastard? *That* bastard nearly took the end of my finger off with a knife. If my nails hadn't needed cutting, he would have done! I am what a pussycat is to a sabre-toothed tiger, compared to that man!'

'So why did you stay?'

He shrugged, and got two plates out from the cupboard. 'He knew about food, he took me on completely untrained. I was learning a lot.'

'And?'

'I think I needed to prove I could take it. That I wasn't the dilettante City boy I seemed to have become.' He looked up and grinned. 'Perhaps I felt my backside needed kicking. It certainly got it. Literally and figuratively. Now, do you want breakfast in bed? Or will you get up?'

She slid out of bed. 'I'll get up.'

'Then please put some knickers on. That jacket is long, but not quite long enough for my peace of mind.'

She giggled and rummaged in her bag. When she was dressed, below the waist at least, she joined him at the table. 'So how did you get from scullery boy to shit-hot chef?'

'Eat your breakfast, it's getting cold.'

Obediently, she sawed at a piece of bacon. 'Why don't you want to tell me? Surely this is the good bit of the story?'

'It is and it isn't.' He frowned, pulling the skin of his tomato as if it required great skill. 'You really want to know? Well, I poisoned him.'

'What!'

'Not badly, only enough to give him dreadful diarrhoea. The sous was drunk – I'd arranged that too – and so I had the restaurant to myself for the night, apart from the other skivvies, of course.'

He shot her a look which reminded her of the night she had worked for him, and what had nearly happened afterwards. She sighed, regretting her restraint.

'So, what happened?'

'Well, the owner came in. That I hadn't arranged, and wouldn't have done. But he liked my work and offered me a better job in his restaurant in Paris.'

'So, did you become head chef there?'

'Oh no, but I was slightly higher up the food chain. The chef I was working for was livid when he found out. I had to abandon my last week's wages and go to Paris.'

'And the rest is history?'

'More or less. Now, eat up, you know how offended chefs get if people let their meals get cold.'

'I've just had a dreadful thought,' said Perdita, when they'd reached the toast and marmalade stage. 'What are my parents going to say when I tell them we're going to get married again?'

He balanced a large piece of peel on his crust of toast. 'I don't think that'll be a problem.'

'Lucas, you didn't ask my father's permission for my hand, did you? If you did, I'll never speak to you again, let alone marry you!'

'No! Of course I didn't. But before they left, they asked me to keep an eye on you. And your mother – intimated – that she'd be glad if we got married again. I think she wants you off her hands. Now Kitty's gone, she thinks she might have to be a mother to you herself.'

358

'That's very unfair. She did the best she could. I've turned out all right, haven't I?'

He sighed. 'More than all right. Now, have you had enough breakfast? Have we talked enough? Or can we do what we were put on earth to do?' He came round the table and pulled her to her feet. His kiss tasted pleasantly of eggs and bacon with a hint of marmalade.

'You haven't told me about me being an heiress, yet.'

'Later.'

'. . . so Kitty said, would I mind looking at her will, even if I didn't want to be an executor.'

Perdita could imagine her saying it. *'Cast your eye down that, darling, and check I haven't lost my marbles and left it all to a cats' home.'*

'I did tell her it was none of my business if she had, but she insisted.' He sighed. 'Her husband left her very well provided for, she's had some extremely good financial advice and she's lived frugally most of her life. You'll inherit an unencumbered house, if you overlook some major repairs, an excellent portfolio of shares, and some valuable jewellery and pictures, which have lived in the bank for years.'

'But when was this? Unless it was very recent, there was still time for her to change it.'

'It was before she had the first TIA'

'Then it might all have changed. It might be Roger who's the heiress, not me.' She smiled to hide her anxiety.

He shook his head. 'She wouldn't do that. She wasn't taken in by Roger any more than I was. I dare say she's left him something, out of guilt, but she'd never disinherit you.'

'I do hope not – not because of the money, but—'

'The land. You told me. And Kitty wanted you to be well provided for. I asked her why she didn't keep the house up better and she said if you wanted to sell it, it was silly to spend money you might not get back.' He smiled. 'If the worst comes to the worst, and she has left it all to Roger, you'll just have to be a kept woman, and live off your husband.'

She frowned. 'Joking apart, I wouldn't want to do that.'

'Seriously, though,' he went on, 'we could raise the money to buy the land off Roger, and if he was dealing with me he wouldn't dare to ask over the odds.'

'How do you know?'

'I just know. I can be quite frightening, although I know you'll find that hard to believe.'

She was forced to laugh. 'So you think my fortune is safe?'

'Yup. So do you want to sell the house?'

Perdita sat perched on a low three-legged stool. She wasn't conscious of thinking, but after a moment, she said, 'No.' Until that moment, she hadn't allowed herself to think about what she might want to do with Kitty's house. Now she felt she wanted to live in it, fill it with children, stop the roof from leaking and revamp the kitchen. And now suddenly, it wasn't only her decision. 'But where do you want to live?'

He didn't hesitate. 'Where you want to live. With you. By your side.' He gazed at her, for once letting his feelings for her shine through his eyes. 'I don't care where I live. I can do what I do anywhere. If you want to live in your house, I'll happily live in it with you.'

'But supposing you get fed up with Grantly Manor? Supposing you want to open your own place somewhere?'

'Then we'll sort out how later, when it happens. At the moment let's just concentrate on getting married and being happy. Oh—' he paused guiltily.

'What?'

'I've just remembered. They want us to make a television series together.'

'So, you could just give up cheffing, and become a

television personality?' She kept her head down and observed him from the top of her eyes.

'No I could not!'

'Well, you'll have to live with a stigma of some sort. Either you married me for my money, or you're not a proper chef, just a personality.'

'No one,' he said sternly, 'who sees us together, could ever think I married you for your money. And besides, no one need know about the money. We can just carry on the way we were. Talking of carrying on . . .'

'Quite right. We should finish our breakfast and do the washing-up. Do we still do it outside, on the table on the veranda?'

'I wasn't thinking about washing-up.'

'I know what you were thinking of, but I need to wash myself, even if we ignore the dishes.'

'I know, let's have a bath.'

'A bath! You mean, there's an en suite out the back, and you never told me?'

'Sort of. You clear up the breakfast while I fetch it.'

He came back a little later with an old tin bath. 'It'll take a while to fill, and we must put lots of newspaper down, so we don't get the floor too wet, but you'll like it, I promise you!'

Chapter Twenty-five

The days that followed were like their honeymoon had been, only better. Then, anxious to please him, Perdita had followed all Lucas's suggestions about what they should do and how they should do it. Now, she had her own ideas. He wouldn't relinquish the cooking entirely, but she did make him eat tinned tomato soup with white bread in it sometimes.

'This is the food that nourished me for years,' she said.

'Nourished! Ha! No wonder you always looked so pale.'

The weather was golden. The short October days were filled with sunshine, and the mornings with mist. Lucas swam naked in the loch, insistent that at the end of the summer, the top few feet were warm enough to do so. Perdita was happy to watch him, especially when he came out, dripping like Poseidon, and swept her wetly into his arms, but she kept her own ablutions to the minimum, depending heavily on the public lavatories in the local town, and any pub they visited. Every two days he filled the ageing tin bath and watched her splash happily in it, agreeing that as the floor shared the washing experience, carting the water in from the burn was worth it.

If the evening was fine, Lucas put the bars of an old oven shelf over the remnants of the fire they'd used for their billycan tea and had a barbeque. Whatever the weather, the billycan tea was a ritual they never missed.

On the last afternoon, before they were due to go back,

he took her to a spot where, if you were lucky, you could see golden eagles and harriers, mountain hares and distant flocks of deer.

They spent a lot of time gazing across the valley to the mountains beyond, watching the sky darken to the colour of duck eggs, tinged with pink. Perdita hadn't spoken for a long time and eventually Lucas asked her if she was all right.

'I was just remembering something Kitty once said to me about bereavement.'

'What?'

'It was years ago, when I was still at school, and I asked her about Lionel, her husband. She said when you lose someone you love, the days go by so slowly, and the loss leaves a vast, immeasurable hole in your life. But gradually, after years, sometimes, very, very slowly, the hole begins to close. It's like darning, she said. Slowly, slowly, you place threads across the hole and weave them together, until eventually, after decades, maybe, you find the hole has gone.' She turned to him and smiled ruefully. 'There's still a bloody great darn there, of course. The sock is never whole again, but at least your toes don't stick out any more. Your life does function.' She found herself laughing and crying at the same time. 'Kitty told me this and then said, "I don't know how you'll manage, darling. I've never managed to teach you to darn."'

He buried her in his arms and held her very tightly. Eventually he said, 'I'll help you. I'm good at darning.'

Perdita was half excited, half terrified as they swept round the drive to the front of Kitty's house. She had been partly expecting to be confronted with a couple of pantechnicons and Roger filling them with antiques. Or, and she had to admit this was very unlikely, to find the house covered with demolition notices and builders' vans, indicating the site was soon to be 'executive homes with integral garages'.

'I'm glad to see the house is still standing,' she said when he'd stopped the car.

'Why on earth shouldn't it be?'

'I don't know, really. I just didn't expect things to look the same, when other things have changed so much. Like us.'

He caressed her chin with a gentle finger. 'We could try and make love in the front seat of the car, but it might be more sensible to go into the house and see if there's a letter from the solicitor.'

Perdita didn't move. The house hadn't burnt down or anything, but she didn't know what sort of a mess she'd left it in. She felt as if she'd been away for months, not just a couple of weeks. Cobwebs and rats, possibly even weasels and stoats, creatures from the wild wood, could have taken the place over in her absence. Not to mention burglars.

They had spent the night in a motel, halfway home, so that they wouldn't arrive in the dark, and now everything looked in surprisingly good order. The fact that they had driven round without being battered by rose fronds, or wisps of lavatera was a good sign. The front was clearer of weeds than it had ever been, even in Kitty's day, Kitty being fond of so many weeds other gardeners would have happily removed.

'Come on, my little ostrich,' said Lucas, 'you'll feel better when you know the worst.'

'Someone's been doing the garden,' Perdita said, pleased, but anxious lest something precious had been tidied on to the compost heap. 'I wonder what the house is like.'

'I expect Miriam has been in.'

Perdita found the key and unlocked the front door.

Instantly the smell of polish greeted them. A huge vase of chrysanthemums and scarlet Bishop of Llandaff dahlias stood on the hall table, adding their piquant scent to the air. Everything looked shiny and cared for.

'I wonder where all the boxes of papers are.' She was pleased to see the hall without them, but again, she was anxious lest anything had happened to them.

Lucas opened the door to the library. 'They're in here. In fact, I think Miriam must have raided the local public records office for extra supplies.'

Perdita peered in over his shoulder and saw row upon row of boxes, obviously gleaned from the local wine merchant. 'No, that's about how many there were, only Kitty's boxes were scruffier. Let's go into the kitchen. That's where Miriam will have put the post.'

The kitchen also gleamed. The table, cleared of extraneous items, made a lovely centrepiece. There was a note from Miriam leaning up against a little silver jug full of garden cyclamen.

Nothing has been thrown away, it's all still there for you to sort out. Janey and William helped me upgrade the boxes and move them into the library. I'll be in tomorrow. I've made a note of my extra hours. The post is on the sideboard.

'I gave her permission to do extra hours,' said Lucas, as Perdita picked up the pile of letters and took them to the table.

'Spending my money for me before I've even got it, are you?' She flicked through half a dozen seed catalogues and a prize draw before identifying the letter from the solicitor. 'Well, I'd better find out if I've got any.'

She held the thick, manila envelope and tried to get her finger in under the flap.

'Here,' Lucas handed her his Swiss Army knife. 'Use this.'

Perdita withdrew a sheaf of papers and scanned the letter which was on top.

' "Dear Miss Dylan," ' she read aloud. ' "I am happy to enclose the papers . . ." Oh, why don't they cut to the chase?'

'Let me look.' Lucas took the bundle and riffled through it. 'Here's a copy of the will. Do you want to read it yourself?'

'I'd better, I suppose.'

He handed her the will. Perdita took a deep breath and glanced down the page. Then she closed her eyes and handed it to Lucas. 'It's all right. It is all mine.'

'Not quite,' said Lucas after a moment. 'There's a legacy for Roger here.'

'Oh? What?'

' "To my great-nephew Roger Owen," ' he read, ' "I bequeath the entire contents of the cupboard on the landing outside the attic." What on earth's in there, I wonder?'

Perdita started to laugh. 'I know. It's all the cups and saucers Kitty got from jumble sales. We used them for the funeral. Remember?'

'Kitty owned those? I thought you must have borrowed them from the village hall. They had that look about them.'

'I expect a village hall which was upgrading gave its crockery to the jumble sale where Kitty bought it. She wanted lots for when the garden was open.'

'Well, I'm sure it's a very handsome legacy,' said Lucas, obviously a little confused.

'No it's not! It's probably worth about a fiver! God, she was a wily old bird! Even when she was in her death throes she was on to Roger and his interest in her Meissen collection! That has cheered me up. I hated the thought of

Kitty being bullied when I wasn't there to protect her. I should have known that no one bullies Kitty, even when she's ill.' She dumped all the papers onto the table. 'Come on, let's explore the rest of the house.'

'I didn't think that table would stay clear for long,' said Lucas.

It was quite different looking at the house, knowing it was to be their home, and the home of their children. Kitty was still there, in every book and picture, piece of silver or china, but the house no longer seemed to be in decline. Perdita and Lucas had plans for its future.

'Shall we keep the shower room downstairs? It is useful having somewhere to wash when you come in from the garden,' said Perdita.

'But we could close up the doorway from the sitting room.'

'And put back the china cupboard? Possibly, but I don't know if I'd want so much china as Kitty had. Especially if we'd have to stop the children breaking it. I might have a sort through and see if there's any other stuff I can fob off on Roger.' She paused. 'I would like to keep the blue sofa. Kitty felt so sentimental about it.'

'Only if it's comfortable. She wouldn't want us to be burdened by her sentiments when she knows we'll have enough of our own.'

'Shall we test it now?' Perdita asked with mock innocence.

'No,' said Lucas firmly. 'Let's go back to the kitchen.'

Back there, Perdita surveyed the room with a critical eye she had never used before. For years and years, this had been Kitty's kitchen, the way she liked it, not open to criticism or change. Now it was hers and Lucas's.

'I think an Aga, don't you? A four door one. Middle-class-lefty-trendy red,' said Perdita.

'Not while I live and breathe! If you think that I'm going to cook on something which takes half an hour to boil an egg, you can think again! No, we need a professional range, something which gets up to a decent temperature.'

'I just like the thought of coming down to a warm kitchen on winter mornings, like today.'

'We can have central heating.'

'I wanted to make the kitchen a bit more like they made my kitchen in the programme, with a few bits of copper and stuff hanging from the ceiling.'

'You can hang what you like from where, but you're not condemning me to cooking on an Aga.'

She'd lost the battle, but she hadn't given up winning the war. 'OK, I'll settle for an armoire.'

'An armoire? What the hell is that? And where on earth did you hear about them?'

'They're all the rage. With wire netting over the front, to stop the hens getting in – or out. Eileen – one of the carers, you know, the young one? – had a magazine with them in. She was addicted to housey mags. I wonder if she's left any behind.' She glanced at Lucas, to see if he was reacting.

'Darling, do you really want a kitchen like they turned yours into on the programme?' He seemed to have given up fighting and wanted to please her. But on the other hand, he didn't want to share what he considered to be a work space with a lot of clutter.

'It's all right. I'm teasing. We'll keep the cooking end of the kitchen strictly business, as long as it's pretty, and make the dining end all fancy. The table stays, don't you think?'

'Definitely.'

'And the sideboard. What about the bookcase?'

'Useful in a kitchen, and it's full of wonderful antique

cookery books. Kitty never thought about what her first edition hardcover Elizabeth David's were worth.'

'As we don't want to sell them, it's not relevant. Shall we go upstairs now?'

He shook his head. 'I don't think we'd better. We're bound to feel obliged to test the beds and there are probably rather a lot of them.'

She chuckled. 'Let's go and see my poly-tunnels then. I hope everything's not dead.'

'Well, let's just give William a ring first. Janey might be there and they haven't been together long. We don't want to embarrass them.'

Perdita bit her lip in horror. 'Imagine being caught *in flagrante* by both your bosses!'

'Exactly. And we'll take the car. Go round the front, like proper visitors.'

William and Janey weren't in bed, they were waiting by the gate, rather anxiously, holding hands.

Perdita jumped out of the car and ran to them, embracing them both. 'Hi! How are you? How are my poly-tunnels? How is everything? We've brought you some honey and some genuine Scotch whisky. Thank you so much for holding the fort while I just ran away.'

The anxiety faded and was replaced with tentative expectation. Janey let go of Perdita and said, 'Well? Are you two . . . well, you know?'

'Well? Yes, extremely well. How kind of you to ask,' said Perdita, laughing.

'We're going to get married, if that's what you want to know,' said Lucas. 'And I'm not planning to use her great fortune to open a new restaurant. Things'll carry on as before, until Perdita gets pregnant.' He glanced at her. 'If she isn't already.'

'Oh, wow! That's so cool!' said Janey. 'But you'd better get married quickly, then. Imagine the scandal if you went down the aisle with a bump.'

Perdita ignored this. 'And we're going to live in Kitty's house, so you can have this one as long as you like. And take my junk out of it, as well.'

'That's great,' said William. 'We thought we ought to get married, too.'

'Brilliant! I wonder if we've used up all Kitty's champagne? If not, we'll have to buy some and have a celebration!'

Janey and William suddenly seemed a little awkward, as if the thought of getting drunk with their bosses wasn't terribly attractive.

'Just a quick glass,' said Lucas, observing their reaction. 'And then Janey can go back to work.'

Perdita suddenly grabbed Lucas's hand. 'I've just thought of something. Come along.'

She dragged him into one of the poly-tunnels and along the rows to the back. 'I've no idea what I'm going to find, but I think, if we're lucky . . .' She lifted out a large pot. There was nothing much to show from the top except something which looked like faded mint. She took a dibber from a ledge and very, very gently, began stirring the surface of the soil. 'Yes!' Carefully, she dug her fingers into the loosened soil and brought out a curious spiral shape, like an extremely plump maggot. It had a wonderfully pearlescent surface.

Lucas pushed her aside. 'I don't believe it! Crosnes! You've managed to grow crosnes! You little beauty! This is fantastic!'

'Crosnes, also known as Chinese artichokes,' Perdita added, for the benefit of Janey and William, who were following at a safe distance.

Perdita tipped out the soil and then sought for the pearly pink tubers. 'It's like digging for gold,' she said.

'Who would have thought that that dried-up crusty

old thing could have turned into something this wonderful?' said Lucas.

'I know,' said his beloved, fondly. 'And the crosnes are pretty amazing too.'